DIVER DOWN

Mercy Watts Mysteries Book Two

A.W. HARTOIN

ALSO BY A.W. HARTOIN

Bottle Blonde (Mercy Watts Mysteries Book Eleven)

Mercy Watts Mysteries Book Set (Books 1-3, plus bonus short)

Paranormal

Many thanks to the people of Roatan, Honduras.
Special thanks to Bananarama Beach and Dive Resort
Your help made the book.

CHAPTER ONE

Mrs. Lane Sanders was the kind of woman who usually didn't approve of me. Her grey hair flowed back from her widow's peak in thick waves and landed on her white silk blouse that was buttoned as high as possible and, just to make sure, sealed with a heavy amber brooch that weighed a pound at least. No one was getting those buttons undone, by god.

I sat in the walnut-paneled waiting room opposite Mrs. Sanders, very aware that it was her domain, not mine. The room matched her perfectly, cold and dignified. I'd never been accused of being either. She sat behind her oversized desk with arms crossed and refused to say where her boss was. That was nearly the last straw. I'd had enough of lawyers and their critical secretaries. Two days left before vacation and Arlene Cobb, a lawyer my father referred to as the Duchess of Dirt, hadn't even bothered to show up to pelt me with obnoxious questions about my godmothers' sanity in the civil case against them. I had better things to do than be deposed, buy flowered sundresses that I'd never wear again and wax things that really ought not be waxed. In the last month, I'd found myself involved in four high-profile cases, where the lawyers were happy to bill as many hours as humanly possible, wasting my time in cold offices, repeating cold facts. I think they were trying to freeze some sort of confession out of me. Fat chance. All four of the offices were so similar I often forgot which one I was in and which high-priced shark sat across the table. This wasn't going to be one of those days.

I would've walked out and, in retrospect, I should've, but Myrtle and Millicent needed me. Their nephew, Brooks, was trying to get control of their money and their lives. He was using my family to do it. So I sat as far away as possible from Mrs. Sanders, which put me directly across from the stenographer, a spindly redhead that was probably forty but looked twenty. He definitely *did* approve of me and not in a good way. It was all my fault for letting my mother pick out my outfit. She insisted and I'd learned the hard way that it was easier to comply than fight, so I was wearing a wrap dress that was supposed to make me look like I meant business yet be stylish. It did neither job well. Mom's theory that the hideous print of black and yellow daisies would be distract from my chest might've worked if the top would've stopped gapping open and the skirt didn't part to expose my thighs.

Jay the stenographer loved that dress, couldn't take his eyes off it. More to the point, he couldn't stop trying to look up my skirt. So I got to sit there holding my dress together, while listening to my lawyer, Big Steve Warnock, yelling in the hall behind me. Big Steve's voice had been known to go through three feet of concrete and we got to hear every curse word he uttered and there were a lot of them. I say we but Lane and Jay didn't seem to be paying attention. Lane's expression had gone to glaring and Jay had slid down in his seat in an effort to get a better view up my skirt. Why is it when someone's trying to look up your skirt, you get an irresistible urge to cross and recross your legs? Maybe it's just me, but I had to recross my legs. It had to be done. Jay licked his lips and I put my right leg over my left and felt a little pop in the twenty-dollar pantyhose I'd bought for their supposed durability because Mom said I had to wear pantyhose to depositions. I leaned forward and a spidery run raced down my thigh to my knee.

Freaking great.

"I can help you take those off," said Jay, licking his lips.

Just then Big Steve stalked in, still on his cell. "Get her here now!" He tossed me the phone and popped Jay in the head with the back of his hairy hand. "Shut up, fool, or I'll fire you so hard you'll have to sell your equipment for scrap."

Jay blushed as red as his hair. "I'm sorry, sir. It won't happen again."

"Damn straight it won't." Big Steve sat next to me and I scooted over to make room, even though he was in another chair. He was that kind of guy, the kind that took up a lot of space in every room, whether a closet or an auditorium. You just couldn't stop looking at him, even when he was quiet, which was rare.

"We'll give Arlene another fifteen seconds and then we're out of here."

"Thank goodness," I said.

Big Steve looked at his watch. "Ten seconds."

I smiled. Jay the stenographer looked terrified, a normal reaction to Big Steve. Lane sighed and got on the phone.

"Five seconds. Grab your purse, Mercy."

"Got it."

A young man with a receding hairline and watery blue eyes ran through the door, clutching six inches worth of paperwork and a battered laptop. "I'm here. I'm here."

Big Steve pushed past him. "We're out and you're not Arlene. Don't think I don't know the difference, although that is a tie a fifty-year-old woman would wear."

"Please don't leave. Mrs. Cobb will kill me if I don't get this deposition done."

"Where is she? And don't tell me she got caught up in court. She has nothing on any docket today."

"Um..." said the young man and I began to feel sorry for him.

"Um is not an answer." Big Steve gently pushed me out the door.

"Arlene has a new boyfriend!" yelled out the young man behind us.

"Leonard," said Lane, "are you out of your mind?"

We turned slowly. Big Steve looked like it was his birthday. "How old is this one?"

Leonard clapped his free hand over his mouth.

"Too late for that, boy. The new cat is out of the bag. I'm truly going to enjoy my next committee meeting with Arlene."

"Please don't tell her I told you," begged Leonard.

"Alright. I'll give you a break."

"Will you please come in the conference room? She'll fire me if I don't get this deposition done."

I crossed my arms. "I thought she was going to kill you."

Leonard barely glanced at me. "Same thing. Please. I'm begging you."

"She's quite the dragon, isn't she?" said Big Steve.

A bead of sweat rolled down Leonard's cheek. Poor guy didn't know Big Steve made dragons look like house cats. He worked sixteen-hour days because he thought the law was good fun and didn't understand that other people needed to do things like, you know, eat and sleep.

"I'll give you fifteen minutes."

Damn. So close.

Leonard led us into the conference room and I sat in a chair designed to be so comfortable that you'd relax and be off your guard. Fat chance. Big Steve touched my hand. "We're in and out. Remember what I told you."

I nodded. How could I forget? He'd told me a dozen times to answer questions briefly and to offer up absolutely nothing. As if I would. I'd been around. This was my tenth deposition in a month, including the murder cases. If this kept up, I'd have to buy stock in pantyhose or paint my legs.

Leonard settled in across from us and spread out his papers like a fan. Jay set up at the end of the room and tried not to look at me. Nice.

"State your name for the record," said Leonard.

Sigh.

"Carolina Watts." I was named after my mother, but my dad had nicknamed me Mercy. I preferred Mercy to Carolina. I was already too much like Mom for comfort.

"Is that the name you're commonly known by?" asked Leonard.

"No."

Leonard looked up and waited. I could see a flicker of a smile on the edge of Big Steve's lips. He loved it when I did as I was told. My parents loved it, too. I didn't get the appeal.

"Let's move it along," said Big Steve.

"Yes, of course. State the name you're commonly called," said Leonard.

"Mercy Watts." I almost said Marilyn, since I was a dead ringer for the late bombshell, Marilyn Monroe, and got called Marilyn as much as I did Mercy.

"Describe your relationship with Myrtle and Millicent Bled."

"I'm their goddaughter."

Defining my relationship to The Girls went on for another five minutes. I don't know what he was looking for and I wasn't sure he did either. Every deposition was the same. Who are you? What's your relationship? Who's decision was it that you attend Whitmore Academy? Who paid for it? Blah. Blah. Blah. But then it got interesting.

"What did your parents pay for the house on Hawthorne Avenue?" asked Leonard without looking up.

"It was a gift," I said.

"A gift from Myrtle and Millicent Bled to your parents whom they barely knew."

"Yes."

"Are you aware of the worth of the Hawthorne house at the time it was signed over?"

"No."

"Would it surprise you if I said that house was worth over seven hundred thousand dollars the year you were born?"

"No."

"You're not surprised that the Bled sisters gave away a seven-hundred-thousand-dollar house to strangers?"

"No."

"I'd be surprised."

"Is that a question?" I asked.

Big Steve's lips twitched. "She's not surprised. Next question."

"Are you aware that the Hawthorne house was signed over to your mother alone? That your father, Tommy Watts, is not in fact on the deed?"

"No."

"You thought it was signed over to both your parents?"

"I've never seen the deed and I never thought about it," I said, stifling a yawn.

"Do you know when exactly your parents met the Bled sisters?"

"No." What in the world was he getting at?

"Would it surprise you that at the time the deed for the Hawthorne house was signed over to your mother, Myrtle and Millicent Bled had never actually met your mother?"

That stopped me cold and I felt Big Steve stiffen beside me.

"Miss Watts, please answer the question," said Leonard with a smile. The goofy lost lawyer act was gone.

"I don't know that's true," I said.

"Did your mother tell you she had met the Bled sisters at the time the deed was signed over?"

"No."

"Why do you think that the Bled sisters gave such an expensive property to a woman they'd never met?"

"I don't know that's true," I said.

"Do you concede that the house was signed over to your mother?"

"No."

"Do you know what cases your father was working on at the time of this supposed gift?"

Supposed?

"No."

"Your father had just become a homicide detective on the St. Louis police force at the time of the signing of the deed. Correct?"

"I guess."

"You don't know?" asked Leonard with such smugness, I wanted to kick him in the shin, but Jay was taking it all down and looking pretty interested, too.

"I don't know the exact dates, since it was before I was born."

"You don't know the events surrounding the giving of this extraordinary house?"

"No."

"What did your parents tell you?"

"Nothing."

"Tommy Watts, a man known for his attention to detail, told you nothing about how your family got entrance into the exclusive world of Hawthorne Avenue?"

"No."

"I find that extraordinary."

Big Steve stood up and his chair flew backwards and hit the wall. "Your fifteen minutes is up." He took my arm and lifted me out of my seat.

"I'm not done," said Leonard.

"Then you should've been on time." Big Steve opened the conference room door and steered me through.

"She'll have to answer these questions."

"She has answered them. My patience is at an end."

We walked through the waiting room and were met by Lane, who handed me two large safety pins.

"For until you get home."

"Thanks," I said, my head still reeling from Leonard's insinuations.

"Did you pick out this dress?" asked Lane.

"My mother did."

"Burn it. It says everything you don't want to say."

"I will. Don't worry. Thank you."

Leonard came charging out of the conference room. "One more question, Miss Watts. How well did your father know Josiah Bled?"

I started to answer that I didn't know, but Lane stepped in front of Leonard. "You're late for court. The Rina case. The clerk has been calling."

Big Steve pushed me through the office door into the warm hall and began yelling into his phone as we walked to the elevator. "Freya, get Bub over to the office now and I want a list of every damn person in the squad when Watts made homicide." He took a breath. "Every person. Right down to the cleaning staff."

I pressed the elevator button and watched Big Steve order poor Freya to pull up his employee list for the same time period. My mom was his legal secretary for years and she would've been in his office when she got the house. He must've thought that someone in their circle had blabbed, but what could they possibly know? Dad always said the house was a thank-you. I gathered there was some kind of favor involved, but I always thought the truth was more special than that. Myrtle and Millicent fell in love with my parents. They adored them and my parents adored them right back. If Leonard thought the house was payment for some kind of illegal act on Dad's part, he was wrong. I'm not saying Dad wasn't above bending the rules or even breaking them. I'd seen him do it and it was always the right thing. My godmothers didn't pay Dad off. There was no way. If they had, it would've been a dirty back-alley deal. They'd never want to see him again. That didn't remotely happen. I was born in the Bled Mansion. The Girls babysat me, while Mom worked. They taught me to garden and bake, against my will but still. Mom was the one they called when they were sick or wanted to shop for ridiculous hats. Dad took care of their security system and fixed faucets for them. Whatever Leonard thought just simply couldn't have happened.

The elevator opened and Big Steve put his phone in his pocket. "I don't want you to worry about this."

"What exactly is this thing I'm not supposed to worry about?" I asked.

"The lawsuit."

"I'm not worried about the lawsuit. Myrtle and Millicent aren't incompetent. What's all this about the house?"

"Nothing to worry about."

Whenever someone says that, I know there's definitely something to worry about.

"Was that dillweed right? Is the house in Mom's name?"

Big Steve looked at the floor numbers slowly counting down.

"You know I can check. It's public record."

"She's on the deed."

"Alone?"

"Yes."

"Had she met The Girls at the time the house was signed over?"

The elevator hit the first floor and the doors started to open. I hit the stop button and an alarm clanged, echoing off the wood paneling.

"Did Mom meet them or not?"

"Mercy, that was twenty-six years ago."

"Don't pretend you don't know."

"Mercy."

"They're my parents, like it or not. I'm not going to tell anyone."

"It's better if you don't know anything. I won't have you lying under oath."

"So that's a no." I let go of the button, the alarm stopped, and the doors jerked open. A crowd stood there, looking as confused as I felt.

"Everything's fine," said Big Steve as he pushed through the crowd. *Yeah, right. I don't think so.*

He walked me to my truck and opened the door for me. "Don't worry. Tommy will dig up something on Brooks and the lawsuit will be a thing of the past."

That was supposed to make me feel better? It didn't. He might as well have said there was something to find out about our house.

I must've looked worried, because he put a heavy hand on my shoulder. "Your parents are good people. The best. Leonard has nothing."

"Come on. Leonard isn't fishing without bait," I said.

"He doesn't even have a hook. Trust me." He moved to close my door, but I blocked it.

"Did Dad know Josiah Bled personally?"

Big Steve grinned. "I have every confidence that you'll be able to figure that out."

He slammed my door and got into his big gold Lexus and squealed the tires on the way out of the parking lot probably yelling into his phone the whole time. Big Steve was right about most things and he was right about me. I'd figure it out eventually, but wouldn't it be nice if my parents would just tell me and save some time. I googled Josiah Bled on my phone and found his Wikipedia page. I'd seen it before, but it still seemed weird that The Girls' uncle had one. Josiah Bled was famous in his own way. First for being a Bled. The Bled Brewery was known all over the world and so was the fabulously rich family. Second for being a WWI flying ace and third being a spy in WWII. He was known to a lesser extent for building our house and The Girls' house. Pictures of both featured prominently on the page below his picture taken in France next to his bi-plane in 1917. He couldn't have been more dashing with his leather flying helmet and white silk scarf. Myrtle and Millicent said their uncle was bad in the best way possible and he looked it as he smiled a rakish smile at the camera, his eyes crinkled like a great joke had just been told.

I scrolled down to his dates. Josiah Aloysius Bled, born July 4, 1900, died unknown. What the heck? How could they not know? He was definitely dead. He'd be over a hundred and ten, if he wasn't. Come to think of it, I'd never seen his grave in the family plot. I wasn't looking for it, but The Girls took me to the family estate Prie-Dieu for picnics and they liked to visit the family. I didn't remember ever visiting Josiah Bled's grave. Maybe he was in Arlington cemetery or someplace like that, but everyone else was in the family plot, no matter where they died or how. Why would the much loved Josiah be any different?

I called Prie-Dieu to ask and got the answering machine. Since their accounts were frozen, The Girls were staying at the old estate to save money. They spent most of their time tending the grounds and giving tours since the mansion was in trust to the Missouri Historical Society. They'd never been so busy.

Then I tried Dad's cell and Mom's. I got voicemail on both. The home office was a lock. Claire, my old high school rival, had taken over after I did a favor for her in exchange for her transcription skills. She practically lived in Dad's office. He was now a private detective and he'd never been so organized. My parents loved Claire. She was the daughter they never had. Obedient, respectful, and quiet. She did absolutely everything they said right down to her dating life. Dad checked out all potential suitors, so Claire hadn't had a date in six months, which was a good thing. If there was a loser con artist in the vicinity, Claire would find him.

"Hey, Claire," I said. "I'm trying to get ahold of my parents, but they're not answering."

"Hi, Mercy. Let me see. That's right. Your dad's chasing a child molester in Jeff City and your mom's testifying in front of the grand jury in Cleveland. Do you want to leave a message in case they get in touch?"

"Will Dad be back tonight?"

"I doubt it. If he gets the guy, he'll follow the arrest through."

"What about Mom? We're supposed to leave in two days."

"She's flying back tomorrow, assuming the indictment goes through. Why? Is something wrong?"

Is something wrong? Not exactly.

"No. Everything's fine. But you've been going through Dad's files reorganizing, right?" I asked.

"Yes. They were a mess."

"Did you perhaps find anything about our house? Maybe some notes?"

Claire got cagey. "What are you looking for?"

"Nothing in particular, just what was going on around the time The Girls gave it to us."

"You'll have to be more specific."

Groan.

"What was Dad working on back then?" I asked.

"He was a police detective."

"I know. He kept every single notebook he used during his career. I just want to know what he was working on."

"I'm afraid I can't tell you," said Claire.

"Why the heck not?"

"I signed a confidentiality agreement."

"I'm his kid. I think you can tell me what cases he was working on before I was born."

"I can't. The agreement was very specific. You're mentioned by name."

"Dad had you sign an agreement not to tell me stuff? Seriously?"

"I can't tell anyone else either, if that makes you feel better," said Claire.

"It doesn't."

"Before you go, I have a message from your mom."

Groan.

"You have to go shopping for appropriate cruise wear today. She's tired of your procrastination. Sheila at Forever Summer is expecting you."

"What in the world is appropriate cruise wear?"

"I have a list for you."

Great. More dresses that fall apart.

"Never mind. I'll figure it out." I hung up and started up my ancient truck. The engine roared in a most satisfying way and the familiar vibrations rumbled through my generous rump, but I didn't know exactly where to go from there. My parents were hiding something and Claire knew what it was. That just sucked.

CHAPTER TWO

I ended up at Forever Summer forty-five minutes and a double bacon cheeseburger later. Never go to Steak-N-Shake when you're upset. It's a bad idea. I was so bloated I could hardly get out of my truck. Sheila watched me as I waddled to the door and grinned like a deranged pug while holding up a slip of paper.

"I've got the list," she said.

"My mom gave you a list, too?" I asked.

"She wanted to make sure you got everything."

"I'm not totally incompetent, you know."

"You're wearing that dress."

"Mom picked it out. I think she did it to make me look stupid."

Sheila turned up her snub nose. "Carolina wouldn't do that. You're wearing it wrong. Let me find you a belt."

"You can find me a blowtorch. I'm never wearing this again."

"Alright. Alright. Let's get working, shall we? Are you feeling super summery?"

I was, but she wasn't. Mom had been dragging me to see Sheila for years in a misguided attempt to get me to stop wearing cutoff jeans in the summer. I'd never seen Sheila in anything but black cashmere pants and a grey turtleneck, even when it was one hundred and four degrees outside. She looked completely bizarre surrounded by tropical prints and maxi dresses.

"Do your worst," I said.

"Yea! You go look through that rack of one-pieces. Carolina says you need two."

"Why do I need two one-piece swimming suits?"

"Versatility."

The door rang when a new customer entered and Sheila ran to greet whoever it was. I went to the swim rack, trying to figure out what was wrong with my old suit, other than the fact that it was faded and stretched out. I found two suits that might, if I was lucky, hold up my chest and didn't look like grandma suits. A man joined me at the rack and thumbed through size eighteen suits. I moved away. I'd had a bad enough day without being hit on. That might sound stupid, but it wouldn't be the first time a man did something goofy to get my attention. A guy once got a pedicure to ask me to dinner. I was embarrassed for him. He went so far as to get clear polish.

I turned to another rack with something called palazzo pants and the man followed me. I so wasn't in the mood. He moved in closer and I darted forward. "Can I help you?"

He wasn't startled or embarrassed like I was going for. He smiled, revealing a set of slightly crooked, very white teeth and held out his hand. "Mercy Watts, I presume."

"Are you a process server?"

He laughed and gave me his card. "Hardly. I'm Oswald Urbani and I have to say the illusion is perfect."

"That website was not my idea."

"So I've heard. Whoever's responsible did an excellent job representing you. You couldn't be more Marilyn."

I rolled my eyes. People say that like it's a compliment. They never think that perhaps, just maybe, looking like Marilyn Monroe isn't the best thing ever. A couple of months ago, some VFW vets finagled some pictures out of me and made a website, making me world famous as a Marilyn Monroe impersonator. Since then I'd been harassed and stalked. That wasn't totally out of the ordinary for me, but the guys who discovered me via the internet were pretty bold. It only let up when I agreed to do modeling gigs, but I still got a few weirdos a week.

Urbani watched me over the top of the rack with a thoughtful expression. He was my best looking stalker ever, not tall, but fit with a tan and soft dark curls waving back from his angular face.

"What?" I asked.

"I'd like to hire you," he said.

"I don't know what you've heard, but I only do print work. Fully clothed."

"I don't blame you, but that's not the kind of work I'm interested in."

"This conversation is over," I said, going to a rack of bra tops.

Unfortunately, he followed. "I want to hire you as an investigator."

"You're high. I'm a nurse."

Urbani moved in closer and lowered his voice. "You're Tommy Watts's daughter."

"That doesn't make me qualified to investigate anything."

"I disagree, and I think the Holtmeyer family would too."

"I can't talk about that." The Holtmeyers were the family that committed the murders that I'd been deposed to death on. I couldn't talk to anyone about that case until the trials were over.

"This isn't about them. I want you to cozy up to my brother-in-law. It should be a cinch for you. He's a huge Marilyn Monroe fan."

"Not interested."

Sheila found me. Her arms were full of dresses, cover-ups, and an unbelievable amount of tops. "I'm ready."

"Am I trying on the whole store?" I asked as I slipped away from Urbani into the dressing room.

"It's not that much. You have to be prepared for any situation." She put me in dressing room three, the extra-large one, and closed me in with four stacks of clothes that were leaning like my mom after a couple martinis.

"I don't need that much," I said.

Sheila didn't answer. She, like Mom, probably thought cutoffs didn't count. I'm here to say they do. They are clothes. I slipped off the hideous daisy dress and rooted through the first pile.

"I'll make it worth your while," said Urbani through the door.

I shrieked, "Get out of here, you freak."

"Now about my case."

"Sheila!"

"She's busy," said Urbani.

I didn't like the sound of that. "Sheila! Are you okay?"

"She's fine. She found better things to do than hover around you. All I ask is that you hear me out."

I pulled on a pink jumpsuit. OMG. It was even worse than I imagined. Jumpsuits are not made for short girls with curves. I looked like a stuffed bear. What the heck was Sheila thinking?

"Mercy?" asked Urbani.

"Fine. I'll listen and then you'll leave."

"Good. I'm worried about my sister, Lucia Carrow. Her husband, Graeme, may be having an affair. She won't talk to me about it."

"That's her business, not yours." Jumpsuit off and in the thou-shalt-be-destroyed pile.

"She's bruised. I think he's hitting her."

I could hear the pain in his voice, low agony under the words. I grabbed a one-piece and held it to my chest. Dad had worked on plenty of abuse cases over the years, the ones that ended in murder. I'd heard the pacing, watched him prep for trial. They were as bad as it got in his line of work, unless you counted cases involving kids. Dad drank when he caught those.

"I can't help you. Even if you knew for sure, it wouldn't change anything," I said softly.

"I think it would," said Urbani.

"I think this is your sister's life. If she wants to be married to an asshole, that's her business. Interference will just alienate her."

"I need to help her."

"You need to leave," I said.

"I don't give up."

"Then it's time you learn a new skill."

I put on the one-piece and viewed myself through one squinted eye. Not bad. I'd buy it, if it covered my chest.

"Mercy," said Sheila. "How's it going?"

"Crappy. Why'd you let him back here?"

"Who?"

"That guy that was following me around the store."

"He came back into the dressing room?" Sheila's voice went squeaky. "Did he do anything to you?"

I opened the dressing room door and looked into Sheila's panicked eyes. "Where were you?"

"I'm so sorry. I got this weird call from a supplier. I was in the back. Are you okay?"

"I'm fine. Nothing happened. He just wanted to annoy me," I said.

"Thank goodness. I'll stay here."

And she did, right through twenty-eight swimsuits and countless outfits. I picked out things that later I wouldn't remember buying. That call Sheila got wasn't a coincidence. I would be hearing from Oswald Urbani again.

I parked behind a Lamborghini in front of Stillman's Antiques Emporium and slipped into the breezeway between the shops. It was the best way to get onto or off of Hawthorne Avenue without being seen. I'd figured it out during my high school years when sneaking out became the only way I'd have a social life. My parents weren't particularly observant, but other residents of the Avenue were. My parents got no less than five calls when I snuck out and got in Lizzie Meyer's Beetle at the end of the block. Dad made a few calls and I was discovered in West County at a party with (gasp) boys. The Chief of Detectives put me in the back of a squad car and made six arrests for contributing to the delinquency of a minor. You can imagine how popular I was. I'd like to say that was the worst day of my life, but with Tommy Watts for a father, it can always get worse.

I don't know why anyone cared about me, but they did. You'd think the wealthy would have better things to do, like ordering their gardeners around or collecting fine wines. Maybe it was because my family didn't fit and they worried about the cop's daughter bringing in the wrong element. As far as I could tell *we* were the wrong element, but once Myrtle and Millicent brought us in, we were accepted. Even though we never had a servant of any kind and Dad washed his own car.

The giant oak at the back of Harris Field's property afforded the best hiding place. It was three houses down and surrounded by lilacs. I leaned on the rough bark and checked my watch. Claire should be leaving our house any minute. She was punctual, if annoying.

Right on time Claire pulled out into the alley behind our house in her baby blue Accord. See ya, sister. I'll be looking at those files now. The ones you so helpfully organized. Once she'd turned the corner, I trotted up to the back gate and let myself in. Ha. As if a little thing like a confidentiality agreement would stop me. Amateurs.

Mom's flowers were a riot of color and scent. Heavy rose blossoms encroached on the brick walk and brushed my ankles with their silky petals. I lazed up the walk breathing deep and looking at the stacks of raw wood covering the patio. Dad was supposed to be replacing the back porch roof, which had been torn off due to rot. The roof had been gone for a while and buying the wood was as far as Dad got. Actually, I think Claire bought the wood, but Dad was claiming credit. He should just hire someone like everyone else on the Avenue. They'd be happy to have their secretaries make a recommendation, but Dad was stubborn. He wanted to do it himself. Little did he know Mom was researching contractors behind his back. She was waiting for him to be out of town for a couple weeks before she'd strike. I planned on being there when he found out there was a new porch roof and he didn't build it. I'd be sure to add to my cursing vocabulary. Dad was colorful when angry to say the least.

I let myself in the back door and grabbed a tin of Ghirardelli double chocolate out of the butler's pantry. No, we didn't have a butler. But if we had, I would've called him Alastair. I made my cocoa and headed upstairs to Dad's office. The door was open, inviting me in to snoop. I set my mug on Dad's desk. We called it the boulder because it was a remnant of his police days and he'd kicked it round during his long career.

The in and out baskets were just begging to be gone through, so I picked up a stack and prepared to be enlightened on what Dad was up to.

"What do you think you're doing?"

I screamed and the papers went flying. I spun around and saw Uncle Morty sitting at Claire's little desk with his feet propped up on the immaculate wood surface.

Crap. Double crap.

The paper rained down around me like giant snowflakes. Great. Uncle Morty and a mess. This was not an improvement on my already lousy day. Uncle Morty chewed on the end of a plastic fork and eyed me from under his favorite driving cap, a sad affair with a ragged bill and several holes. It usually matched the rest of his ensemble. Uncle Morty loved ancient sweatsuits bought at Walmart in the eighties. That day he had on a shiny black tracksuit with racing stripes. I don't think I'd ever seen him in new clothes before and the sight put me off balance.

He pointed the fork at me. "You think you're smart, Mercy. You ain't."

"Are you trying to scare me to death?" I yelled.

Uncle Morty chuckled. "If that was possible, Tommy'd have done it long ago."

"Why are you here?"

"You know why I'm here, Nosy Parker."

"Did Claire call you? That little traitor," I said, trying to look wronged instead of being wrong.

"You two was never friends. You got all the looks. She got all the dates. Boys are smarter than they seem."

I plopped down in Dad's comfy chair. "What does that mean? Guys were right to ask out Claire instead of me? Claire doesn't have two opinions to put together."

"Looks ain't everything. You are trouble with a capital T."

"I am not."

"What are you here for? Dusting, I suppose."

"I could be."

He snorted. "You're here to find information that's none of your business."

"It's my family and I want to know what happened with our house."

"Get used to being in the dark. It's where Tommy wants you," he said.

"No way. I'm getting deposed on this crap."

"That's an easy deposition for you then. You don't know nothing and that's how it's going to stay."

I crossed my arms. "You have to leave sometime. I'll wait you out and get in those files."

Morty picked up a black nylon briefcase and dropped it on the desk. "Ain't nothing to find."

CHAPTER THREE

Right after Morty left my parents' house with his briefcase and all the information I wanted, I got called in to work a twelve-hour night shift in a Pediatric ICU. I took the shift, despite the heartache it would inevitably bring, because I worked PRN, which meant I filled in when someone was short a nurse. Peds was my least favorite work, but I have to admit there was something about taking care of a child when a family was living their worst nightmare. I could do a good job. I could help. Sometimes I needed to be what other people needed. It was a quiet night and nothing much happened. There were about ten people on that floor who didn't think I was trouble, so that was a bonus and I scored a second shift the next night.

I got home in the morning and into bed while managing to ignore cellphone messages. Six hours later, the landline Dad insisted I have for his own nefarious purposes began ringing with a decidedly crabby tone. I ignored it. That never worked out for me, but I tried it anyway.

After ten separate calls, the answering machine picked up. "Mercy, don't make me come over there."

Dad. The writer of confidentiality agreements and ruiner of many a date.

The phone rang again. This time I picked up. "What?"

"Is that how you greet your loving father?" he said.

"It is today."

"Were you asleep?"

"I worked a twelve-hour shift last night," I said.

"Well...this is important."

"It always is."

"Did you meet Oz Urbani yesterday?" he asked.

I didn't know what to say. That was fast, even for Dad.

"Mercy. Oz Urbani. Did you meet him?

"Um...yeah. I guess so," I said.

"Did you or didn't you?"

"I did. Why?" I asked.

"Don't speak to him again."

"Why not?"

"Can't you just listen and obey?" asked Dad.

"Hello. This is your daughter speaking."

"Alright. This is how it is. His full name is Oswald Fibonacci Urbani. Get it?"

"Not really." I yawned. This conversation wasn't nearly as interesting as Dad thought it was.

"He's a Fibonacci as in *the* Fibonaccis."

"Are you talking about the Mafia family?" I asked.

"That's the one. Oz is the nephew of Cosmo Fibonacci, the supposed head of the family."

"Supposed?"

"Rumor has it that Cosmo's twin, Calpurnia, is the power behind the throne, but it seems unlikely."

I blinked. A woman heading a Mafia family? That was unexpected, and, if it were true, the Fibonaccis would be a very well run organization. I shuddered to think what my mother could do with such an army at her beck and call.

"So Oswald's in the mob," I said. "I didn't see that coming."

"He's not officially. He's a golf pro," said Dad.

"Then why can't I talk to him?"

"He's a Fibonacci. What did he want?"

"Maybe he wanted a date," I said.

Dad made a grunt full of sarcasm. "What did he want?"

"He wanted me to find out if his sister's husband is an asshole."

"Stay away from him. You don't want to owe him or have him owe you."

"No problem."

Dad hung up after giving me a dozen dire warnings about getting involved with a Fibonacci. They sounded eerily similar to the warnings he used to give me about boys. I almost asked him about the house, but it was pointless. He'd never tell me anything. I'd have to find out the hard way. I wondered what Claire liked more, vodka or tequila. She looked like a lightweight. That would make it easier to get information out of her.

I fell asleep thinking of the best way to booze information out of Claire. After much less sleep than I wanted, I went in for my last shift before vacation. It ended up being one of my worst nights as a nurse ever. Two children died, one from a head wound sustained falling out of a second story window and the other leukemia. I managed to keep my crying to a half hour in the bathroom and vowed never to return. I told my service not to book me any more shifts on Peds, but I don't think they took me seriously.

I got up when it was dusk and started packing, only to realize my one suitcase was too small for everything Sheila made me buy. I put on one of Sheila's favorites, a sleeveless shirtdress that managed to cover all my bits and decided to walk over to my parents' house to borrow one of Mom's suitcases. I left my apartment barefoot and swinging my sandals in one hand. The day's heavy humidity had lifted, leaving a slight chill in the air and a smell that only happened in St. Louis in late August, a sort of clean dirt smell. I did my best to push those two kids out of my mind. I don't know how Dad worked on cases involving kids as much as he did. He seemed to handle it pretty well with the help of a bottle of Tullamore Dew. I wasn't much of a drinker, so the best I had to cope was to put those faces into a little box deep inside my mind and promise myself I'd visit them again one day.

"Hey, Mercy!" A man waved at me from the door of Black Heart

Books, the best bookstore on the planet and the only one in the Central West End.

I waved back but didn't cross the street. It was Nardo, a photographer who'd started stalking me after the public became aware of my uncanny resemblance to Marilyn Monroe. There was a market for pictures of me and he didn't care how he got them. Eventually, we came to an understanding. Nardo would be my official photographer and would keep the rest of the paparazzi away from me. Since then he'd taken to hanging out in my neighborhood and I saw him nearly every day.

"I have some jobs for you!" he yelled.

"Vacation! See you in a couple weeks!"

He saluted, turned back into the shop, and joined his book group on the cushy sofa next to the front window. Nardo, after he stopped stalking me, turned out to be a pretty reasonable person. He belonged to multiple book groups and made fantastic salsa verde.

I took a right onto Lexington and then found myself walking on the gaslit sidewalk of Hawthorne Avenue. The houses were huge on our end of the street, but not as big as the ones on Myrtle and Millicent's end. I'd avoided their side, since they left for Prie-Dieu. Their house looked so lonely and sad without them. Mom went over to water the plants, but I couldn't bear to. It made me feel like Myrtle and Millicent had died and I'd never see them again. Most of the houses on our end were just as quiet and dark. Their inhabitants were spending the hot summer months in Europe or on private islands in the Caribbean. My parents, on the other hand, were home. The lights were blazing on all three stories. Mom liked light and music, all kinds, and reggae blared out into the night.

I let myself in and yelled, "Mom!"

"In the kitchen!"

I dropped my sandals and found Mom packing snacks in a gallon Ziplock bag, like they didn't have snacks on cruise ships.

"How many granola bars do you think we need?" Mom asked, holding a box of the really dry crusty ones.

"None," I said.

"Don't be difficult. We have to have snacks."

I groaned as my Aunt Tennessee came in. She was wrapped in an enormous orange shawl thing. Since she weighed well over two hundred pounds, you can imagine the size of it.

"Mercy, I bought a new swimming suit. Do you want to see?" she asked, her face lit up with hope.

I'd been through this exercise every year of my life. Aunt Tenne bought a suit every year, hoping it would be different, that something called "Magic Suit" or "Hope on a Hanger" really would be the answer, and it never was.

"Sure," I said, hoping I sounded more confident than I felt.

Aunt Tenne opened her arms like a joyfully dramatic butterfly and my mouth dropped. Holy crap! It *was* a magic suit. There was a waist where there'd never been one before. Curves. A lovely line.

"That is the best suit I have ever seen," I said. "I want one."

She wrapped her arms around me and kissed me on the cheek. "It's perfect, isn't it?"

Mom watched me over Aunt Tenne's shoulder, her pretty face puckered in a frown.

"What?" I mouthed.

Mom shook her head and Aunt Tenne stepped back. "It's going to be different this year. I won't think about it. I'm going to be happy." She flounced out of the kitchen, singing Bob Marley's "Waiting in Vain."

"What's she talking about?" I asked.

"Nothing," said Mom, avoiding my eyes. "She's turning over a new leaf. That's all."

"Doesn't sound like you believe it."

"Sometimes it's just hard hoping for things to get better."

"What's supposed to get better? The weight?" I asked.

"It's not about the weight."

"What's it about then?"

"Never mind. We need to talk," she said.

I didn't like the sound of that. Usually I came out on the losing end of our mother/daughter talks. "I just came for a suitcase."

Mom brightened up, thoughts of Aunt Tenne forgotten. "That's what I want to talk about. You don't need to pack all the stuff you bought from Sheila."

"Why not?"

"Don't sound so suspicious. We've been upgraded."

"To what? A nude cruise?"

"Don't be disgusting. It's not a cruise anymore." Mom shook the entire box of nasty granola bars in the snack bag and looked at me, triumphant.

"What happened to the cruise?"

"Ava called this morning from the travel agency and she found us an even better deal."

"I can't believe you still use a travel agency."

"Ava is a specialist and I don't have time to search for deals. Do you?" asked Mom.

I did, but I said, "No."

"Alright then. We're going to...Roatan." Mom flung out her arms like she was presenting an award.

"Where's that?" I plopped down on a chair and picked through Mom's pile of Belgian chocolate bars, looking for a seventy percent. No luck.

"Honduras. Haven't you always wanted to go there?"

"To Honduras? Um...I'm going to go with no."

"It'll be fantastic. We're going to scuba dive. It's all included."

"Do we want to scuba dive?" I asked. Scuba diving was right up there with base jumping. I had enough excitement just being Tommy Watts's daughter.

Mom rolled her eyes and ran her fingers through her hair. The fluffy curls that always behaved landed and framed her face. At forty-seven, she could've passed for my sister easily. I can't tell you how many of my dates liked her better than me. Between her and Claire it's a wonder I ever got a boyfriend. Maybe I was trouble. I snatched a sixty percent Galler bar and inhaled it.

"Where's your passport?" Mom asked.

"In my dresser."

Mom handed me a printout of airline itinerary and reservations at La Isla Bonita Beach and Dive Resort.

"What about Dixie?" I asked. "The cruise was kind of her thing."

"She's fine with it. Very excited."

I couldn't tell if Mom was telling the truth or not, but I doubted Mom's best friend was okay with the change. Her husband Gavin had died two months ago. He was one of the murders I'd been deposed about. Gavin never wanted to go on a cruise. He thought they'd be boring. The cruise was supposed to be some sort of a fresh start for Dixie.

"Mercy." Mom came over and hugged me. "She's okay with it. I promise. We can go on a cruise anytime."

The door to the butler's pantry flew open and my cousin by marriage, Chuck, strode in carrying a sparkly pink gift bag. He wore St. Louis police department workout clothes and shone with sweat. Every muscle stood out on his long, lean limbs and he smelled like man. Another one for my think-about-later box.

He dropped the bag on the table. "Why the long faces? Isn't it girl trip time?"

"We're going to Honduras," I said.

"I heard. You two will be something in wetsuits," said Chuck.

"I'm not sure about the scuba diving."

"I'm advanced certified. It's not that difficult. They'll take good care of you." His blue eyes twinkled at me and his mouth suppressed a grin.

"You say that like you think I need coddling or something."

Mom laughed and packed the chocolate bars. "Well, honey, you're not known for your toughness."

"What?" I jumped up. Only later did I discover that I had flecks of chocolate all over my face. "I'm tough. I brought down Gavin's murderer, didn't I?"

"Technically, your partner brought him down and I arrested him," said Chuck.

"Aaron is not my partner, and I figured it out."

"Aaron clocked him," said Mom. "You make a good team."

"We are not a team. Nobody could team with Aaron," I said.

This had been an ongoing argument for the last two months. Dad had declared Uncle Morty's friend Aaron and I a team after I solved his best friend, Gavin's, murder with, I suppose, a tiny bit of help from Aaron. So every time I did something for Dad now, Aaron was right there *helping*. That mainly meant boring me senseless with talk of Dungeons and Dragons, Star Wars, and hot dogs. Actual help was not on the list.

"Aaron's a good guy and he saved your bacon. I won't hear anything against him," said Mom.

"I'm not saying he's evil. He's Aaron. And I am tough."

Mom put her hands on her hips. "You're difficult. Can't you be more accepting of the special people in your life?"

"Yeah," said Chuck, stepping closer. "Can't you accept the special people?"

"Aaron's special alright." I backed away. "You stink."

"What's in the bag, Chuck?" asked Mom.

"Present for Mercy. Wear it in good health," he said.

I opened the bag and pulled out the smallest bikini I'd ever seen. It had pink polka dots and couldn't have been used to cover an entire melon much less me.

"It's adorable," declared Mom. "I love the color."

"Are you kidding? You said I had to have one-pieces with under-wires," I said.

Mom snorted. "This is a gift."

"I can't wear that. It's illegal in fifty-eight countries."

"But not in Honduras." Mom left with the snack bag and yelled over her shoulder. "Thank your cousin."

Chuck pursed his lips. "I'm ready to be thanked."

"Ooh, gross."

Chuck wasn't a real blood relation. His mom married my uncle when he was thirteen and he'd been bothering me ever since.

"No kiss?" he asked.

"Not a chance. I do have a question for you though."

"Yes, I'll help you try on the bikini. It's the least I can do."

"It's more than you can ever hope for. My question is about our house," I said.

Chuck crossed his arms. "Oh, yeah. What about it?"

"Do you know when Myrtle and Millicent signed it over?"

"Before we were born. I don't know the day."

"Do you know why they signed it over?" I asked.

He watched me for a second and then said, "Why are you asking?"

"Because I got deposed about it."

"Then it's good you don't know."

"But you do?" I asked. "Did Dad tell you not to tell me?"

"Nope. He didn't have to. If he wanted you to know something, he'd tell you. End of story." Chuck opened the pantry door and a rush of coldness came in from my favorite space.

"But he told you?"

Chuck moved so quickly I didn't have time to flinch. He gave me a peck on the lips and went into the pantry. I followed, a little breathless. "What do you think you're doing?"

He gave me his best rakish grin. "Getting my thank-you."

"Did Dad tell you about the house and how they got it?" I asked.

"No, but it doesn't take a genius to know something weird's going on there." Chuck left through the back door and I stayed standing on the marble pantry floor, feeling the cold creep up my ankles.

CHAPTER FOUR

An hour later, I found my boyfriend, Pete, in an on-call room, sleeping off back-to-back bowel resections. He claimed his surgical residency would end someday. I had my doubts.

I slipped in the room and knelt by the bunk bed and pushed the dark blond hair off his broad forehead. He didn't move. His phone began vibrating away on the floor next to his slack hand that hung off the side of the bed. The screen said ICU Stat. Great. Foiled again. We'd had a few romantic moments in on-call rooms, but that night wasn't going to be one of them.

I kissed his cheek and shook his shoulder. "Pete. They're calling for you in the ICU."

"Mercy?" he said in a rough throaty voice full of exhaustion.

"Sorry to wake you." I gave him the phone.

He texted the nurse back and then groaned. "I have to go. The cops are trying to get in to see my patient."

"In the ICU?"

"Gunshot victim. Happened in front of Plaza Frontenac, if you can believe that. She didn't see anything. But I guess they don't believe me." He sat up and went to put on his shoes, only to discover that he'd slept in them.

"They're paid not to believe." I tried to quell my curiosity but failed as usual. "So the victim talked to you before surgery?"

"Yep. She was walking out the door and someone shot her. She has no idea why. I'm off tomorrow. Let's go see a movie or something."

Pete followed me to the elevator. I pushed the up and down buttons.

"Are you mad at me?" he asked.

I hugged him, breathing in his smell. Not cologne, sterile gloves and antiseptic. "No. I wish I was here tomorrow."

"Where're you going to be?"

"Vacation on Roatan. Mom changed it from the cruise."

"Sorry. I totally forgot about the girl trip. So it's Roatan, Honduras now?" he asked as the elevator doors opened.

"Apparently so."

Pete stepped inside and held the door. "Take your full kit. Jonas did a Doctors Without Borders in Coxen Hole. They had expired antibiotics and no opiates."

"Fantastic." I kissed him and had a brief but disturbing flash of Chuck's peck.

Pete must've read my mind. "Hey, is Chuck working tonight?"

"No," I said with a twinge of guilt. I don't know why. I didn't kiss anybody. "He was just at my parents'."

"Damn. I'd rather deal with him than some other detectives I don't know. Be careful," said Pete, getting out his prescription pad and writing out two for me. "Fill these just in case. Jonas said it's like the Wild West down there."

"Thanks. I'll see you when I get back," I said.

"I'll try to be conscious."

The doors closed and I took Pete's prescriptions to the pharmacy, one for the antibiotic, Keflex, and the other a painkiller, Norco. Never leave home without them, especially when going to a Third World country. After that I got waxed and wished I hadn't. Don't believe them when they say it only hurts for a second. I'd been kicked with less sting. I nearly brought my Norco collection down by one, but I took a Motrin instead. I'd had my fill of painkillers after the Holtmeyers in Gavin's case got through with me.

When I got home, I packed both my kits. Pete only knew about one, the medical one. It had sterile gloves, tweezers, alcohol pads, syringes, Betadine, and the like. I added the Keflex and Norco to the other medications I'd collected, zipped it shut and tossed it in with my bras. Then it was on to the kit Pete didn't know about, Dad's kit. It included less, shall we say, benign things, like zipties, three kinds of mace, two antique pistols, because one is not enough, and the recently added Universal Taser Dad gave me on the 4th of July. Thanks, Dad. Just what I always wanted. I left the pistols and the taser snug in between Christmas sweaters. Somehow, I thought the TSA would take a dim view of them, even in checked baggage. I threw in an assortment of the clothes Sheila picked out, my two one-pieces, and Chuck's bikini. Mom would be on me if I didn't bring it. After that I passed out in front of a Denzel Washington movie with my cat, Skanky, and an untouched bag of baby carrots.

"Find that damn cat! We've got to go!" Dad stood in my living room at six in the morning with his arms crossed and his red hair standing on end. He was not a morning person and I doubted it was his idea to drive us to the airport.

"Stop yelling," I said as I dropped to my knees and peered under the sofa.

"I'm not yelling."

"Yes, you are. I'll never find him now." I'd been looking for Skanky for an hour. He always knew when I was going to take him over to Mom's and leave him with her evil Siamese.

Dad walked past me. "I'll get him."

"You'll never find him. He's scared to death of you."

"No, he isn't. He likes me." Dad went into my bedroom, which was a mess. At least it wasn't Mom. She'd pause to pick up and lecture me.

"Skanky hates you. You're always threatening to turn him into a cat taco."

Dad walked back out, holding a wide-eyed Skanky by the scruff of the neck. "He knows I'm not serious."

"How'd you do that?" I stuffed Skanky into his carrier and he didn't even yowl. Dad must've petrified him.

"It's a cat and you named him Skanky. How smart do you think he is?" Dad grabbed my suitcase and went out the door.

I locked up and chased him down the stairs. "He's not stupid."

"He's a cat. Enough said."

"Does Mom know you think her Siamese are stupid?"

"The Siamese aren't stupid. They're evil."

We went out the front door of my building to find Dad's car stuffed with Mom, Aunt Tenne, and Dixie. Dad somehow wedged my suitcase in the trunk and then grabbed my arm before I got in. "You got your kit?"

"Yes, Dad."

"The taser, too?"

"We're not supposed to bring those on aircraft."

"Jesus, Mercy. I got you the export license so you could carry it."

"Why would you do that? I'm not going to run around foreign countries tasing people."

"You never know when you might need it. Especially now that the Fibonaccis are in the picture."

"They're not in the picture."

I tried to get in the car, but Dad turned me around. "Go get it. We'll wait."

"I don't need it. This is a vacation, crazy person."

Mom rolled down her window. "Get in the car, Mercy. We're going to be late."

Dad gave me a little push toward my building's front door. "Flight's at eight-thirty. We have time."

Mom got all squinty-eyed. "Time for what? You better not be doing anything. This is a vacation. No work."

"Dad wants me to get my taser," I said.

Dad groaned.

"No tasers. Get in the car," said Mom.

"She needs it. Just in case," said Dad.

Mom started to get out of the car. "If you've arranged any work for our daughter in Roatan, so help me I will—"

Dad held up his hands. "No. No. There's no work in Roatan." Out of the side of his mouth, he said to me. "For god's sake, get in the car."

I squashed in beside Aunt Tenne, who was wearing an enormous sun hat and fushsia lipstick. "What was that about?"

"Dad's crazy," I said.

"I heard that," he said.

"You should be used to it. I say it all the time."

Dad growled and broke about ten traffic laws on the way to Lambert International. He dropped us at Departures with dire warnings about third world countries and a whisper in my ear about not talking to any Fibonaccis ever.

Fine. I'll try to hold myself back.

Dad squealed his tires and was gone. I have to say it was a relief. He'd been glaring at me in the rearview the entire way over. I turned around and Dixie, Mom, and Aunt Tenne were standing in a line with their hands on their hips. Small, medium, and large suspicion.

"What?" I asked.

"Mercy," said Dixie. "You know this trip is very special to me."

"Yeah."

"I loved Gavin, but he ruined every vacation we ever had with work. There was always a case. Someone always needed help. I need a fresh start."

"Don't worry. There's no case. None at all," I said.

"You promise?"

"Cross my heart. If a dead body lands at my feet, I'll step over it."

"That's all we wanted to hear." Mom grabbed her suitcase and led the way into the terminal. The crowd parted for her with all the usual smiles and whispers. Mom said she hated the Marilyn Monroe comparisons, but you'd never know it. She was dressed like a fifties movie star with a full-skirted dress cinched at the waist with a wide belt and a pair of oversized sunglasses. That was Mom incognito. She couldn't help herself.

We walked through the terminal with people pointing first at her and then me. A woman ran up to me and asked for my autograph for her husband. I signed her notebook while Aunt Tenne rolled her eyes.

"My husband loves your website," the woman said. "He says it's like Marilyn is with us again."

"Thanks, I guess." I'd been getting more autograph seekers lately and it made me feel like apologizing to the real Marilyn. She worked hard to cultivate the image I was born with and I didn't appreciate it. When people were staring at me, or worse, asking if I was a female impersonator, my face seemed more like a disease than anything else.

"You look so natural," she said.

"I try." I don't know what that woman was thinking. It was six forty-five in the morning. I had no makeup, hair in a ponytail, and was wearing yoga pants and flip-flops. I couldn't be more natural, but she still thought I was putting on a show.

We ended up at security with plenty of time to spare and I stood bleary-eyed, hoping the line would move someday soon. Then I smelled something. One of those smells that seeps into your brain and kicks it right in the crotch. Hot dogs. I squinted and looked over my shoulder. Aaron was standing directly behind me, holding a bottle of chocolate Yoo-Hoo and munching on a snowball snack cake. I looked forward. I did not just see Aaron. That would be ridiculous. Aaron never went anywhere unless it was with me. He would never be at the airport.

Mom turned around. "Mercy, take off your shoes." She raised her sunglasses. "Aaron, what are you doing here?"

"Waiting," he said.

Nooooo. It's real.

"Mercy," said Mom. "It's Aaron."

I closed my eyes. "I'm pretending it isn't."

"Have you come to see us off?" asked Dixie.

"I'm going," said Aaron.

I opened my eyes in time to see him chug some Yoo-Hoo. "Where are you going?"

"Wherever you're going," he said.

"Why?"

"Mercy, don't be rude," said Mom.

"It's not rude. It's a question. Aaron, where are you going?" I asked.

"Isla Roatan."

"Why?"

"Cause we're partners," said Aaron.

"Not in life."

"I got to go. We're partners. Tommy said." He bit the snowball and coconut flakes stuck to his upper lips like he was in a Got Milk ad.

"This is a vacation. You don't have to vacation with me."

"Got my tickets."

Mom, Dixie, and Aunt Tenne exclaimed how happy they were to have him with us. Not an ounce of suspicion between them when it came to Aaron and there should've been plenty. Aaron wasn't there by accident. Mom went through security, followed by Dixie, and Aunt Tenne. When they were through, I asked Aaron, "Dad told you to go to Roatan, didn't he?"

"Yep. Said you need me."

"What for exactly?" I asked.

"Just in case."

The security guy pointed at me. "Your husband can't take that through."

Husband?

"Madam," he said again. "Your husband can't take that through."

That's when I realized he was talking about Aaron, a guy that was two inches shorter than me, fifty pounds heavier, and sported a permanent case of bedhead. "Are you kidding? He's not my husband. I'm not married and I'm especially not married to him."

"He still can't take that through."

Aaron chugged the Yoo-Hoo and stuffed the rest of the snowball in his mouth. I followed him through the x-ray and past a security lady that told me my husband was a sweetheart. When it was time to board the plane, the gate attendant said my seat had been moved so I could sit next to my husband. WTF! So there I was, stuffed in a middle seat between Aunt Tenne and Aaron, who immediately got out the sandwiches he'd packed. Salami and shaved parmesan with arugula on a skinny garlic baguette. He brought one for each of us and half the plane wanted the recipe before they were seated. They smelled that good.

Aaron and Aunt Tenne munched on either side of me and I fought the urge to stuff the whole sandwich in my mouth at once. But Aaron was looking pretty pleased with himself and I didn't want to encourage him. This whole vacation thing was a one-time deal, no matter what Dad thought.

"Phone," said Aaron between bites.

Before I could say a word, Dad was yelling in my ear. "What did you do?"

"About what?"

"Judge Panesar just extended the freeze on The Girls' assets. And she signed search warrants for our bank accounts," he said, so enraged I could barely understand him.

"*Our* bank accounts? You mean yours and mine?" I asked.

"Yes, Mercy. Mine, your mother's, and yours."

"Why?"

"The Duchess of Dirt is alleging that your mother and I are blackmailing The Girls and the money's being funneled through you."

"That's ridiculous."

"Of course it is. I want to know who you've been talking to about the case."

"Nobody. There's nothing to say."

"You have to tell me."

Aunt Tenne furrowed her brows at me and I shrugged. "I didn't talk to anyone about it. The lawsuit's totally lame. They can look at my accounts until their eyes bleed. I don't care."

"Well, I do care. You better think long and hard about this, Mercy."

He hung up on me and I stared at the phone.

"What happened?" asked Aunt Tenne.

"I honestly don't know."

The captain announced that we were cleared for takeoff and for the flight attendants to secure the cabin. I put my phone away and tried to shake the feeling that Dad was hiding something and Arlene Cobb was on the trail. It was a new and wholly unexpected thought that Dad might've done something wrong, really wrong, and it had to do with The Girls and our house. I'd never started a vacation feeling crappier, but at least we were flying away from all that and I'd have time to breathe.

I tugged my seatbelt tight and watched a flight attendant hurry down the aisle. For a second, I thought she was headed toward me. Because, let's face it, that's just my luck. But she wasn't going for me. She stopped at the row in front of us and said, "Lucia Carrow?"

Lucia Carrow?

"That's me," answered a dark-haired woman in front of me.

"Sorry about the delay. Here's your gate check ticket," said the flight attendant.

The woman thanked her and I leaned over into the salami cloud surrounding Aaron. "Did she say Lucia Carrow?"

"Yep. Bet you're glad I'm here now," said Aaron.

Not really.

CHAPTER FIVE

The plane landed and taxied across a bumpy tarmac, stopping next to a concrete building that looked straight out of the fifties with lots of rectangular windows and a certain tired aura. Aaron had finished giving out recipes to passengers and was back to me. Fantastic. He'd already told me about every restaurant deemed worthy of attention on the west end of the island and a few that weren't.

"We should kill our own lionfish for dinner," he said. We'd been on lionfish for the last fifteen minutes.

"No."

"They're good eating."

"I'm not killing anything," I said, unbuckling my seat belt.

"They're killing the native species, Mercy," said Aunt Tenne. "We have to help the environment."

"I want to help *my* environment, which is full of noise pollution right now. Let's all be quiet."

The woman who was called Lucia Carrow squeezed into the aisle to deplane and I got my first good look. She was small, delicately boned with thick curly brown hair and large eyes. Crap. She had to be

Urbani's sister. They looked too much alike and how many Lucia Carrow's could there be?

"So you take a Hawaiian sling," said Aaron.

What did I do to deserve this?

"Graeme, you forgot your camera," said the woman.

Her husband, a medium-built blond with thinning hair, reached under the seat for a large black camera case. Graeme Carrow. There could be no mistake. It was them.

I must've done something really bad.

"You got to shoot it in the head," said Aaron.

I punched his fleshy shoulder. "I don't want to shoot anything. Stop talking. I can't take it anymore."

"Mercy!" said Mom.

"You need ice cream," mused Aaron as I pushed him down the aisle toward freedom.

We deplaned onto the tarmac into the tropical humidity that wasn't as bad as St. Louis and dragged our carry-ons across the blacktop behind Lucia and Graeme Carrow. He had his hand on the small of her back and guided her into the building. We followed them through Customs. It was so quick, I almost didn't know what had happened, and we were shunted into a holding area the size of my mom's bedroom, except without the air-conditioning. An older man rushed up to me, said his name was Enzo, and asked something I couldn't quite make out. Aaron answered him in Spanish.

"What does he want?" asked Mom.

"Where we're staying," said Aaron, producing a half-melted Mars bar from his carry-on.

"You speak Spanish?" I asked.

"No."

"La Isla Bonita," said Mom with one of her dazzling smiles.

Enzo stood there dazed for a second. "Marilyn. Bonita, Marilyn."

Is there no place on earth that doesn't know Marilyn Monroe? Seriously.

I must've groaned, because he looked at me. "Dos Marilyn!"

I smiled and waved. Enzo led us to the luggage carousel. "La Isla Bonita!" Then he charged through the small room and passed through a door in a glass wall. There was a crowd pressing against a rope on the other side. Enzo spoke to someone and he turned to us, flashing a broad smile and holding up a sign that said "La Isla Bonita" in big pink letters. Whoa. This trip just got better. The resort guy made Channing Tatum seem average. I think I blushed and I don't blush.

Get it together, girl.

The older guy rushed back in and, in a flurry of Spanish, indicated we should wait.

"There are eight more guests," said Aaron.

Enzo herded a couple over. The woman had amazing hair. It defied gravity, rising six inches off her forehead in stiff curls and down her back, reaching to her elbows. If Aaron had been a normal guy, he'd have been staring at her breasts that defied gravity in a very missile silo way. Her husband introduced them as Frankie and Linda Gmuca. He was a good twenty years older than Linda and wore a conservative dress shirt and a pair of Versace sunglasses perched on his balding head. They loved Aaron instantly and got into a loud conversation about salami.

After that we were joined by another couple and their two kids. They looked like they could've modeled for the Land's End catalog, being incredibly perfect and bland next to the Gmucas. Todd and Tracy Pell introduced their exceedingly bored children as Tara and Tyler. They liked T names and told us so.

While Tracy was schooling Mom on the long history of T names in her family, I spotted Lucia and Graeme Carrow across the room. They were happily comparing cameras with another couple, who had enough equipment to be photojournalists for *National Geographic*. Lucia looked okay to me. She smiled and stood close to Graeme, cuddling up to his side. That might not mean anything. She could be currying favor with her abuser.

Stop it! Don't look. She's not your problem.

Dixie stepped in front of me, her pretty face free of the heavy makeup she used to wear before Gavin died. Now it took me a second to recognize her. "I don't know what you're doing, but knock it off."

"I'm just standing here," I said.

"No, you're not. I remember that look. I saw it for thirty years. You're curious about something."

I shook my head. "I'm not really. Just tired."

Dixie spoke to Mom and I saw the Carrows speak to another native guy, probably about their resort. Thank goodness. It's a coincidence that they're here. Coincidences happen. They happen all the time. I couldn't think of any that happened to me, but still.

The luggage carousel creaked to life and scattered pieces of luggage started coming through the opening in the wall. Ten minutes later, we had all of it on a rickety metal cart. I could practically taste the fruity drinks already.

"The gang's all here," said Mom, fanning herself and Aunt Tenne with Aunt Tenne's big hat.

"I'm glad we found you. We were getting worried," said a man behind me.

No!

I turned.

Yes.

Lucia and Graeme Carrow stood behind me, smiling with their arms linked. Graeme's mouth fell open when he got a load of Mom and me, but he concealed his gaga for the Marilyn thing pretty well. I shook hands and tried not to look incredibly shocked at their going to our resort. Coincidence, huh? I don't think so.

"Are you *the* Mercy Watts? The one from the website?" Graeme looked hopeful.

"That's me," I said.

"I know this is awkward, but could I take a picture with you later? My friends will lose their minds."

"Sure." I watched Lucia out of the corner of my eye. She was interested, but I didn't see any signs of discomfort or jealousy. Either her brother was wrong about the affair or Lucia had no idea.

Enzo piled Lucia and Graeme's luggage on top of the pile and led us through the door in the glass wall. The hot guy stood smiling on the other side. He introduced himself as Mauro, a dive master and sometime driver. His accent was soft and exotic, but I couldn't even enjoy it, hot as he was. I was too mad. What were the chances I'd be on a vacation with Oz Urbani's sister? I'll tell you how many chances. None. Zero.

Mauro brought us outside to a short line of resort vans and loaded our luggage in the back of a van with "La Isla Bonita Beach and Dive Resort" painted on the side. Everyone started getting in, but I held Mom back.

"How exactly did we end up getting this trip?" I asked.

"Ava called and told me about it," said Mom.

"Just out of the blue, she called you?"

"Yes. The trip came in and she thought we would like it better."

"There were no penalties for canceling the cruise?"

"No. It was all taken care of."

More than you know.

La Isla Bonita sat on the West Bay near the tip of Roatan. The whole thing was tucked away from the main road and only when we drove through the gate did I realize we were there. The armed guard was the giveaway. I guess Pete was right about the Wild West comparison. Heavy tropical foliage surrounded the wooden buildings and the resort sign was nearly obscured. Mauro stopped at a little building that had "Reception" carved into a wooden plaque and a stocky man in his forties wearing a La Isla Bonita tee came out. He introduced himself as Bruno and began unloading the luggage. I waited next to a fat palm tree while Mom checked us in. Skinny brown birds that resembled crows flew overhead, yelling something that sounded like, "Spaghetti." I took off my shoes and my toes sunk into the warm sand. There were no sidewalks, just sand paths. I hadn't looked at the website, but I knew there wouldn't be any TVs or phones or clocks in our rooms. Fabulous.

Mom came out with our keys and Aaron appeared at my side with two ice cream cones. "Chocolate or coconut?"

"I didn't see an ice cream shop," I said.

"You didn't look."

"True. Thanks." I chose chocolate, of course.

Aaron licked his cone and took his key from Mom. Aunt Tenne and Dixie were still in Reception, so we waited under a red bougainvillea bush. I'd never smelled such air. It was sweet with flowers but dirty and earthy all at the same time. Lucia came out of Reception with Tracy, the Land's End Mom. They were discussing sunblock. Was fifty SPF enough or should they get one hundred?

Tara and Tyler ran up and interrupted their mother mid-sentence, wailing that they were hungry, tired, and bored. Tracy fed them chocolates out of her purse like they were two and promised that she would do anything they wanted as soon as they were checked in. The kids kept whining and tugging on her arms. Lucia hurried down the stairs with a glance of distaste over her shoulder and began rifling through her purse, searching for something. She kept talking, but the rifling got worse and worse.

Graeme came out, grinning and holding up their key. Then he stopped short. "What's wrong, Lucia?"

"I can't find my inhalers. I know I put them both in my purse," said Lucia, her cheeks red. "I have to have them on me at all times."

Inhalers. The one thing I didn't bring.

"Are you sure?" asked Graeme.

I pictured Urbani's worried face. Crap. An asthmatic without her inhaler wasn't a good thing.

"I'm sure. They're not here." Lucia's voice rose up in panic.

Graeme hugged her. "It's okay. I packed extras. They're in my suitcase."

Lucia's shoulders relaxed. "Thank goodness. Why'd you pack them?"

"Because you forget them." He gave her the key and picked up their suitcases. "See you all later."

We said goodbye and I watched them wander down a narrow path between palm trees. Lucia was saying she was sure she packed them and I got a feeling, a nervous Tommy Watts kind of a feeling. Dad was famous for his feelings. He knew when something wasn't right and I'd started to develop his skill. Graeme said Lucia forgot her inhalers, not that she would lose them altogether. Where did they go?

I looked up to find Aaron watching me through his thick glasses. He already had drips of ice cream down the front of his Spiderman tee and sand in his hair that was standing up in weird cowlicks all over his head. My partner. Right.

"Got a feeling?" he asked.

"Maybe."

Aunt Tenne and Dixie came out of Reception with a load of brochures, gave Tracy and her still whining kids a wide berth, and trotted down the stairs smiling. Dixie hooked her arm through mine. "Let's go check out our rooms." Her voice was cheerful, but her face couldn't have been sadder.

"Are you okay?" I asked.

She sighed. "Just thinking about Gavin. For some reason, your face reminds me how much I'm missing him."

"My face?"

"You were looking so intense just now. Like you were on the scent. Gavin loved the hunt. I can see that in you."

"I'm sorry. I don't mean to do it. I'm not up to anything."

"Good. Let's keep it that way," said Dixie.

Mom came over. "Bruno will take our bags to the rooms. Let's see the beach instead."

"I'll go with Bruno," said Aunt Tenne.

"Suit yourself," said Mom.

She led us down the path, whistling an aria I couldn't place. We passed the dive shop filled with divers tugging on tight wetsuits surrounded by posters of native fish and maps of Roatan. A well-tanned woman with a tangle of sun-streaked hair waved to us. "Welcome to La Isla Bonita."

We waved back and entered the heart of the resort. Curving paths took us past small bungalows with deep front porches and hammocks.

"That's our building," said Mom, pointing to a two story with four rooms. An outdoor staircase led up to the second floor. Brightly colored hammocks were hung next to each of the doors and a wide pail of water for cleaning sandy feet sat at the base of the stairs. No high-rise rooms with waitstaff for us. It felt slightly gritty but well-kept. I really didn't need the white linen capris Sheila insisted I buy. For once my beloved cutoffs were perfect.

The path widened and we found the on-site restaurant and bar. I'd never seen a restaurant with a sand floor and birds' nests in the rafters. To the right was a small pool with comfy deck chairs and a small waterfall, but straight ahead was the money shot. The ocean, ice blue and framed by palm trees. Dixie's grip on my arm tightened and her lips pressed together so that they went pale.

"Dixie?" I asked.

"It's so beautiful," she choked out.

Mom turned around, gave me her purse, and hugged Dixie. "It's alright that you're here. It's okay that you're happy."

"I should've made him come to places like this. He was always working. I should've made him rest and enjoy things," said Dixie, tears streaming down her face.

"Aaron," said Mom.

Aaron walked around us and went to the bar without another word from Mom. I followed him partially because I wanted to know what he was supposed to do and partially to get away from the crushing grief that hit Dixie at the most unexpected times. I didn't know what to do with it. Waves of agony flowed out from her waif-like body and went through the restaurant, making strangers take notice. Their faces instantly changed to expressions of concern or remembrances of their own past pain. That grief made me think of things I'd rather forget, like Gavin's body on the gurney, the face of his killer glaring at me from across a crowded courtroom. I had to do something, change something. Solving that crime wasn't enough. It didn't change anything and gave Dixie no relief that I could detect. My skin went all itchy. I wanted to run or fight. Something. Instead, I perched on a stool next to Aaron.

"Four Monkey Lalas," he said.

"What's a Monkey Lala?" I asked.

"Signature drink."

"What's in it?"

"Happiness."

"Well, I could use some of that."

The bartender, a smiling man with ebony skin and a lovely voice, sang a Shaggy song while he made our happiness. I rooted through my purse and found Oz Urbani's card stuffed down in a corner. The bartender set a glass in front of me and Aaron was right. It tasted like happiness with a touch of Bailey's and rum. Aaron took Mom and Dixie their drinks and I watched Dixie's eyes crinkle when she tasted it. Just what she needed, that and an adventure all her own.

I got out my phone and walked down to the beach. Pete had sent me a couple incoherent texts. If it had been anyone else I would've thought they were drunk, but since it was Pete, I knew he was exhausted. I texted him back and pondered the card in my hand. Calling Urbani probably wasn't the best idea, but my skin was still itchy, even with the help of a Monkey Lala and that Dad feeling just wouldn't go away. I hated being manipulated, especially on my vacation.

The phone rang twice before Urbani answered, sounding quite smug.

"Ah, Mercy Watts. I was wondering when I'd be hearing from you."

"You bastard. Do you know where I am?"

"Near a beach wearing a fetching bikini."

"When pigs fly. Guess who happens to be at this resort?"

"Pretty woman. Looks a lot like me," he said.

"What the hell do you think you're doing?"

"Helping my sister."

"I'm not working for you," I said.

"Let's not say you're working for me. Let's say you're observant and you hear things. Maybe you see some things."

I thought about the missing inhalers and decided to keep it to myself. I didn't want to encourage him.

"And maybe I call you when I get back to chat," I said. "Is that it?"

"We might bump into each other."

"I'll make sure we don't."

"You'll like Lucia. She's a wonderful person. Volunteers at Children's Hospital. Packs food for the homeless. Does those breast cancer runs."

"There are other detectives, if you're so worried."

"None like you," he said.

"Alright. I'll grant you that, but I can't work for you."

"Me specifically or my family?"

"Same thing."

"It is and it isn't. You checked me out, didn't you?" he asked.

"My dad did."

"Then you know I'm clean."

"You're a Fibonacci," I said. "You're all clean. Technically."

He laughed. "Some more than others, but I don't think it makes a difference really. You can't help yourself."

I took a big gulp of Monkey Lala for strength. "What makes you think that?"

"Because I checked you out. You're your father's daughter. He specialized in crimes against women and had the best conviction rate in the state, maybe the country."

"I didn't go into the family business." More Monkey Lala.

"Not officially, but a rape case comes into an ER, if you're working, you get it. You've got good victim rapport. You're known to follow up with victims, make sure they get services, etc. And there's the Holt-meyer case, among others."

"It's my job, dillweed. What's your point?"

"My point is that your dad never walked away from a victim and you don't either. If that asshole is hurting my sister, I don't think for a minute that you'll leave her hanging."

"Do you really think Graeme Carrow would be fool enough to beat up your sister?" I asked.

"Men do lots of things they shouldn't," he said, softly.

"I'm surprised your family hasn't done something already."

"They don't know and I have to be sure before they do. Understand what I'm saying?"

I hung up on him. "Shit." I understood alright. Payback was a bitch and the Fibonaccis didn't play.

Mom trotted down the stairs and looked at the phone in my hand. I quickly stuffed it and Oz's card back in my purse.

"I'm not even going to ask," she said.

"Good. How's Dixie?"

"Better. Sometimes she just needs to cry."

"How long is this going to go on?"

"As long as it takes. You know that better than most." Mom rubbed my shoulder. "So they have spots for the open water certification class tomorrow."

There was that pesky feeling again. "Who's going?"

"The Gmucas. I don't know what she's going to do with that hair."

Whew!

"Oh, and Lucia and Graeme."

"Are you kidding me?" I asked.

"No. Why?"

"Nothing. I'm in."

Mom clinked her glass against mine. "To the island. Who knows what adventures await."

I smiled, but I was starting to get an idea of what awaited me. An asthmatic *loses* her inhaler on an island known for subpar healthcare. Her husband, who might be beating her, just happens to have spares. And she's going scuba diving. A sport contraindicated for asthmatics with meds she hasn't had under her control. I was definitely in that class. Damn that Oz Urbani.

CHAPTER SIX

I got woken up by the crazed spaghetti birds at the crack of dawn. They'd added a new call of "meatball", which did not make their racket any better. Sleeping in would've been nice. Aunt Tenne was snoring in the other bedroom, having come in at two o'clock in the morning. I knew because I was up sitting on our porch, thinking about my parents and The Girls, while listening to Graeme *not* beating Lucia in their bungalow across the path. I'd turned into some kind of freaking stalker. Our internet was in and out, but I'd been able to research Graeme just enough to know he was boring. He had a thriving dental practice on The Hill, the Italian section of St. Louis. He'd met Lucia at St. Louis University and they'd been married five years. That was all on his website. I didn't have Uncle Morty's skills when it came to web snooping and I couldn't ask him. He'd tell Dad first thing. There were several competitors I could hire. Spidermonkey was Uncle Morty's arch nemesis and it was sure to get back to him that I'd gone to someone else. It wasn't worth the asspain. I didn't know if anything was going on for sure other than the nagging feeling that something was up.

Aunt Tenne snorted and began snoring even louder. I slipped out of bed and wrote her a note. I was getting coffee, not telling Mom she'd been out until two. I was definitely not going to be the one to let that news out. Mom was the younger sister, but you'd never know it. She hovered over Aunt Tenne and fretted about her all the time. Once when I was fifteen Aunt Tenne went away for the weekend without telling Mom. She nearly called out the National Guard. Mom called every ER in the city and made me sit at a cemetery with her for hours. It was the weirdest thing. Mom wouldn't say why she was so worried just that it was August, like that somehow explained things.

I threw on a cover-up and decided not to wear shoes. The morning was clear and sunny and the smell of coffee wafted around the palm trees. No sound from Graeme and Lucia's bungalow, so I walked down to the restaurant to find a coffee bar had been set up. Dixie stood in front of it with her finger on her lips.

"What's up?" I asked.

"Their milk's sitting out," she said. "Should I tell them?"

I picked up a carton and checked the side. "It's UHT milk. You don't have to refrigerate it."

"That's weird. I don't know," said Dixie.

"It's fine. They use it all the time in Europe."

The Girls had taken me to Europe multiple times when I was a kid. The boxes of warm milk freaked me out at first, but you get used to it. Dixie's face changed and the corners of her mouth pulled down.

Oh, no. What'd I say?

"Gavin never wanted to go to Europe."

I poured her a big mug of coffee. "You should go now. I recommend Paris. You'd fit right in."

She perked up. "That's right. The Girls took you. You're one lucky girl, growing up the way you did."

"I was. I am. I wish The Girls had a touch of luck right now," I said.

"Case not going well?"

"Judge extended the freeze," I said.

"I wish I knew what all the fuss was about. At least I'd know what to expect," said Dixie.

"You've been subpoenaed?" I took a sip of my coffee and tried to look uninterested.

"Yes. Big Steve's going to prep me when we get back."

We found a swing overlooking the ocean and sat down gingerly so as to not spill our coffee. I watched the Land's End couple's children splash around in the water while I worked up the nerve to get nosy.

"So what's he going to prep you for?" I asked.

"He wants to go over everything that happened the year before you were born. I told him I was in grad school. I barely remember anything but that."

That's right. Dixie knew my parents back then.

"Were you there when the deed to the house was signed over?"

"No. I wouldn't be there for that," she said.

"Were you surprised when The Girls gave Mom the house?"

"I barely remember it happening. I think Gavin helped your parents move in. I must've been working."

"Did Mom say anything at the time about getting the house?"

"No."

"When did you meet The Girls?" I asked.

Dixie took a sip and peered over the rim of her mug at me. "Are you interrogating me?"

"No. Just curious."

"You've got that look again," she said.

"I'd just like to know how we ended up with that house."

Dixie looked out at the ocean, and her face lit up from the sun's reflection off the perfect blue. "You'll have to ask Carolina."

I suppressed a groan. Lucky for me that I did. Mom ran around the side of our swing. "Where's Tenne?"

"In bed," I said.

"She's not answering the door." Mom's cheeks were flushed.

"I just left her. She was snoring her head off."

"So she's acting fine?"

"She's asleep," I said.

"But nothing unusual has happened?" asked Mom.

"Like what?"

"Like anything."

Does staying out until two count?

"Um...no, she's good," I said with a twinge of guilt. I lied on a regular basis when I was doing stuff for Dad, but I'd never gotten comfortable with lying to Mom. Probably because she usually caught me.

Mom took my coffee and downed the remainder.

"Why are you acting like Aunt Tenne's a crazy person you have to watch?" I asked.

Mom and Dixie exchanged a look. Great, more stuff people won't tell me.

"We're not going to go sit in a graveyard today, are we?"

"Did you see a graveyard? Did Tenne see it?"

"No and no. What is up with you?"

"Nothing. Let's get breakfast. Class is at eight thirty. Did you study your materials last night?"

"Yes, Mom. And I have to say studying on my first night of vacation was awesome."

We found a table with a fabulous view and ordered banana pancakes.

"Stop complaining," said Mom. "You'll be certified in three days."

"Great. Crossing off a goal I never had."

Dixie laughed at us and then smiled out at the glaring sand and water. It was going to be a hot one.

Mauro was waiting for us at the dive shop, wearing a pair of European swim trunks and by that, I mean very, very small. And tight. And small.

Stop looking, you freak.

"Mercy," said Mom.

"What?" I asked.

"Mauro asked you a question."

I blushed so hard I think my skin sizzled. "I'm sorry. What did you say?"

"Did you take all of your tests on PADI?" asked Mauro. His face was totally deadpan, but his eyes were laughing at me.

"Yeah, I did."

"Alright then. We will start our classwork as soon as the others arrive."

On cue Lucia and Graeme walked in, holding hands, and I couldn't stop looking at her suit either. It was made for old ladies, an oversized tankini with a skirt that went down to mid-thigh. Lucia had a nice figure, beautifully proportioned. What was she covering up? Graeme had a beach bag the size of a sofa cushion. I hoped Lucia had her inhaler in there.

Mauro asked them about their tests and the rest of our class arrived. The Land's End dad, Todd, came in carrying a backpack. He asked if they had lockers and where he should put his water. Mauro showed him the lockers and the Gmucas came in. Frankie had the kind of suit I was used to men wearing, to the knee with lots of pockets. Linda wore a leopard skin confection that looked like it may have been stuck on with tape. Last to arrive were three guys about my age. We heard them well before they came into the dive shop. Their laughter echoed off the walls and palm trees.

"Dude, you were so drunk," said the first to enter, a short, stocky blond with a military style haircut. Next was a taller man, thin with wavy brown hair and a large diamond stud in one ear. The third was same height as the second. He had espresso-colored skin and light brown eyes. He struck me as the kind of guy who wouldn't wear a diamond stud if his life depended on it.

"Welcome," said Mauro, extending his hand. "You are?"

The blond shook his hand. "Hi. I'm Joe and this is Andrew and Colin."

Colin, the brunette, let out a piercing whistle. "This resort gets better and better."

He was looking at me in a way that wasn't flattering, but clearly, he thought it was. He elbowed Joe in the ribs. "Did you arrange this?"

The smile Joe had on for Mauro froze on his face. Andrew fidgeted and looked at his feet.

"Arranged?" asked Mauro.

"You know," said Colin, "a festive little treat to send Andrew off into wedded bliss. Come on over here, hottie. Let's see what you've got. We can afford it."

Holy crap. He thinks I'm a prostitute.

I was about to give him the mother of all tell-offs, when my mother marched across the shop and put her finger in his face. "Who the hell do you think you are? This is my daughter. Not some sort of thing to be purchased like a car."

Colin stared at Mom. "There are two of you. This is awesome."

"Boy, you better—"

Mauro put his arm between them. "Mrs. Watts and her daughter are guests at the resort. They are not here for your entertainment."

"I don't know about that," said Colin.

Joe slugged him hard in the shoulder. "Shut up, man. This isn't APO."

"I'm so sorry," said Andrew with a faint tinge of pink on his cheeks. "Colin speaks before he thinks."

"APO?" asked Mauro.

"Our fraternity," said Andrew, looking hard at Colin. "But those days are over. Long over."

Colin put up his hands. "Sorry. Sorry. What can I say? When it comes to beautiful women, I lose my head."

"You are about to lose something else," said Mom.

The way Mom was looking at Colin, he should've been terrified, but he wasn't. He just grinned at her in a way that was supposed to be charming, but it was making Mom want to neuter him.

Andrew pushed Colin away into the shop and then stood between us and him. I smiled and he gave me a slight nod. I'd never been terribly fond of frat boys. My chest always seemed to cause a serious loss of critical thinking in their beer-addled brains, but I thought I could learn to like Andrew and Joe. They were working hard to keep their eyes up where they should be.

"Well, we are all here now," said Mauro. "Please come this way."

We sat at several rickety wooden tables on the deck next to the dive shop and were forced to listen to a lecture that was one hour and forty minutes longer than I was prepared to sit through. My head started nodding after twenty minutes and Mom kept poking me with her sharp elbow. I did learn how not to die, which was important.

Lucia seemed to be paying attention but didn't say anything about her inhaler during the medical portion.

"Okay," said Mauro. "If we are all ready, we will put on our bay say days and go to the shore."

Bay say days?

Nobody else looked confused, so I followed the crowd back under the dive shop overhang. Mauro and the woman from behind the counter, Marcella, started asking everyone their sizes for wetsuits. Lucia picked women's small. When she stepped into it, her swim skirt slipped and I saw the bruises her brother Oz must've been talking about. Three large purple circles covered her hip and thigh, like she'd been slammed against something. Maybe a bannister or wall. Lucia hastily pulled the wetsuit up and I looked away, picking up a women's medium. Wrong. I sat on the bench and yanked the thick foamy material up over my thighs, which until that moment I thought were fairly slender. I managed to get my arms in but couldn't get the zip in the back to go up. I was trying to get Mom's attention as she struggled with her own suit, but Mauro saw me and came over. I think his swimsuit got smaller.

OMG. What is wrong with me? I have a boyfriend. A very nice boyfriend who I hardly ever see and has the body mass of an underfed greyhound. But he's smart. And kind. Did Mauro just ripple? Ahhhh!

"Problem?" he asked, his accent soft and musical.

"No. I'm good."

Back away from the crazy girl.

"I'll help you." Mauro turned me around but didn't try to pull up my zipper. "It's too small. I get you a large."

"But I'm a medium," I protested.

"Not today."

He came back with a large. A large! I've never worn a large anything in my life. Why did I drink all those Monkey Lalas? They must have a thousand calories a piece.

"Put it on," said Mauro. "It's not bad."

But it was bad. He could zip it up farther, but it still wouldn't go up all the way. Then he did it. The incredibly hot dive instructor did it. He got me an extra large. That would've been bad enough, but that one wouldn't zip up either. By this time everyone was in their wetsuits and was watching me. Mauro yanked on the back of my wetsuit and muttered under his breath. I don't speak Spanish, but I think fat girl was in there.

"I can't do it," he said. "Your—how you say—top half is too big."

Colin laughed and Joe hit him again.

"Well, that's it, I guess," I said, turning to slink away. "No scuba for me."

Mauro grabbed my zipper lanyard and held me back like a dog on a leash. "It's okay."

"No, it really isn't."

Marcella said something in Spanish and Mauro agreed. She went to the rack and got another wetsuit that looked enormous. I mean, we're talking really big. Tent big.

"We try another size," said Mauro.

I looked at the tag. Men's medium. Kill me now. Yes. That one zipped up and as an added bonus, the crotch was at my knees, so I got to walk like a penguin. I would've run out of the shop, if I could've waddled fast enough.

Lucia came over and patted my back. "You look fine. Really. It's just that you're so well-endowed. I have a friend who had the same problem. No one will notice in the water."

Oz was right. I did like her. Damn it. Why couldn't she be a snotty crab that turned up her nose at my penguin suit? It would be so much easier to ignore the bruises. "Thanks."

She started back toward Graeme who was with his bundle of equipment on the bench, but I held her back.

"Lucia, I don't mean to be nosy, but do you have asthma?"

"How'd you know?"

"I'm a nurse and you packed inhalers."

"Oh. Why do you ask?"

"Scuba is contraindicated for asthma sufferers."

"I know, but I got clearance from my doctor. I just have to have my inhaler close at hand."

"Are you sure about this?" I asked. There was that feeling again.

"I'm sure it will be fine. Graeme really wants to get certified together," said Lucia.

I bet he does.

Marcella, the shop assistant, came over and handed me a black vest. "This BCD should fit you."

"Oh," I said. "Bay say day."

She laughed and we looked at Mauro.

"What?" he said.

"Bay say day," said Marcella with a laugh.

He frowned. "I don't say that."

"You really do," I said and he frowned deeper, making him absolutely adorable. I turned away before I launched myself at him and packed my own bundle, wrapping my regs, mask, and fins inside my BCD. Mauro had us start loading our tanks into the back of a golf cart parked beside the shop. I came and saw Lucia sitting next to her bundle talking to Todd.

"Everything okay?" I asked.

She smiled. "Just a little nervous."

"Me, too. Grab your stuff. We nervous Nellies will do it together."

We loaded our bundles into the back of the golf cart and followed it down a narrow sand road to the ocean. The shore dive turned out to be a piece of cake. Although every time I cleared my regulator, I got a nice spray of seawater in the mouth. Gag. Mostly, I was just glad Lucia was fine and I didn't do anything to further embarrass myself, like shoot to the surface in a panic. Todd did that twice. Linda once. Even Mom had a mini freakout when she had to fill her mask. Only Dixie got through it without a problem. When we surfaced, she wore a smile I hadn't seen since the Easter before Gavin died.

"That was amazing," she said. "Gavin would be so proud of me."

And he would. Dixie did everything perfectly, but he always thought she was perfect to begin with. Me, he would've teased. I could just see him sneaking up on me, doing a shark routine.

We tromped back to the dive shop, unloaded our gear, and were told to be back there in three hours. I immediately broke my vow and had a Monkey Lala and a huge cheeseburger with Aunt Tenne who looked happier than Christmas. Mom kept watching her and asking how she was feeling. Aunt Tenne finally made a run for it, saying she had to get something from our room, but Mom and Dixie followed, still peppering her with questions.

I watched them bothering the crap out of Aunt Tenne, grateful that for once it wasn't me. I was totally alone and nobody was bothering me. Sure I got some of the usual double takes, but nobody came over and said how much I looked like Marilyn or anything worse. Everything was perfect. I scubaed. I hadn't seen Aaron all day. But that couldn't last and I should've known where he'd be. That cheeseburger was fantastic, too fantastic. It had a hint of the Tommy Watts Burger, Aaron's restaurant, Kronos, was known for.

I asked the waiter, "Have you seen a little guy, crazy hair, food obsessed, likes Spiderman?"

"He's in the kitchen," he said.

Of course he is. Aaron was the only guy in the world who would spend his vacation in the resort kitchen, probably because he hadn't located a Dungeons and Dragons game to invade.

Aaron came out of the kitchen, wearing a pink hairnet and carrying a platter of chili cheese fries with a side of poblano garlic aioli. That wasn't on the menu.

"What are you doing in the kitchen?" I asked as he sat down next to me.

"Cooking."

"Why?"

I had to ask, so I deserved what I got. Aaron told me about every fish available on the island and how to cook them. He was going to invent a fish hot dog because that needed to happen. But his chili cheese fries were amazing. The secret ingredient was plantain and he planned to introduce an island submenu if he could talk Rodney, the other owner of Kronos, into it.

While Aaron was explaining fish gutting against my will, I saw Mom trailing Aunt Tenne down to the beach. Christmas was over and my aunt looked like she might crack Mom in the head with a coconut.

"Hey, Aaron," I said. "Do you know why Mom's acting so weird about Aunt Tenne?"

He stopped mid-intestine sentence and said, "She's okay this year."

"Who? Mom or Aunt Tenne?"

"Tenne. Your mom's the same."

"What do you mean this year?"

"It's August," he said with a mouthful of fries and a huge splat of aioli on his chest.

"Why wouldn't she be okay in August?"

"August is bad. Got to make the cobbler." He headed for the kitchen and I chased after him.

"What is it about August?"

Aaron shrugged and went into the kitchen. Even Aaron wasn't talking and he had chronic diarrhea of the mouth. Usually, I couldn't shut him up. But it was something about August. I walked back to the dive shop and went through every August in memory. Other than the year of sitting in the cemetery, I couldn't think of anything that happened in August.

The Gmucas were already in the shop, making out in a corner. Everyone else filtered in after me. Colin kept trying to stand close to me and Joe and Andrew were annoyed with him. Mom was last and came in with her worried face. We loaded up our gear into the golf carts and got to take one of the resort boats out to Turtle Crossing. We had to sit on the edge of the boat and fall off backwards. Mauro straight up laughed at me as I waddled over in my penguin suit, the last one to go in. Everyone else was bobbing around like corks, waiting for me. I sat on the edge and was about to put my regulator in my mouth when Mauro stopped me.

"You're worried about Lucia," he said in that fabulous accent that I couldn't quite place.

I bit my lip, not sure how much to say. I might come off like some conspiracy theory nut.

"She did get clearance from her doctor to be certified," he said.

"I know," I said.

"Is there something else?" His eyes were so brown and he smelled like Hawaiian Tropic.

Focus.

"Yes," I said.

"You won't tell me?"

"I have nothing concrete. Just stay close to her. Okay?"

"You have me worried. Scuba can be a dangerous sport."

"That's why I'm worried." I put the reg in my mouth but found I couldn't make myself fall backwards. It's so unnatural, falling backwards on purpose. Mauro shook his head and pushed my forehead with his finger and there I went. Under the water in a rush and then right back up again. Awesome.

Mauro came in and one by one we went down the guide rope to the bottom, forty feet down. Ten minutes later we were all exploring an open sandy area surrounded by high coral walls. It was breathtaking in its grandeur. I felt like I was outside myself on another planet. There was a whole world down there. One that was totally unconcerned about us. Mauro led us through our lessons, basically the same stuff we'd done in the morning. We all succeeded and then we fanned out to explore. I followed Lucia and Graeme around the perimeter. Discreetly, I hope. Mauro stayed close, but he had a lot of us to watch.

A school of little box-shaped fish went under me and I hovered around a clump of sea anemones and coral, watching them feed on lacy fan coral. Dixie swam up and pointed. It took me a second, but I finally saw something odd moving slowly along the ocean floor. It was bulbous and opalescent with narrow fins lining the side of its body. Oh, a squid. I looked back to signal to Lucia. She was thrashing around and making a slashing motion across her throat. Her primary reg was floating free in the water beside her. No air. I darted towards her, but Mauro shot past me. He took her spare reg out of her mouth, put in his spare, and cleared it. I came up beside them and watched Lucia's sides heave. Her brown eyes were huge and focused on Mauro. He gave her the okay sign and she gave it back. Then he pointed at me and gave me a thumbs up. Go to the surface. I okayed back.

Graeme swam up and wanted to know what happened. Mauro indicated a problem with Lucia's tank. Lucia gave him the okay sign and he relaxed. Mauro told him to stay down and we slowly ascended. My ears were not loving it. They creaked and popped painfully, despite our slowness.

We surfaced five feet from the boat, blew up our BCD vests, and removed our regs.

"Are you okay?" I asked Lucia.

"I think so." That's what she said, but she was still huffing and puffing.

"Slow down. Mauro had you. You were never in any danger."

She nodded and her eyes darted around.

"Look at me," I said. "You're not having an attack. This is just panic."

Lucia focused on me.

"Blow out a breath with pursed lips." I demonstrated and she imitated me. Her face relaxed into its normal soft lines. "Better?"

"Yes. Does this mean I fail?" she asked Mauro.

He laughed. "No. Equipment failures are not your fault. You did exactly what I want. Spare reg and then signal. Perfection."

She smiled. "Oh, good. Graeme would be so disappointed."

Well, we wouldn't want that, would we?

We swam over to the boat and the captain, Alex, helped Lucia on board.

Mauro asked me, "Will you stay with her? I must go down."

"Sure," I said.

"Is this what you were worried about, Mercy?"

"I didn't know it at the time, but yes."

"We must talk." Mauro went under and Alex helped me on the boat.

Lucia sat on a side bench and wiggled until her tank dropped in the storage hole. I waddled over and sat opposite her, dropped my tank, and took off my vest. Alex helped Lucia off with her vest and disconnected her regs. She stretched and went up to the prow to her beach bag. Alex tested both Lucia's regs, his forehead creased. Then he connected a fresh set of regs and tested each one.

"Tank's good?" I asked.

"Yes. It is problem with regs," said Alex in his heavy Honduran accent.

"Both regs were bad?"

"Yes." He rubbed the graying stubble on his chin.

"How often does that happen?" I glanced toward Lucia. She was digging around in her bag and not paying attention.

"Never." More stubble scratching.

"Did you hear what Mauro and I were talking about before I went in?"

"Yes."

"Did you see anyone messing with Lucia's equipment?"

"No one touched it."

Lucia called over. "Well, it's a good thing I didn't have an attack."

"Why's that?" I asked.

"I forgot my inhaler." She paused and rooted around again. "And my wallet. I don't know where my head is."

"Seriously?" I glanced at Alex and he raised an eyebrow at me.

"I could've sworn I put them in here, but I must've left it in the room," she said. "Do you want some chocolate?"

Lucia, Alex, and I shared a Bissinger's milk chocolate bar. Lucia chatted away how crazy it was that both her regs failed while Alex and I nodded. I wasn't sure what to say. Hey, Lucia, maybe somebody's trying to kill you. The missing inhaler didn't make things any better. I leaned on the edge of the boat. It would be so easy to get the inhaler out of her bag and drop it over the side, never to be seen again. We were all so busy getting our equipment squared away, the whole bag could've been tossed over and no one would've been the wiser.

Twenty minutes later, everyone surfaced and got in the boat. There was little discussion about Lucia's regs. She was fine and everyone seemed to accept the failures as the price of doing business, everyone except me, Alex, and Mauro. Mostly the talk was of the five sea turtles everyone saw. Lucia apologized to me a thousand times for making me miss it. I couldn't have cared less. If someone was really trying to kill the niece of Calpurnia Fibonacci it was bad. Very bad.

Back at the dive shop, the manager, a grizzled old diver that went by the name of Spitball, took apart Lucia's regs. It was just Spitball, Mauro, and me in the equipment room standing over a small table made from driftwood.

"Well, that's a new one," said Spitball.

"What's wrong with them?" I asked.

Spitball held up reg number one. "The first stage spring failed." Then he picked up the spare. "The diaphragm's gone."

"So they were tampered with."

"Not necessarily. The spring could've failed with age."

He was blowing me off. Freak accidents are easier to believe than murder attempts, I guess.

"What about the diaphragm? Where'd that go?"

Mauro took the reg from Spitball. "It could disintegrate under the right conditions."

"What conditions are those?"

"No servicing for years. It could happen. But all our equipment is checked daily," said Mauro. "I did the work myself."

"Someone could've switched the regs, right? All our bundles were sitting on the bench while we were at lunch. Anyone could've come in and done it," I said.

"Marcella was here," said Spitball.

"All the time? Every minute?" I couldn't keep the sarcasm from my voice. He didn't believe me. I hate that.

"Does the diver want to continue in the class?"

"Yes," I said. "She doesn't suspect anything."

"It could be a freak accident."

"Or not."

Mauro set down the reg. "I will test her equipment before each dive. There will be no repeat."

I threw my beach bag over my shoulder. "I'm guessing you won't have to worry about it."

"Why not?"

"He'd have to be an idiot to try the same thing again."

"Who are you really?" asked Spitball.

"Just another tourist."

"Right. We get tourists that look exactly like Marilyn Monroe, who think someone's trying to murder another guest all the time." Spitball looked down at the regs, not seeing what I saw.

"The world is weird," I said.

"And so are you, I think."

"Speaking of weird, why are you called Spitball?" I asked.

"Call sign. I did three tours in Vietnam in an F4."

"My grandpa did three tours in a helicopter."

"What battalion?"

"I have no idea, but he's still tough as nails. He once beat up his brother over who got the last burrito."

"When was that?"

"Last year."

Spitball rubbed his chin. "I punched a guy over cheddar cheese once. It was worth it."

Spitball and I laughed, but Mauro looked confused. I guess he didn't have a lot of contact with crazy Vietnam vets.

"Does your grandpa go to reunions?"

"Hell, no. He wants to forget."

Spitball nodded slowly. "You're sure about this whole murder thing?"

"Pretty sure."

"Well, Mauro will do whatever you want. We'll keep that girl safe." Spitball threw the broken regs in a backpack and went out the back door.

"I need a drink," I said, going out the front door into the waiting area where someone—probably Graeme, but I wasn't saying that out loud—tried to kill Lucia.

"You should go to your room first." Mauro gave me an odd smile. Was he hinting that he'd like to come with or what? He kept looking at me and for a second I almost considered it.

Remember Pete. Remember Pete.

"I'd like to, but I better just get a drink," I said.

Marcella walked in and said, "Oh, wow."

"What?" I asked.

She pointed at a mirror hanging behind one of the tubs where divers rinsed their masks and snorkels. I went over and shrieked. I actually shrieked out loud, not in my head or anything, but a big shriek. Something terrible had happened to me. My hair had gone bat shit crazy. It was all piled on top of my head. I don't know how it got up there or stayed for that matter. It was frizzy electrified straw. My face wasn't any better. I had big red lines between my brows, giving me the world's worst angry eyes. And there was a mask ring around the upper half of my face and for some reason my nose was pushed to the right.

"Why didn't you tell me?" I yelled at Mauro.

"I said you should go to your room. You have to fix that, if you can." Mauro got thoughtful. "What did you think I was doing?"

"I thought you were hitting on me."

He lifted his upper lip in distaste. "No."

"That happens, you know. Men hit on me all the time," I said.

"Not today they won't."

Marcella had her hands over her mouth and her body shook so much that she had to brace herself against the wall. I put my crooked, red nose in the air and stomped out.

I trotted back to the room as far off the regular paths as possible, hoping no one would see me. But the person I really didn't want to see me, Mauro, had already seen me, so I don't know why I bothered. I went around the back of the last bungalow and saw Aunt Tenne jogging down our stairs. I've never seen her run anywhere in my entire life. She was singing and wearing a flowing green sarong. She looked down the main path and then hung a right in between two buildings. The coast was clear. I sprinted for the stairs and jumped in the pail to rinse my feet. Then Mom came out of nowhere.

"Mercy, have you seen Tenne? I've been looking for her everywhere."

"Mom, why didn't you tell me I look like...like this?"

"Oh, you're fine. Where's your aunt?"

"I'm not fine. I look like someone attacked me with perm solution and something's wrong with my nose."

"Your nose looks the same as it always does," said Mom.

"No, it doesn't." I thought for a second. "It doesn't, does it? OMG."

Mom rolled her eyes. "Where's Tenne?"

"I think she went snorkeling," I lied. Whatever Aunt Tenne was up to, it was her private business. Not that Mom would agree. The word privacy wasn't in her language.

"Are you sure? Did she look okay? Was she crying or anything like that?" Mom wrung her hands and looked around like Aunt Tenne might drop out of a palm tree.

"Why would she be crying on vacation?"

"No reason." Mom tucked her sleek blond hair behind her ears.

Fine. Don't tell me anything. Two can play at that.

"Hey. Why's your hair all nice?" I asked. "And you don't have any marks on your face at all."

"Good genes. Let's go to the bar."

"I have your genes. I'm a carbon copy of you."

"I put conditioner on my hair before I went. It keeps the seawater off," said Mom.

"Why didn't you tell me to do that?"

"I assumed you knew."

"How would I know that?" I asked.

"Well, I knew it."

Groan.

Mom hooked her arm through mine. "Let's get some Monkey Lalas. Dixie says she's going to do the limbo tonight."

"Pass. I can't be seen like this."

"Mauro's already seen you."

I made a face at her and ran up the stairs, flung open the door and felt the rush of icy air-conditioned air. Ahhh.

"Hey, Mercy."

Shriek. Aaron sat on the sofa, still wearing his hairnet.

"How'd you get in here?"

He shrugged.

"Ewww. It smells like a taco shop."

"You hungry?" Aaron held up a bulging bag with water dripping off the bottom onto the white tile floor.

I cringed. "What is that?"

"Lionfish. Mauro gave it to me. Let's cook it."

"How about you go cook it far away and I take a shower."

"Nope."

"Why not?" I asked.

"Cause I got to help you."

"What makes you think I need help?"

Aaron ignored my question and jiggled his fish bag. "Gotta cook it now, while it's fresh."

"I'm not cooking anything. Look at me." I pointed at my head.

Aaron looked, but as usual I wasn't sure if he actually saw me through his thick smudged glasses. He sat there, holding his bag, and for some reason I had the urge to tell him about Oz Urbani and the rest of it. But if I did, he'd call up Dad and tell him I'd gotten myself into a situation as he would call it. Oz was expecting me to take care of Lucia, whether I agreed to it or not. If she got killed...I didn't even what to think about it. If Aaron told Dad that Lucia was a Fibonacci, he would come to the rescue. She wouldn't die, but I just might. Mom would kill me for ruining our girl trip and Lucia wouldn't be thrilled when she found out about Oz trying to hire me.

I grabbed Aaron's wrist and hauled him to his feet. I opened the door and booted him through. "Go fry your fish."

"But Tommy said—"

I slammed the door and locked it. Then I propped a chair under the knob and wedged it closed. That should hold him for a while. I had to think and the best place for that was in a hot shower. But since my life is my life, the shower was lukewarm and smelled like bad well water. I did what Dad called a sea shower and jumped out as fast as possible. The thirty seconds of conditioner didn't do my hair much good, but it didn't look quite so angry. My nose had moved back into its normal position and the red lines on my face had diminished. I fixed the rest with coverup and powder.

It was nearly six o'clock and time for the limbo contest. I picked up my purse and got one of Dad's cards. Lucia had to be told about the regs. I didn't expect her to believe me, but Dad's reputation might make an impression on her, even if I didn't. I put on my favorite cutoffs and a tank. For once, Mom wouldn't be able to say they were inappropriate. I left the bedroom and got a whiff of smoke. I jerked open the front door and found Aaron squatting in front of a hibachi. There was a whole lionfish, complete with spines and eyeballs, sizzling on it. Nothing, absolutely nothing, could've been less appetizing than that fish. It was still orange and kind of looking at me.

"You ready?" asked Aaron, poking the side of the lionfish.

"I don't know what you're talking about, but no."

I edged around him and ran down the stairs. The light was on in Lucia and Graeme's bungalow. The sun had dipped low and there were shadows everywhere. I walked across the sand path. It was still warm from the heat of the day and I never wanted to wear shoes again. Lucia's path was to my left. Time to tell her about the regs. I glanced over my shoulder as I swerved toward her path, but Aaron stood on the porch watching me. Fantastic. I went straight until I thought he couldn't see me anymore and then doubled back. I was sure he'd be back to his fish, but he'd stayed at the railing.

Crap!

Maybe the bungalow had a back door. I stepped off the path and jogged between stumpy palms around the back of the bungalows. The shadows were darker back there and I kept kicking coconuts. Maybe shoes weren't such a bad idea. I found a back path and practiced what I'd say to Lucia. Hopefully, she'd be alone. That would make things easier.

I found the back of Lucia's bungalow and started for the door when I heard whispering. Someone ran from behind a fat coconut tree and disappeared between two maintenance sheds. I couldn't make out who it was. There was just this sense that it was a man. Nothing else. Lucia! I ran to the back door and pounded on it.

"Lucia!" I yelled. "Open up!"

What if she's dead in there?

"Lucia!"

A hand tapped me on the shoulder.

Being a cool customer, I shrieked good and loud.

"What are you doing?" asked Mauro, squinting at me in the dim light.

I straightened my tank top and said, "What are you doing?"

"Following you."

"There was someone out here and now Lucia's not answering the door. Something might've happened to her."

"The Carrows are at the restaurant. Who did you see?"

"It was too dark. I couldn't make them out, but they were definitely lurking out here."

Mauro smiled and moved in closer. He smelled fresh and clean with a hint of allspice. "Lurking? Are you sure you're a nurse?"

"Of course, I'm sure." I backed up and bumped my head on the coconut tree that loomed over me.

Mauro held out his arm. "I'll walk you to the restaurant before I go."

"Where are you going?"

"Home."

I instantly pictured his house, small, slightly messy with a big—

Stop it.

"You don't have to walk me," I said, just a little breathless. "Um... did you happen to tell Lucia about the regs?"

"Spitball did."

"And?"

"And nothing. They weren't concerned," said Mauro.

"They? Graeme was there?"

"He is her husband. You don't suspect him, do you?"

I thought of the bruises on Lucia's hips, but kept it to myself. "I don't know what I think."

"You don't like Graeme?" Mauro took my arm; his strong fingers wrapped all the way around my bicep.

"No, he's fine." I shook him off. "Got to go. See you bright and early."

I took off down the path and glanced back to see him go between the sheds where the other person had gone.

"Got it."

Shriek. Aaron stood on the main path, holding the lionfish with a long two-pronged fork.

"Are you trying to scare me to death?"

"No."

"Are you following me?"

"No."

I threw up my hands and passed him. I hoped he wouldn't follow, but he did. He always did. I went down to the restaurant. There was a small band on the makeshift stage made of bamboo and the smell from that night's special, roast pig, hung heavy in the air. Lucia and Graeme were there at the bar with the Gmucas and Todd. They raised their glasses with smiles stretching their sunburned cheeks. I couldn't talk to Lucia with so many people around, so I went in search of Mom. I passed the frat boys sprawled out at a table covered with empty glasses and beer bottles. Colin leered at me but didn't get up thankfully. Eventually, I found Mom sitting on the deck overlooking the sea. She had her arms crossed, not a good sign. Dixie was on the dance floor in a queue for the limbo. Aunt Tenne was behind her, wearing that new sarong and smiling like I'd never seen her smile. A waiter brought Mom a plate of fish tacos and set a tiny salad in front of an empty seat. Must be for Dixie. She was forever on a diet.

I sat down next to Mom and Aaron sat next to me. He held the lionfish out like an Olympic torch.

"Aaron," said Mom. "What's with the fish?"

"I cooked it."

"Nice." She looked out over the dance floor with a serious frown.

One of the lionfish's spines brushed my face and I inched my chair closer to Mom. "He barbecued it on our porch."

"That's nice."

"No, it's not."

"Do you see what she's doing?" asked Mom.

"Dixie? I think she's going to limbo." It was unexpected, but she was giving happiness a shot.

"Not Dixie. Tenne."

"She's going to limbo, too. So what?" I asked.

"So what? Do you see who she's with?"

"Um…"

The waiter brought a platter and a carving knife over. Aaron slapped his crusty fish on it and smacked his lips.

"The pool boy," said Mom. I hadn't heard that edge in her voice since I dated Lorenzo Stern for about five minutes before I met Pete. Lorenzo was the son of Lorenzo Stern, Sr., a defense attorney that hated my dad like herpes.

"There's a pool boy?" I hadn't seen any pool boys. La Isla Bonita was kind of a self-serve joint. A few pool boys would've been nice, especially if they kept a steady stream of Monkey Lalas coming. I needed them to forget my hair, man-sized wetsuit and the Fibonacci situation.

"Bruno." Aaron carved a hunk off the lionfish and held it out to me. "Try it."

"You named the fish?"

"Bruno's the pool boy," said Mom.

Then I saw him. He stood behind Aunt Tenne, swaying to the music. Bruno had helped with the luggage on the first day. He seemed alright, even if he was wearing a Hawaiian shirt. "I think he's a porter."

"That hardly matters."

I had no idea what did matter, other than keeping Lucia alive until we got back to the States. Aaron poked the fish in front of my face again. "It's good."

"Aren't they poisonous?"

"Venomous."

"That does not make me feel better," I said. "You first."

Aaron poked the white flakey meat into his mouth and groaned with happiness. Lucia and Graeme left the bar and took to the dance floor. I had to admit they looked like a happy couple. That is until Graeme spun her and her blouse slipped off her shoulder, revealing a fresh reddish bruise on her back. I had to talk to her. She wasn't running into doors. Oz was right. Something was going on.

Aaron carved me a piece of lionfish and before I could say no, he'd shoved it in my mouth. Not bad for a venomous fish.

"You like it?" asked Aaron.

"It's okay," I said. "I could do without the eyeballs watching me."

Aaron began telling me all about the gutting and the batter he used. I tuned out when he got to the venom sacs. I'd rather not know. The waiter came. I ordered a salad to make up for all the Monkey Lalas and a Monkey Lala to make me feel better about eating a salad.

I chewed slowly, watching Lucia dance and laugh. I couldn't shake the feeling that she wouldn't be laughing for long.

CHAPTER SEVEN

Night three of the girl trip from hell I slept on the hammock, trying to listen for trouble in the Carrows' bungalow. I hadn't been able to see Lucia alone. Graeme was always there hovering. A lot like Aaron actually, only without the food. I saw Lucia and Graeme come out in the morning, arm in arm. We all got through our last certification dive without a problem, although the frat boys were hung over and miserable. Mauro stayed close to Lucia the whole time and I stayed with her during our two-hundred-meter swim. After it was over, we filled out paperwork and went to lunch. I thought maybe I could talk to her at the restaurant. Graeme had to go to the bathroom sometime, but they took their lunch back to the bungalow and came back to the beach together.

I did my best to keep an eye on Lucia and avoid Mom. Aunt Tenne had come in at about three in the morning, whistling. I lied to Mom again, but she was getting suspicious. Aunt Tenne was still asleep and that wasn't normal for her.

I lay on the hot floating platform, sunny-side down with a lizard an inch from my nose. The sun was so hot it felt like it was pressing me down. I could've stayed there all day if it weren't for Tyler and Tara, the Land's End kids, arguing about scuba diving on the other side of the platform.

"We are old enough," said Tara.

"Dad said we aren't," said Tyler.

"I asked that scuba guy. He said you only have to be eight."

"So what?"

"I'm ten. I could get certified."

"No, you couldn't."

"You can get certified when you're ten. I'm ten."

"You're stupid." Tyler ran past my head and did a cannonball. Cool seawater pebbled my sizzling body, making me jerk and gasp.

"I hate you!" yelled Tara.

I hate both of you. Isn't it time for naps?

"You're still not scuba diving," Tyler yelled back and then he hawked a lugie into the water. Awesome.

"I'm going to make Dad take me this afternoon."

"No, you're not."

They went on yelling and I closed my eyes. I went to my happy place, which happened to be as cold as the platform was hot. The butler's pantry in my parents' house. I pictured the little drawers and cubbies with their little brass plaques. They hid all manner of good things, chocolates, cocoa, cognac, flavored sugars, and prosciutto. I'd never discovered all their secrets, but I wanted to.

"Mercy!" Mom came walking down the broad wooden stairs to the beach, oblivious to the guy that was trailing her and trying to work up the nerve to speak. He had a camera. Great. Mom saw me and tromped across the sand with her hips swinging. The guy's eyes widened when I lifted myself onto my elbows. He raised the camera. Mauro came across the sand and pointed his finger at the guy. "Beat it."

He turned tail and almost knocked over a waiter bringing Lucia a fresh iced tea. She lay under an umbrella wearing a coverup that left everything to the imagination. Graeme was right there, reading a paperback thriller and blocking my access.

"Are you ready?" called Mauro. "The boat leaves in fifteen minutes."

I dropped back on my chest, and Mom picked up my beach bag

from beside my chair. "Come on, Mercy. This is just for fun. We're certified divers now."

I glanced at Lucia. "Maybe I'll just stay here."

"Everyone's coming," said Mauro, his rich voice carrying well over the water.

"Everyone?"

"Of course," said Mom.

Tyler chased Tara through the water toward the platform, both screaming like sugared-up three-year-olds. My happy place wasn't enough to combat them, so I slipped in the water that always seemed to be the perfect temperature and wished my lizard luck, but he scampered over the side to hide under one of the chains that held the platform in place.

I swam to the beach while Mauro went over to Lucia. I half-hoped Lucia would shake her head no. I'd had about enough diving. Every time we went down, my nerves tightened one more notch. I didn't need the stress. Dad had called and ranted about The Girls' lawsuit. I asked him if he ever met Josiah Bled, which only made him madder. It's a good thing I didn't ask anything really insulting like 'Was our house a payoff?' After that, Dixie'd started crying again during lunch. Aunt Tenne was the only one who was happy and Mom seemed determined to ruin it.

Lucia got up and I groaned. Why couldn't she lay on the beach where I could read and watch her without worrying about regs or oxygen levels? Lucia smiled at me and I followed her and Graeme to the dive shop, where I put on my hated wetsuit and coated my hair with a half cup of conditioner. Todd, the Land's End dad, was the last to arrive and we all walked down to the beach behind the golf carts. Colin patted my rear three times and smacking his hand only seemed to encourage him. I was starting to wear down my teeth from grinding them so much. To distract myself, I asked Lucia if she had her inhaler. She did, but it was her last one. I didn't like that. She had no idea where the other one went. My guess was over the side of the boat, because her other inhaler and wallet hadn't turned up in her room and that was worrisome. Graeme wouldn't take Lucia's wallet. What would be the point? Her money was his and vice versa.

Alex the captain took us out to Pablo's Place, a dive spot known for great coral and lobsters. The boat skipped over waves as the wind picked up and I yawned.

"Tired?" asked Todd.

"Just a little," I said.

"So's Tracy. Not sleeping well on the hotel bed."

Frankie leaned forward. "Maybe they can switch out the mattress. Ours is great."

Linda nodded and braided her long hair. "I'm sleeping like a rock."

Alex turned the boat and we all leaned to the right. Then he cut the engine and we coasted to a stop. Mauro went around helping with gear and stopped in front of me, so close my chest brushed his BCD.

"I've checked everything," he said.

"Twice?" I asked.

"Three times. No worries today."

We queued and the line went fast. Lucia and Graeme were in first. She had no fear and I admired her for it. From my point of view, she had a lot to be fearful of. On that dive there was no lead rope and we all deflated our BCDs to descend together. The spot was beautiful but different than our previous dive areas. The coral was larger with lots of fanciful formations and big schools of colorful fish darting around them. We descended to forty feet and began to spread out. Mauro clinked on his tank and the sharp metallic sound echoed through the water. He made the sign for turtle and everyone got out their cameras. It was a hawksbill, if I remembered the dive book pictures correctly. The shell was at least two feet across with a jagged section at the back.

Mauro clinked again and made the sign for shark. Five feet from the turtle was a nurse shark lying on the sandy bottom between two walls of blue and yellow coral. He was maybe nine feet in length and reminded me of a catfish with its broad head. Mauro indicated that we should spread out and look for seahorses among the coral. Lucia was to my right, swimming behind Graeme. He pointed to some tall formations of coral, the kind that looks like crusty old vases. Around them were lots of fan coral, black and red, and brain coral that always made me want to touch its lovely swirls and grooves.

I followed Graeme and Lucia into the coral maze and we spent fifteen minutes looking before Graeme found a little yellow seahorse hanging on a fan coral branch. He had a long snout and spines running down his back. I couldn't stop looking at him. He was so small and delicate, the size of my little finger.

Lucia took a picture and then swam deeper into the maze. I tore myself away to follow. There was a tug on my foot. Mauro gave me the okay sign and I gave it back. He asked how much air I had left. Plenty. Over fifteen hundred PSI. I turned back to where Lucia had gone and saw her drop down between the edge of the drop-off and a large area of brain coral. Lucia emerged again, twisting in the water, a cloud of red around one thigh. I darted over, my knees scraping the coral. Her hands were on her thigh. A shaft of white stuck out from between her fingers.

I yelled through my reg, "Don't take it out." But she yanked it out anyway and dropped it. I got a glimpse before it disappeared into the depths, a five-inch serrated piece of bone. Lucia shot up, headed for the surface through a cloud of red. I held her foot. She'd give herself the bends. Graeme was there. He gestured wildly. I didn't think. I grabbed his hands and pressed them on the spewing wound. Then we started the ascent, painfully slow. I tapped on my tank with my finger-nails. The noise wasn't nearly as effective as Mauro's bottle opener, but he heard me. His brown eyes were wide beneath the mask. I shrugged and made the sign for stingray. He made us slow down further and it took an extra five minutes to get up top.

By the time my ears broke the surface, Mauro was yelling for Alex. Then the boat was there. In the movies, they like to show things happening in slow motion as if that's the way people see action. In my experience, traumatic situations happen so fast the brain can't even track it. I saw Alex's face. I saw the boat. Then it was there beside us. I swear I didn't see it move. Alex took Lucia's hands and hauled her onboard. A stream of blood coated her leg the instant Graeme let go of her thigh. He went for the ladder, but I shoved him out of the way and tried to climb with my fins on. Not going to happen. Alex grabbed me and I flew over the side, cracking my head on the bench and slipping in Lucia's blood, which coated the floor.

"I need a belt or a strap!" I yelled.

Alex yanked off his belt and I wrapped it around Lucia's thigh. The puncture was an inch in width and deep. Once I had the tourniquet in place the bleeding stopped and I looked up at Lucia's white face.

"I didn't even see it," she gasped.

"It's okay. It's all under control." Yeah, right. My voice was shaking like I was sitting on top of a dryer.

Graeme knelt beside Lucia. "What the hell happened?"

"Stingray, I think," said Lucia.

Mauro yelled from the water. "How is she?"

"The bleeding's under control," I said. "We have to get her to a hospital. I think it was a stingray."

He gave me a look that said, "No way." And then he told Alex, "Take them to shore and send another boat. I can't leave. I've got divers down."

Alex got on the radio and asked for an ambulance to meet us on shore. He turned the boat around and we sped off. Graeme lay on the bottom of the boat with Lucia. He cradled her, not noticing how his head banged against the spare tanks with every wave. I slipped on the blood and landed painfully on my scraped knees. Lucia's pulse was racing, but she'd pinked up. I liked that. I wrapped her leg in my towel and said stupid things like we're almost there and relax. Because telling people to relax always makes them do it.

We passed another La Isla Bonita boat going out at full speed and then landed on the beach like we were under a hail of gunfire. Spitball jumped into the water to tie us up.

"Who is it?" he yelled, but his eyes said he already knew.

"Lucia!"

"God damn son of a bitch fuck!"

Graeme gathered Lucia into his arms. He leaned over the boat's side, every muscle strained to the limit, and gingerly gave her to Spitball. He carried her onto the beach and laid her on a towel. Graeme turned to me and I pulled back in surprise. His eyes were full of tears. "Is she going to be okay?"

"Yes. Absolutely."

He jumped over the side and ran through the water to Lucia.

Either he was one hell of an actor or Lucia was just incredibly unlucky. How many stingray attacks could there be a year?

Alex helped me off with my tank and BCD and I went over the side into the perfect water. I had a flash of the plume of blood flowing out from Lucia's thigh. That didn't feel like an accident. It just didn't. A siren sounded in the distance as I sank down beside Lucia. Her face was twisted in pain.

"Did you get a glimpse of anything?" I asked.

"There was something there." She gasped.

The ambulance pulled up next to us on the sand and two EMTs got out. Graeme and I stepped back, while they assessed her. When they were done, they each took an arm and started to pull her to her feet.

"Wait," I said. "What are you doing?"

"Taking her to the hospital," said the older of the two. He had the air of someone who's seen too many accidents to care much anymore.

"Put her on a stretcher. She can't walk."

"No stretcher. We carry her."

"What do you mean no stretcher?" I looked in the ambulance and sure enough there was no stretcher in the back and, frankly, not much else. "Where is it?"

"It's on the other side of the island. Car accident."

"Are you saying you have one stretcher and you share?"

The EMT narrowed his eyes at me. "This is not America. You don't get everything you want all the time."

Graeme put his finger in the EMT's face. "She doesn't want a stretcher. She needs it."

Spitball pushed Graeme's arm down. "It doesn't matter. Let's get her to the hospital. ASAP."

Graeme insisted on putting Lucia on the small pallet in the back of the ambulance. It was crazy. A patient lying on the floor.

"Mercy," said Lucia, drool rolled down her chin and her words slurred. "I don't feel good."

"That's not right," I said, trying to get in the ambulance.

The EMT pushed me back. "It's just a puncture."

"Not with drooling. It's something else. Let me in."

Lucia slumped and her hand hit the floor. Graeme looked at me. "What is it?"

"I don't know." I tried to push past the EMT, but he knocked me aside.

"We have rules in this country," he said.

"Oh, yeah," I yelled. "You have rules, but no stretchers apparently."

Graeme looked around the ambulance with increasing panic. "Is this okay?"

"They use clean needles," I said.

His sides started to heave as he began to panic. "But what about the rest of it?"

"You don't have a choice."

"But—"

The EMT slammed the doors and the ambulance peeled out, spraying me with sand.

"Shit! Spitball, where's the hospital?" I asked.

"Coxen Hole. I'll take you."

We ran through the alley between our resort and another, ending up next to a group of scooters.

"Are you kidding me?" I asked.

"Hey," said Spitball. "I flew missions over hot zones. I don't do slow."

And he didn't. I have no idea what he did to that scooter, but it went like a crouch rocket. We zipped through traffic, weaving around rusted-out vehicles and fruit stands. When we got to Coxen Hole I was glad I had a grizzled old guy named Spitball with me. That town made North St. Louis look like a retirement community. Grungy concrete buildings were packed together and the narrow twisted roads were filled with vehicles that appeared to be held together with baling wire. Some of the houses or shops were painted bright pastels, that only made them sadder with all the dirt and exhaust giving them a grayish tinge.

Spitball zipped around an ancient Toyota pickup with at least ten kids in the bed. They smiled and waved. I waved back and was struck by their faces, happy, full-cheeked, and bright-eyed. Would American children be so joyful in such circumstances? I doubted it. I wouldn't have been. Actually, everyone on the street seemed equally cheerful. They moved about their day in colorful clothes, kicking up dust on the sidewalk and not noticing that the buildings they passed looked ready to topple over on them.

"There it is," said Spitball as he braked hard.

I saw nothing that would pass for a hospital. Maybe it was on the other side of the prison ahead to our left. It had high concrete walls with razor wire on top. I knew prisons as well as hospitals. Dad visited some of the people he helped to convict, usually women, but sometimes men. Dad didn't look like he had any soft spots, but they were there. He understood circumstances make you who you are and he insisted I understand it, too. Mom didn't know, but Dad took me on his visits sometimes. Some of the people I met when I was ten were still there, wearing orange and eagerly waiting behind plexiglass for Dad to appear.

We idled behind a late model Ford covered in scuba stickers. I tried not to look at the prison. There was no one to visit. No information to gather. But I still felt the heaviness settle on me. It came every time, that thick darkness, it said you go in, they might not let you out. Dad never asked me how I felt as a kid going in those places or how I felt as an adult going in to get some information for him. He said it was important to see what we do. How things end up. People don't disappear. They go into a kind of stasis. It was important to know. I think he also thought it would keep me on the straight and narrow. I didn't have any real criminal tendencies, so I think we could've skipped it.

Our tires squealed as Spitball hit the gas and we sped through a narrow opening between resort vans. He hung a left, pulled up to the prison, and stopped at the guard shack. A guard in a green uniform stepped out, carrying an AK47.

"Hey, Mr. Spitball. How you doing?" asked the guard.

"Can't complain. Ambulance come in?" asked Spitball.

"Yeah. A couple minutes ago. It got one of yours?"

"Sure does. Stingray barb in the leg."

"That's some nasty shit." The guard waved us in.

Spitball parked under an overhang and we went in the emergency entrance. There were dozens of people waiting in gray, uncomfortable chairs like any other ER. Spitball waved down a nurse in green scrubs and asked about Lucia. She was back with the doctor. The nurse didn't know much, except she was conscious. I blew out a breath and leaned on the wall. Between Lucia and the whole in-a-prison feeling, my legs were shaking.

"She's a nurse," said Spitball. "Can she go back?"

"Family?"

I almost lied. "No."

"You'll have to wait out here," said the nurse.

"She's talking and coherent?" I asked.

"She was when she came in." She looked down at her chart. "Stingray barb. Not serious."

"She was drooling in the ambulance. I think she passed out."

"Drooling?"

"Yes. Definitely," I said. "Something else is going on. There might be poison involved."

The nurse didn't raise an eyebrow or look remotely interested. "I'll tell Dr. Navarro."

We found a couple of chairs in the corner between a man holding a bloody rag over his face and a kid throwing up in a bucket. This was way too much like my regular life. Where was the vacation in my vacation? I went back and forth between wanting to assess patients and wanting to get the hell out of there. Since my kit was back in the room and I didn't have any gloves (gloves were absolutely required) I went to sleep on Spitball's boney shoulder.

A half hour later, I woke to the smell of hot chocolate. I opened my eyes to see a chipped mug under my nose. It held a thick foamy brew. Heaven.

"Where'd you get that?" asked Spitball.

"Made it," said Aaron. He looked down at me from behind glasses that had a couple of dead bugs spattered on them. I'd never been so happy to see him. Which isn't saying much, since I'm never happy to see him at all. Except when he's saving my life. That happens more than I liked to admit.

He gave me the mug and I took an experimental sip. Perfection with a hint of cinnamon. Aaron rubbed his hands together and bounced up and down. "How's it?"

"Wonderful. Where'd you get hot chocolate?"

"Jesse let me make it in her kitchen."

"Who's Jesse?" I asked. When Aaron looked confused, I said, "Oh, never mind. How'd you get here?"

"I brought him," said Mauro.

I don't know how I didn't notice him before. His taut brown leg was a foot away from me. Mauro looked so good. His hair was all mussed up from the wind, not like Aaron's mussed. Mussed good. He exuded confidence, and I was stressed out and exhausted. It was one of those times I wanted a handsome man to hug me, chastely of course. Well, mostly chastely. Because handsome helps. Don't try to say it doesn't. Spitball would've hugged me, but he smelled like cigarettes and had skin like leftover toast. Aaron didn't bear considering. Before I could launch myself at Mauro, a new nurse came out. She pointed at me. "You can come back."

I stood up and that's when I realized I still had on my penguin wetsuit. I couldn't take it off. We were in a hospital and all I had on underneath was a swimsuit. I sighed, gave my mug to Aaron, hitched up my crotch and waddled out of the waiting room behind her. The rest of the hospital was better than the outside portrayed. The walls were whitewashed and the floors were clean. I did feel a bit like I'd stepped back in time to the fifties. Everything was utilitarian and hard. There were no fountains or music, carpet or cushy chairs.

We went around a corner and passed a long line that extended down the corridor. The patients stood back-to-back but looked like they shouldn't be standing at all. Their skin sagged on their sallow cheeks. Several had Kaposi's sarcomas, purplish tumors on their arms and faces. All the patients hung onto the handrail. Without it, I don't know if they could've stayed upright.

We turned another corner and I touched the nurse's arm. "Were those AIDS patients?"

"Yes. The clinic is always busy."

"Why are they standing in the hall?"

She glanced at me, her dark eyes angry and resigned all at once. "There's no room. We're not exactly the Taj Mahal here."

Since the Taj Mahal was a mausoleum, I had to disagree. "You can't find chairs for them?"

"I would if I could. We have one of the highest rates of AIDs in Central America."

"I had no idea."

"Nobody does." She stopped at a door. "We'll release her after they pay."

"Release her? She's been here like a half hour. What about the drooling?"

"They say she can go. It's a minor stab wound."

She ran to catch up with another nurse and I went inside. Lucia lay on a narrow hospital bed. Her leg was well-bandaged, her eyes shut, and she was very relaxed. Graeme sat next to her on a wooden chair with her hand pressed to his cheek.

"How's it going?" I asked as I took her pulse. Not bad.

"I'm okay," said Lucia, slightly slurring her words.

"I don't know what to do," said Graeme. "They're going to release her like this."

"What did they give her?"

"Nothing. Can you go to the pharmacy for us?" Graeme asked. "I don't want to leave her."

"She's this relaxed with nothing? What about a local? Where's the IV?"

"The nurse said it's near the end of the quarter and they're running out of everything."

Lucia's head rolled around on the pillow. "I feel so weird."

"How's the pain?" I asked.

"It hurts, but I don't really care."

Graeme kissed her cheek. "I don't understand what's going on."

I put on my it's-totally-fine face. "What did the doctor prescribe?"

Graeme handed me a script for penicillin. That wasn't good enough. Lucia needed a broad spectrum antibiotic.

"What about a painkiller?" I asked.

"They don't have any opiates," he said. "But he gave her a tetanus booster. Is that right?"

"Yes. We always want tetanus up to date with a puncture. Mind if I take a look?" I asked.

"Go ahead."

I undid Lucia's bandage. The wound looked clean, but there was significant swelling and reddening around the site. Lucia reacted to the pain, but she was loopy and it was freaking me out.

"Excuse me," said a man behind me.

I turned to find a doctor in a crisp white lab coat. I felt like I'd been caught sticking quarters up my nose. He had that disapproving grandpa thing going on.

"Hello," I said, trying to muster up as much dignity as I could given what I was wearing. "I'm Mercy Watts, friend and nurse."

He relaxed and put out his hand. "I'm Dr. Navarro. I've treated the wound and Lucia's ready for discharge."

"Great. Can I speak to you outside?"

He didn't look surprised. He probably got that a lot from tourists. We stepped outside and closed the door.

"How can I help you?" asked Dr. Navarro.

"When Lucia was put in the ambulance, she was drooling copiously and I believe she passed out. There may be poison involved."

"Yes, the nurse told me. But Mrs. Carrow was conscious when she arrived. There was some drooling, but it dissipated when I irrigated the wound. There must've been minimal venom involvement. There's no evidence of poison."

"Did you do any blood work?"

His brow wrinkled. "No. She recovered quite quickly. What do you suspect happened?"

"Succinylcholine chloride to be exact."

"That's very specific. Why in the world would you think that?"

"She's oddly relaxed and drooling isn't exactly common after a stab wound of any kind. This is the second *accident* Lucia's had since she's been on the island."

"You think the stingray injected her with succinylcholine chloride?" He raised a bushy eyebrow at me.

"I don't think it was a stingray."

"Well, it presents like one."

"The barb could've been dipped in it," I said.

"I'd say it was possible, if she wasn't underwater at the time. The water would've washed it off before it got in her system."

"I know, but something's not right. We need to call the police."

He sighed and put a hand on my shoulder. "It won't do any good. This island it's...not well-policed. They come over from the mainland, do their time, and get out. And today they've got their hands full. We've had three assaults and a murder in the last twelve hours. Even if they believed you, we couldn't prove it. Succinylcholine chloride clears the system quickly and that's with a large dose."

"The perfect poison," I said. "Do you believe me?"

He gave me a patronizing smile. "I appreciate your concern. My advice: send her home early. Home is the best place for her to recover."

Unless it's not. Graeme will be there and I won't.

"Don't the police care about the tourists? If something happened to Lucia, it would be bad for business," I said.

"This was an accident. It happens, especially with tourists," said Dr. Narvarro.

How convenient.

"You have her prescription. I'll have her wheeled out to a cab."

"We don't need the penicillin. I brought Keflex."

"You came prepared."

"Nurses," I said. "It's what we do."

"Any painkillers?"

"Norco."

"That will work fine for her."

I reached for the doorknob, but he held me back. "You seem like a girl with connections."

"Really," I said, indicating my awesome saggy-butted wetsuit. "You think so?"

"I see past that. You have a certain confidence about you. The kind of confidence that comes from wealth and security."

I kept my face blank. I wouldn't have mentioned Myrtle and Millicent, if my life depended on it.

"We need help. You can see the state we're in. Medications are hard to come by. Tourists bring them in, but they are often expired. We run out of painkillers, antibiotics, and insulin nearly every quarter. We were lucky to have the tetanus booster. If you have any connections. If you can do anything, it would be a great good."

A great good. How The Girls would like that. Their money was this unseen ocean that I always knew about and stood on the edge of with it lapping my toes. That ocean was unreachable now because of Brooks and his ridiculous lawsuit. My parents were paying their expenses for the moment. Even if they could access their fabulous wealth, I didn't know how to ask them to do something. I'd never asked for anything. It would've been ridiculous to do so with all they'd done for me. But Roatan might be the right thing to ask for, if I could stomach it.

"I'll see what I can do. I can't promise anything."

"All I ask is that you try."

"I'll figure something out."

Then he hugged me. I was so surprised, I didn't react. Not counting Pete, the only time a doctor ever hugged me was to cop a feel.

Dr. Navarro pulled back. "Thank you."

"I'll do my best. Tourists really bring you expired meds?"

"It's better than nothing most of the time."

"I guess so," I said.

A nurse called Dr. Navarro away and I went into Lucia's room. "Okay. Here's what we're going to do. I brought Keflex and Norco with me. That's what we're going to use."

Lucia pushed herself upright. "That sounds good."

"I don't know about that," said Graeme. "Dr. Navarro prescribed the penicillin."

"What I have is better," I said.

Graeme shifted in his chair and avoided looking at me. "I don't mean to be rude, but..."

He doesn't trust me. One point for Graeme.

I smiled. "I wouldn't trust me either, but I am who I say I am."

"Graeme, it's fine," said Lucia.

"You don't know me," I said. "You should confirm my qualifications. I suggest you call St. James ER and ask for Evelyn. She'll vouch for me."

"You don't mind?" asked Lucia.

"Not at all."

Graeme searched on his phone, got the number, and called the ER. Evelyn was there as she always was. Graeme told her the situation and she told him to listen to me. A nurse came in with the discharge paperwork and Graeme paid the bill with a credit card.

Aaron and Mauro were still in the waiting room, now eating baleadas with their feet propped up. Spitball had gone back to the resort.

"Want some?" asked Aaron, holding up the remains of a folded tortilla.

"What's in it?" I asked.

"Rice, beans, and crema."

"I'll pass, but Lucia needs something in her stomach."

Aaron stuffed the rest of the baleada in his mouth and ran out the exit as fast as his little legs would carry him. We followed him outside with Lucia in a wheelchair and signaled for a cab. By the time we got her into the cab, she wasn't loopy anymore and she was in considerable pain. Aaron ran up, but he didn't have the baleada I expected. He gave a large Styrofoam cup to Lucia.

"What's this?" she asked.

"Banana smoothie. Better for the stomach." Then Aaron trotted off to Mauro's scooter. I was this close to saying I'd ride with Mauro and he could go in the cab with Lucia and Graeme. Only the thought of Pete kept me from doing it. That and the fact that I'd be putting Lucia in there with the guy who might be trying to murder her and Aaron, who'd probably tell them all about how he found a chicken toenail in a hot dog once. He kept the toenail and if they were really lucky, he might have it on him. Lucia had suffered enough for one day.

I got in beside Lucia and shut the door. Lucia took a tentative sip and proclaimed the smoothie to be just what she needed.

"Your little guy really has a nose for food," said Graeme.

"He's practically a legend," I said.

The cabbie pulled out of the hospital and it took me about thirty seconds to realize there was no air-conditioning. The day had gotten increasingly hot and muggy. The breeze from the open windows made me feel like we were in a convection oven. The wetsuit wasn't helping. I unzipped and folded the top down, but it didn't help much.

"What happened to your suit?" asked Lucia while grimacing and clutching Graeme's arm.

"Awww crap." All the stitching had come out of the cups and one of the underwires stuck out like a horn.

Graeme grinned at me. "Do you think Marilyn had these problems?"

"Nobody has these problems except me," I said as I tried to stuff the wire back in. But it boinged out and thwacked me in the nose.

"I wish I had a picture of that."

Lucia sipped her smoothie and said she was full. I put the cool cup against her bandage, hoping it would help until we got to La Isla Bonita, but after that I didn't know what to do. I had little doubt that someone was trying to kill her, but I was starting to like Graeme. He didn't fit my idea of a wife-killer at all. But sociopaths were able to mimic normal emotions I reminded myself. He could be fooling me the way Ted Bundy fooled everyone he met. Dr. Navarro said to get Lucia off the island, but that wasn't a solution. If I was wrong about Graeme and he was trying to kill Lucia, it was best to keep her on the island. At least I could keep an eye on them until I got some evidence of his guilt.

The cab sped out of Coxen Hole and I stared out the window at the countryside. It was beautiful with the crashing surf to one side of us and the jungle on the other. Almost beautiful enough to distract me, but not quite. We made it back as Lucia started to cry in pain. We put her in bed and I gave her the first doses of both medications. She drifted off as soon as the Norco hit her. Once she was asleep and feeling no pain, I changed her dressing and frowned.

"What's wrong?" asked Graeme.

"There's more swelling than I'd like." I didn't mention the heat coming off of the wound. There was definitely an infection and it'd set in at record speed.

"Will the antibiotic take care of it?"

"It should. We'll keep an eye on it."

Graeme stretched out on the bed beside Lucia. "God, it's been a long day."

I stood up to go. I didn't like leaving her there with him, but no excuses to stay came to mind and I left. Surely nothing would happen in their bungalow. He'd have to be crazy to try anything where he'd be the prime suspect and nothing the killer did said he was crazy. Every attempt could be seen as an accident. It was done so well, even I wasn't sure. Lucia was in danger. I just hoped she could survive her own bed.

CHAPTER EIGHT

I woke the next morning to the sound of the spaghetti birds going batshit crazy overhead. The hammock had sagged and my rump brushed the porch. The only time I'd been less comfortable was on a Girl Scout camping trip when our clueless leader, my mother, decided that setting up tents in a field full of rocks was a grand idea because the view was excellent. My view from the porch was excellent, too. Lucia and Graeme's bungalow was quiet and had been all night. They'd had dinner in their room, and I'd checked the wound before bed. It hadn't improved, so I put an ice pack on it, in hopes that would help.

I thrust a leg over the side of the hammock and my foot touched something soft and warm. There was a body on the floor. I shrieked because I'm cool that way, spun over in the hammock and landed with a thunk on the floor.

"What's wrong with you?" asked Aaron from a pile of towels. He'd made a nest like some sort of rodent on my porch.

"You scared me to death. What are you doing here? You have a room," I said.

"Helping."

"Why do you always think I need help? I'm fine."

"I'm your partner. Tommy says I have to help you."

"Well, I'm not doing anything. I'm on vacation."

Aaron rubbed his eyes. They were blue. I didn't know that. His glasses were always so dirty it was hard to tell. "You're out here."

"Yeah. So?" I asked.

"It's not safe."

"There's guards all over the place."

"They're not helping Lucia," he said.

I stood and straightened my robe. "Um...what do you mean by that?"

"Someone's trying to kill Lucia and you're trying to stop them. You hungry? They got banana pancakes today. Not plantains, regular bananas. Plantains would be too starchy. They might work in a sort of potato pancake way. I could try that. What'd you think? Shredded plantain cakes with maybe a boysenberry chicken roulade."

"Stop talking!"

"Huh?"

"What was that about Lucia?" I asked.

"What?" asked Aaron.

"OMG. Someone's trying to kill Lucia?"

"Guess so."

"Holy crap. How'd you know that?" I asked.

He shrugged and I could tell he was thinking about pancakes again.

"I'm halfway to crazy town. Why didn't you tell me you knew?"

Aaron shrugged again and started to go in our room.

"Don't go in there. Aunt Tenne's still asleep."

"No, she's not. She left at six," he said.

"Really? That's a first. Was she okay?"

"Sure." Aaron went inside and got a bottle of water.

I passed him and put on my last one-piece and a cover-up. Nice and wrinkly, just like I felt. When I came out Aaron was still there with his water, unopened. I don't know why he got it. Then again, I didn't know why he did most things.

"Aaron, would you know if Aunt Tenne was okay?"

"Sure."

"How would you know?"

Aaron looked at the ceiling and seemed confused. Ha! Stumped him.

"Was she smiling?" I asked.

"No."

"Was she crying?"

"Yes," he said.

I slapped my forehead. "Aaron, for future reference, when a woman is crying, she's not okay. Understand?"

"Sure."

"What am I right now? What's it look like to you?"

Aaron scratched his head. "Um....mad?"

"Yes, Aaron, I'm mad. You're driving me crazy," I said.

Aaron grinned like he'd just fed me crab. "Hey, I got it."

"Yes, you got it. Let's go find Aunt Tenne because she isn't okay."

We found Aunt Tenne on the chair swings overlooking the ocean. She was bent over, her shoulders heaving. I would've expected Mom to be with her, she'd been so worried, but it was Bruno the porter sitting next to her. He had his arm over her back as he looked out over the ocean, his face wet with tears. I'd never seen a man cry like that and it stopped me ten feet away on the cool morning sand. Dad had cried when Cora, his first partner died, and when Gavin died, but it was a restrained kind of grief. Never out of control and there was always a drink in hand. Bruno had no drink, nothing to contain him. He sat with Aunt Tenne and cried with her.

"You know what this is about, don't you?" I asked Aaron.

He looked at me with the blank expression he did so well.

"Never mind. Would you do me a favor?"

"You hungry? I can make those plantain cakes. You like those?"

"Maybe later. I want you to go back and hang around Lucia's bungalow. I feel weird about not having one of us around. You can't tell Dad anything about this, okay?"

I'm sure Aaron's eyes would've gone all shifty, if I could've seen them.

"Aaron, I'm totally serious."

"Tommy said—"

"I don't care what he said." I took off his glasses and cleaned them on the hem of my cover-up. "You're supposed to be my partner. Where's your loyalty?"

He put his glasses back on. It was amazing how different he looked when you could see his eyes. Not better, but different. He was still wearing his favorite Doctor Who tee shirt that featured the Doctor from twenty seasons ago and a multitude of unidentifiable food stains. Unidentifiable to me, that is. Aaron probably knew exactly what they were and where he got the food.

"I'm your partner?" he asked.

Groan.

"I'm your partner," he repeated.

This hurts me. It really does.

"You are my partner. Are you going to tell Dad or not?"

"What about breakfast?"

"Fine. I'll eat whatever you want. Just watch over Lucia," I said.

Aaron trotted off in the direction of our rooms. I yelled after him. "Except crab. No crab."

I headed for the bar and much needed coffee and spotted Mom and Dixie. They were perched on stools and completely still, watching the display of tremendous grief on the swings. I walked to them, feeling every grain of sand under my feet and having a weird out-of-body feeling. I knew we were in a tropical paradise having that moment, but I kept thinking any second I'd wake up at home with Skanky on my chest, wondering why I had such a crazy dream.

Mom and Dixie didn't look at me when I got to them. Their eyes were red and a pair of steaming coffee cups sat untouched on the bar behind them.

"What happened?" I asked with a thick, heavy voice.

"Nothing," said Mom.

"How's Lucia?" asked Dixie, her eyes not straying to me.

"Well," I said. "She did take a stingray barb to the leg yesterday, so she's been better. What's with all the crying?"

Dixie focused on me. "You should go check on Lucia. She needs you."

"Don't change the subject," I said. "What's going on with Aunt Tenne?"

"She's just having a good cry. Let's get back to Lucia," said Mom. "She sure is accident prone."

I kind of wanted to tell Mom what was going on. She was way more experienced in crime than I was. The bartender brought me a cup of coffee and I blew into it, pondering my choices. Every one ended with Dad knowing that I was involved with a Fibonacci. The last thing I wanted was a lecture or worse Dad flying down to bother the crap out of me. I couldn't trust Mom or Dixie to keep Lucia's family a secret. They'd probably knock me over trying to get to a phone.

"Lucia should be fine. I'm a little worried about infection," I said, trying to sound breezy, but I needn't have bothered. Mom's focus was back on Aunt Tenne. "Hello."

"What is it, honey?" Mom asked.

"What's wrong with Aunt Tenne?"

"Women need a good cry now and then."

"What about men? Bruno's not exactly a happy camper. Aren't you going to go over there and chase off *the pool boy*?"

"Not hardly. It's Tenne's day and she can have it any way she wants."

"But—"

Mom waved me away. "Stop interrogating me and go do something."

"Like what?" I asked.

Mauro came up behind me. I smelled him before I saw him. Hmmmm, Hawaiian Tropic. "Like come with me to look for Lucia's barb," he said.

"Now?"

"Have you got something better to do?" he asked.

Aunt Tenne was still sobbing on the swings, which bore investigating, but Mom was giving me the stink eye. "Okay. Let's go."

Mauro drove the smallest La Isla Bonita boat out to Pablo's Place and we put our equipment on. I didn't bring any conditioner. I was going to pay for that with giant snaggle hair, but it would be worth it, if we could find the barb.

"How big was it?" asked Mauro as he clipped on his BCD.

"About six or seven inches."

His head jerked up. "Are you certain of this?"

"I didn't measure it, but yeah, it was big."

"Our native species don't usually get that big. How wide was it?"

"At least an inch. Lucia's wound was that size."

Mauro sat next to me and double checked my equipment. I became very aware that we were alone on the ocean with no witnesses. My chest tightened until I remembered Mauro wasn't a suspect. If he was trying to kill Lucia, she'd have been dead that first time. He was the one who gave her his spare reg. He could've sat back and pretended not to see.

"You know where we're going?" I couldn't have got us back to the exact place where Lucia had been attacked if my life depended on it.

"Yes, I remember the spot. Mercy, I think you're right about Lucia. Someone is trying to kill her."

As soon as he said it, I wanted to deny that it could be true. It was so much more awful when it couldn't be an accident. "Why's that?"

"That doesn't sound like a native barb and the place where it happened isn't a place where stingrays would normally be. They don't like coral and narrow areas. They're flat."

"So someone brought in a barb to make it look like an accident. It's our best evidence."

"We must give it to the police immediately," said Mauro, lowering his own mask.

"Your island cops won't take this seriously, unless she's dead," I said. "Dr. Navarro clued me in on how it works around here."

"It's not the best system, but they do try. Why are you so interested?"

"My dad's a detective. I can't just sit by."

"You think Graeme did it?" he asked.

"He's the natural choice. He had access all four times," I said.

"Four. Did I miss something?"

I checked my regs twice. Paranoia was setting in. "Lucia said she packed two inhalers in her purse. They disappeared. Second, both her regs were tampered with. Third, another inhaler disappears from her beach bag on the boat along with her wallet. Fourth, the stabbing. Graeme was there at every incident."

"Why would he hurt his own wife?"

"Have you seen the bruises?"

Mauro looked down; his handsome face somber. "I have."

"All is not well. That's all I know," I said.

"There were others around." He smiled. "You and me, for instance."

"And the Gmucas, Todd, the frat boys, my mom and Dixie. None of us have a history with her though, and the husband is always the first choice. But Graeme, I don't know, he doesn't seem the type. This is pretty cold-blooded."

"Maybe you should consider the rest."

"I should, but one suspect is just so much easier." I smiled. "I'm all about efficiency."

"Do you want me to make it worse?" he asked.

"Not really."

He put my reg in my mouth. "There were other boats in the area. Someone could've swam over."

Crap! Double crap!

Mauro pushed me back and I fell in cursing. I descended a little too quickly, causing my ears to pop painfully. Mauro came to my side and gestured for me to follow him. I thought maybe I would recognize something once we got down, but I didn't. Pablo's Place was all new to me. A parrotfish glided by and I spotted a large lobster backing into his spot under the coral. I was so busy looking around, I was surprised how quickly we made it to the attack spot. We went over every inch of the area and found nothing. Mauro's eyes got increasingly worried the longer we looked. He'd put it together. Whoever attacked Lucia had cleaned up after himself. We took Lucia to the surface and he retrieved the barb. The evidence.

Mauro gave me the thumbs up and we surfaced. Bobbing next to the hull of our boat, we raised our masks.

"He planned it all out, didn't he?" he said.

"Looks like it," I said. "I wonder how many other ideas this genius has."

"What do you mean?" asked Mauro.

"He planned for failure. If the regs didn't work, he had the barb and whatever he dipped it in."

"You think he might have more."

"I would. Two backups is prudent." I took off my flippers and tossed them over the side of the boat. "You know, this degree of planning, it just doesn't sound like a husband killing a wife."

Mauro helped me onto the ladder. "I thought Graeme was your suspect."

"He is, but we couldn't find the barb. I don't know. It just feels wrong. Husband's beat wives to death. They strangle them. Shoot them. How many men make a three-part plan and clean up? Besides, Graeme got to Lucia quickly and went to the hospital with her. He didn't have time to retrieve the barb."

"Graeme could have a partner and they could've gotten it. Maybe you should ask your dad?"

I climbed over the side of the boat. "Not if I can help it."

Lucia and Graeme were on the beach under a pair of pink striped umbrellas when we pulled up onto shore. Ever faithful, Aaron sat ten yards away watching them like a nerdy owl. Lucia and Graeme didn't seem to know he was there. Thank goodness. If I had a guy like that following me, I'd be pretty freaked out and that's saying something. I'd had some pretty weird guys follow me.

Mauro and I unloaded our tanks and equipment while I watched Graeme out of the corner of my eye. Was he the kind of guy that would hatch an elaborate plan to off his wife? If I knew his financial situation, that might help. Divorce was expensive. Divorce from a Fibonacci, well, that might be straight up unhealthy. Maybe Dr. Carrow, DDS, thought her accidental death was preferable to his.

Graeme kissed Lucia's forehead and walked off the beach in the direction of the restaurant past Colin the frat boy passed out on a lounge chair with his hat over his face. Finally, a moment alone with Lucia.

"Are we done?" I asked Mauro.

"Yes. What are you going to do?"

"I'm going to tell Lucia someone's trying to kill her."

"Good luck with that." Mauro drove off and I walked over to Lucia. She put down her book, *"P" is for Peril.* "Mercy, where have you been?"

"Actually I wanted to talk to you about that. May I sit down?"

"Of course."

I looked to wave Aaron over. He could be my character witness or at least Dad's character witness. But Aaron was gone. He abandoned his post, the twerp. I sat and tried to look reliable, not something I'm great at, especially with the hair from hell.

"How are you feeling?" I asked.

"Not great. I think I just need to rest. The painkillers help. Thanks for those."

"Don't mention it. I don't know how to tell you this, but Mauro and I went out to try and find the stingray barb. He thinks it wasn't a native species."

"Really? That's weird."

"I agree. It's even weirder that it's not where you dropped it. The barb is gone."

"Oh." Lucia looked so pretty with her big eyes and fluffy dark hair. I hated to wipe that innocent expression off her face.

"Somebody took it," I said.

"It would be a cool souvenir, I guess."

"I don't think it's a souvenir. I think it's evidence."

There. I did it.

Lucia tilted her head. "Evidence that I got stung?"

I guess I didn't do it. Second try. "Evidence of attempted murder."

She gasped and put her hand on her chest. "There was a murder? Who was it? Oh my god!"

Wow. I really stink at this.

"No. No. Of an attempted murder of...um...you." I bit my lip and waited for her to freak.

Instead, she laughed. She laughed so hard, she had to wipe the tears away. "Oh, Mercy. That's a good one."

"I'm serious, Lucia. Truly I am. Look at what's happened on this island, since you got here. The missing inhalers. Two broken regs and a stabbing. You have to listen to me."

"Who would try to kill me? I'm a housewife. I volunteer and walk the dog."

"Well, usually in cases like this, the police look at the husband."

She laughed again with fresh tears and everything. I felt like an idiot. Surely a woman with a violent husband wouldn't think this was so crazy.

"Graeme's a dentist for heaven's sake. A dentist," she said.

"Dentists can kill people."

"Name one killer dentist."

Oh, crap. She had me. I couldn't think of one.

"There are a lot of killer husbands," I said.

"How would you know that?" She held up her novel. "Have you been reading a lot of murder mysteries?"

This was not going the way I thought it would. "I never read them. My father's a retired police detective. I've lived with crime my whole life. I don't want to read about it."

Graeme walked up. "Ah, the two most beautiful ladies on the island." I think he cringed when he looked at me. "What are you talking about?"

Lucia took a mug of coffee from him. "Mercy thinks you're trying to kill me."

"Well, that is on my bucket list." He sat on the end of Lucia's chair and they clinked mugs.

I'm sure I've felt stupider at some point in my life, but I sure didn't know when.

"Look, I have some experience in this area. You should listen to me," I said.

"Are you a cop or something?" asked Graeme. I detected no worry in his eyes. Confident bastard.

"My dad's Tommy Watts." I hated to do it, but I had to pull out the rep. "He's kind of a famous detective."

Lucia brightened up. "Tall guy with red hair. Kind of gangly?"

"That's him."

Lucia pushed Graeme's shoulder. "The master of ceremonies at the last Policeman's Benevolent Association dinner."

"That's your dad?" asked Graeme with a shocked look. "There's no resemblance at all."

"It's all on the inside. So you two were at the PBA dinner?"

"I organize fundraising for the Widows and Orphans Fund," said Lucia.

Didn't see that coming. A Fibonacci at a dinner for cops. WTF.

"Um...that's nice. So I'm trying to tell you that I know what I'm talking about. Nobody has that many accidents, Lucia."

Graeme took a sip of coffee and looked at me quietly. I think he was trying to detect some Tommy Watts in my face. Good luck. I was all Mom on the outside. "Accidents happen, Mercy. This has just been an unlucky trip."

"Or very lucky trip, depending on how you look at it," I said.

Lucia patted my shoulder. "I appreciate your concern, but I'm not worried. No one would take the trouble of murdering me. I'm not that interesting."

In other words, you're crazy.

"Please be careful," I said. "There is cause for concern. You should stay on the resort where there are guards."

"We're not letting some freak accidents ruin our vacation," said Graeme.

"Once I feel better, we're going on a glass-bottomed boat tour," said Lucia, smiling. "Don't worry. Those are pretty benign, unless a fish jumps in the boat and bites me."

There was nothing I could do. Lucia couldn't conceive of a killer husband or any threat at all. As a bonus, Graeme now knew I suspected him and could come after me, if he was the one. I suppose I should've been afraid, but I sensed no malice from him. I'd been fooled before, so all I could do was cross my fingers and hope.

"Mind if I take a look at your leg?" I asked.

"Absolutely."

I lifted the skirt of her long cover-up and frowned at the stain of yellow pus that had soaked through the bandage. Lucia winced as I peeled back the tape and gauze. The wound had swollen to twice the size it had been the night before. It was gaping open, red, and hot to the touch.

"That doesn't look good," said Graeme.

"No, it doesn't. You definitely have an infection. The Keflex should be taking care of it. Did you take your dose yet today?"

"I thought I should wait until the same time as yesterday," said Lucia.

"Let's go ahead and take it now. I'd like to soak it in Epsom salts as well."

"You brought Epsom salts with you on vacation?"

"I wish I had. I'll get Aaron on it. If there are Epsom salts on the island, he'll find them," I said.

"Your little guy is pretty interesting," said Graeme. "So are you two—"

"Oh my god no. Why do people think he's my significant other?"

Lucia laughed. "You're always together."

"Not by choice. He's kind of my partner. He's supposed to look after me, if you can believe that," I said.

"I can believe it. He's always right there with whatever you need."

"And it's not that weird," said Graeme. "Beautiful women marry odd men all the time. Have you seen Bill Gates' wife?"

"He's loaded," I said.

"I wouldn't be surprised if Aaron had money," said Lucia. "He's a genius in the kitchen."

"I'll give you that. I'm going to see about those salts. Graeme, can you go get the Keflex?"

He headed to the room. I ordered an ice water for Lucia and rewrapped the wound. "I'll put new bandages on after we soak it." I bit my lip and glanced around. The beach was packed. Colin was awake and now pounding beers with Andrew and Joe. A bunch of cruise ship passengers were totally wasted and dancing in their Brazilian bikinis and nearly flattening small children if they wandered too close. If it wasn't Graeme and I wasn't ready to concede that yet, it could be anybody. There were a lot of anybodies on that beach.

Lucia patted my hand. "You don't have to stay here with me. Nothing will happen. Even if you're right, I'm right out here in the open."

"I just can't leave you," I said.

"You're wonderful for caring, but I'm telling you it can't be true. It just can't. I have good luck, not bad. It's kind of a family thing."

It was the first time I'd heard a hint of her family connections. Fibonaccis were famous for their luck as well as other things. Lucia had been pretty lucky so far.

"Sometimes we have to make our own luck," I said, still looking around.

Aunt Tenne and Bruno weren't on the swings anymore. But Mom and Dixie were coming down the path to the beach carrying mimosas. "My mom's coming. Please don't tell her what I said."

"Why not?" asked Lucia.

"No crimes or talk of crime allowed. We're supposed to be having a girl trip."

"You brought Aaron on a girl trip?"

"I don't bring him anywhere. He just shows up. So you'll keep mum about the whole suspicious accident thing?" I asked.

"I will, but I kind of want to see what would happen."

Mom tells Dad. Dad finds out you're a Fibonacci. Dad hits roof.

"Probably just a stern lecture, but I try to avoid those whenever possible. You know how family can be."

She settled back on her lounge and tipped down the brim of her broad sunhat, so that I couldn't see her eyes. "Yes, I certainly do."

I left and intercepted Mom and Dixie while they were ordering lounge chairs to be brought down for them.

"Hey, Mom. Can you keep an eye on Lucia for a little bit?"

"Why? She's not three."

Cause someone's trying to kill her a lot.

"Her leg is worse and I need to find her some Epsom salts. If she throws up, or does anything unusual, come get me immediately. I'll be in the room."

"Sure," said Dixie. "We'd be happy to."

Dixie did look happy, but Mom gave me the suspicious look she usually reserved for Dad. "Isn't this unusual for such a minor wound?"

"I wouldn't call it minor and stingrays are poisonous. Just watch her. Okay?" I rushed away down a back path before Mom could question me further. She wouldn't have needed to question me, if she gave the situation a moment of thought. She knew everything that had happened to Lucia. She just needed to string the events together. If she did, I was toast. The last thing I wanted was Dad flying down to Roatan to take over between sessions of yelling at me.

Since I had no discernible sense of direction, I wandered around on those twisted, shady paths for a good ten minutes. Getting lost doesn't usually work out for me. I tend to end up at the right place at the wrong time. The most notable incident was in tenth grade when I got lost under the gym trying to find the tennis equipment lockup and discovered my crush, Brennan Glock, kissing our English lit teacher who happened to be a dude. I still said yes two weeks later when Brennan asked me to Homecoming, because he was the only one who asked, being the only one who really didn't care if I said no. I told him what I saw over dinner and we became a special kind of friends. It turned out that I was the only who knew he was gay (besides Mr. Heck), and it remained that way for another decade.

Most recently, I'd found a fellow nurse stuffing a patient's Schedule II drugs in her panties. Don't ask me why. She had pockets. On this unlucky day, I saw the Gmucas sneaking down the path behind the bungalows. Frankie whispered to Linda and they disappeared behind Lucia and Graeme's. I crept through the foliage to the bungalow next door and peeked around the corner. Frankie was jiggling the back door handle.

Holy crap!

Linda whispered in Frankie's ear and kissed his cheek. How touching. You just became suspects with a capital S.

I stepped out into the open. "Hi, guys. What's ya doing?"

Frankie and Linda turned matching shades of red. "Um...Um..."

"Is that your bungalow?"

Linda looked at the door and feigned surprised. "Oh, my gosh. It isn't. This is so embarrassing. Let's go, Frankie."

"We were just, you know, going back to our room," said Frankie.

"Through the back door?" I asked.

"We...um."

"Come on, Frankie." Linda dragged her husband away before he could finish his sentence, which certainly didn't make them look any better.

I watched them go into their bungalow three doors down and then got on the right path to the room. Before I came out of the palms, I smelled the most amazing smell. Aaron. Not Aaron personally. He usually smelled like hot dogs or crab, but Aaron's cooking. I was getting so that I could pick his style out of a lineup. Aaron was the only person I would ever know that could make the air succulent.

The water pail next to our steps was clean and fresh. I wrecked it and ran up the stairs to find Aaron squatting next to two hibachis. One had a small saucepan, bubbling with a light brown liquid. The other was covered in fruit, pineapples, mangos, peaches, and, oddly, watermelon. Opposite Aaron sat Todd the Land's End dad on the deck chair, wearing a pink polo, ironed, and with a perfect tan.

"You hungry?" asked Aaron.

"I am now," I said. "Hi, Todd."

"Hello, Mercy." Todd winced when he looked at me. I pictured my hair resembling something Lady Gaga would have, only worse. "Aaron offered to make breakfast and there's no way I could resist. Tracy's taking the kids snorkeling for the morning at Half Moon Bay. I hope you don't mind."

"Why would I mind?"

"You might've been hoping for a romantic breakfast, just the two of you."

"Not you, too. Aaron and I aren't a thing. He's...he's my dad's best friend's Dungeons and Dragons buddy."

"And World of Warcraft," said Aaron.

"That, too."

"And Star Wars: Force Unleashed."

"You're not helping," I said. "We're not together. We're really, really not together. Please tell people that."

"But you're on vacation together," said Todd.

"It's complicated."

"We're partners," said Aaron.

"Really not helping. We're sort of partners in work. We do research for my dad. It's boring," I said. "What's for breakfast?"

Aaron lifted the edge of a pineapple. "Grilled fruit salad with honey lime syrup."

"Smells great," I said. "Do you happen to know where I can get some Epsom salts?"

"Yeah."

I waited for a second, but nothing more seemed to be coming, so I asked, "And where would that be?"

"Julia's."

I tried to run my fingers through my hair, but they got stuck. "Aaron, you make me tired. Can you get them for me? Lucia needs to soak her wound."

He mumbled something I took for a yes and I went in for a quick shower. It didn't help much. I looked like I'd angered my hair permanently. When I came out swathed in towels and leave-in conditioner, Aaron was chopping fruit on top of our little apartment fridge in the corner. I watched him for a moment, peeling and chopping with precision. I'd never seen him in action before. I have to say it was impressive. It would've been even more impressive if he hadn't had a foot wide ketchup stain on the seat of his shorts. How do you sit in that much ketchup and not notice it?

"Are you going to get the Epsom salts," I said.

"Got 'em," he said, holding up a small wrinkled paper bag.

"Already?"

He shrugged and kept chopping.

"Thanks." I took the bag out on the porch and found Todd engrossed in a paperback, *Catch-22*. I couldn't ask him to take the salts. As benign as he seemed, he was still a suspect. I passed him by, ran down the steps, and found Marcella coming onto the path from the dive shop. "Can you do me a favor?" I asked.

"Sure," she said.

"Take these salts down to my mother on the beach. She'll know what to do."

"Any new suspects?"

"Not yet."

Marcella took off for the beach and I went back to find Aaron still in my room, muttering over a mixing bowl.

"Aaron, I need a favor." *Not sure how to ask this.* "Do you have Spidermonkey's phone number?"

"Spidermonkey the hacker?"

"How many Spidermonkeys do you know?"

"Morty hates Spidermonkey."

"I know, but I need information and I can't ask Uncle Morty."

"How come?"

"Cause he'll tell Dad."

"So."

Because I'm trying to hide stuff, you nutbag.

"Because I can handle this Lucia thing on my own. I don't need Dad calling me up and interfering. You know how he is."

You should anyway. You're on my girl trip.

"I'll get him to call you. Don't tell Tommy. Tommy'd be pissed, if he knew," said Aaron.

"I will never tell Dad. Believe me." I went in the bedroom, tried to find some clean clothes, but settled for my surviving one-piece and a rather crusty cover-up. It was kind of nice not worrying about shoes or clothes. If it weren't for the hair, I might consider island living.

My phone rang and I answered without looking at the caller ID. Mistake. "Hello."

"What the hell, Mercy," said Chuck.

"Shit!"

"Weren't expecting me, were you?"

"No. No. I just stubbed my toe. It's fine," I said.

"Yeah, right. You were expecting Spidermonkey."

"Who?"

"He's one of my informants. He hears something about you, he calls me first thing."

"Why?"

"Because you're family," he said.

"That is not working out for me." I waited while a burst of raucous laughter drowned out what Chuck was saying.

"Shut up, you pricks!" yelled Chuck.

"What's that about?" I asked.

"You don't want to know."

"If it's at your expense then I do."

"I guess you'll find out eventually. I arrested a woman this morning and she attacked me with a frozen bratwurst."

I laughed until my stomach clenched in pain. "I so needed that!"

"Yeah, that's great. So what are you doing that you have to hide it from Tommy?" asked Chuck.

"How many times did she hit you?"

"Mercy!"

"I'm not hiding anything from Dad," I said, still chuckling.

"Do you want me to refer Spidermonkey to him?"

"Can't you just leave me alone?" I asked.

"Not a chance, sweet cheeks."

"Don't call me that."

"I'm trying out pet names. I think we should have pet names for each other."

"Eww. No."

"You know you want to tell me, love muffin," said Chuck.

I hung up. I needed to wash out my ears. The phone rang again and I swear the ring was sleazy.

"What?" I said.

"Mercy," said Chuck with all the sleaze gone. "Tell me what's going on."

"I can't."

Chuck paused and I pictured him sitting at his desk with his Timberlands propped up. The boots gave him an extra couple of inches in height, not that he needed it, but he liked the intimidation factor.

"I'll just be going now," I said.

"I won't tell Tommy."

"Yeah, right."

Chuck was my dad's protege and he'd never gone against him since the moment he invaded our family.

"I'm serious. I'd rather keep it from Tommy than have you out there on your own," he said.

"I have Aaron."

"So you're digging the partner now?"

"Not exactly, but the food is good and he does have a tendency to keep me alive," I said.

"You need information. I can provide that."

Chuck was right. I couldn't do the research on my own and Dad had a broad reach. Anyone else I called might be his source.

"If you betray me, I'll never trust you again. You get that?"

"I do. What's the deal?"

"Now don't freak out, but I need you to look at Graeme Carrow," I said.

"The Fibonacci woman's husband? Why? What the hell, Mercy? Is Oz Urbani down there? I will kick his ass. You have to stay away from those people."

"You promised not to freak," I said.

"I promised not to tell Tommy. I can freak the fuck out if I want."

"Oz isn't here."

"But you're on a first name basis," said Chuck.

"Calm down. He isn't here."

"But..."

"His sister is."

"Shit!"

"And someone's trying to kill her."

"I'm coming down there. I'm leaving now."

I rolled my eyes and lay down on the bed. The woven mat ceiling looked particularly nice from that angle, all nice and orderly, unlike people. "How about you act like I'm not an incompetent asshole and get me the information."

"You don't get it, Mercy. If Lucia Fibonacci gets killed and her brother thinks you're supposed to be protecting her, they will kill you. It will look like an accident or an act of God or some such shit, but you will get dead with a quickness."

"I get it. I'm not stupid." I told him the events as they happened, half hoping he'd disagree with me. He didn't.

"It sounds like you don't like Graeme for it anymore," he said.

"Her reaction just didn't fit with an abused woman. I've treated enough to know how they behave. She's not scared of him."

"There's something you should know. The Fibonaccis are in a war right now. It looks like they had an underboss in the Todaro family of New York executed and they are pissed."

"Pissed enough to have Lucia killed?"

"Only if they want to start a war. Civilians aren't fair game. Besides, it's notoriously hard to kill a Fibonacci."

"Or indict them apparently."

"We've never indicted a Fibonacci for so much as public lewdness. It's freakish, considering how many players they have and they're into everything from racketeering to drug smuggling."

"I do not feel better about this situation," I said.

"I'm scared shitless for you and I'm coming down there. First flight I can get."

I would've thrown a fit, but I was having a quiet little freak out of my own. A murderous husband was one thing. A mob hit was quite another. Wait. Mob hit?

"If someone was trying to kill a rival family member, would they take the trouble to make it look like an accident? This is Roatan. Land of what-the-hell. They could just shoot her and be done with it. The investigation would be minimal at best."

"Yeah. Somebody's pretty worried about getting caught."

"And they're not that great at this. They keep missing," I said.

"I admit that doesn't make sense. New York knows what they're doing, but she is a Fibonacci."

"You really believe all that stuff about their invincibility?"

"The evidence is hard to deny. I'll get you that information and I'm on a plane," he said.

"Fine."

I hung up and felt somebody watching me. Aaron stood in the door, holding a barbecue fork with five kinds of fruit on it. "Lucia's a Fibonacci?"

"Yes. Don't tell Mom, Dixie, or Aunt Tenne, and especially not Dad. They will freak," I said. "Dad will do more than freak."

"The Fibonaccis will kill you, if she dies."

"I know. I know."

"You hungry?" asked Aaron.

"Not so much."

Aaron sat on the edge of the bed and gave me the fork. I had no choice but to eat the best fruit of my life.

"Oh my god, Aaron. This is incredible."

"You like it?"

"It's like fruit crack." I licked the fork.

Aaron ran out of the room and for a second I thought I'd somehow insulted him with the crack reference, but he came back with a heaping bowl. I ate and he watched me.

"We gotta keep her alive," he said.

"No kidding."

"Call Tommy."

"No way. Chuck already knows and he's coming down. We just have to get through this with her alive and Dad in the dark," I said.

"Tommy's good."

"Dad's a genius for sure, but he told me not to have anything to do with the Fibonaccis. He'll say I should've gotten the hell out of here the minute I knew who she was."

Aaron scratched his head and looked incredibly dim. "They'll kill you."

"They'll have to stand in line. Dad first," I said. "Now get out, so I can get dressed."

"Is it good?" he stared at my half-empty bowl.

"You know it is. Stop being so needy." I pushed him off the bed.

"Needy?" he asked.

"Yes, you are needy. Go!"

Aaron trotted out of the room and I got dressed, while managing to stuff my face. I enjoyed the air-conditioning for an extra five minutes before stepping into the sticky tropical heat and was instantly sweaty again. I swear it was worse than St. Louis. I blame the palm trees. Aaron and Todd were on the porch, discussing Star Wars something or other. The hibachi was still fired up and now had a lionfish on it. It was bigger and spinier than the last one. Gack!

"Where'd you get that thing?" I asked.

"Bruno," said Aaron.

"Bruno the porter?"

"Huh?"

"The one that was on the swing with Aunt Tenne."

"He's an artist," said Aaron.

"Bruno the porter is an artist?"

"Huh?"

I edged around the hibachi, trying not to notice the fish's eyeball staring at me. "Never mind. See you, Todd."

"I hope Lucia's okay," he said.

"I'm sure she will be. I can handle infection."

Everything else, well, we'll see.

I ran down the stairs and checked my watch. Not too bad. I'd get Lucia back to the room and away from absolutely everyone. Chuck was coming to Roatan. If I knew him, he'd be pestering the crap out of me within twelve hours. That wasn't too long to wait for backup. I never thought I'd find myself looking forward to seeing him, but the Mafia added something. I was in over my head. That didn't happen very often. I float like nobody's business.

Bruno walked across the path, carrying luggage. He didn't see me and I fought the urge to hang a left and question him. Who was Bruno the artist for one? And had he seen anything suspicious, like with Lucia's bags? But I didn't have the time and went to the beach. A breeze was kicking up, whipping through the palms and yanking at my skirt. When I reached the restaurant, instead of blue skies greeting me, there were rolls of dense clouds pushing toward the island. They reminded me of dough when Millicent went after it with her French pin. There was force and determination in the sky. I broke out into a run and zigzagged past tables.

"Mercy!" Dixie appeared at the top of the stairs and Tracy and her kids ran past, nearly colliding with me.

I dashed toward Dixie as the first raindrop pelted me between the eyes. "I'm coming. Where'd this storm come from?"

"It just happened. One minute it was clear and the next this."

Lightning flashed behind her and then two more bolts. I ran past Dixie and down to the beach. Mom and Lucia were under a beach umbrella. She was worse. Much worse. It was in her eyes. Another bolt and I was half-blinded by the light. I stumbled into the table next to Lucia's chair. Two glasses went over and sloshed onto my legs.

I put my hand on her forehead. "Did you throw up?"

"No." Lucia's face was flushed. She had a fever. I put it at a hundred and two.

Graeme hunched over us. "She took the antibiotic."

"Good." I raised the towel she had over her legs and peeked at the wound. Not good.

"I just mixed up the Epsom Salts," said Mom.

"I'll carry her back to the room," said Graeme.

"We're going to the hospital!" I yelled over a roll of thunder.

"What?" asked Mom.

"Hospital! Get a car. Now!"

Mom, Dixie, and Graeme stared at me for a second.

"Pick her up, Graeme! Mom find a car!"

Mom ran up the stairs and Graeme scooped up Lucia. Sheets of rain hit us and everything went gray. There was so much water in the air, it was almost like being underwater. One of the bartenders ran up with an umbrella. Graeme struggled through the wet sand to the stairs. He lurched side-to-side as the rain hit him first from one way and then the other. What the hell kind of weather was this?

Graeme headed for the bar's overhang, but I pulled him back onto the path. "We can't wait it out. She needs to go now!"

"What is it?"

"The infection has spread. Come on!"

Graeme put on speed and ran down the path to the front office building. Mom met us halfway. "There are no vehicles. They're all at the airport. All we have are the golf carts."

"We'll call a cab!" I yelled.

The front desk building was open. My hands slipped around on the doorknob. The burst of rain thrust me into the door's glass and I cracked it with my forehead. A girl was on the other side. She pushed the door open. I barely got out of the way before the wind whipped the door back and crashed it into the wall. Graeme went past me into the office followed by Mom and Dixie.

"Are you alright?" asked the young woman. Her name tag said Elena.

"Holy crap!" said Graeme.

"Is it a hurricane?" asked Mom.

"No. No," said Elena. "Just a storm. They can come up fast. This is a bad one though."

"We need to get to the hospital," I said.

"Not in this weather. No one will be moving."

"Call a cab. She's got an infection. She needs IV antibiotics."

Elena looked at Lucia, still in Graeme's arms. She shook wildly and her cheeks were flaming. Elena picked up the phone and went down a list taped to her desk.

"No one's answering. They don't want to come out in this," she said.

"How long will this last?" I asked.

"A couple of hours probably."

"We need a car. Where's Mauro?"

"Out on a dive."

"Are you kidding? They're out in this? They could be killed."

"Don't worry. The minute their captain saw this, he pulled the divers up, and went to shore. They're at another resort."

"What about Spitball?" asked Mom.

"He's out too."

"Do you know anyone with a car?" I asked.

"Most of us ride scooters," said Elena.

Hours. Hours was not good. Lucia had gone from okay to bad within forty minutes. If she was developing sepsis, we didn't have that long.

"What about Bruno?" I asked.

"The pool boy?" asked Mom.

"He's not a pool boy! Holy crap, Mom. Be quiet. Where's Bruno?"

"I don't know," said Elena. "He might be in his room. He lives in the maintenance building."

Mom threw up her hands. "That's just great."

"Who cares, Mom. Aunt T is fifty-two," I said.

"I care. She's my sister and she's vulnerable. I have to look out for her."

I opened the door and a gust of rain hit me so hard I was surprised I didn't have welts afterwards.

"You can't go out there," yelled Mom. "You're bleeding."

"I'm not bleeding. Where's the maintenance building?" I asked Elena.

"Through the alley behind the security post. There's a parrot on the door."

"Mercy!" yelled Mom.

"I'm going, too," said Graeme.

He laid Lucia on a little rattan sofa at the back of the room and she clutched his hand. "Stay with me."

"I'll be right back. We're going to get you that car."

We plowed out into the storm and fell off the office's tiny porch into water three inches deep. I grabbed Graeme's hand and he yanked me up. We ran behind the empty security post into the alley. Instantly, the wind was gone. Only the pelting rain remained, coming at us from between the two buildings. Unfortunately for me, the alley was graveled and I had no shoes. I picked my way through as Graeme went ahead.

"I found it!" he yelled down the alley. Then he came back, tossed me over his shoulder, and ran to the door with an elaborate parrot painted on it.

He put me down and we pounded on the door until Bruno opened it. I had a flash that Aunt Tenne might be in there doing something I didn't want to know about and nearly turned around. Graeme pushed through and we slid around on a white tile floor in a room with a bed.

Shield your eyes!

"Sir, what is wrong?" asked Bruno, fully dressed. Thank goodness.

"We need a car," said Graeme.

I bit my lip and glanced at the bed. Empty.

"I don't have a car," said Bruno.

"You know my Aunt Tennessee, right? I'm Mercy."

"Yes, of course. Your aunt speaks of you often."

"So you know I'm a nurse. Can you find a car? We need to get to the Coxen Hole hospital."

"In this storm? It's not a good idea."

Both men looked at me. "We have to," I said, wiping the water out of my eyes. "His wife suffered a stab wound yesterday and it's infected."

"Can't that wait a little while?" Bruno's voice was low and calm and it made my breathing slow down.

"I'm afraid not. Her condition is deteriorating fast. Too fast for a normal infection. There must be a spine lodged in the wound." I hesitated. Graeme looked positively terrified. "The combination of whatever was on the barb and the foreign object may be causing sepsis."

"Oh, shit. That kills people," said Graeme.

"Yes, it does." I turned to Bruno. "Please?"

"My friend Penny has a car." Bruno put on a raincoat and opened the door. A rush of water held back by the door flooded the room. "I'll be right back."

Then he was gone, leaving me with Graeme. The guy who might've caused this problem in the first place.

"I can't believe this is happening," he said. "This was supposed to be the perfect vacation, but it's a nightmare."

Graeme put his face in his hands and I considered him. The more I talked to Graeme the less I thought he hurt Lucia. But I could be wrong. Maybe he was a world-class actor and I was alone with him. I'd recently been reminded not to isolate myself when I knew a murderer was around and there I was, alone with Graeme, the prime suspect. Idiot. I backed away from him, sloshing in the cold water until I stepped on fabric. A thick canvas cloth lay on the floor under my feet. It covered a fourth of the floor space and in the center was a large easel. A canvas the size of my bathroom sat on it.

"Is that your aunt?" asked Graeme.

The painting was only half finished, but there was a woman done in a style I'd never seen before and I've seen a lot of art, thanks to Myrtle and Millicent. The woman reclined on a bench, surrounded by flowers, birds, and clocks. Part of her was made up of the flowers, birds, and clocks and the rest of a combo of cubism, expressionism, post-impressionist styles. I stepped closer. And pointillism around the eyes and mouth. The painting was the strangest thing I'd ever seen and I'd once been forced to go through an exhibit at the Museum of Modern Art in New York that consisted mostly of toilets and mannequin heads. This, in contrast, was breathtakingly beautiful. It was right in all the wrong ways and it was Aunt Tenne.

"Yes," I said. "It's her."

"I've never seen anything like that," said Graeme. "Is it good or just insane?"

I was no art critic, but I was pretty confident about that piece. "It's good. It's amazing."

"And there's a lot of them."

One wall of the small room was covered in paintings. They were butted up against each so as not to waste an inch. There were two more of Aunt Tenne. One was photorealist and the other impressionist. Each executed perfectly. Every painting on the wall was a different style or combo of styles and they had life, a kind of glow that comes with greatness, not merely skill. My eyes filled and overflowed. I'm not a crier. I rarely cry at movies, unless a kid or dog dies, but I cried then, because I was in the presence of something amazing. Myrtle and Millicent had taught me to know brilliance when I saw it.

The door burst open behind us and Bruno came in holding up a set of car keys. "I got it."

"Thank god!" said Graeme.

We returned to the storm, but for some reason it didn't seem as bad, even though it was. The rain was just as hard. The wind just as wicked. But it didn't matter. All I could think of was Aunt Tenne in that painting, so beautiful, crazy, and totally unexpected. Great art can take you out of your life. I'd never been so happy to leave mine.

Mom flung the office door open when we got there and I stumbled inside. Bruno yelled that he'd get the car and disappeared in the sheets of rain. I sucked in a deep breath. I didn't realize I'd been holding it.

Lucia was still on the sofa, but Dixie was on the floor next to her holding a trash can. I sloshed over and touched Lucia's forehead. One hundred and three at least.

"She's vomiting now," said Dixie.

"I see that." I took Lucia's hand. "It's alright. Bruno found a car for us. We'll get you to Coxen Hole in no time."

"Okay." Lucia's voice was so weak, I had to lean in to hear it.

Bruno burst in. "I've got it."

Graeme picked up Lucia and charged back into the storm.

"Mom, you two stay here," I said.

Mom pulled me back from the door and crushed me against her chest. "Be careful, honeybabe."

"I will."

The worry in her eyes deepened. "Did you see Tenne?"

"Like I never have before." I rushed out the door and dove into the front seat of a beat-up Chevy Cavalier.

One thing about driving around in a tropical storm that's making you think you're going to die, nobody is on the roads. Bruno drove down the center of the street with the windshield going on high, but it didn't begin to combat the rain. Graeme held the shaking Lucia in his arms in the back. The bandage had fallen off her leg. The wound had opened up, gaping to an oval the size of an egg. The flesh was fiery red and must've been incredibly painful even with the Norco on board. But what scared me most was Lucia herself. She wasn't crying. Her face was pressed against Graeme's chest and she was breathing hard.

"How long?" I asked Bruno.

"Twenty minutes."

Okay. Okay. We're not going to have organ shutdown in twenty minutes. But I'm not positive what was on that damn barb. Shit.

Bruno swerved around a car that had been abandoned in the middle of the road. We were between rows of shops, but there wasn't a person in sight. It reminded me of some disaster movie. All we needed was zombies in hot pursuit.

I looked back at Graeme. He had his face pointed at the ceiling and a tear slipped past his ear.

Say something, idiot. Be distracting. Conversation is good. Talk. Damnit!

"Bruno!"

"Yes." He didn't look at me. He was sitting so far forward, trying to see, his chest was practically pressed against the steering wheel.

"Did you paint my aunt?"

He blushed, I think. His skin was dark enough that the barest amount of pink shown through.

"I saw the painting in your room. It was fantastic."

He said nothing.

"My godmothers collect art," I said. "They've taken me to museums all over the world. Your work should be in museums. Isn't that right, Graeme."

Graeme focused on me. "Yes. The paintings are beautiful."

"Do you know art?" I asked.

"Only what Lucia has taught me."

"Lucia, are you into art?"

She raised her head and looked at me, unfocused. "Yes."

"Bruno is a fabulous artist. You should see his work. What's your favorite artist?"

"Toulouse-Lautrec."

Didn't see that coming.

"He's a dadalist?"

She focused, not a lot, but I'd take anything. "No. Post-impressionist."

"That's right. My godmothers took me to his museum in Albi."

"Really?" she asked. "You've been there?"

"Twice actually. Have you been?"

"Not yet."

"It really is a must. We stayed in a great little hotel." I went on and on, gabbing about art and museums. Lucia perked up and by the time we made it to the hospital, Graeme looked less like he was going to fall apart. Bruno pulled up to the gate guard shack and found it empty. He drove up to the emergency room door and Graeme ran Lucia inside. I touched Bruno's shoulder, but he kept looking out the windshield.

"Thank you," I said. "You may have saved my life along with Lucia's."

He looked at me with small but expressive brown eyes full of concern and I got what Aunt Tenne saw in him and how it had happened so quickly. "What do you mean?"

"I'll explain when I can. Don't tell Aunt Tenne what I just said."

"I don't keep secrets."

"Not for long. Just until Lucia's out of danger."

"Okay. Just until then."

"You are a wonderful artist. Can we talk about that sometime?"

He looked away and the pink in his cheeks flared up. I got out of the car and ran into the ER. Graeme was at the desk yelling at a nurse, who was shaking her head.

"What's happening?" I asked.

"She won't take her back," said Graeme. "She doesn't care."

"We are very busy," said the nurse. Her name tag said Louise. Nice name. Not a nice woman.

I was about to climb over the desk and take her by the throat but decided as my knee hit the edge that perhaps a more diplomatic approach would be best.

"Okay, Louise. I see where you're coming from. I'm a nurse in the States. I get it, but we have a situation here." I put my hand in Graeme's back pocket and took out his wallet. His eyebrows went up, but he didn't say anything. "I should explain the situation a little better."

Louise gazed at me with scorn. I could practically see the words "Uppity American" racing through her mind. "I don't need anything explained to me."

"You'd be surprised." I came around the desk and took her by the arm. I gave her a look that would freeze lava and she allowed me to walk her through to the back and close the door.

"Look, Louise. I don't expect you to recognize the name, but that's Lucia Fibonacci out there. She's a member of one of the biggest Mafia families in the States. You understand Mafia?"

She stepped back. "So?"

"So you don't want her to die on your watch. It wouldn't be healthy for you," I said.

"Are you threatening me?"

"Absolutely. I'm glad we understand each other." I produced Graeme's wallet.

Please let there be money in here. Lots of money.

I opened the wallet and found a stack of twenties.

Thank you, dentistry.

"I'm not unreasonable. Take this for your trouble." I gave her the whole wad. Probably close to three hundred dollars. "How about calling Dr. Navarro. He saw her yesterday."

Louise stuffed the bills in her pocket and picked up the phone on the wall. "Dr. Navarro to ER. Dr. Navarro to ER."

"Thank you, Louise. We needed that."

I went back to Graeme and Lucia. He'd sat down in a chair with her on his lap. Her teeth were chattering so hard, I could hear them across the room.

"You talked her into it?" asked Graeme.

"I threatened and paid her. A winning combo."

"Thank god."

"I cleaned you out," I said, holding up his empty wallet.

"I do not give a flying fuck. Whatever it takes."

Dr. Navarro ran into the waiting room and I waved to him.

"What happened?" he asked.

I pointed to Lucia's leg. "This happened in the last hour and a half."

"Louise!" yelled Dr. Navarro. "Bring me a wheelchair!"

She ran over with a rusty wheelchair and Graeme put Lucia in it. Navarro patted Louise's shoulder. "It's good you called me. I'm taking her to three."

Dr. Navarro wheeled Lucia out and Bruno came in.

"They're taking her back," I said. "Can you wait?"

"Yes. It's better than going out there again," said Bruno.

"Mercy!" yelled Dr. Navarro. "Come back. I'll see to that cut."

Cut?

Bruno pointed to his own forehead and I touched mine. My hand came away bloody. Ah crap. I followed Dr. Navarro to room three and watched as they put Lucia on the gurney. The doctor pulled up a stool and examined her leg while another nurse, Rosario, took her blood pressure, pulse, and temperature. Blood pressure was low. Pulse and temperature were high. I was only off a half point, one hundred and three point five.

"The infection is spreading. I must've missed something on the x-ray," said Dr. Navarro.

"Like what?" asked Graeme.

"A spine from the barb, perhaps. I'll have to get in there and see if I can find it."

Lucia stiffened and her grip tightened on Graeme's arm, so that a flash of pain crossed his face.

Dr. Navarro gently patted her hip. "Don't worry. You're in luck. We received a donation of Propofol from a drug company in the States as well as IV antibiotics. We'll have you back at the resort in no time."

Graeme looked at me. "Isn't that the drug that killed Michael Jackson?"

"He wasn't in a hospital setting," I said. "It wasn't Propofol that killed him. That was the doctor."

"It's perfectly safe," said Dr. Navarro. "You can stay with her, if you like."

"And Mercy?" asked Graeme.

"If you like."

Dr. Navarro had Lucia taken to an outpatient surgical suite and I breathed a sigh of relief when I saw it. The room may not have been American grade, but it had the basics and they were spotless.

"You were expecting a hut?" asked Dr. Navarro.

"I don't know what to expect anymore," I said.

"We get that a lot in Roatan."

The anesthesiologist came in and administered the Propofol drip. Then he left, which didn't thrill me, but we were lucky to have the stuff in the first place. Lucia was out immediately and it was nice to see her lovely face relaxed in sleep. Dr. Navarro scrubbed in and laid out his own instruments. He palpitated the wound and started digging around. Graeme was sitting on a stool at Lucia's head and the stool's wheels started squeaking. I looked over just in time to watch him do a header into the gurney and fall to the floor.

"Any blood?" asked Dr. Navarro, not looking up.

I rolled Graeme over. "Nope. Just your basic pass out."

"Drag him out of the way, in case we have any problems."

I grabbed Graeme's limp arm and dragged him across the room like a bag of wet laundry and propped him up in a corner. He moaned and I patted his cheek. "Graeme, wake up."

"What?"

"You passed out," I said.

His eyes fluttered. "Why?"

"Cause you're not a murderer."

"Huh?"

"Don't worry about it. Stay here until it's over." I went back to my stool. "How's it going? See anything?"

"Yes, I do," said Dr. Navarro in a low whisper.

"Well..."

"You know your theory about this not being an accident?"

"Yeah," I said slowly.

Dr. Navarro inserted a pair of forceps into Lucia's wound. It made a juicy squelch and he pulled out an inch-long strip of bloody, pus-covered plastic. "You were right."

CHAPTER NINE

Lucia lay sleeping in her hospital bed with Graeme crashed out in the chair beside her. Dr. Navarro took two stitches to close my forehead wound and gave me a Band-Aid with Hello Kitty on it, donated by a tourist he said. Then the doctor, Bruno and I gathered around a small procedure table, looking at the bloody strip lying in a metal basin.

"What is it?" asked Bruno.

"Evidence," I said.

"Of murder?"

"Exactly."

Dr. Navarro rubbed his forehead and then began pacing. "Mercy thought Lucia had been drugged with succinylcholine in addition to the stab wound. But her blood tests were clear. If that's what was used, it wasn't a large enough dose to kill her." He did an about face and glared at us with an intensity that reminded me of Dad on a case. "I didn't doubt Mercy, but I couldn't figure out how the drug could've been administered. She had no needle marks. There was only the stab wound and that was done under water."

"What's that got to do with this?" asked Bruno, pointing to the plastic.

"That's how he did it," I said. "The stingray barb was coated with the drug and kept in a Ziplock. He stabbed Lucia through the bag, delivering the poison into her system."

"But it didn't work."

"No," said Dr. Navarro. "But it could have. He was unlucky. Mercy was right there with her. There wasn't time for the poison to take effect under water where Lucia would've been most vulnerable."

"And she pulled out the barb immediately. The sea water probably washed out most of the dose." I didn't mention that I wanted her to leave the barb alone. That was procedure and the thought made me sick.

"I've called the police, but I don't know what they can do," said Dr. Navarro.

"You have proof," said Bruno.

"Yes." Dr. Navarro didn't sound so sure. "They could choose to see this as an accident. It's not the usual shooting or stabbing. That's what they are used to dealing with. We don't have test results to back up our claims."

"The plastic will have to be tested," I said. "There may still be traces of sux on it."

"I will send it to a lab on the mainland. Results won't come for weeks."

"We'll just have to convince them."

And we tried. The National Police came and took our statements. They looked at the bloody plastic and nodded, but, in the end, did nothing. It wasn't that they didn't believe us. It's just that they didn't know what to do about it.

Officer Tabora stayed behind when his colleagues left. He was a tiny man with three hairs to call his own. He paced around the room, much like Dr. Navarro. "You must get her off the island."

"I agree," I said.

"You can't do anything?" asked Graeme. "What about your CSI unit? What about figuring out who did it?"

"We don't have a CSI unit. This island is about containment, not control."

"It's the Wild West," I said.

"Yes," said Officer Tabora. "The expats that come here to either retire or hide, say that it's a sunny place for shady people. They're right. If you're looking to escape something, it's a good place to come. I believe someone wants your wife dead, Mr. Carrow, but I'm telling you I don't think I can do anything about it. There are any number of people on this island who could carry out such a mission and it's the perfect place for it."

Graeme rocked back on his feet. He was a guy who believed in law enforcement, despite being married to a Fibonacci. The cops couldn't fix this or even contain it and it was blowing him away.

"But..."

"You have to leave," I said. "We've been lucky."

"What makes you think they won't follow her back to the States?"

"I think they will, but our cops are equipped to handle this. Whoever did this, did it here for a reason. Roatan can hide a crime. They don't want to get caught. They might find another target now that we're on to them and being back where any attempt can be properly investigated will be a deterrent."

"We'll get on the first flight out," said Graeme.

"I'm keeping her overnight as a precaution, but that plastic was the problem," said Dr. Navarro. "I expect her to be up and around soon."

Bruno and I said goodbye and went back to the Cavalier. The storm was over and except for the palm leaves and trash strewn around the parking lot, you'd never have known anything happened. The sky was back to perfect blue and there was a light, warm breeze. We dragged a large branch out from behind the car and got in. It was sopping wet in there and the seat squished when I sat down. I didn't know what I was going to say to Bruno's friend. The car wasn't cherry, but holy crap we'd turned it into a gray sponge.

He was so quiet; he was probably thinking the same thing. We drove through Coxen Hole in silence, looking at the aftermath that wasn't an aftermath at all. The streets were once again crowded with people and cars. The debris had been pushed to the gutters and forgotten. The Coxen Hole residents were once again laughing and shopping, but I was still shaken. The storm wasn't over for me. Aside from the two stitches in my forehead from where I hit the glass door, the damp hair, and the chafed thighs from wet cutoffs, I was shaken on the inside. I guess maybe I was holding out hope that I was wrong. That Chuck was wrong. I always wanted him to be wrong, but this time especially.

Think about something else.

"Bruno, what's up with you and my aunt?"

Silence.

"You may as well tell me. I'm the nice one, believe it or not. My mom will chase you around with a stick to get the truth."

He glanced at me sideways and a hint of a smile appeared on his thin lips.

"Seriously. She knows I brought mace and she's not afraid to use it."

"You think your mother would hurt me?" he asked. "She's so..."

"Beautiful? Yeah. But behind that Marilyn exterior is the heart of a hard ass. She'd take you out and make it look like an accident."

"Your aunt is, how you say, a unique person."

"I agree. Are you having an affair?"

"We are having love. Does that offend you?" He stared hard at the road and his chest had moved closer to the steering wheel. Tense, anyone?

"It surprises me," I said.

"Why? She is beautiful, like you and your mother."

I didn't know what to say. When it came to looks nobody and I mean nobody saw us in Aunt Tenne. The weight masked so much. She was easily the kindest person I knew. The one who kept my childhood secrets and sided with me against my crazy parents. But she was always alone. I'd never known her to not be alone.

I looked out the window and blinked back stinging tears. "If you hurt her, my mother will kill you."

And she'll have to wait in line.

He chuckled softly. "You don't have to worry about me hurting her."

"Do you know how old she is?" The weight masked that, too. Her face was full. Any wrinkle didn't stand a chance.

"Fifty-two."

I'll be damned.

"How old are you?" There I went being nosy, just call me Mom.

"I am thirty-five."

I nearly swallowed my tongue. "Are you serious?" I would've put him at forty-five easy.

"My life...it's not an American life."

I turned to him. "Neither is mine. Nobody is typical. So you don't care about the age difference?"

He looked at me right in the eyes for the first time. "No, I don't. Neither does she."

"We're leaving soon."

"I know."

"You're coming with us, aren't you?" I asked, but it wasn't really a question.

"Yes."

"My mom is going to flip."

"I know," he said.

"She'll think you're using Aunt Tenne to get to the States or something."

"I know."

We drove into the West Bay and turned onto La Isla Bonita Drive. "Um...are you?" I asked.

"No."

"Care to elaborate?"

"No."

Swell. This is going to be fun.

"It would help if Mom knew you better. Where did you study? How long have you been painting?"

Silence.

"Come on! Being an artist isn't a capital crime. I know. I've almost been the victim of a capital crime. Twice."

He pulled up at the front office and stopped with the motor running.

"You're a pain in the ass," I said. "And you don't know what you're getting yourself into. If you don't tell us who you are, my father will hound you into the dirt. It's what he does. Hell, it's what we all do."

"I have to get the car back," he said, softly.

"Fine. Make your own bed. My parents will staple you to the mattress." I got out and Bruno drove away. Damnit. I didn't handle that right. So what's new?

Aaron appeared from behind the office, holding a tall glass and a square pastry on a stick. "You hungry?"

"What the heck! How is that you just happen to be standing there with food the moment I arrive?"

He shrugged.

"Did you know I was coming?" I asked.

"You hungry?"

"Yes. For the love of god, yes. I am starving. What have you got?"

"Monkey Lala and mango pie on a stick," he said.

"That's a thing?"

"It is now."

"I'll take it." I took the luscious Monkey Lala and sucked down half in a gulp. I didn't even need to bite into the pastry. The smell was so good it nearly filled me up with just that. "You're amazing."

Aaron didn't answer. He stared at the mango pie. I almost didn't want to try it, just to bother him. I was his taste tester. That's what he came for.

I took a small bite and he went up on the balls of his feet. Pastry flakey, buttery with a hint of salt, but not regular salt. Something special. The filling? OMG! It was orgasm on a stick. There aren't words. Seriously, there aren't.

"Why aren't you famous?" I asked, once I'd gotten ahold of myself.

"I am."

"Where?"

"In Star Trek: The Force Unleased, Comic Con San Diego, Comic Con Denver—"

"I meant in the food world."

He shrugged. "I got another lionfish."

"Why in the world?" I asked.

"Mauro gave it to me."

"Remind me to kick him."

Aaron looked confused, but that was nothing new.

"Do you know where everyone is?" I asked.

"Who?"

"Mom and company."

"They're shopping," he said.

"Good." I went down the path to the room with Aaron on my heels. "You don't have to come."

"Chuck said."

"What did he say?"

"I have to watch you," said Aaron

Fantastic. First Dad and now Chuck. "When is he flying down?"

"No flights."

I stopped and Aaron bumped into my back. "No flights at all?"

"Nope."

"How about out?" I asked as I put on some speed.

Aaron jogged beside me. "No."

"Shit."

I jumped in the water bucket next to our stairs and then jogged up while sucking down the last of the Monkey Lala. I'd thrown open the door and had one foot inside before I realized Aunt Tenne was sitting on the porch.

"Where are you going in such a lather?" she asked.

"Nowhere."

Aaron squatted next to his beloved hibachis and poked the cold coals around. Aunt Tenne smiled at him, not the sad smile I'd grown up with but a lovely one that touched every one of her features. "Your phone's been ringing, Mercy."

Please don't have looked at the ID.

"Chuck's missing you quite a lot." Her smile deepened to devilishness.

Crap.

"You want to tell me something?" she asked.

"Nothing to tell. He likes to bother me," I said.

"That he does, but he's not usually so insistent."

"He's stepping it up. I've got to take a shower."

Unfortunately, she heaved herself off the deck chair and smiled expectantly. "Okay."

"Where are you going?"

"Inside with you. We haven't talked at all since we got here," she said.

"Yeah, well I've got to shower. You're not coming in there," I said.

"You're trying to avoid talking about Chuck."

I'm trying to talk to Chuck without a witness.

"Aaron, where's that lionfish?" I asked.

"You want it?" he asked.

No!

"Yes," I said, trying to look honest. "Where is it?"

"I got it in the restaurant fridge."

"Aunt Tenne, why don't you go get that fish and Aaron will get the fire going while I take a shower."

She cocked her head to the side and I tried to appear innocent. "Well..."

"We'll have lunch and talk," I said, edging inside the door.

"I have a feeling you have big news."

None that I'm telling you.

"Sure. News. Go get that fish." I stepped inside the cool room and shivered. I'd gotten so used to the tropical humidity, the room felt frigid, although the thermometer was set for eighty. I peeked out the curtain and watched Aunt Tenne go down the stairs. Aaron was still squatting next to the hibachi, but now rubbing his hands like a mad food scientist, which I guess he kind of was.

I turned the lock extra slow, so he wouldn't hear it, and jogged to the bedroom. My phone was laying on the bed all exposed and showed twenty calls from Chuck. Thank god he knew not to text. Aunt Tenne was no fool. She'd be able to piece together the Fibonacci situation in minutes or at the very least know I was doing something Mom had banned.

I stripped off my damp clothes, found some that weren't too sandy, and dressed while I waited for Chuck to answer.

"Where the hell have you been?" he yelled into the phone. "I've been going crazy."

"Hospital."

"Oh, shit!"

"She's still alive. The stab wound developed an infection." I gave him the rundown and he got quiet.

"This is not good," he said.

"Understatement of the day." I found my dad kit stuffed into the corner of my suitcase. Inside, taking up most of the space, was my twenty-three-piece lock pick kit. Dad put it in my Easter basket when I was twelve. Mom was not amused.

"I can't get down there directly," said Chuck. "There are no flights to the island. I'm going to try and fly into the mainland and take a boat over."

"How long will it take?"

"A couple of days, if I can do it at all."

"What about flights off the island?" I tucked the pick kit in my waistband.

"Totally booked."

"I could take Lucia to the mainland, I guess."

"No. I think our best bet is to arrange emergency transport. I've got a friend looking into it. The mainland is iffy. At least you're in a tourist area."

"That's not helping us so far."

"I know, but there's nowhere you can go that you can't be followed. The mainland isn't safer. I'd say it's worse."

I opened the bedroom window and stuck my head out. There was a downspout right next to it and it looked fairly sturdy. I got my butt onto the sill and one leg through the window.

"Mercy, what are you doing?"

"I'm climbing out the window. Talk to you later," I said, hanging up and tucking the phone in my pocket. "Oh crap this is a bad idea."

I grabbed hold of the downspout and got one foot on the brace that secured it to the building. Aunt Tenne's voice came around the building. "Now that's a lot of spines."

All I had to do was skinny down the drainpipe, get in the Gmucas' bungalow, and do a quick search. Then do Lucia's and Graeme's place. Not more than a half hour, if I didn't fall to my death. I heaved myself onto the drainpipe and the brace bit into my feet. The metal creaked and groaned, but it held. Okay. Right foot down to the next brace.

More creaking. A lot more. Left foot down. Snapping metal. Quick. Right foot down. Big snap and a shudder. The drainpipe shifted. Quick. Foot down. Super loud metal creaking, like *Titanic's* going to split in half creaking. I pressed my cheek against the pipe.

Don't scream. Don't scream. The fall can't be more than fifteen feet. Oh, crap.

There was a loud snap and the pipe bent backwards. I watched as each brace popped free from the wall. I swung backwards in slow motion. I closed my eyes, ready for the impact that never came. The pipe came to a stop when I was horizontal. I opened one eye and saw a faded black tee with Obi Wan on it. I opened my eyes and found Aaron and Aunt Tenne watching me hang from a drainpipe like some kind of brain-damaged monkey.

"I got the lionfish on the grill," said Aaron as if it wasn't unusual for him to find me like this.

"Oh, yeah? Good," I said.

Aunt Tenne crossed her arms and did her best Mom imitation. "Going somewhere?"

"We need ice."

"Really? You climbed down a drainpipe for ice?"

"Seemed like a good idea at the time." I lost my grip and fell the remaining three feet into the sand with an oomph. "Maybe not."

She gave me a hand up and waited as I brushed myself off and tried to think of a reasonable excuse, but there weren't any. Nobody climbs down drainpipes if they can avoid it. "I'll just be getting that ice now."

Aunt Tenne snagged the hem of my tee. "Not so fast." She swooped in and plucked the lock pick kit out of my waistband. "Now where have I seen this before. I know, Easter basket thirteen years ago."

"Oh my goodness. I thought I grabbed my makeup kit." I snatched the case out of her hands.

"Spill it or I'm telling Carolina what you've been doing," said Aunt Tenne.

I walked backwards and bumped into a palm. "I haven't been doing anything. We're on vacation. I'm vacationing. See the sunburn."

"Right. Chuck's calling you like his pants are on fire and I catch you climbing down a building with lock picks. Tell me now."

"I can't. You just have to trust me," I said.

"It's to do with Lucia Carrow, isn't it?"

I can not catch a break.

"Lucia has an infection. She's at the hospital. She's fine."

"Yeah, right. How many people have that many freak accidents on vacation and have you dogging their footsteps?"

"I don't know what you mean. I'm a nurse. I help when help is required," I said.

"That's not all you are. You're Tommy Watts, the sequel. What's going on? And remember all I have to do is mention Lucia's name to your mother and you are toast."

"That's not necessary."

"I think it is. You're ruining our vacation."

"What are you talking about? We've hardly seen you. You've been off falling in love."

Aunt Tenne gasped. "That's not true."

"Please. Bruno drove us to the hospital. I know all about it."

She fidgeted and blushed. "Are you going to tell Carolina and Dixie?"

"Let's make a deal. I don't know anything and you don't either," I said.

Aunt Tenne took me by the shoulders. "If anything happens to you, I'd never forgive myself."

"Then I'll make sure nothing happens. One more thing." I smiled. This was my chance.

Aunt Tenne groaned.

"What do you know about The Girls and our house?"

"That's easy. Nothing," she said.

"But you were around when they gave it to Mom. I just want to know why," I said.

Aunt Tenne looked away. "I wasn't...doing well at the time. We weren't talking much and it was none of my business anyway."

"Mom never told you? Seriously."

"Some things you don't ask about." She touched Aaron's shoulder. "You stick with her. I'll watch the fish."

He rubbed his hands together again and said, "I'm ready. Where're we going?"

Ah, come on.

"I can do this myself."

"That's the deal, Mercygirl. It's Aaron or we're both in a world of hurt. I don't have the information you want."

"Fine. Have you seen the Gmucas this morning?" I asked.

"Why?" Aunt Tenne tapped her foot in the sand, not nearly as effective as practically any other surface. No tapping impatient noise, just swish.

"Cause I'm going to search their bungalow. Happy now?"

"Not hardly. Is that necessary? They seem like such nice people."

"I agree, but they had access to Lucia at each incident."

She stopped tapping and ground her toes into the sand, digging in deep. "They're having lunch, but you better hurry."

"Come on, Aaron." I dashed off between the palms and took the long way around. At least until I got to a maintenance shed that I'd never seen before. It had stacks of old rusted scuba tanks and a golf cart with blown out tires. Aaron didn't say anything. He stood behind me, huffing and puffing.

I took a guess and went right onto a path between two large hibiscus plants so laden with blossoms that they were almost flat on the sand. I got about ten feet when I realized the huffing and puffing was gone. Aaron still stood at the shed.

"What are you doing?" I asked.

"Wrong way."

"Why didn't you tell me?"

He shrugged, but surprisingly didn't ask if I was hungry.

"You lead then."

Aaron navigated through such a complicated series of turns and twists that I'd never find my way back on my own. I'd die out there and be eaten by spaghetti birds and jackals, if Roatan had them. It seemed like they would. The island, beneath the sunny happiness, had a distinct jackal aura.

Aaron halted at the back of a bungalow and dug a pack of Bubble Yum out of his pocket.

"Is this it?" I asked. There was no number or sign. It looked like every other bungalow.

"Yep." He popped a purple square in his mouth and began chewing the huge wad.

"You be the lookout. Knock on the back door if they come back."

He just chewed and looked at me, totally dim. I groaned, pulled out my bag o' lock picks, and attacked the backdoor lock. It was a standard five pin and I had it open in under two minutes, which was good for me. But Dad would've been ashamed, not that I was breaking and entering but that I was so damn slow. Locksport was one Dad's weirder hobbies. He and Uncle Morty went to Def Con, the conference for hackers, lockpickers, and other odd ducks every year. He kept trying to take me. It wasn't happening.

The Gmucas' bungalow hadn't seen the maid yet, lucky for me. The place was messy, not as bad as my apartment but close. I started in the bathroom. La Isla Bonita didn't do medicine cabinets, so everything was strewn across the dark blue tile countertop. Everything included twelve prescription bottles, five kinds of shampoo, four conditioners, six body lotions, and so much makeup Linda could've operated a store out of there.

All the meds were prescribed to Frankie. Apparently, he looked good, but had the physiology of an eighty-year-old. He had scripts for high blood pressure, cholesterol, impotence, nerve pain, chronic heartburn, and more. There weren't any bottles of succinylcholine on the counter or in the trash. I searched every suitcase and drawer and found nothing that directly linked either Frankie or Linda to the attempts on Lucia's life. Of course, any one of Frankie's prescriptions could kill in the right amount, but those hadn't been used.

I went to the jackets that were hanging up on hooks next to the front door, hoping I'd find a stingray barb. A nice detailed murder plot in the form of a short story would be nice. You laugh, but it's happened. Dad had two cases that involved fiction. I didn't think my guy was stupid enough to write out his plot and try to sell it to a magazine, but you never know.

If he or she was that stupid, the evidence wasn't in the bungalow. A soft knock echoed through the room and the door handle next to me turned. I dashed across the room toward the back door, but the front opened and I juked left into the bathroom.

"That burger was amazing," said Linda. "What kind of cheese was that?"

Oh crap, they're inside. Damnit, Aaron.

"I think it was some kind of pepperjack," said Frankie.

I got in the shower and hid behind the curtain. There was two more bottles of shampoo and conditioner in there. What the heck, Linda? Even you don't have that much hair.

"I think I'll take a shower."

I gasped and clamped a hand over my mouth. This was bad. I had nowhere to go.

"Let me taste that cheese first, babydoll," said Frankie in what I guessed was his sexy voice.

There was lots of lipsmacking soap opera style, nice and juicy. Gross. I peeked out from behind the curtain and considered making a run for it, but Linda's giant hair swung in front of the bathroom door. I had one option. The cabinets under the sink. The doors weren't big, but I should be able to squeeze my big hips through. Everything fits when you're desperate.

Linda's hair disappeared and more kissing ensued. "Oh baby, you are so hot."

"No, you're the hot one."

"You know you're hot."

"You're smoking hot. Oh my god, I'm gonna get burned."

Barf.

I crept out of the shower and opened the middle cabinet. It creaked so loud that I clenched my teeth, but the you're-so-hot duo was too busy to notice. One look inside that cabinet made me want to march into the other room with my hands up. "You caught me. My standards are pretty low, but that cabinet...no."

"Oh my god," said Linda. "This whole plan is turning me on so much."

"I'm so glad we decided to do this," said Frankie.

Plan? Oh, no. I have to hear this.

I crouched in front of the cabinet, pushed aside the grimy cleaning products, peeled the roach spray can out of the amber pool it was lying in, and forced myself in. My rear crunched one of the roach motels. There were a bunch of big juicy ones in there. Tropical paradise, my foot. I closed the door just as Frankie and Linda came in, bumping into the wall from the sound of it.

"You are the hottest woman in the world. You're amazing. You're vicious. You're an animal."

"It can't fail. We're almost there, baby."

"You never fail. We have this in the bag."

"Tony will pay through the nose."

A payoff?

"That money will come in handy," said Frankie.

"Mama needs a new set of shoes."

"Mama can have anything she wants."

Clothes hit the floor with soft flumps. They were naked. It couldn't get any worse.

"On the counter. On the counter."

Not the counter. Anything but the counter. Go to the shower. Listen to me, you horny freaks. Go to the shower.

"I love it on the counter."

Damnit.

The countertop creaked above me, but I almost couldn't hear it over the groaning. Maybe it would collapse and kill me. That was my only hope.

"I never want this to end!"

Please let this end.

"Those pills are fantastic. You're just my big horny toad."

"I could go for hours."

Nooooooo!

They proceeded to go at it like nothing I'd ever heard. Butchering pigs would've been quieter. I leaned to my right and fell against something on the wall that was both crunchy and sticky. Gack. I inched my hand in my pocket and managed to pull out my cellphone.

I squinted in the dark and texted Aaron. "I'm trapped."

He didn't answer. No surprise. Half the time he didn't answer when I was standing right in front of him.

"They're having sex over my head. Help me!"

No answer. I was in for the duration, which, I had to guess, was going to be a long while.

"You're the best!" yelled Linda.

"No, you're the best!"

I seriously considered crawling out of the cabinet and hoping they didn't notice. I probably would've had a decent chance of making it, if one of them hadn't been banging their knees against my door. I hoped they got splinters.

"Did you hear something?" asked Frankie.

"Don't stop, you crazy bag of man candy!"

I need a lobotomy so I can unhear that.

"I am your man candy, aren't I? Say I'm your man candy."

"Man candy!"

I could eat the roach spray. It's okay. I had a good life. I've seen Paris. I've seen Rome.

"I'm your man candy!"

Roach spray can't taste any worse than Dad's Hungarian goulash.

"You are the master of man candy!"

Where's that can?

"Did you hear something?" asked Frankie. "I think I heard something."

"It's the door. Do you think they can hear us?"

"Yes!"

"Yes!"

Take the lid off the can.

"Yes, baby, yes!"

Maybe I should text Mom first. I could tell her she was awesome, despite all the mothering.

"They're still knocking," cried out Frankie.

"Let 'em knock. We're never stopping."

There was a huge snapping noise. The countertop shifted on top of me and a gush of water erupted from the sink, hitting me on the side of the head. The Gmucas screamed and fell to the floor in front of my door. I got an unwelcome glimpse of naked wet flesh through a new gap as they raced out.

"What should we do?" screamed Linda.

"I'll call the front desk."

"I'll get the door."

"Put something on!" yelled Frankie.

I opened my door and plopped out onto the floor, slipping around and gasping like a caught fish.

"Aaron," said Linda. "Do you know anything about plumbing?"

Aaron said something about lionfish and I put one eye around the corner. He stood in the doorway, chewing his Bubble Yum while Linda flailed her arms around, explaining how the sink exploded for no reason whatsoever. Frankie was on the phone with one hand over his eyes. He was redder than a fire hydrant. I didn't know if it was the embarrassment or the sex. I bit my lip and watched him for a split second. The guy was on four different heart meds and he'd taken Viagra. Did he have a death wish?

Just get out. You can save his life later.

I tiptoed to the back door and slipped out through the river that was flowing out of the sink. I closed the door and stood dripping onto the sand. I was out and they didn't catch me. Bruno ran up the back path, lugging a yellow toolbox. If I'd been thinking straight, I would've run around the corner before he saw me, instead I stood there, hearing Gmuca sex echoes in my head. It was horrible.

"What are you doing out here? Like that?" he asked when he reached me.

"Being punished for my bad behavior," I said.

Bruno ripped open the back door. "Did you flood the bungalow?"

"Actually, no. I didn't do that."

Bruno ran inside and I trudged off down the path, making squishy noises. That was the second time in four hours that I'd been soaked to the skin. The feeling was not growing on me. I was doing something wrong in my life that I was being punished for. I should go to confession the instant I got off the plane. Father Tim would absolve me. Of course there was the problem of telling him exactly what happened. God already knew. Did I really have to say it out loud? Father Tim was a delicate sort. He could only talk to me behind confessional screen. Face-to-face made him go all fluttery.

Aaron ran up beside me. "I saved you."

Crappy construction saved me, but okay.

"Thanks, Aaron," I said. "The Gmucas are now serious suspects. They're getting money from a guy named Tony."

"Okay. You hungry?"

I sighed. "I could eat your foot."

"What do you want? I could make you something. I got lionfish."

"Make whatever you want."

"Really? I got this idea for lionfish consommé."

Gag.

"Go crazy, Aaron."

He trotted off ahead of me, rubbing his hands together and saying ingredients under his breath. I trudged along behind him, getting looks from the other tourists that ranged from pity to suspicion that I might be insane. They were right, only an insane person would break into people's rooms and let them have sex over her head. The whole vacation was crazy from Aaron being on it to the multiple murder attempts. Grandma George would say that I must be living wrong. Maybe I was, but what else could I do. This was my life. I had to live it.

I lost track of Aaron, but somehow found myself on the main path leading to the room. The scent of hibiscus and cooking lionfish wafted around me. They smelled right together, tropical and sort of homey. Not that I wanted to touch that consommé with a toe much less my tongue. I could stand it as long as I had to eat it after a long shower and a nap. I reached the foot of the stairs, stepped in the bucket and Mom appeared from around the corner of the building.

"What happened to you?" she asked.

"Tropical storm Bettina."

"That was over a while ago and you're still soaking."

"Yeah, well it's me, so that's what happens."

"The stitches look good. It probably won't scar." Mom leaned in and sniffed me. "You smell like Lysol and bug spray."

"Thanks."

"Honeybabe, you look exhausted. Let's get you upstairs." Mom put her hand on my shoulder and then jerked back. Amber goo covered her palm. "What the heck is that?"

"Roach spray."

"That's disgusting. How'd you get roach spray on your shoulder and what happened to your leg?"

I blinked. My leg? Mom pointed down and I got tired. Really tired. My right leg had red slightly swollen spots from the kneecap down. I stepped out of the water and found my ankle was much worse, but it diminished at the foot, becoming only mildly pink.

Mom squatted and examined my leg. "It's only in the front. What did you do?"

"I must've come in contact with some kind of irritant during the storm."

"It's not the roach spray?" Mom asked, standing up and crossing her arms.

My arm and thigh had smears of the sticky amber stuff, but no redness. "No. I'm not reacting to that."

"We need to get you to the doctor. It could be some kind of tropical disease, like sleeping sickness or malaria."

"It's not malaria. It's contact dermatitis. No big deal. I'll clean up and put some hydrocortisone on it."

Mom pursed her lips and twisted them sideways. "I don't know. We should go just to be on the safe side."

I rubbed my eyes. So tired. "Look, I'll be at the hospital tomorrow morning to check on Lucia. I'll have Dr. Navarro take a look. Will that make you happy?"

"Lucia's not at the hospital. I just saw her and Graeme get out of a cab."

My brain snapped awake. "Are you kidding?"

"Of course not." She went to take my arm, but I dodged her and sprinted across the way to the Carrows' bungalow.

I pounded on the door. "Lucia! Are you in there?"

Mom grabbed my arm and spun me around. "Are you crazy? Pipe down. It looked like Graeme was taking her down to the beach."

"Are you kidding?"

"Stop asking that. I never kid."

That was true, Mom wasn't much of a joker. At that moment I wished she was. I shook off her hand and ran down the path to the beach with Mom hard on my heels. We passed two couple following Bruno to their rooms. They, including Bruno, looking at me with distaste. I guess I looked pretty bad. Then their expressions changed to a more familiar state, shocked fascination. For once, I wished it was for me. I wasn't all that crazy about being disgusting, but, of course, it was Mom. And she was running. She and Dad had a deal that she'd never run in public, since it was bad for humanity and husbands in particular. As we passed one of the men got punched in the shoulder and the other got a "Hey" in the face.

"Stop running, Mom!" I yelled.

"You stop running. I'm chasing you."

I didn't stop. Graeme brought Lucia back. He goddamn brought her back. Gee, I wonder if he figured out it would be a lot harder to kill her in a hospital than at a resort. Just when I was feeling better about that dude.

I'm such an idiot. I started to trust him. You can't trust anyone when it comes to murder. Anyone is capable of anything.

"Mercy! Stop!" yelled Mom.

"No."

I'm not stopping until I've wrung his lying, trying to kill a Fibonacci, idiot neck.

Mom lunged and grabbed my roach spray arm which gave her grip. She yanked me to halt just as we passed under the restaurant overhang. "Stop now."

"I have to get to Lucia," I said, panting and slightly light-headed.

"Why?" Mom was in my face. She was thinking finally and it wasn't working in my favor. "The hospital released her. She must be fine. Isn't that right?"

"That's a serious infection, Mom. She should be in the hospital."

"Then they would've kept her."

I clamped my lips together and we glared at each other.

"What have you been doing? No excuses. Tell me now," said Mom in her best I-brought-you-in-this-world-I-can-take-you-out voice. Thanks, Mr. Bill Cosby, for giving her that idea.

"Nothing, "I replied through gritted teeth.

Mom's fingers dug into my arm. "Nothing. I don't think so. You're soaking wet, covered in roach spray, and have some kind of skin disease. Not to mention the stitches in your face. Your face, Mercy."

"That was the storm. You saw me do it."

"Be quiet. And Lucia Carrow keeps having freak accidents and you're running around after her, like a maniac." Mom paused. She sucked in a deep breath and the pink vanished from her perfect cheeks. "They're not accidents. Nobody has that many accidents. What have you gotten yourself into?"

"I haven't gotten myself into anything." I forced myself to sound calmer than I felt.

"You're involved." She had me by both shoulders and lowered her voice. "Why didn't you tell me?"

"We're on vacation."

She shook me until my chin hit my chest.

"Better?" I asked.

"Don't be obnoxious," said Mom.

"Too late. Can I go now?"

"You are going to explain this whole thing to me later and then you're going to tell your father."

I stepped backwards out of her hands. "I think you should tell him for my safety."

"Why?" Mom went another shade of pale.

"Lucia's a Fibonacci." I darted away and ran through the restaurant, dodging tables and waiters. I ran down the steps past Colin, who was so drunk he didn't even try to grope me. My feet sank into the sand and I frantically scanned the beach for Lucia. I didn't see her and ran down the rows of lounge chairs. At the end of the first row was Tracy with her bratty kids, fighting over a paddle.

"It's mine," yelled Tara.

"Mine," said Tyler.

I ran to the foot of Tracy's chair. "Have you seen Lucia?"

She lowered her sunglasses. "Lucia Carrow?"

I could barely hear over her repulsive offspring. "Yes. Have you seen her?"

"I don't think so." Tracy yawned. "I thought she went to the hospital for her leg."

"She did."

Tara and Tyler were out of their seats and tussling over the paddle, spraying sand on people and screeching at the top of their lungs. The other guests tried to disguise their irritation and failed. Those kids were enough to make anyone consider sterilization.

"Knock it off!" I said to them. "You're disturbing people."

"Hey," said Tracy. "Don't discipline my kids."

"Why not? You're not doing it."

Tara and Tyler continued yelling.

"You don't even have a boat!" I spun around and went through to the second row. Tracy may have been yelling something at me, but I couldn't have cared less. I wasn't going to take it anymore. Kids screaming for no reason. People trying to kill people right under my nose. Roach spray. Skin disease. Endless supplies of lionfish. I had had it.

I stomped down the row, ready to take Graeme by the neck and squeeze. Take your wife out of the hospital, will you? Perhaps you'll enjoy passing out.

"Mercy!" Mom yelled. "They're over there."

I followed her finger to a secluded spot in front of the resort's five star restaurant, The Aviary, at the edge of the property. That's just what Lucia needed. Seclusion. But she was sitting up with her back to me. I recognized the dark brown curls under the wide sunhat. I assessed her posture as I ran across the deep dry sand, my thighs burning with the effort. She was sitting without support. Good. But she was leaning toward the other chair with one arm extended tense. Crap!

I put on speed and ran past Joe, Andrew, and Todd hauling BCDs off a dive boat. I tripped and went down on my knees. Sand dug into my scrapes and I winced as I scrambled to my feet. "Lucia!"

She didn't turn and I ran up behind, gasping for breath. "Lucia!"

"Mercy!" She lifted the brim of her crazy hat. "What happened to you?"

"What happened to you? Why aren't you in the hospital?"

"They needed the bed. Something happened on one of the cruise ships."

"Mercy." A weak voice came from the other chair. Graeme. He laid back on the lounge chair, limp with red cheeks.

I pushed the hair off my forehead. "Graeme?"

His head lolled to the side. "Uh huh?"

My anger evaporated. "Has he been drinking?" Graeme's left hand was wrapped around a tall glass on the table between.

"No," said Lucia. "But he just started acting funny."

Mom joined us. "What's going on?"

"I'm not sure yet." I walked around their chairs, my feet sinking into the sand, cool under the shade of the palm trees. Graeme wasn't focusing on me or anyone. I sat on the edge of his chair and turned his face toward me. "Graeme, can you see me?"

He said yes in a slurred voice that sounded like he'd been pounding tequila shots. I picked up his trembling wrist and took his pulse. One hundred and forty beats per minute and he was at rest.

"Did he take anything, Lucia?" I asked.

"Like what?" Her voice went up in pitch.

"Like anything. Any medications at all."

"No, nothing. He got the pills you gave me, but he didn't take any."

"You're sure?"

"Absolutely. He doesn't like to take medication, if he doesn't have to."

My eyes fell on the glass, still in Graeme's hand. I leaned over his body and took it. Smelled like sweet tea. Maybe raspberry. The glass was nearly empty.

"What is this, Graeme?" I asked.

He slurred something incoherent.

"Lucia, what is this?"

"I don't know. I don't know. The waiter just brought it. What's wrong with him?"

"You didn't order it?"

"No. The guy said it was for me, but I didn't want it, so Graeme drank it."

I shot to my feet. "Mom find a car. Any car. We have to get him to the hospital now."

"What is it?" she asked.

"Just go. Find Spitball or Mauro. Somebody now."

I took Graeme by the shoulders and tilted his torso over the edge of the chair. He groaned. I pinched his nose shut and pried his mouth open. He fought me, but I got him in a headlock. My fingers got past his teeth and he bit me. Now that's a special pain.

"What are you doing?" screamed Lucia.

"He's been poisoned." I don't know how I wasn't screaming, the pain was that bad.

"I'll help you!"

"No! I can do it!" The trouble was I couldn't. Graeme was totally out of it, but it didn't stop him from biting the hell out of me and thrashing around like a toddler waiting for a shot.

Aaron dropped into view next to me. "Need help?"

"Got to make him throw up," I said through clenched teeth.

Aaron grabbed Graeme's face and muscled his jaws open. Those stumpy little hands were amazingly strong. Years of chopping, I guess. I shoved my fingers deep into Graeme's gullet. His body convulsed and a stream of brown gushed past my hand.

CHAPTER TEN

Louise aka Nurse Crabby didn't require a bribe to put Graeme on a gurney. Maybe it was his sweaty, shaking body lying on the floor in front of her desk or Mauro screaming in Spanish or maybe it was me. I caught a glimpse of myself in the ER door. I would've been afraid of me. No question. I was halfway to crazy town and I looked it.

Louise and I pushed Graeme through the corridors into Room Three where Lucia had been only hours before. Louise took his vitals while I stood at the door, screaming for a doctor. A page went out and it was in English, but so heavily accented that I couldn't tell what they said. Dr. Navarro ran around the corner with a stack of charts in his arms. My reappearance in his ER startled him and he dropped four of the heavy metal folders with a clatter.

I ran over. "I'll get them. He's in Three. Go."

Dr. Navarro shoved the rest of his charts in my arms. "Lucia?"

"Graeme. Poisoning. Antifreeze, I think."

He cursed in Spanish and ran into Graeme's room. At least I think it was cursing. It had that ring. I gathered up the charts and followed him in, dumping the charts in a chair. Dr. Navarro tested Graeme's pupil response with his penlight and smelled his breath.

Graeme was still out of it, but conscious. He knew his name, but that was about it.

"What makes you think it's ethylene glycol?" Dr. Navarro asked.

"He drank a glass of sweet tea and this happened. Antifreeze is easy to conceal and the symptoms are right."

He ordered Louise to draw blood and get a urine sample.

"That will take too long. Do you have dialysis?"

"There's a clinic in French Harbor."

"Not here? You're the hospital."

"No fluid, but we have sodium bicarbonate and ethanol." He scribbled on Graeme's chart and told Louise to set up the IV.

I picked up Graeme's trembling hand and he turned his head towards me, eyelids at half-mast. "He's not too bad," I said. "It should work."

"It should. We'll get him to French Harbor if he goes into renal failure."

Louise ran back in and did the IV. Another nurse hung the bag of sodium bicarbonate and got ready to pour the ethanol down his throat. He wasn't going to like that, but it was drink or take it through the nose. Not a great choice either way.

"Graeme, you have to drink this stuff, okay?" I squeezed his hand.

The drip started and I watched as the bicarbonate headed towards Graeme's vein. The nurse put a cup to his lips and poured some in. He shook his head and the fluid ran out of the side of his mouth.

"Graeme! You have to drink it or they'll shove a tube up your nose," I said.

That got his attention with a quickness and he drank the cupful, coughing and sputtering, but he got it down.

"Now it's just wait and see," said Dr. Navarro, watching the heart monitor.

Graeme was resting comfortably and his pulse and breathing had slowed. But ethylene glycol poisoning wasn't an exact science. It affected different people differently. Graeme's kidneys could still shut down or he could walk away. We just didn't know.

"Are you going to admit him?" I asked.

"I would, but all our beds are full."

"How is that possible?"

"We have thirty-three beds and a population of sixty-five thousand," he said quietly.

"Holy crap. I don't even know what to say."

"It's a whole different world out here. Have you given any thought to our medication situation?" he asked.

"I haven't. I'm sorry." I ran my hand through my hair, which was only slightly less tangled than a cat's hairball.

"Mercy, let me see your hand."

"Huh?"

Dr. Navarro took my hand out of my snarled hair and flattened it on his palm. Red raised splotches covered my hand and extended up my arm to the elbow. "Looks like contact dermatitis." Then he saw the roach spray and cocked his head to the side. "What have you been doing?"

"You don't want to know," I said.

He bent over my hand and sniffed. "It smells sweet."

"Yeah. I sort of shoved it down Graeme's throat."

"And you didn't wash it?"

"There wasn't time."

"You're having an allergic reaction in addition to the usual irritation. Louise, can you get a colloidal bath for Mercy?"

"Yes, doctor."

The hospital's intercom crackled to life. "Dr. Navarro to Room Twelve. Dr. Navarro to Room Twelve."

He left and Louise came back with a pink plastic basin with cream-colored bits floating around in the water.

"Yum," I said.

Louise frowned. No sense of humor. She set me up next to Graeme's bed and put the basin on the rickety arm of the chair. I put my arm in. Ahhh. Warm and soothing. Just what the doctor ordered, literally.

Louise hesitated and glanced at Graeme. "Someone tried to kill him, didn't they?"

"Yes."

"And his wife, the one with the stab wound."

"Her, too. Actually, her mostly. I think she was the intended victim."

Louise straightened the thin sheet over Graeme's legs. "I'm sorry I was difficult earlier. I shouldn't have taken your money."

"I get it. You're understaffed and underpaid. You're under everything, I imagine," I said.

"Yes. We're out of medication one third of the time. I'll give your money back. You came here expecting help, not blackmail."

"Keep it. Donate to the hospital or whatever. We got what we came for."

"Thank you. We can use it," she said. "I'll go see if I can find a bigger basin."

"I'm fine. This is plenty big."

"It's for your leg. He vomited on your leg too, right?"

I extended my right leg. The swollen redness from earlier was still there, but it was considerably better. "No," I said slowly. "He didn't."

Louise squatted in front of me and palpitated the area. "It looks like the same reaction."

"Oh my god." I yanked my cellphone out of my still wet pocket. The screen was fogged with water and the damn thing was dead. "I've managed to drown my cellphone. Louise, can I borrow yours? I have to call my mother."

Louise gave me her Nokia, so old that I was surprised it still worked. Mom answered after the third ring with a suspicious hello.

"Mom, it's me. How's Lucia? Is she with you?"

"Mercy, thank goodness. Yes, she's right here and she's fine. How's Graeme?"

"I think we caught it in time, but this wasn't the first attempt," I said.

"We've established that. Don't think our discussion is over," said Mom.

"Whatever. I meant that this isn't the first poisoning. They tried before."

Louise placed a metal bucket in front of my chair and put my leg in.

"What do you mean? Lucia's fine, other than the leg thing."

"Remember my leg being swollen and red? I just figured out the cause. Graeme barfed all over my hand and arm. Now my arm looks like my leg."

"It wasn't the vomit?"

"It didn't get on my leg, but when we were getting Lucia off the beach during the storm, I knocked over a glass. It went all over my leg."

Mom gasped and told Lucia.

"Ask her where that first drink came from," I said. "It was on her side table before the storm."

Mom asked and I waited. I wanted to jump out of my chair and run around the room.

"She doesn't know," said Mom. "Can you ask Graeme?"

Graeme was snorting and thrashing around trying to avoid his next dose of ethanol. Plus, he wasn't so much coherent.

"Not now," I said. "Don't let Lucia drink anything that isn't out of a sealed can or bottle. You have to be the one to open it. Not the bartender or any of the staff."

"Got it."

"Is Aaron there?"

Mom gave the phone to my partner. "Hey. What's ya doing?" he asked.

"I need you to cook for me," I said.

He inhaled and, unless I missed my guess, jumped to his feet and was looking for a frying pan or, god help me, a lionfish.

"Aaron, focus. Someone is trying to poison Lucia. They put antifreeze in her drinks. They could try food next, since we're on to them. You need to cook every meal for her and the rest of us, just in case."

"I'm on it. Do you want ribeye?"

"Really?"

"I got ribeye and blue cheese."

"That sounds fabulous but see if Lucia can handle something that heavy first. How about the consommé you were talking about?"

"Yeah, yeah. We'll start with consommé and then—"

I didn't have time to listen to the full menu and I was starving. That didn't help. "You rock, Aaron. Give the phone to Mom."

"Okay. I got more lionfish," he said.

"That's a dream come true. Mom, please."

He handed over the phone before he got to making lionfish hot dogs. It was coming. I was starting to get a sense for these things.

"When are you coming back?" asked Mom.

"I have no idea. They don't have a bed for Graeme, so as soon as he's mobile I'd guess."

"We've got to get off this island."

"I know, but Chuck said there aren't any available flights."

Mom's voice got all oozy. "You called Chuck."

"Sorta kinda. Anyway, can you call him and find out if he's got any information? My phone is dead," I said.

"What kind of information?"

"He'll know."

"You two talking a lot these days?"

"Only when absolutely necessary," I said.

"You could've called Morty, but you didn't. You called Chuck."

"Uncle Morty would tell Dad," I said. This conversation was almost as annoying as Chuck. I could hear the huge smile on Mom's face.

"Chuck doesn't keep things from your father or does he now...for you," she said.

"Mom, drop it. I asked him and he's doing me a favor. Did you tell Dad?"

"Not yet. There's nothing he can do and I don't want to hear the yelling."

I agreed and hung up. The less yelling the better. I settled back in my cracked vinyl chair and got mesmerized by Graeme's heart monitor, the steady beep beep.

I woke two hours later with my head on Graeme's bed and my leg and arm still in the warm water. Contrary to middle school beliefs, I did not pee.

"Hey," slurred Graeme.

I rubbed my eyes. "How are you feeling?"

"Like I drank antifreeze."

"So not great then."

"I've been better and more sober," he said.

I smiled and lifted my arm. My swelling was down and the red had gone to pink. "Ethanol is an effective treatment for ethylene glycol poisoning, believe it or not."

"What's up with the baking soda?" he asked, pointing to the sodium bicarbonate drip.

"That corrects the metabolic acidosis and increases the elimination of renal glycolic acid."

"It makes me pee."

"Something like that," I said with a smile.

"When can I leave? I gotta get back to Lucia," he said, his eyes still unfocused.

"I don't know. It's not up to me."

"Someone tried to kill her."

"Yes."

"You were right all along. I thought you were crazy," he said.

I patted his leg. "It's a common opinion."

"What are we going to do? We can't get off this island. I called the airline."

"I know. We're just going to hunker down and wait it out."

"I hate this."

"Me, too."

After another half hour, Dr. Navarro came in and checked Graeme's chart. "You were lucky."

"It runs in the family," said Graeme with his eyes half-closed.

"I'm going to keep you for another hour and see how it goes. No more sweet tea."

Graeme smiled. "Never again."

Dr. Navarro hooked his chart over the end of the bed and said, "Mercy, can you step outside with me?"

"Sure." I dried off my arm and leg with a towel he gave me and we went into the hall. Officer Tabora was waiting. He had two other officers behind him and they looked distinctly serious and not in a we're investigating an attempted murder way and you're a witness. More like we think you're the suspect way. I can't explain what the difference is exactly, but I'd been Dad's suspect in several crimes ranging from sneaking out to stealing his booze. I could always tell when he thought I'd done something. The Roatan cops had that same aura about them. I guess cops are all the same.

"Miss Watts, you must come with us," said Officer Tabora. He had a sheen of sweat on his brow and his hand on his weapon.

Seriously, dude. No need for that. I think the three of you can take me.

"Where would we be going?" I asked.

"We'll be more comfortable at the police station here in Coxen Hole."

I laughed. "I've been in a lot of police stations and I mean a lot. They are never comfortable."

"You'll have to come with us," Tabora said.

Dr. Navarro stepped up. His cheeks were flushed and he fidgeted with his lapel. "Is this really necessary?"

"It is."

The good doctor glanced at me and I said, "You had to call them. Don't worry about it."

That's what I said, not how I felt. I was worried as all get out. In a Third World country suspected of attempted murder. I'd seen too many episodes of *Locked Up Abroad* to think this was okay.

Tabora took my arm and I stepped back out of his grasp. "Am I under arrest?"

"We'd like to question you."

"Go for it. I'm quite comfortable here," I said.

"It's not appropriate."

"This is the Wild West remember? Appropriate hardly seems important."

Graeme called out behind me, "Mercy, what's going on?"

"The cops want to question us about your poisoning," I said, over my shoulder.

"They can come in," he said.

I raised an eyebrow and gestured to the door. The three shuffled their feet and looked vaguely confused. They wanted me, not Graeme.

"You were going to question the victim, right?" I asked.

"In time, after he's recovered," said Tabora.

"He can be questioned now," said Dr. Navarro. "We're thinking of discharging him soon."

Tabora stomped past me and we all followed. He questioned Graeme about the drink and where he got it. Tabora got the same answers I got. Graeme didn't know who sent it or why. He did know I saved him, which was a relief and a huge irritation to Tabora and crew.

"Has it occurred to you, Mr. Carrow, that Miss Watts has been orchestrating all these attempts herself?" asked Tabora.

Graeme yawned and a small, boozy smile crossed his lips. "Why would she do that?"

"In order to play the hero."

"Does she look like a publicity hound to you?"

Everyone looked at me and lifted their lips simultaneously in a snarl of distaste.

Okay. So I didn't look great. Geez!

"She may be after something other than publicity," said Tabora.

"Like what?"

"We need to question her to find that out."

I crossed my arms. "Go ahead. Ask me anything."

"Where were you when the tainted drink was being delivered?" Tabora asked.

Anything but that. Stall. Stall.

"Why do you care?" I asked.

Crap. He knew he was on to something. I could see it in his increasingly beady eyes.

"I want to know if you could've poisoned the drink."

"I didn't." I couldn't exactly tell him I was breaking and entering the Gmucas' bungalow. What incredibly bad timing.

"Tell me where you were and who you were with."

Uhhhh....

"Miss Watts, I'm waiting," said Tabora.

"I was..." *Think, you idiot!* "I was—"

"With me," said Aaron, trotting into the room, carrying a picnic basket.

"She was with you? Doing what?" asked Tabora.

Aaron scratched his rear. "I don't want to say."

"You'll have to say or I'm taking you both in."

Graeme sat up, lurched to the side, and grabbed his bed's metal railing. "Mercy didn't do anything. She saved me. She saved Lucia. Look at her. She's had the crap beat out of her."

"Looks can be deceiving. You know what they say about an angel face," said Tabora and his two companions looked at me with expressions that said, "Angel face, my ass."

Thanks, guys. I needed that.

"I don't care about her damn face. She didn't do anything," said Graeme.

Tabora glared at Aaron. "Where were you and what were you doing?"

Aaron chewed on a fingernail and then inspected his handiwork. He couldn't have looked less creditable. Then he said it. The words that would haunt me for years. "We were having sex next to a trash can."

Did he put trash can, sex, me, and him in the same sentence? No, he didn't. That could not have happened.

The cops gave Aaron and me the once-over and nodded. They nodded! Those dillweeds thought it was possible that I would actually do that. I kept a straight face. At least I kept a not shocked and disgusted face.

"I knew you were a couple," said Graeme.

"Me, too," said Dr. Navarro.

"Makes sense."

No, it doesn't, you brain donors.

"Well," I said, weakly. "You know how it is when you just...have to have...it."

A little part of me died in that moment. I had absolutely no pride left.

Tabora eyed me like the sexual deviant I apparently was. "Do you have any witnesses?"

"To us"—*Gag*—"having sex?" I asked. "Um, no." I would've asked what kind of a girl he thought I was, but that was already clear.

Aaron chewed another nail and pointed to my knees. All the cops nodded again. Graeme and Dr. Navarro turned pink at the tips of their ears. I looked down and sure enough there was evidence of me, Mercy Watts, humping next to a trash can in the dirt, if one chose to see it that way, which they did. My knees were scraped up and still had some sand crusted in the cuts.

"Alright then," said Tabora. "But I'll need your passport to ensure you stay on the island."

"I'm not surrendering my passport," I said. "You need a court order for that."

"Where do you think you are?"

"I think I'm an American citizen who's committed no crimes and isn't being arrested. Besides, I don't have it on me. My mother has it. You'll have to pry it out of her cold dead hands and she's got quite a grip."

I guess Tabora got the whole mother and her cub thing, because he left, saying something vague about interviewing me later. Dr. Navarro followed him out to check on Graeme's bloodwork. I waited until they were long gone before I turned to Aaron. I didn't know whether to hug him or rip his lips off, so he could never repeat his story again ever.

"You hungry?" he asked, holding up his basket.

"Aaron...you...I...what the what?"

"What's wrong?" asked Graeme from the bed, reminding me there was a witness.

"Ah nothing," I said. "What did you bring?"

"Food," said Aaron. "You said you needed me to cook for you."

"I did say that, didn't I? What did you make?"

Please not lionfish. Please not lionfish.

"Crab cakes."

Now I wish it was lionfish.

"What else?"

"Poblano remoulade, tomato corn salad, and parmesan pepper orzo."

Why couldn't there be chocolate? I'm a girl. I need chocolate.

"And baked hot chocolate," said Aaron.

"I think you just made it up to me," I said.

"What?"

I glanced at Graeme. It was best, although humiliating, if he thought we were a couple for a while longer. "Nothing. Let's eat."

"Can I eat?" asked Graeme in a little boy voice.

"If you think you can handle it. Do you like crab cakes?"

"Love them."

You can eat mine. Hoorah!

Aaron opened an orange container and the smell of crab filled the room. "I brought two for each of us."

Damn.

He made a plate for Graeme first. It had two oversized juicy crab cakes on it. Yuck. Then he made mine and the crab seemed even bigger. I admit they looked tasty. If only they didn't smell like crab on steroids. I tried everything else on the plate first. Delicious. Those cakes were sitting there like crusty eyeballs. Aaron watched me, leaning forward and biting his lip. I was going to have to eat that crab. He just saved my bacon. I had to do it. Plus, Graeme was watching and we were supposed be a couple. A guy would know if his girlfriend hated crab with a burning passion. Not a guy like Aaron, mind you, but a normal guy would know. Pete knew. Even Chuck knew of my crab loathing. I had to fake it.

"Hmmm. Looks incredible, like everything you make," I said.

Coward. Just do it.

And I ate one crab cake. I got it down with a smile and only two involuntary heaves. It was juicy. Oh so juicy. Thinking about it later made me dry heave. That actually came in handy later in life, so I ended up appreciating that cake, but that's another story.

"Aaron, you are a genius. That was the best crab cake I've ever eaten," I said.

And the only one.

He grinned at me and then looked at the other cake on my plate. Nope. I couldn't do it. My mouth had sacrificed enough.

"Maybe you should have this one...honey. You know I'm on that diet and I really want that baked hot chocolate."

Aaron looked at the ceiling, probably contemplating the words Mercy and diet going in the same sentence. A feat that had never happened before or since. While he was occupied, I scraped the hated cake onto his plate and captured the first—and still the best—baked hot chocolate of my life. He'd made them in red mugs and when my spoon broke the crust nothing else mattered. So people thought I'd do things in the dirt next to trash cans with Aaron. So what? I had chocolate. The Beatles were wrong. All you need isn't love. It's chocolate. Of course, when Chuck found out he would make my life a living hell, but at that moment everything was perfect. Too bad it couldn't last.

CHAPTER ELEVEN

W e got Graeme back to his bungalow and in bed two hours later. Lucia was hobbling around and fussing over him. He was loving it. She tucked him in and got him a bottled water. Pretty good for someone with an open infected stab wound, but I've noticed that women usually rise to the occasion when someone they love is wounded or ill, no matter their own condition. I wanted to tell her to knock it off and lie down, but it would've done no good. She had to take care of him. It was nice to see them together like that. They smiled and touched each other's hands. I don't know how I could've suspected him. Oz had totally thrown me off the trail with his suspicions. Of course, there were the bruises he'd noticed and he was right. Lucia was bruised to an unnatural extent and I hadn't explained that yet. I supposed I couldn't really eliminate Graeme from the list of suspects until I did. Plus, I was curious. I couldn't help myself. Too much Dad in me.

"Do you mind if I use your bathroom?" I asked.

"Sure," said Lucia as she got on the bed and cuddled up to Graeme.

I went into the bathroom and closed the door. It was a duplicate of the Gmucas' bathroom, except it didn't have any butt prints on the counter and had a stunning lack of shampoos. Lucia and Graeme were as neat and orderly as I expected. She had a small makeup bag and he had a man's travel bag hanging open from a hook with guy stuff like a nose hair trimmer, tweezers, and Icy Hot. They also had something else the Gmucas didn't have. Another travel bag, black nylon in the shape of a little suitcase. I'd seen those before and it wasn't for shampoos. I didn't bother to open it. There was no need and I felt guilty, the way I always did when I found out a secret that I had no business knowing.

I flushed the toilet and went back into the other room. Aaron had come in and was unpacking another basket. Lucia and Graeme had realized their mistake, because they were sitting bolt upright and were watching me with big eyes.

"Aaron, can you keep a secret?" I asked.

"Huh?"

I sat at the end of their bed. "He can, mostly because he won't remember it, but still whatever you say is safe. We won't tell."

"What are you talking about?" asked Lucia in a high voice.

"You're a diabetic."

She didn't answer and picked at the coverlet.

"That's why you have all those bruises."

"Yes." She slumped.

"Why are you hiding it?" I asked.

"You don't know my family. If they found out, they'd be all over me. They'd want me to fly to a special doctor. They'd want to go with me to the doctor. You just can't understand."

"That's where you're wrong. I understand overbearing. I think my family finds new definitions for the word."

"My family's special. I can't explain why," said Lucia.

"When were you diagnosed?" I asked.

"Six months ago."

"Have you considered a pump?"

"My endocrinologist wants me to have one, but I just..." Her eyes filled with tears.

I patted her foot. "You're not ready."

"No," said Graeme. "She's not. I'm not either, I guess. Our lives have changed so much already."

"I understand." I swallowed the desire to lecture, to persuade. If she wasn't ready to be hooked up to an insulin pump, she wasn't ready. "So that's why you didn't drink that sweet tea either time it showed up at your chair."

Lucia wiped her cheeks. "I can't drink that stuff."

"So..." said Graeme. "The diabetes kind of saved your life. Suddenly, I feel better about it." He kissed her forehead.

"I'm glad you do." Lucia laughed a little and it was good to hear.

"Do you mind if I check your leg? I meant to do it earlier, but what with Graeme almost dying, I got distracted," I said.

"Excuses. Excuses." Lucia grinned. "Go ahead. It feels a lot better. I didn't think it would."

"That plastic was quite the irritant. Now that it's out, you should heal quickly, assuming your blood sugar levels are under control."

I lifted the blanket and peeled back the bandage. Not bad. There was only a little seepage and the wound was packed correctly. I was worried that proper wound care wouldn't be followed in a hospital on a shoestring budget, but they'd done a good job.

"Looks good. I'll repack it tomorrow for you."

"That looks good?" asked Graeme. "What's with the gauze stuffed in there?"

"It makes sure the wound heals from the inside out, leaving no pockets of infection."

Aaron came to my side and held up two plates. "You hungry?"

For once, he wasn't asking me and I wished he was. The smell coming off those plates was straight up amazing.

"I'm starving," said Graeme.

"I thought you just ate?" asked Lucia.

"I can always eat, unless it's broccoli, then I'm full."

Lucia rolled her eyes. "What did you make, Aaron?"

He lowered the plates and I almost cried. Burgers. Big fat ones, dripping with mayo and covered in bacon. I got the crab cakes. I was being punished for the whole breaking and entering thing. That was the only explanation.

Must distract myself from burger.

"Do either of you remember which waiter brought the sweet tea?" I asked.

Graeme swallowed and wiped his chin of the heavenly juices of what was probably the world's best burger. "It wasn't a waiter. It was Bruno. I think he's some kind of handyman."

"Bruno?" Oh, no. That's not good. I had to clear him before Mom found out and threw a fit. "Did he bring the first sweet tea?"

Please say no.

"I really don't remember," said Graeme. "You don't think Bruno had anything to do with this? He seems like such a nice guy."

"He's a suspect. Everyone is, except the four of us in this room and my family. They didn't have access."

"Why would Bruno want to kill me? He doesn't even know me," said Lucia.

Time to come clean.

"He doesn't have to know you, if he was hired," I said.

Graeme and Lucia lay on their bed with their mouths firmly shut.

"I have to tell you something and I don't think you're going to like it but try to remember that I saved you both."

"Okay," said Lucia, slowly.

"I know your brother," I said.

"Darrell?" asked Graeme, hopefully.

"No, Lucia's brother, Oz."

"You know who I am?" Lucia sat up and pushed her plate away. Aaron whisked it away. "You've known this whole time. Did my dear brother send you here to spy on us?"

"This is unbelievable!" said Graeme.

"I'm sorry but yes, he did. But I was unaware of it until we arrived on the island."

"How the hell can you be unaware that you've been hired to spy on us?"

"I met Oz a few days before this trip. He found me in a boutique and wanted to hire me. In his defense, I'd say he loves you very much and he thought Graeme was abusing you. He'd seen the bruising and you wouldn't talk to him."

"Love isn't an excuse for everything," said Lucia.

"In my family it is." I went on to explain how we ended up on Roatan and that it was her brother who made sure she'd be watched, which ended up saving her. Not such a bad thing, considering.

"I can't believe this," said Lucia.

"So you think someone's trying to kill Lucia because she's a Fibonacci," said Graeme.

"Yes, I do. It may be payback for a hit done in New York recently. Although I admit my theory isn't perfect," I said.

"Why not?"

"Because hitmen are usually more direct. The tampering with your regs, the stingray barb—those were designed to hide that a crime had ever taken place. Somebody doesn't want to get caught. I'd expect a hitman to shoot you in the back of the head in a parking garage or something like that."

"What about the poisoning?" asked Lucia. "That's direct."

"It is. I think he's desperate. The regs were planned ahead of time and so was the barb with the succinylcholine, but they didn't work. Antifreeze is widely available. That plan was on the fly."

"But I've never been involved with that part of the family," said Lucia. "Never."

"I know, but somebody's gone to a lot of trouble to arrange your death and I don't think it's because you do charity work."

Lucia laid back on her pillows and her face became soft and tired. "Why didn't you tell my brother what was happening? If he knew, he'd hijack a plane to get down here."

"I know and I'm sure my father's keeping an eye on your brother. He found out about Oz's offer and had his own freak out. If my father knew I was on vacation with you, I'd never hear the end of it. Honestly, I wasn't completely convinced the regs weren't an accident. I was holding out hope that I was wrong, then the barb happened. I thought I could handle it."

"Why? You're not a cop," said Graeme.

"It's in the blood. I'll tell you my story sometime. Right now, I'm going to find Bruno and see if I can trace those drinks."

I got up and Graeme grabbed my hand. "I'm not thrilled that you were spying on us for Oz and I'm not even sure why you did it, but I'm glad you did."

"I saw the bruises, too. Oz was right about me. I couldn't leave his sister hanging."

I found Bruno cleaning the pool with a long-handled net. The storm had blown palm leaves, coconuts, flowers, cups, and two deck chairs into the normally crystal clear water. Bruno hauled out a coconut and carefully placed it on a pile with five more. My patience was at an all-time low and my rough edges had the bite of a cheap steak knife. Only one thing stopped me from stomping over there and accusing him of giving Lucia those drinks. Aunt Tenne was stretched out on a lounge chair with eyes so full of hope and unguarded love that I just couldn't ruin it. So she watched Bruno clean and I stood behind a wide palm tree thinking it over.

Bruno could've snagged Lucia's asthma inhalers when he unloaded her bags when we arrived. He'd helped load scuba equipment on the day her regs were sabotaged. The regs were out where anyone could've switched them, so that could've been Bruno or practically anyone else. He could've gotten into her beach bag and taken the third inhaler and wallet as well, but he wasn't diving the day Lucia got stabbed and I'd seen him hauling luggage before we went out. Theoretically, he could've hopped on a boat and following us out, but all the dive boats in the vicinity were for tourists. He would've stuck out. There was still the drinks. He could've poisoned them, but would he? Bruno didn't strike me as the kind of guy that would do anything for money and it had to be about money. He was a native Honduran. He didn't know the Carrows, a couple from St. Louis, Missouri. It wasn't personal. Sure his clothes were ragged and those canvases didn't come cheap. I didn't see an artist doing murder for hire. Maybe all my time in museums and galleries was coloring my vision. Artists could be criminals like anyone else. But I didn't like the idea, especially with Aunt Tenne in the picture.

Mom came up beside me and started to put her arm around me but stopped. "Are you ever going to shower?"

"Got a lot going on, in case you haven't noticed," I said.

"There's always time for hygiene."

"Good tip."

She groaned and asked, "What are you waiting for? Go interrogate him."

The wind picked up and wrapped her long flowing skirt around my still crusty legs, warm comforting feeling, like her strong arms around my shoulders. "The right moment," I said. "Where's Dixie?"

"She's having her hair colored."

"Really? Is she better?" I asked.

Mom sighed. "She's broken-hearted. I think she always will be. If she and Gavin had had children, maybe it would've been different. She'd have someone left."

"Hey, she has us. We've always been her family. What, are we getting demoted?"

"No, but she built her life around Gavin. Her center is gone."

"So if Dad died, I'd be your center."

"You already are."

That was disturbing. Mom and Dad were so together. I always felt like the third wheel. Certainly not the center of anything; that would be Dad's career. We all served the job. I was more like a satellite in orbit around them, occasionally caught in the gravitational pull.

"Now whatever Dixie's hair looks like, we love it. You understand me?"

"Why would it look bad?"

"She found a shop in West End that doubles as a tackle shop."

"Oh, lord."

"Exactly. Now let's get this show on the road. I have some choice words for that man." Mom pointed at Bruno up to his waist in the dirty pool, trying to grab a submerged deck chair.

"No," I said. "No choice words. He hasn't done anything for sure."

"He's seduced your aunt. He's lucky if I let him live."

"Mom, you can't." I lunged for her arm, but Mom was striding across the sand. Aunt Tenne saw her and smiled, then the smile dropped off her face. Fantastic. And I always thought Mom was the calmer of my two parents. Maybe not. I chased after her, spraying sand every which way.

"Mom, I will handle this."

"Please," Mom said over her shoulder. "You think he's harmless."

"We don't know that he isn't."

She spun around. "He's after her money."

"Aunt Tenne doesn't have any money," I said.

"Of course she does. She inherited from the uncles, just like I did."

"But she lives like she's on disability."

"Self-flagellation, pure and simple," Mom said.

"Why? What did she do?"

"Nothing. She never did a damn thing." Mom stepped on the pool deck and pointed a long perfectly polished finger at Bruno. "I would like a word, sir."

Bruno froze and Aunt Tenne jumped to her feet. "Whatever you have to say, Carolina, you can say it to me."

I stepped in front of Mom. "No, she can't. It's about Lucia's sweet tea. That's what it's about. That's it."

"No, it isn't," yelled Mom.

"Go ahead and say it!" Aunt Tenne yelled back.

Bruno and I looked at each other. A sad kind of pleading came into his eyes, but I didn't know what to do. I'd never stopped my mother from doing anything and, as far as I knew, no one else had either.

"Tenne, you know how you get. This man is trying to take advantage of you," said Mom, pushing past me.

"You don't know anything," said Aunt Tenne.

"I know you. You can't handle this. Not right now. Not today."

"Today has nothing to do with it."

"It's always about today. It has been since you were eighteen."

What the hell are we talking about?

"Well, not anymore. It's over." Aunt Tenne's face was flushed and her green eyes glittered. She was stunning and Bruno saw it. I watched him looking at her and I could tell. He saw her. The her that everyone else missed.

"Just like that. Do you know how many times we've been through this?" asked Mom.

"Who cares?"

"I do. We are going home soon and he is not coming with us," said Mom.

"You're just jealous."

"Jealous. Are you crazy? I guess I shouldn't ask that. I already know."

"You're jealous because Bruno is talented and handsome and you can't stand that," said Aunt Tenne.

Mom stomped up to the side of the pool. "Are you saying I don't have that?"

"You have Tommy."

Don't bring Dad into this!

"Tommy is handsome and talented at many things," said Mom.

"He looks like a giant Howdy Dowdy with all those gangly limbs and red hair."

"He's charming," yelled Mom.

"Thank goodness for that." Aunt Tenne spun around on her heels and went to the beach. She passed a waiter carrying a tray of drinks, snatched one off his tray, and chugged it on her way down to the sand. The waiter stared at her, then shook his head and went back to the bar.

"Well," said Mom to me. "What do you think about that?"

"I don't know." I really didn't. Mom and Aunt Tenne rarely fought and when they did it was a pretty quiet affair. More miffed silence than screaming accusations.

"I am not jealous."

"Are you sure about that?" I asked. It seemed reasonable.

"That is utterly ridiculous. Tenne is acting like a fool. I'm trying to save her from herself."

I rubbed my tired eyes. "She's having fun. Can't you just let her?"

"No, I can't. Do not say you're in favor of this. He's using her." Mom pointed to Bruno still in the pool and wrestling with the water-logged chair. "You're using her."

He ignored her. Good choice. Mom had lost it. Where was Dad when I needed him?

"Mom, what is he using her for?"

"To get to the States. For money. I don't know."

"Just let it alone, Mom! For crying out loud," I said.

Mom gave me a blistering look and stomped away. "Fine. I'm getting a Monkey Lala."

"Get eight. That should cover the crazy!" I yelled after her.

Then I turned back to Bruno. "That went well."

"Maybe in America." He pushed the chair to the edge of the pool and tried to heave it onto the side.

I ran around and grabbed it. The thing weighed a ton with its water-logged cushions. I dragged it over the lip and sat down, panting.

"Bruno, my mother is crazy, but I still have to ask you some questions about Lucia and Graeme Carrow."

"Yes." He went for the second chair.

"Neither of the Carrows ordered the sweet tea you brought them."

"I don't know whether they did or not," said Bruno, then he dove down and pushed the chair to the surface.

I waited for him to come up, then said, "I do and they didn't. Where'd the drink come from?"

"The bar. It had a note to take it to Mrs. Carrow."

"A handwritten note?"

"Yes." He struggled with the chair and I got down on my knees and reached for one leg.

"Do you still have it?"

"I left it on the bar."

Damn.

"You didn't question a note with a drink? Where was the bartender?"

"Christopher was making Tequila Sunsets on the other side of the bar. I just took the drink and gave it to Mrs. Carrow." He looked up at me, his black hair slicked back and shiny. I detected none of the tells I was supposed to look for. Nothing. He didn't appear to be lying.

I sighed. "Did you notice anyone lurking around waiting for you to take it?"

He smiled for the first time. "Lurking? No."

"Did you bring Mrs. Carrow a sweet tea this morning?"

"No, I was at the airport picking up new guests."

"Where were you on Sunday between 11:30 and 1:30?"

His brow furrowed and he heaved the chair the last two inches to my hand. I pulled it onto the side and gave Bruno a hand up. He climbed dripping onto the deck and squeezed out the hem of his shirt. "I was fixing the shower in Room Eight. Alberto was with me. You can ask him, but why?"

"Someone sabotaged Lucia's regs during that period."

"Ah, yes. Tenne told me your theory on that. Anybody could've gotten to her bundle. People come and go."

"I know. Security doesn't hang out in the scuba shop. Where were you when Mrs. Carrow got stabbed with the stingray barb?"

A little pink came into his tan cheeks. "I was with your aunt."

"You don't seem surprised that I'm asking you all this," I said.

"Tenne told me you would." He picked up the net again and scooped out another coconut.

"It's not personal," I said.

"To you."

"You're wrong about that. This whole thing is very personal to me. I meant that I don't have anything against you. About my mother and Aunt Tenne, do you know what they were fighting about? I mean, other than you."

His face which had been open and honest, closed like a brochure. "No."

Now that was lying. He had it all, a slight yes nod, he stepped back and put the net between us, and tapped his foot. I smiled at him. "So you know, but you won't tell me."

He frowned and I laughed. "Don't worry. I get it. You promised Aunt Tenne. I won't pester you."

Bruno clamped his mouth shut and went back to skimming the pool. I went to the bar, feeling grimier with every step. The sand I'd kicked up when I ran to the pool had stuck to my legs and was rubbing my thighs raw. Mauro was at the bar. He was very clean, tan, and tall. Before he saw me, he tilted to the right with his elbow on the bar and about twenty muscles flexed on his side. I stopped and rethought. Did I really want to be investigating attempted murders looking like a tropical vagrant? Oh, well. It didn't matter. He was gorgeous, but, covered in sand and roach poison or not, I had a boyfriend.

"Hi, Mauro," I said.

"Whoa," he said, baring his teeth.

Okay. Maybe it does matter.

"It's not that bad," I said, trying to sound confident in that fact, but coming off like a second grader denying that she ate the cookies. I always ate the cookies and I never got away with it.

Christopher the bartender came over with a fresh Monkey Lala. "Whoa."

"It's not that bad!"

Christopher didn't reply. He reached over and opened the glass fridge door where he kept all his fresh fruit, and I saw myself. It *was* that bad. I'd had the crap beaten out of me and looked better.

"Is my forehead purple?"

"And green," said Mauro.

"You might want to clean up them stitches. You've got a little pus going on," said Christopher.

"What's that smell?"

"There's goo on your shoulder."

Mauro took a long splinter out of my hair. "How'd this get in your hair?"

"Long story."

He gave me his Monkey Lala. "You need this more than I do."

I sucked down a fourth of the drink. Everything's better with a Monkey Lala. "Did my Mom order some of these?"

"Two," said Christopher. "She's beautiful when she's angry."

Mauro nodded. "She's beautiful all the time."

Then they looked at me and not in a good way. I wasn't used to such disdain and it made me feel like I didn't fit in my dirty, smelly, damaged skin. I drank another fourth for strength. "I need to ask you some questions, Christopher."

"Shoot."

"Did you make a sweet tea for Mrs. Carrow this morning and another this afternoon?"

"The police already asked me that," he said.

"They were here?" I asked.

"Yeah, but they didn't seem all that concerned. I think they're just hoping nothing else happens before the Carrows leave."

"What did you tell them?"

"I didn't make any sweet tea. It's not a bar drink. I have plain tea, but nobody ordered that either."

"Did you see the drink that Bruno delivered on the bar?" I asked.

"No. Sorry."

A pretty girl with a pixie cut framing her face scooted over close to Mauro and he grimaced. She leaned over the bar, giving a good view of her small high breasts. "I saw that drink."

Christopher grinned and said to her breasts, "Did you now?"

"I did. It was sitting on the bar right there with a slip of pink paper next to it." The girl leaned on Mauro's bulging bicep and he inched away.

"Did you see how it got on the bar?" I asked.

"No. It was just there and then Bruno came. He read the note and took the drink. Gary, the owner, said someone tried to poison a guest. Is that true?" She was talking to me but looking at Mauro. He was not digging it.

"It's true. There was another sweet tea delivered right before the storm this morning. Did any of you see that?"

None of them were even aware of a second drink. I hadn't told Officer Tabora about it, so I guess that made sense. The bar phone rang and Christopher answered. He looked at me and then nodded. "Yeah, she's here. Yes, sir. I understand."

"What was that about?" I asked.

"You're a suspect," he said. "We're not supposed to talk about this with you. The island police will handle it." Then he looked at the girl. "They want you in the office, Laurie. You better move it."

Laurie gave Mauro a longing look, which he ignored. Then she sauntered off with a lot of hip swing and very little hip. Mauro reached over the bar and grabbed a bottle of Coke. "The police. That's a laugh."

"Do you think I tried to kill Lucia?" I asked.

He took a swig and then grinned. "Not for a minute. Look at you."

"What about what I look like?"

"You're beating the hell out of yourself to save her and Graeme. If you wanted them dead, I'm pretty sure they would be."

Is that a compliment or an insult?

"Thanks, I guess."

Christopher went to make some Island Breezes and Mauro set his bottle on the bar. He gave me the once-over, twice. "You really don't have any respect for it, do you?"

I drank the rest of my Monkey Lala and let the calorie-laden goodness wash over me. "Respect for what?"

He gestured to the whole me. "You're one of the most beautiful women I've ever seen, but this is what you do to yourself."

"I'll heal."

"You really don't care."

"It is what it is. What am I supposed to do, let Lucia die because I don't want to break a nail?"

"No, of course not," he said. "But I don't know what to make of you."

"Join the club." I paused. "One of the most beautiful women?"

He laughed. "Yes. One of. You're not the only beauty around. Your mother is unbelievable. She's so graceful. When she looks at you, you start to feel—"

"Alright. Alright. That's my mother, my married mother, you're talking about."

"But you're not married, right?"

I put my glass on the bar. "Does it really matter? I'm a walking FEMA project."

He leaned in and the smell of Hawaiian Tropic was intoxicating. "It doesn't matter. The bones are good. How serious are you and Aaron?"

"I'm seriously disturbed that you think I'm dating Aaron, a guy for whom clean tees and combs are optional."

"I heard you were together and..."

Don't say it.

"Had some kind of a tryst next to a..."

Noooooo!

"Trash can."

I jumped to my feet, knocking over my stool with a clatter. "I did not have a tryst or anything else in the dirt next to a trash can."

"That's a relief," said Dixie from behind me. "I have to say from the look of you it was a possibility."

Mauro laughed and picked up my stool. I was afraid to turn around. Hair color in a bait shop. That was a huge risk. I had to manage the right reaction. It was absolutely required.

Please let the hair be good. Please let the hair be good.

I plastered a I-just-ate-chocolate look on my face and turned. Dixie stood with her elbow on the bar, but I didn't recognize her for a second. She'd gone all the way to platinum blond with tousled curls framing her face. Mauro leaned over my shoulder and whispered in my ear. "Say something."

"Whoa."

"What do you think?" asked Dixie.

I'm shocked. I'm freaked. No. No. I'm supportive. I'm a good girl in the loosest terms possible.

"Dixie, you're transformed. It's like you're a whole different person," I said with warmth, I hoped.

"That's the idea, but do you like it?"

"It's a little shocking, but I do. It's growing on me by the second. Why did you do it?"

"My life is different now. I thought I should look different."

"I like it, Mrs. Flouder," said Mauro. "You look like a fifties bombshell."

"Hey, that's my shtick," I said.

"Not today," said Dixie. "Take a shower and, for goodness sake, put some ice on your forehead. You're starting to look like a unicorn."

Mauro went into the bar and got me a Ziplock bag of crushed ice. I gingerly put it on my forehead and winced in spite of myself. "Well...I guess I'll go take a shower, since everyone seems to think I need one, for some reason."

"We'll talk later," said Mauro with a smile that made me think of him in his tiny swim trunks.

I didn't trust myself to answer. I was beat up, smelly, and exhausted in the middle of an investigation that wasn't exactly going well, and, worst of all, Pete was a million miles away. I could barely picture his face at that moment and that wasn't a good thing.

Dixie frowned and took my arm. "You have a boyfriend. Don't forget that."

"I knew it," said Mauro.

I groaned.

Dixie pushed me away from the bar. "Go take a shower. A cold one. And call Chuck. He's been pinging me every ten minutes, but he won't say why he has to talk to you. It's driving me nuts."

"I killed my phone," I said.

"Take mine and go," she said, turning to Mauro. "You're quite the looker, but stop looking at Mercy."

I caught the words, "I can't" as I headed down the path to my room. Great. Now I had to control myself, not one of my gifts. The to do list in my head kept growing longer and longer. Find the source of the sweet tea. Fix the locations of the Gmucas and frat guys during the tea delivery and everyone else that had been on the boat. I assumed antifreeze was widely available on Roatan, so there was no use chasing that down.

I hung a right onto Lucia and Graeme's path and knocked softly on their door. Aaron opened it a crack. His eyes darted around like he was expecting a visit from the boogeyman.

"You alone?" he asked.

"Duh. Let me in."

"Alright then."

I passed Aaron and went to the bed. Lucia and Graeme were both asleep. Graeme snored like a sick buffalo while I took his pulse. It was back into the safe range. He smelled pretty boozy and the ethanol bottle I'd left with him had a cup less than before. I'd insist that he see a nephrologist when we got back to the States just to be on the safe side, but I thought he'd recover fully without liver damage.

I checked Lucia's wound without waking her somehow. The

redness and fever were down and no additional pus. Her pulse was good. I would've liked to take both of their blood pressures but lacked the equipment. Instead, I tucked them in as Dixie's phone started vibrating against my hip. Chuck and he wasn't happy. I think he would've been texting curse words if it hadn't been Dixie he was talking to. Dad would hurt him, if he found out.

Chuck would just have to wait. My shower was long overdue.

"Hey, Aaron," I whispered. "Can you stay with them?"

"Huh?" He was bent over a small pad of paper and writing so fast I'm surprised the paper didn't catch on fire.

"Can you stay here? I have to shower, then I'll take over."

He looked up from his pad, but I couldn't see his eyes. His glasses had become hopelessly smudged again. "Yeah. Yeah." He closed the pad and pressed it against his chest. "Can I trust you?"

"I should hope so. We're the couple who humps next to trash cans."

"Don't tell anyone about this notepad."

I hesitated for a moment, but I just had to ask. "Why?"

"I just developed my recipe for lionfish hot dogs." He glanced around the room. "It's top secret."

"You really think there's a market for lionfish hot dogs?" I asked.

"There will be when I make them."

I thought about it. Everything Aaron made was wicked good, except crab. There was no hope for crab. "It's hard for me to imagine, but you're probably right. Just promise never to tell me what's in them or how they're made."

He pressed the pad harder against his chest. "But I can trust you, right?"

I rolled my eyes and opened the door. "I'll be back."

I stepped outside and found the Gmucas walking up the path. For a second, their bathroom caterwauling echoed in my ears and I shuddered. If I could've avoided them, I would've. But they were also prime suspects what with the trying to get into the Carrows' bungalow and all that talk about money. I had to head them off.

"Hi, Mercy," said Linda. "How are they doing? We brought get-well treats."

Frankie held up a basket with baked goods and various bottles.

Over my dead body.

"That's so nice of you," I said.

"Can we see them?" asked Linda.

"They're asleep. Why don't I take that and we'll tell them you came by?"

Frankie gave me the basket reluctantly. "Can't we come in for just a minute?"

Hell no!

"Maybe in about an hour. They've had a rough couple of days," I said

Linda lowered her voice. "Is it true? Did someone try to poison them?"

"Yes. The police are involved. We'll catch them." I gave them a hard look. "They won't be leaving this island free."

"I should hope not."

"Let us know if there's anything we can do to help," said Frankie.

"I will." I slipped back inside, closed the door, and looked through the peephole. They were pretty smooth. Were they lying? I couldn't tell. There was no head nodding or anything obvious, but it was a short interaction.

I carried the basket past Aaron, who was back to scribbling on his pad. "Don't give them anything from this basket."

He grunted and kept scribbling. I hugged the basket. What to do with it? Hell, I would've thrown it out the back door, but the Gmucas were known to lurk around on the back paths. I took it into the bathroom, got a bath towel, and tied every single item up in it with a knot. Lucia had one eyeliner pencil and I used it to write in big black letters on the towel. "Do not eat or drink contents. May be contaminated." I put the bundle in the shower and pulled the curtain closed.

I left out the back door, so I wouldn't have to have a conversation about lionfish hot dogs or anything else in a hot dog. I turned to the left and spotted two of the frat boys. Andrew had his head down with his hand over his eyes and Joe guzzled a beer. Neither looked happy. I tiptoed between two bungalows and peeked at them from behind an overgrown hibiscus. I hadn't seriously considered those guys. They mostly seemed like drunken idiots out for one last screw before getting Andrew married, but since Graeme wasn't a suspect anymore, everyone else had to be. They did have access.

"We have three days left," said Andrew. "Three days."

"No shit. Anything can happen." Joe finished his beer and tossed the bottle into the sand.

"Anything will happen. He's fucking crazy."

"He's desperate."

Andrew looked up at the sky. "We can't keep him in the room forever. Maybe we shouldn't help him."

"You want to give him tough love or whatever that shit is?" asked Joe. "That'll get him killed. I say we pay the debt ourselves."

"I can't do that."

"I don't think we have a choice. Come on. Let's talk to him before he comes up with some other idiotic plan."

"You know what?" asked Andrew. "This is the worst vacation of my life. If Anita finds out, she'll kill me."

"She won't find out. We're in fucking Roatan, Honduras. What happens in Roatan and all that. The cops don't even know we're alive."

Andrew and Joe walked around the bungalow and Andrew said, "For now."

Great. Three more suspects and no waiting.

I went back to the main path and saw Andrew and Joe talking to the maid on their bungalow's front porch. Then they went inside and slammed the door. The maid stood there for a moment, holding her basket of cleaning supplies and sporting a worried frown. She walked off finally. No one came out and I'd have to wait until they left to search it. The thought made me overwhelmingly tired. The only thing I wanted to search out was a bed and a new ice pack. My bag was now a bag o' water and not terribly useful.

I dipped my feet in our bucket and trudged up the staircase. I swear it was getting taller and taller every time I went up it. And every time I went up, a new disaster awaited me. That time was no different.

"Mercy. My girl. Come sit with me," said Aunt Tenne from the hammock. She was so heavy; her rear was firmly planted on the porch.

"I have to take a shower." I couldn't have been less enthusiastic, but that didn't deter Aunt Tenne. She smiled and pointed at the lounge.

"Just for a minute. We need to talk."

"No offense, but I have had about as much talking and listening as I can take."

Her mouth tightened around the edges and she raised her eyebrows. "Mercy. I need to talk to you."

I sat on the lounge and wished a coconut would hit me on the head. Being knocked out was starting to sound restful. "What is it?"

"I want you to help me with your mother."

"What makes you think I have any influence? She's my mother. She gives me orders, not the other way around." I leaned back, closed my eyes, and took a deep breath. The smell of barbecued lionfish still lingered in the air. Way to ruin breathing, Aaron.

"You have influence. Talk to her. Tell her how happy I am. Tell her how wonderful Bruno is. He loves me. He does."

"Aunt Tenne, you've known him for six days. Six days. That's barely enough time to know what his favorite color is much less fall in love."

"How long do you think it took your parents?"

I squinted at her. "I don't know and I don't care. Can I shower and go find a murderer now?" I didn't mention the nap, but I had a nap coming in a big way.

"They haven't murdered anyone yet, have they?"

"Let's not get into semantics, okay?" I staggered to my feet and Aunt Tenne rolled out of the hammock, a lot more graceful than me, that's for sure.

"I'm sorry to put this on you," she said.

But you're still going to do it.

"But I really need you to make her understand."

"Fine, but you owe me."

Aunt Tenne smiled, the big light-up way she did when looking at Bruno and my hard heart melted just a teeny bit. "I'm counting on you."

That's what I need, another person counting on me.

"Stay away from Mom for a while. Okay? Don't poke the bear."

She touched my shoulder with one finger. I guess I was too gross for more. "I'll tell Bruno." She jogged down the creaking stairs.

I went inside and got in the shower. I was in there a good five minutes before I realized I hadn't taken off my clothes. I'd sunk to a new level. Wet clothes are amazingly hard to get off. They wanted to stay on. They really did. In retrospect, somebody might've been trying to tell me something because staying dressed really would've been better. But I did take them off, squeezed them out, and rolled them into a tight bundle. I pulled back the shower curtain to toss them in the sink and saw Dixie's phone start vibrating. Probably Chuck. It had that insistent, annoying kind of buzz and started bumping across the counter toward oblivion. I heaved the bundle at the sink and lunged for it. My feet slipped and I did a slow motion twist, grabbing for the shower curtain, tearing it from its rings, and landing half in the shower and half out.

"Ow," I whispered.

Dixie's phone jumped off the counter and clattered to the tile. The faceplate shattered, but it continued to buzz next to me, and then my clothes, which had not made it into the sink, fell off the counter and landed with a wet splat on top of the phone.

"Hey." Aaron stood in the doorway. "What's ya doing there?"

"Oh my god! Cover your eyes!" I rolled over and yanked the torn curtain over me.

Aaron did not cover his eyes. He said, "Lucia wants to go to the beach."

"What the what? Get out!"

He chewed on a ragged fingernail, which was apparently more interesting than my half-naked body. Thank goodness for that bit of weirdness. "Can she go?"

"No." I struggled to my feet and wrapped the curtain around me. "She has an infection and we need to keep an eye on the both of them."

"He's going, too." More fingernail biting.

The water still spraying into the shower turned from hot to luke-warm. Fantastic. "No, he isn't. What is wrong with these people? Go stop them. I'll be right there."

Aaron didn't leave. I really didn't expect him to, because it would've been somebody else's life. Water was flooding the bathroom. I wasn't close to clean and the water was now cold.

"What are you waiting for?" I asked.

"You hungry?"

"What do you think?"

That's when he looked at me. "Yeah. Let's go to The Aviary tonight. They got good crab."

The Aviary had a great reputation, but crab was a deal-breaker.

"Aaron, if you don't get out of here, I might rip your nostrils off."

"They got soft shell and Alaskan King Crab."

"Aaron, if you think I won't kill you and make it look like an accident, you're wrong."

"And crab kabob and crab po'boy."

I almost told him I hated crab with the fiery hell of a thousand venereal infections, but I just couldn't. The little weirdo loved to feed me crab and somehow, I couldn't ruin it for him. If he wouldn't leave under a threat of death, I would have to distract him. "Do they have steak? I'd like a good steak."

He rubbed his hands together. "I can find out."

"You do that at Lucia's bungalow. Go on now."

"I gotta go over to The Aviary."

"You can call them on Lucia's phone. Leave me your phone. I have to call Chuck. I'm pretty sure I killed Dixie's phone."

He went back to his biting. "I gave it to Lucia, so she could call me if something happened."

"How's she going to call you, if she has your phone?"

"Huh?"

"Never mind. Get over there and call the restaurant."

Aaron left with a quickness, probably not because he had left two invalids alone to make a jailbreak. I dropped the curtain and flinched as I stepped under the icy water. Who knew the best part of my shower would be the part where I was wearing clothes? I made Guinness World Record time for the fastest shower, mopped up the floor with every towel we had, got dressed in the last clean dress I had. And finished up by smearing triple antibiotic cream on my forehead, which made it nice and shiny, just in case someone happened to miss the lovely purple and green surrounding the stitches.

Dixie's phone was indeed dead. One more casualty of the worst vacation ever. Oz Urbani owed me big. There was no avoiding it. How he would decide to pay me back, scared the crap out of me. Of course there was the possibility that I wouldn't catch the killer and the more I thought about it, the more that freaked me out. Oz sent me to Roatan to protect his sister. I had a feeling the Fibonacci family wouldn't care if Lucia survived Roatan, only to be killed in St. Louis because I couldn't catch the guy. What would they do then? I ran out the door determined not to find out.

CHAPTER TWELVE

I met Lucia and Graeme halfway down their walk. Aaron was on the phone, not stopping the crazy invalids like I asked. Graeme was so drunk; he was embracing a palm tree like a lover. Lucia was still pretty pale, but she'd gotten a cane from somewhere and was moving at a pretty good clip. By good clip, I mean six inches a minute.

"Do you two have a death wish?" I asked with my hands on my hips.

"We've been talking," said Lucia.

"Don't talk. No good can come from it."

"We're not letting him win," slurred Graeme.

I took Lucia's arm. "You know they say living well is the best revenge. Well, in your case it's living at all. Get back in that bungalow."

"We want to go to the beach, so he knows we're not defeated." Lucia's eyes were fiery. It was the first hint of what I assumed was Fibonacci spirit.

"What can happen?" asked Graeme. "You'll be there."

"In case you haven't noticed, I'm getting pretty worn down," I said.

"You look good to me."

"Then you're blind drunk."

Lucia rammed her cane into the sand. "He's not ruining our vacation."

"Well, he's ruining mine. Please go back for me, if not yourselves."

Aaron trotted around Graeme. "They can take us in fifteen minutes."

Graeme perked up. He almost held his head straight. "Take us where. Where're we going? I'm ready."

I rolled my eyes. "He wants to have dinner at The Aviary."

"Oh, we don't want to intrude on your romantic dinner," said Lucia. "We'll have dinner at the regular restaurant." She hobbled forward an inch.

Groan.

"Fine. Aaron, call them back and see if they can seat us all. Drop the words victim and poison. That should help."

Aaron called The Aviary back and got us in. Then I had him call the front desk and ask for a golf cart. Lucia and Graeme protested, saying they could walk. By the time we got to the restaurant I was seriously questioning their sanity. If anyone had an excuse to stay in bed, it was them. Instead, they hobbled up the wide stone staircase, read the sign that shoes weren't allowed, and kicked them off as the sommelier opened the door to best restaurant on the island all smiles and charm.

The Aviary was as I expected having eaten at a lot of best restaurants with Myrtle and Millicent, starched tablecloths, clean lines, good art on the walls, but not great. The difference was the staff. They were dressed in casual island wear and all barefoot. Lucia and Graeme chatted up the bartender and found out the no shoes policy had to do with the atmosphere they were going for and a strong dislike of sand on the floor. Lucia proceeded to meet three of the five other tables. She was as bad as Dad. We couldn't get through a meal without meeting someone new or talking to someone he knew on a case eight years ago in Seattle.

To my relief, the restaurant wasn't dedicated to crab. The menu was small, but varied, and they had steak, thank goodness.

"Okay. Don't drink anything that isn't opened in front of you. Aaron, how about you order for me?" I said.

He rubbed his hands together so fast I thought he'd start a fire.

"But no crab."

The rubbing stopped.

"Because you already made me crab cakes today."

"Okay. Okay. They got cucumber chawan mushi."

What the what?

"Okay," I said, weakly. "Go with your instincts."

Aaron looked so happy; it was almost worth it. I left him explaining the menu to Lucia and Graeme and I escaped outside with Lucia's phone to call Chuck.

"Hello," said a gruff voice.

"Chuck?" I asked.

"Mercy?"

"Yeah, I had to use Lucia's phone. You don't sound so good. Where are you?"

"In Venezuela."

"What the hell are you doing in Venezuela?"

"Trying to get to you."

I got teary-eyed. I never thought that would happen in regard to Chuck, unless he was dead or something.

"Mercy?"

"Yeah."

"Are you...crying?"

"I'm not crying, you dufus. What are you doing in Venezuela? That's not even close to Honduras."

"Closer than I was. Actually, I was flying into Belize, but there was some kind of situation at the airport, so we got sent to Venezuela. I'm getting on a plane to Nicaragua in an hour."

"Can't you fly into Honduras?"

"No, I'm taking a bus over, baby."

"What a nightmare."

"But I'll get there."

"What did you find out?"

Chuck's connection, Spidermonkey, had found out quite a bit, but none of it was particularly helpful. The Gmucas were connected to the Belotti family in Las Vegas. They specialized in cocaine trafficking but were fairly minor players with no ties to the Fibonaccis or the Todaros in New York. The Gmucas, themselves, had little credit card debt, no history of gambling, but they had been arrested twice for breaking and entering. The charges were dropped, but it wasn't clear why. There was nothing in Lucia or Graeme's histories that would make them targets other than Lucia's family.

"Any large deposits?" I asked.

"Just regular income. Why?"

"They're getting money from a guy named Tony."

"And you know this because?" asked Chuck.

"It's a long story. So there's no suspicious transactions?"

"None at all. There's no reason to think the Gmucas are involved."

Groan.

"It could be random," said Chuck. "It's been known to happen."

"Multiple attempts by a random assailant? Isn't that more of a drive by shooting kind of deal?"

"I'm grasping at straws here. Who else was on the boat during the stabbing?"

"Todd Pell was on the boat. He's on vacation with his wife and kids and Aaron was with him during the second poisoning attempt."

"I'll check him out anyway. Who else?"

I told him about the frat boys and that got him interested. His reaction to Colin grabbing my ass made me smile. Colin might find himself with a bloody nose. The airline announced that Chuck's plane was boarding and before we said goodbye Chuck said, "Call your boyfriend."

"What?"

"You aren't answering his texts, so he called me."

"Why would he call you of all people?" I asked.

"The last time he called your mother, she asked him how many children he wants."

"What did he say?" I asked.

"He doesn't know," said Chuck.

I wasn't surprised. Pete's plans didn't usually go beyond his next shift.

"He's busy," I said.

"So am I, but I have plans," said Chuck. "Want to know what my plans are?"

"Not if they have anything to do with me."

"They do."

"Goodbye."

I hung up, but stayed on the front deck of The Aviary, watching the small orange sun dip into the ocean. Beautiful and calming. Well, it was until Mom and Aunt Tenne walked by. They were fighting again. Something about dinner. I'm guessing Aunt Tenne was having dinner with Bruno and Mom wasn't thrilled. I was supposed to be doing something about Mom. I did promise, but Mom was crazy. There was no cure for that.

"Miss Watts?" Our waiter smiled at me from The Aviary's door. "Your appetizer has been served."

"Thank you. What is it?"

"Cucumber chawan mushi."

"Give it to me straight. How bad is it?" I asked with a grimace.

"It's a Japanese egg custard with cucumber and tomato gelee. It's unusual, but quite good."

"I'm going to hold you to that."

He grinned and held open the door for me. "I'm not worried."

The mushi sat in the middle of a dessert plate in a highball glass and the waiter was right. It was kind of good once you got used to savory custard and jellied tomatoes. I ate the whole thing and then had a great steak that Aaron had ordered specially for me. It had aspic of something on it and I've learned to stop listening when the word aspic comes up. Lucia and Graeme had all kinds of crazy stuff that Aaron had ordered for them and ate more than I expected. We were waiting for dessert, a flourless chocolate cake with a concord grape reduction in my case, when the frat boys walked in. I should say two of them walked in. The third was dragged. Colin had a split lip, a black eye, his diamond earring had been ripped out of his ear, and, unless I was seeing things, he had handprints on his neck.

"Do you see that?" asked Lucia. "Maybe someone tried to kill him, too."

"We should ask," said Graeme.

"I'll look into it, but I don't think it's the same person," I said.

Lucia leaned closer to me. "Why not?"

"Beating someone up is pretty direct. All the attempts on you have been on the down low."

Colin shoved Andrew away from him and made for the door. Joe got him by the back of the shirt and steered him toward their table.

"I don't want to be here," said Colin.

"Too freaking bad," said Joe. "Andrew wants a nice dinner. This is supposed to be his week."

Colin glanced around the dining room, spotted me, and his angry face turned lecherous. Great. I'm catnip to the criminal-minded.

"No, you don't," said Andrew. "Sit down and shut up."

It took both Andrew and Joe to get Colin in his chair and a double scotch to get him to stay there.

The waiter put my cake in front of me with a flourish. I took a huge bite and melted like the chocolate drizzled on the plate. It was so good I almost didn't mind Colin staring. Halfway through my cake, I caught him looking at Lucia and then Graeme. Actually, it wasn't Graeme he was interested in. It was the heavy Omega Seamaster watch on his wrist. Colin caught me looking at him and he licked his split lip.

Yeah, you're real enticing.

I looked at Graeme's watch again. It was five grand easy. Colin wasn't looking at it because he admired it. Lucia's wallet had gone missing along with her inhaler. Colin could be the one. Joe said he was desperate and in debt. Maybe he was a low-rent hitman. That would explain why he was so bad at it.

"What do you know about Colin, Andrew, and Joe?" I asked Graeme.

"Nothing," he said. "They're here to celebrate Andrew's wedding. Colin's some kind of screw-up, I gather."

"Have you ever met them before? Or heard of them?"

"No," said Lucia, her cheeks flushed. "Do you think they did it?"

"I think everybody did it for now."

Aaron had the menu in front of him and was studying like there was going to be a final. I tapped it and he lowered it just enough for me to see his glasses. "Huh?"

"What do you know about Colin, Joe, and Andrew?"

"Andrew likes his burgers with avocado. Joe likes burgers with bacon and barbecue sauce. Colin doesn't—"

"Stop right there," I said. "Do you know anything about them that isn't food-related?"

"No."

"Never mind."

Aaron put the menu back up and muttered something about sriracha sauce. Not helpful.

"You know what? I have an errand to run. You three stay here," I said. "I'll be right back."

"What about your cake?" asked Lucia.

"Don't let them take it. I'm totally going to eat that."

"Where are you going?" asked Graeme. "I can help."

"You can't stand up straight. I'll be fine." I slipped out the side door when Colin and company were ordering and crossed my fingers.

The frat boys' door picked as easy as the Gmucas' did. I stepped inside and the smell of boys' locker room hit me. But there was something else, too. I couldn't quite place it with all that guy stink floating around. I flipped on the light and gasped. Yes, I actually gasped. The room was that gross. They must've kept the maid out all week. There was dirty underwear everywhere on every surface, bloody towels wadded up on a chair, half-empty takeout containers, and a few pizza boxes. But that didn't account for all the smell. I opened the bathroom door and it made me fondly remember the cabinet under the Gmucas' sink, roach goo and all.

Somebody had been sick and I mean *The Exorcist* kind of sick. They had spewed. Having spent serious time in ERs, it smelled like drunk sick to me. I was guessing scotch and Colin. There was a pool of yellow next to the toilet and I wished it was pee. It was bile, the kind of stuff that comes out when a person only drinks and eats nothing. Come to think of it, I'd never seen Colin eat. Maybe that was what Aaron was going to say when I cut him off. The little guy did know something. I didn't know how useful it was, but alcoholics were known to get desperate.

I stood there with my hand over my mouth. That wasn't all though. There was another smell. I closed the bathroom door and picked my way through the room. I ended up where I started next to the back door, standing beside their metal ice bucket and that was it. The bucket had ashes in it. Quite a few actually. One little corner of paper had escaped the inferno and it looked like a receipt to me. If I were Hercules Poirot, I would've had a handy hatbox with me and a mustache wax melter thingy, so I could figure out what the burned papers said. I made a mental note to ask Dad if the hatbox trick would really work, but I probably shouldn't. I was always disappointed with his answers and I looked stupid in the process.

There were no drugs anywhere in the room, except for aspirin. No stingray barbs, antifreeze, or regulators. It was pretty disappointing. I was so ready to find some concrete evidence. I tiptoed over underwear and relocked the door to ultimate grossness and forced myself to go back to The Aviary instead of the front desk to report the biohazard bungalow.

As I walked down the path, I heard whispering. I ducked behind a flower-covered bush and the Gmucas tiptoed onto the path from another bungalow, not their own. What the heck? They were sweaty and flushed.

"That was so hot," whispered Linda.

"Cause you're hot," said Frankie.

"We are so going to win this time. Seven rooms and we're just getting started. Tony's going to be so jealous."

Hot. Sweaty. Other people's rooms. Ewwww.

This didn't exactly clear Frankie and Linda of the attacks on Lucia and Graeme, but at least I knew why they were trying to get into their room. I only hoped they hadn't gotten into mine. I'd have to check my counter for butt prints. It was a new low. Somehow, I just kept finding new and grosser ones.

Lucia, Graeme, and Aaron were still at our table. Graeme could hardly keep his eyes open, but he generously paid the check. Aaron and I put them back on the golf cart and drove them to their bungalow. By the time we got there, Graeme was awake again and wanting to go to karaoke night.

I got out of the golf cart. "Are you kidding? You're lucky I let you go to dinner."

"I'm feeling pretty good," he said. "I'm alive and that's something to celebrate."

"Well, I can't argue with that, but we don't know the aftereffects of the antifreeze. You should take it easy."

"What will we do?" asked Lucia. "I've had enough of those four walls."

"Sleep. Get better," I said.

"When will that be?"

"Everyone heals in their own time. But resting will speed things along."

Graeme gave me a lopsided grin. "So we could heal fast and get back to our vacation."

"Uh…yeah, sure. Please go to bed. Do it for me. I'm exhausted."

Lucia climbed slowly out of the cart. "Okay. We'll do it for you, but tomorrow's another day."

And I hope you survive it.

"Yes. We'll start fresh tomorrow."

Aaron helped Lucia inside and Graeme clung to me. He was a lot heavier than he looked and I swear I had a hernia popping out before I got him on the bed. I did a quick wound check, made sure Lucia took her meds, and locked them in.

"Aaron, can you return this cart for me?"

He got in and did a quick three-point turn.

"One more thing," I said. "You know that hot chocolate you made for me at the hospital, could you do that again? I really need it."

Aaron hit the gas or electric, whatever golf carts run on, and peeled out, spraying sand everywhere, including on me. I walked up to the room and put on one of Pete's tees that I borrowed and never gave back. I curled up in bed with my Kindle with the neck pulled up over my nose. The shirt smelled like Pete. It smelled like someone who never ever investigated crimes on vacation, who knew exactly what to do all the time and rarely made mistakes. It smelled nothing like me.

Aaron came in record time, carrying a large mug. He gave it to me and watched while I sipped the comfort.

"I don't know what to do next," I told him.

"About what?"

"About Lucia and Graeme."

"What about them?"

I took a big gulp after that one. "Hello, Aaron. Someone's trying to kill them and I have no idea who. The cops' best idea is me."

"You didn't do it."

"I know that." I drank the rest of my hot chocolate. "I'm going to sleep now."

Aaron made no move to leave. If it were any other man on the planet, I would've thought he was hinting at joining me in bed, but since it was Aaron, I figured he was confused.

"You should go to your room and I'll stay here."

"I got to watch you. Tommy would want me to watch you."

"Trust me. Dad doesn't want you to watch me sleep."

"Someone might try to kill you. I got to watch you."

"I am too tired to have this conversation," I said. "You go out to the sofa. Please don't watch me while I sleep. It's creepy."

He left reluctantly and I dreamt that he slept curled up on the rug outside my door like a dog. He might've done it. I wouldn't put it past him.

CHAPTER THIRTEEN

"Mercy, wake up."

After some severe shoulder shaking, I rolled over. Aunt Tenne sat on the edge of my bed, holding the largest coffee mug I'd ever seen. Her hair was slicked back and held in place with a dozen red blossoms and she smelled like the ocean.

"You look nice," I said.

"Thank you." She lifted a lock of hair off my forehead and grimaced. "I was hoping this would be better this morning."

"It has to get worse before it gets better."

"Isn't that always the way?" She gave me the mug. "Speaking of worse, the cops are here?"

I sipped the hot, but not terribly flavorful brew and sighed. "What now?"

"A tourist is missing."

I jerked at her words and coffee slopped out, stinging my fingers and soaking the sheets. "What happened?" I shoved the mug at her and rolled off the bed.

"It's not Lucia or Graeme. I didn't mean to scare you."

I bent over, breathing hard. My life had flashed before me. It was really short and there wasn't nearly enough chocolate.

"Mercy?" Aunt Tenne patted me.

"I'm okay. Have you ever had your life flash before your eyes?"

She frowned and looked away. "Yes, I have."

I took the mug back and gulped down half the remainder. "Are you ever going to tell me what's going on with you?"

"The cops are here. Better put on some clothes."

So I guess not.

Aunt Tenne left. I went in search of something clean and didn't find it. I put on last night's dress, which smelled faintly of the frat boys' room and went out into the living room. Officer Tabora stood next to the door with his hand on his weapon. A younger cop fidgeted beside him until he got a load of me. His mouth dropped open. For once, I would've liked the compliment, since I felt so crappy, but it was probably my forehead and knees he was impressed with.

"Miss Watts," said Tabora. "We'd like you to come with us."

"Pass. Who's missing?" I asked.

The younger cop smirked at me. "As if you don't know."

"If I knew who it was, I wouldn't ask. My aunt says it's not Lucia or Graeme, so I give up."

"Andrew Thatcher," said Tabora.

It was my mouth's turn to drop. "The groom. No way. We just saw him last night."

"We know. Mr. Thatcher disappeared sometime after dinner at The Aviary and before six o'clock this morning. How well do you know him?"

My mind raced. Andrew missing, not Colin. Colin was a better candidate in my book.

"Hardly at all," I said. "We got open water certified together, but that's about it."

"You want to stick with that?"

"Yes. I don't really know him. I don't know everyone."

"You were seen coming out of his room last night," said Tabora.

Oh, shit! Do I lie? What would Dad do? Oh, hell. Dad wouldn't have gotten caught. He wouldn't have left fingerprints. Idiot.

I set the coffee mug on the mini fridge and put up my hands. "You got me. I was in their room last night for about ten minutes."

Tabora couldn't have been more surprised to hear the truth and that alone made it worth it. I loved surprising men. They always think they know me.

"You admit you were in his room?" he asked slowly.

"Yep. It was stupid, but I'd had a few."

"A few what?"

"Glasses of wine. I'm a lightweight." I grinned and tried to look like a saucy minx.

"So you were drunk and you broke into Thatcher's room."

"Not break in, went in."

With the help of lock picks.

"Why did you *go* into his room?"

I swallowed. *Just do it. He already thinks you're a sleazy slut.*

"Andrew is really hot, so you know…"

"Spell it out for me."

"Well…"

It's okay. It's not as bad as the trash can thing.

"I was going to hide in his room and seduce him, but he didn't come back," I said.

"You wanted to get naked in *that* room?" asked Tabora with a snort.

It is as bad. That room's like the inside of a trash can.

"Like I said, he didn't come back. No harm. No foul."

Tabora's young partner jiggled his handcuffs and a bead of sweat ran down his cheek. His eyes scanned my injuries. He flushed and his breathing sped up. What did the lie spotting handbook say about that? Sexual attraction.

Oh, crap. That's just what I need.

"Mercy Watts, you're under arrest for breaking and entering," said Tabora. "Cuff her, Pinto."

Pinto unclipped his cuffs so fast, you'd have thought it was his birthday. I stepped back and bumped into the mini fridge and the mug fell onto the tile, shattering in a million pieces. Aunt Tenne ran out of her bedroom. "What's going on?"

"We're arresting your niece," said Tabora.

Aunt Tenne barged over, shoved me behind her, and put her finger in his face. "You are not. She's a United States citizen."

"I don't care if she's a citizen of Mars. I'm arresting her for breaking and entering."

"No, you're not," I said. "You think I kidnapped Andrew Thatcher."

"That's ridiculous," said Aunt Tenne. "She was here all night."

Pinto tried to dodge my aunt's large form and grab my wrist.

"That guy isn't putting handcuffs on me," I said.

"It'll be worse if you resist me," said Pinto.

"I doubt it."

"Get her, Pinto," said Tabora.

That's when it hit me. Aunt Tenne could hold them off only for so long. I was going to be arrested in a foreign country. Scenes from *Locked Up Abroad* ran through my mind. For the first time in my life, I was beyond Dad's long reach. He couldn't help me. Pinto would put handcuffs on me and I wouldn't be able to protect myself. He liked my bruises and he'd make more.

"She was here all night," said Aunt Tenne. "Mercy doesn't even know that man."

"She wanted to have sex with him," said Tabora.

"Mercy!"

"I don't know. It seemed like a good idea," I said, jumped to her other side away from Pinto's grasping hand.

"What about Pete?"

"Who's Pete?" asked Tabora.

"Her boyfriend," said Aunt Tenne.

"You have two boyfriends?"

"Yes!" I yelled as Pinto grabbed the hem of my dress and I slapped the crap out of him. "No!"

"Which is it?" asked Tabora.

"Neither."

"Mercy!" said Aunt Tenne. "I'm ashamed of you."

"Me, too," I said.

"Pinto, arrest her!" yelled Tabora.

"I'm trying to, but she won't stay still. I like that." He lunged at me and we went down on the tile.

Aunt Tenne smacked Pinto on the back of the head. "Stop that.

She didn't do it."

Tabora yanked her back. "You weren't here last night. You don't know where she was."

Aaron walked in, eating a foot-long hot dog. He chewed and watched Pinto trying to cuff me.

"Tell him, Aaron!" I yelled.

"Huh?"

"Where I was last night!"

Pinto pinned me and got one cuff on.

"Where?" asked Aaron.

"Aaron, he's arresting me in Honduras. Honduras! Tell him where I was last night. He thinks I kidnapped Andrew Thatcher."

"Oh." He took a bite and thought about it.

"Aaron!"

"She was here. I put her to bed," he said.

Tabora looked at the ceiling. "And where were you?"

Aaron chewed.

Oh, god! Please be a normal guy. Be where a normal guy would be.

"In bed with her?" he asked.

Yes!

"You aren't sure?" asked Tabora.

Aaron looked at his dog. It was more interesting than me on the floor with one handcuff and a cop on top of me.

Aunt Tenne poked him.

"We had sex like next to the trash can," said Aaron finally.

I want to die.

Aunt Tenne stared down at me. "Mercy, what is he saying?"

"I'm disgusting. It's time you knew the truth," I said. "But I don't know anything about Andrew. I would've thought Colin would be the one, if anyone."

Pinto grabbed my free wrist and inched it closer to the other cuff.

"Stop, Pinto," said Tabora.

You never saw a man so disappointed, but he did roll off, thankfully. That wasn't a banana in his pocket.

"What was that about Colin?" asked Tabora.

Aaron helped me up. I held out my wrist with the dangling cuffs to Pinto. "Key, please."

He reluctantly unlocked me but stood way too close.

"You were saying?"

I rubbed my wrist. "I overheard Colin's friends talking about him. Something about a plan and a debt. Joe wanted to pay the debt and Andrew didn't."

"Why were you eavesdropping on them?" asked Tabora.

"Right place. Right time. I thought it might have something to do with Lucia. They were pretty upset."

"What do you think now?"

"I think Colin's a raging alcoholic and he's gotten himself into a bad situation. I don't know if it has anything to do with the Carrows, but anything's possible. Colin needs money for something. Killing pays."

Tabora rubbed his chin. "There's still the matter of you breaking into their room."

"That was a mistake. You saw that place. It was a cesspool."

"And you wanted to get naked in it."

"Mercy, my god. What is wrong with you?" asked Aunt Tenne.

As nauseating as it was, I had to keep up the lie. "I was only going to get a little naked," I said. "I'm young. I'm stupid. You can't hold that against me."

Pinto jiggled his cuffs again. "I say we arrest her to be on the safe side. She did resist me."

"Every woman resists you," said Tabora. "Miss Watts, give me your passport and I won't arrest you. I can't have you leaving the island before this is resolved."

Not the ideal solution, but I got my passport and handed it over. Pinto tried to take it, but Tabora intervened. His radio crackled and a voice said something about a bloodstain.

"Stay where I can find you," he said and went out the door.

Pinto grinned and said in my ear, "Where I can find you."

Tabora yelled outside and Pinto hustled out the door. Aunt Tenne slammed it behind him and crossed her arms. "You want to tell me what's going on around here?"

Not really.

"Mercy." There was a warning in her voice.

I peeked out the curtains and watched Pinto knock on Lucia's door. She didn't answer.

"They're gone," said Aaron.

"Where are they?"

"Down at the beach."

"You took them to the beach?" I asked.

He shrugged. "They just went."

"On foot?"

"Yeah."

I flung open the door and about a dozen island cops looked up at me and snickered. I ran down the stairs and went toward the beach. Aunt Tenne was yelling my name, but I kept going. Aaron was right behind me, if I went by the huffing and puffing. The oceanside restaurant was packed. A cruise ship must've docked. I couldn't see them anywhere. My heart rate went up another notch. The last time I couldn't find them, Graeme had been poisoned. I ran to the bar and went up on my tiptoes. An arm went around my waist. Pinto. I raised my hand and a well-tanned one grabbed my hand and spun me around into a broad chest. Mauro.

"Thank god," I said.

"I'm not usually called a god, but I'll take it."

"Where's Lucia and Graeme? I have to find them."

"You're panicking."

"Not helping." I struggled in his arms. "Let go."

"They're with your mother and Dixie. They're fine." He pointed at the best table in the house, next to the railing overlooking the ocean, and then pulled me to his chest. My head ended up on his very hard pec, sexy but not comfortable. "Try to relax. Everything isn't on your shoulders."

"Oh, you think not? Andrew Thatcher is missing and I almost got arrested for it. We can't get off this island ahead of schedule and now Tabora has my passport."

"Let's hope they find Andrew," said Mauro, his chest rumbled beneath my cheek.

"They found blood," I said.

"That doesn't mean anything."

"In my world it does." I heard Mom's voice calling me. "I have to go."

"I wish you wouldn't," he said.

"I have a boyfriend."

"You and Aaron don't seem that serious."

"It's hard to explain our relationship," I said.

Aaron's voice came over my shoulder and chilled me. "We had sex last night."

Not now. Not when a super-hot guy is hugging me.

I looked over my shoulder at my so-called partner who was sweaty and holding a fresh hot dog.

"You don't have to tell him that. He's not the cops," I said.

"That's what happened." He looked pretty sure about it, too.

Mauro's chest shook. "So you want to tell me something."

The truth would be nice, but no.

I took one more breath of his coconutty scent before pushing him away. "Yes. It was a fiery night of...passion."

Aaron stuffed the rest of his hot dog in his mouth. My lover. Sexy. He swallowed so hard, it looked like it hurt, and then said, "You hungry?"

"Yes, but no crab," I said.

Aaron did an about-face and trotted into the restaurant. His cutoff acid-wash jeans slipped down and I got a flash of his hairy rear. Now the morning was perfect.

"You got a great guy there," said Mauro, grinning like Dad when he was bothering Mom senseless.

"Don't tease me. I can't take it."

"I'm not teasing you. Aaron is great. No one cooks like him."

"I'll give you that."

Linda and Frankie Gmuca came around the other side of the bar. Linda carried two tall glasses filled with orange foam. Frankie pointed to Mom's table and they headed over.

"Oh, no," I said.

"What?" asked Mauro.

I didn't answer. Linda and Frankie marched over to the table and Linda placed the glasses in front of Lucia and Graeme.

"Gotta go." I ran through the restaurant, dodging early drunks from the cruise ships and narrowly missed stepping on a toddler getting ready to stuff sand in his gullet.

Mom spotted me and her perfect, unbruised brow wrinkled. Lucia reached for the glass and Mom's eyebrows shot up, but she seemed frozen. I dashed up to their table, just as Linda and Frankie were ready to sit down. "Hey," I gasped. "What's going on?"

"We feel so good today," said Lucia, "you wouldn't believe it."

Back away from the glass.

Since Lucia couldn't read minds, she extended the straw to her pursed lips.

Noooo!

"Oh, my gosh!" said Dixie, jumping to her feet. "There's that guy who...who got bitten by a shark."

Linda and Frankie turned to look. I grabbed glasses and tossed the contents over my shoulders.

"What the fuck!" yelled a guy on the beach behind me.

Luckily, the restaurant deck was over his head and Linda and Frankie couldn't see the undoubtedly drenched tourist below when they turned back.

"What was that?" asked Frankie.

"What?" I asked.

"Somebody's yelling."

Mom turned on the charm and believe me that's saying something. I'd never known anyone to resist Mom. She smiled and batted her eyes that somehow grew two sizes. "You know those rowdy cruise ship passengers drunk at this time of the morning."

Mom's magic was working but the yelling below us was only increasing.

"Hey," said Linda. "What happened to your drinks? We had those made special."

I bet you did, you horny lunatics.

I put my hand on my chest and batted my own eyes. I admit I don't have the track record of Mom, but I've been known to get my way. "I'm so sorry. I thought those were for me."

"You drank both of them?" asked Frankie, astonished.

"I was starving. It's been a long couple of days," I said. "Those were delicious by the way. What was in those?"

An enraged howl came up from the beach. "I will freaking kill somebody, man!"

Oh, no.

"It's my special elixir," said Frankie. "I developed it after teaching fourth grade for a couple of years. Keeps you healthy."

A man covered in orange goo came stomping up the restaurant stairs, looking around like a crazed Sissy Spacek from the movie, *Carrie.*

Mom saw him, too. "Dixie, you have a pen. Can you write down that recipe for me? I have to see a man about a thing."

Dixie produced a pen from her purse and bent over her napkin with Linda and Frankie. Mom ran for my drink victim and rage melted into "There's Marilyn Monroe, running right for me." Half the restaurant had that look. The other half was too drunk to notice. Mom stopped him. She touched his shoulder and flipped back her hair. Shameless, thank goodness.

Aaron came trotting out of the kitchen, carrying a full platter. I didn't know what it was and I didn't care. I met him halfway, took him by the arm, and steered him in the direction of the drink guy.

"I don't have time to explain," I said. "Just go with it."

"Huh?"

We reached Mom and the guy, who looked worse close-up. He had a formerly white tee on that was now orange and he'd wiped the orange out of his eyes, leaving a strange kind of mask.

"Sir," I said. "We apologize for this accident."

He squinted at me. "There are two of you? What happened to your face?"

"Scooter accident." I took the platter from Aaron. "Please accept this gourmet brunch as an apology."

He took the platter from me, probably because he didn't know what else to do and Mom was purring at him. "What is it?"

"That is the famous breakfast from the Kronos Café in St. Louis. And this is Aaron the chef."

"Hey," said Aaron.

"You'll love it," said Mom. "Aaron's the best in the world."

"It does smell good, but what about my clothes? I don't go back to the ship for another five hours."

Mom dimpled at him. "We'll take care of you." She turned him around and had him back down the stairs before he knew what happened.

I put my head on Aaron's shoulder. "Dude, I owe you one."

"You owe me eleven."

"Eleven?"

"Yeah. I cracked the guy that was trying to kill you and—"

"That was a woman," I said.

"And I went to Lincoln with you on that case," said Aaron.

"That was not my idea."

"I stole Rodney's car for you."

"Never mind," I said. "I owe you eleven." If it were any other guy, I would've said, "Don't get any ideas about how I might pay you back," but Aaron's idea of payback was probably getting to feed me. I could live with that.

"You still hungry?" asked Aaron.

"Well, since I didn't eat anything, yes."

He trotted back to the kitchen and I returned to the table.

Dixie looked up from a laundry list of ingredients. "This sounds great. Mercy, do you want to go to the bar and have them made while we order?" She was pretty beady-eyed, so I took the list and went back to the bar. Mauro was still there, now talking to two girls in Brazilian bikinis. They kept turning and flashing their buns at him. Classy.

I leaned over the bar and spoke to Alex the bartender. "Did you make a couple of drinks with this stuff?"

He looked at my list. "Sure did. Weird combo but smelled good. Why?"

"Because the Gmucas were trying to give them to the Carrows."

Alex squinted at me. "There's nothing in there that could hurt them, I swear."

"Did you leave them alone with the drinks before they took them to the table?"

"Yeah. I've got other customers. These cruisers are total lushes."

I put my head on the bar. "Great."

"You don't think the Gmucas did the antifreeze thing, do you?" asked Alex.

"They had opportunity," I said.

Mauro waved goodbye to the girls and their bare bottoms and whispered in my ear, "No, they didn't."

"Since when?"

"Check out Frankie's shirt."

Frankie had on a Gumbalimba Park tee.

"So what?" I asked.

"They went yesterday and did the canopy tour and the whole deal."

"I saw them yesterday. They could've done it."

"You saw them yesterday morning, so did I. They were here for the storm, but they spent the afternoon at Gumbalimba."

"How do you know?"

"They told me," he said, bending a little closer than necessary. I liked it.

"People lie," I said. "They lie, even when they don't have to."

I should know.

"I asked Chanda in the tour office. She booked the tour and put them in a cab."

"You're sure?"

"I am."

I kissed his cheek. "Finally, somebody off the list."

"You can thank me again. Maybe at dinner tonight? That is if you and Aaron aren't exclusive."

"Aaron and I are exclusive only because he won't leave me alone." I sighed as Pete's distracted face came into my mind. "But I am exclusive with someone else."

"Let me understand. You're exclusive, but you and Aaron are still humping next to trash cans?"

"If you actually believe that, why on earth would you ever want to take me to dinner?" I asked.

"I don't know what I believe, except that you are unusual. I like that."

"You are a sick man."

"And you like that?"

"If I was allowed to like it, I would. But I'm not, so I don't. Understand?"

"No."

I started to explain, but Officer Tabora came into the restaurant. The tourists parted and gave him a clear path. At first, I thought he was coming for me. But all he did was squint at me and head for the table with Dixie and the Gmucas. I gave the list to Mauro. "Can you have these made?"

"Where are you going?"

"I've got to get a look at the crime scene. Don't let those drinks out of your sight."

I thrust the napkin at him and ran out of the restaurant. If it wasn't the Gmucas, Colin was now heading my list. I took the back way to the bungalow and passed through the parking lot. Four cops and a couple of guys that seemed like crime scene technicians, except they were wearing shorts, were getting in a van. Pinto leered at me and leaned out the window. "Be seeing you soon."

"Don't count on it," I said, turning onto the path. I managed to suppress the shiver that went up my spine. I could not get arrested by that man. It would be a very bad thing.

Now that I was out of the public areas of the resort, it was all quiet. The cruise ship passengers weren't allowed in the paying guest parts and all the cops were gone, leaving the spaghetti birds yelling in the palms and an isolated feeling that made me think of Andrew Thatcher. Whatever had happened to him was Colin's fault. And from the look of Colin last night, his friends didn't play nice.

I turned onto the back path, so I could get a look at the crime scene without being observed. I'd forgotten to get my lock picks and almost went back when I saw a foot sticking out from behind a palm. For a second, my heart seized. I thought it was Andrew, but, of course, it wasn't. Even Pinto wouldn't have missed him sitting next to his bungalow.

I went around the palm and found Joe sitting with one leg drawn up and his forehead resting on it. He had a cell phone in one hand and a napkin in the other.

"Joe? Are you okay?" I asked.

He glared at me. "What do you think?"

"I think you're having the worst week of your life."

His expression softened. "You got that right."

I sat beside him in the sand and looked at the crime scene tape wound around the bushes and blocking the back door. "Any news?"

"No."

"What did Colin say?"

"Not a damn thing. They can't find him." Joe spat the words. "Fucking typical."

"But they do think he had something to do with it?" I asked.

"Oh, he had something to do with it. He always does. If there's bullshit going down, you can count on Colin to be right in the middle of it."

"What was he into?"

"You name it? He's probably done it. You know, I didn't want him on this trip at all, but Andrew insisted. He said it was for old time sake. We were best friends in college and Andrew just couldn't let go. He said Colin will settle down and we have to stick by him. Fuck that."

We sat in silence for a moment. Sometimes there's just nothing to say, no comfort to give. Aaron appeared beside me with another platter. The smell of sausage, hash browns, and general goodness settled over us.

"How do you always know where I am?" I asked.

Aaron shrugged and put the platter in front of me. Food. Glorious food. I never imagined I'd spend half my vacation starving.

Joe glanced over. "Is that one of your creations, Aaron?"

Aaron rubbed his hands together. "I made the sausage this morning. The browns are a mixture of Yukon Gold and Idaho potatoes. The eggs are made the French way with heavy cream." He took a deep breath. "I grated the garlic and onion for the sauté and used cognac to deglaze."

Joe started looking at my platter longingly. Poor guy was having a terrible vacation. At least he could have the best food. I passed the plate to him. "And it's for you. Better eat it before it gets cold."

He tried to give it back. "Aaron made this for you."

"No, he didn't. It's for you. When's the last time you ate?" I asked.

"Last night."

"Chow down. You need your strength."

Aaron pulled a small backpack from behind him and produced a thermos full of milky coffee, silverware, and a napkin.

Joe took a bite and moaned. It hurt deep inside me.

Breakfast, I love you.

"This is the best thing I've eaten in my life. You're like a food genius. I don't know how to thank you," said Joe.

"Now that you mention it, you can thank us with information," I said.

"Like what?" He moaned again.

"Like what you know about Colin's activities, since you've been here. I assume you don't owe him any loyalty."

"Hell, no. Ask me anything."

"Did Colin try to kill Lucia and Graeme Carrow?"

Joe's head jerked up and a piece of sausage fell out of his mouth. "Are you serious?"

"I gather he's desperate for money. Killing pays," I said.

"He is desperate. Actually, Andrew and I were fighting about that. Colin gambles and I mean serious high-stakes gambling. It started in college along with the drinking and drugs. We thought he'd get over it, when we graduated. Everyone else grew up, but he didn't. It just got worse."

"He gambled here on the island?" I asked.

"Of course, he did, the idiot. These are guys you don't want to know, much less owe. They're freaking terrifying," said Joe.

"How much did he lose?"

"Thirty thousand in the first four days we were here, and who knows how much since then."

Aaron sat down. "Thirty thousand dollars?"

That was the first time I'd ever seen him surprised. Usually, he was kind of blank.

"Yep. Dollars, not pesos or whatever. Colin's got a problem, but he thinks he's cool."

"Did he have anything to do with the attempts on Lucia and Graeme?" I took the thermos and poured myself a generous amount of lovely coffee into the lid.

"I don't think so," said Joe, after he finished the sausage. "He just gets hurt himself, but…"

"But it's possible," I finished for him.

"I hate to say it, but he could've done it."

"How did you end up on this island anyway? It's not exactly Cancun."

"It was Colin's idea. I didn't know why he was so set on it, but we found out after we arrived that he already had connections." He looked away for a second and I felt the pain coming off of him in waves. "I should've said no. If anything is Colin's idea, you know it has to be bad. Maybe I'm the idiot."

"Has there been a ransom demand?" I asked.

"No, and Tabora is really worried about that." He pointed to the bungalow. "They took Andrew when he was trying to get in the back door. There's a little blood on the door and bushes. He was just coming back to get his camera during dinner."

"Why the back door?"

"The front door sticks," said Joe.

"When did that start? I saw you using the front."

"Yesterday afternoon. It was a bear to get open."

I bit my lip.

"Oh shit," said Joe. "You think someone messed with the door, so we'd have to use the back." He pushed the platter away and Aaron swiftly took it off his knees.

"I think it's probable. It's easier to nab someone in the back than the front. Tell me what happened."

"When Andrew didn't come back, Colin and I went looking for him. We called the police, but they said tourists get drunk and wander off all the time. They didn't even come over here."

"When did you find the blood?" I asked.

"This morning. I got up and Colin was gone. I walked around, looking for him and Andrew, and that's when I saw the blood on the door."

"It could be Colin's."

"I wish." He looked at me, defiant. "I really do wish it were Colin's and I don't care how that sounds."

I rubbed his shoulder and gave him the coffee. He took a swig and continued, "But it's not Colin's. There was a struggle. I was in the bungalow all night. I would've heard something. Colin took off, like the asshole he is."

"No ransom," said Aaron and we both looked at him.

Aaron looked as dim as a fifteen-watt bulb, but his words lit up an idea in my head. "They got the wrong guy."

"Wrong guy?" asked Joe. "How'd you confuse Andrew with Colin? Andrew is black, for Christ's sake."

"There's no light back here. It gets pretty dark and they're about the same height and build. We're not talking about rocket scientists here. They meant to take Colin. They already tried beating the crap out of him to get the money and that didn't work. You and Andrew wouldn't pay. I bet they were planning on ransoming him to you."

"But there's no ransom note."

"Because they've got Andrew instead and he's supposed to have the money, right? How much have you got on your own?" I asked.

"I could come up with twenty grand, if I had to."

"And that's not enough. They want the full amount, which I'm guessing is more than thirty."

"Will they kill Andrew? He didn't do anything. I'll give them what I have, the whole twenty. I wouldn't give them twenty cents for Colin at this point."

"I don't know what they'll do. *They* probably don't know what they're going to do. That's why there's no ransom demand yet."

"Andrew could get killed a week before his wedding. I can't believe this. Andrew's the best of us. He's the reason I got through college. I'll pay it. They just have to ask. But I swear, if Colin shows up, I think I'll kill him. Do you think they'll take the twenty?"

"I think they'll cut their losses," I said. "Where did you meet these creeps?"

"At a bar in Coxen Hole. I thought I was going to get tetanus just from walking in that joint and I've pulled Colin out of some pretty sleazy places."

"I want you to go there and let it be known that you want Andrew back and you're willing to pay. I'll get Spitball and Mauro to go with you."

"Shouldn't the cops handle this?"

"I don't know if Andrew has that kind of time. Let's keep it simple. We want Andrew. They want money. I assume you don't care whether they're caught or not as long as Andrew comes out alive."

"That's all that matters," said Joe.

"Then that's what we're going to do."

CHAPTER FOURTEEN

Spitball and Mauro took off with Joe five minutes after I told them what was going on. Spitball was armed like he was invading Afghanistan. I think he would've packed a harpoon, if he could've fit it into his backpack. They sped off in the resort's van, looking grim but determined. They'd tell a select few that Joe wanted Andrew back, alive, and he didn't care about anything else. Spitball knew the bar and the people in it by reputation. He agreed with me. They'd be willing to deal. Nobody wanted U.S. officials getting involved in Roatan affairs. It was better to take the money and call it good.

I watched them drive away and squeezed the key in my hand. Joe had given me his front door key, so I could check out the lock. Aaron trotted along beside me as I went through the resort. My stomach was growling so loud, I could barely hear the spaghetti birds, but I couldn't ask Aaron to make a third breakfast for me. That was just ridiculous.

The area around Joe's bungalow was clear, so we went right up and unlocked the door. I expected the lock to grind or perhaps for the key not to go all the way in, like someone had done the old superglue technique, but the lock was fine. The doorknob wasn't. I could barely turn it. Aaron yanked the door and it took so much effort that he got red-faced and sweaty.

I sniffed. "What is that smell? Have you been eating lionfish again?"

"Hot dog."

I sniffed again. "Please don't tell me those were lionfish hot dogs."

"I invented them. The trick is to combine lionfish with chicken to get the right texture."

"I'm sorry I asked." I squatted and looked at the latch. There were faint traces of blue on the metal. "I need a screwdriver."

Aaron gave me a butter knife, because of course he would have one on him at all times. I unscrewed the faceplate and took it off. Inside the latch assembly was more blue stuff. It was stiff and tacky and reminded me of plumber's putty. I'd never seen blue putty, though, and Dad had about six different kinds. At some point he'd gotten the idea that I should be able to do simple plumbing repairs. I thought I should find a hot plumber instead, but Dad insisted on teaching me how to do stuff I never actually intended to do.

I sniffed and, although it was hard to detect over Aaron's fishdog stink, it did smell like putty. Someone had messed with Joe's door. It wasn't a crime of opportunity. They planned it, but not well enough to get the right guy.

"You're just asking to get arrested, you know that?" Tabora came up beside me and squatted.

"I have a key and Joe's permission. You can call him," I said.

"He's not here?" It wasn't really a question. Tabora wasn't surprised.

"Not at the moment."

"He's going to pay the kidnappers, isn't he?"

"How should I know?" I asked.

"Because you're calling the shots. I looked you up. Your father's famous in the law enforcement community."

"He is. I'm not."

Tabora peered in the latch assembly. "What have you got there?"

I broke down and told him my theory about the putty. He stood and leaned on the doorframe. "Where's Joe?"

"That depends on what you're going to do," I said.

"I'm supposed to catch the perpetrators and charge them with multiple crimes."

"But..."

"I'd like Mr. Thatcher to live and get off this island."

I leaned on the doorframe and sized the cop up. He seemed sincere and local law enforcement wouldn't want an international incident anymore than the local hoods. An American man kidnapped and murdered a week before his wedding would garner some serious interest. "Joe's in a bar, letting his intentions be known," I said.

"What about the money?" asked Tabora

"What about it? Joe says he can get it."

"He could in the States. This is Roatan. Nothing moves quickly."

I screwed the faceplate back on. "What do you suggest?"

"I might be able to get access to some lempira. Joe will have to pay it back. Call me when they contact him," said Tabora.

I stood up and stepped inside, wrinkling my nose at the smell. "I will."

"What do you expect to find in there?" he asked.

"Maybe something to do with Lucia and Graeme. It doesn't hurt to check again," I said.

Tabora smiled. "I knew you weren't in there to seduce Thatcher."

"What gave me away?"

He put a gentle hand on my shoulder. "Your eyes. There wasn't an ounce of truth in that statement."

I couldn't resist. "You bought the trash can thing."

Officer Tabora laughed. "Not even for a moment, but we didn't have enough to hold you anyway."

"So I was humiliated for nothing."

"My companions believed every word, if that makes you feel better."

"It doesn't," I said.

He paused and became thoughtful. "Miss Watts, are you planning on being with Joe at the exchange?"

"If it's possible, I'll be there."

Tabora nodded and walked away with his shoulders hunched. Aaron and I went inside and the situation had not improved. I should've brought gloves. Going through pockets and reaching under beds without them wasn't the best idea.

We went through the room, every pocket and every drawer. Nothing that pertained to Lucia or Graeme. The burnt paper was gone out of the trash can. I guessed that Colin had flushed it. Probably lists of his markers. As if flushing them would erase his debt.

"That it?" asked Aaron.

I nodded and we left, locking the door.

"Mercy, what are you doing?" Mom was on the path with her hands on her hips.

"Uh...nothing," I said.

"Nothing. You just broke into a kidnap victim's room."

"I have a key." I held it up to prove it.

"You have a key? That's great. Just because someone lets you in, doesn't mean you have to go," said Mom.

It kinda does.

Mom's voice went up. "Are you listening to me?"

No, not really. When do I ever?

"Yes, Mom. I'm listening."

"You can't get involved with that kidnapping. It's bad enough that you got involved with the Carrows' problem."

"I thought you liked them," I said.

"I do," said Mom.

"Then what's your point? You want me to let Lucia get killed, so I won't mess up our vacation?"

"Don't be ridiculous. I want you to stop looking for trouble."

"Trouble comes to me. Giftwrapped," I said.

"Well, don't open the package. I've had enough of this with your father. You're supposed to be a girl."

"There are girl detectives, you know."

"But you're not one. You need to remember that," said Mom.

I crossed my arms. "Then stop making me work for Dad, if you don't like it."

That stumped her, a feat I'd never before accomplished. She couldn't have it both ways. I don't think she'd ever thought she couldn't have exactly what she wanted. I had to admit her track record said she could.

"We'll talk about this later," said Mom.

"If later means never, I'm totally for that," I said.

"It means later. Come on. You have to talk to your aunt. She's serious about this gardener."

Now she's my aunt.

Mom took my arm and I gave a pleading look to Aaron, who was polishing his butter knife on his shirt. Hopeless.

"Just let it go, Mom," I said. "He's a nice guy."

"You don't know the whole situation."

"Because no one will tell me."

"That's beside the point," she said.

"Not to me. And I'm not going to talk to Aunt Tenne about this. She can do what she wants."

"She doesn't know what she wants. I'm her sister. I always take care of her."

I walked off toward the restaurant with Aaron trotting behind me.

Mom yelled after me. "I made some calls!"

I halted and Aaron ran into me with an oomph. "What calls?"

"I know people. Your father knows people."

"Tell me you didn't have Bruno put on the terrorist watchlist."

"Not yet. Talk to Tenne. She'll listen to you. She thinks you walk on water," said Mom.

"No!" I yelled. "I will not!"

"Yes, you will!"

"Then tell me why!" I yelled so loud; my throat felt like it'd been strip-mined.

"I can't!" Mom yelled back.

"Fine! Stay right there." I stomped up the stairs to my room, flung open the door so that the glass rattled, and grabbed my lock picks. I went back down and took Mom's arm.

"Where are we going?" she said, while trying to wiggle out of my grip.

"To see why you should leave Bruno and Aunt Tenne alone."

"There's nothing on earth that could convince me of that."

"Don't count on it."

I dragged Mom through a maze of paths and promptly got lost. Aaron took over and we arrived at Bruno's door in five minutes, instead of the twenty it would've taken me. I knocked on the door. No answer, so I opened my lock pick case.

"No, no, no," said Mom. "This is breaking and entering. We are not doing this."

"Why'd you let Dad give me this kit then, if I'm never supposed to use it?" I asked.

"I...I..."

Score!

"This will only take a second and then I want you to back off Bruno, okay?"

"Fat chance."

I stuck my picks in the lock and listened for the click, which came faster than I expected. I turned the doorknob. "You know, Mom, I've never understood that phrase. Fat chance means the chance is big, right? So in this case it's accurate."

Mom crossed her arms. "I'm not going in there."

"Aaron," I said.

He poked Mom in the back with his butter knife. She yelped and turned on him. "You think I should go in there?"

"You'll listen to Aaron and not me?" I asked.

"Aaron is sensible."

"How can you tell?"

We looked at my partner, who was now picking his teeth with the butter knife. Sensible was not the word I'd use.

"Go in," he said with the knife still in his mouth.

"Alright. Then I will." Mom flounced in and I waited outside.

"Why does my mother like you so much?" I asked Aaron.

He kept on picking his teeth and shrugged. "Everybody does."

I considered the statement and it was true. I'd never met anyone who didn't like Aaron. He was like a panda, fat and odd-shaped, but nevertheless irresistible to the general population. I've never been a panda person, though. I didn't get it.

Mom stepped out of Bruno's room, white-faced and silent.

Oh, crap! Has Bruno slashed the paintings or put blood on them or something?

I squeezed past her and peeked in the room. The paintings were intact and there were a few more. Bruno had moved on to yet another technique. Chiaroscuro, if memory served. Aunt Tenne was painted as the Madonna, nude from the waist up, and so beautifully done in light and shadow it made me a bit breathless. Rembrandt would've been jealous. I left the room reluctantly and relocked the door.

"So what do you say now?" I asked.

Mom gazed at me with big green eyes filled with tears. "He's a genius."

"He is, but even if he only loved Aunt Tenne that would be enough. Call off the dogs. If she's making a mistake, so be it. She's been sad my whole life. Bruno makes her happy. Who cares if it doesn't last? At least she'll be happy for awhile. That's better than nothing."

"I'm worried about the fall," said Mom. "She can't handle it."

"We don't know what will happen, but I do know something should happen. She's been alone too long."

Mom hooked her arm through mine and we walked back to the restaurant. Dixie and the Carrows still sat at their table, laughing. The Gmucas were at the bar, probably ordering more drinks for me to throw on cruise ship passengers.

"There you are," said Dixie. "We were just talking about taking a glass-bottomed boat tour. What do you think?"

I looked over at Lucia and Graeme. Their color was good and they'd both eaten. "How do you feel?"

"Great," said Lucia. "This whole thing has been weighing on me. I'm so glad it's over."

"Over? Since when is it over?"

"We heard that the cops are looking for that Colin character."

"I never liked him," said Graeme. "He always looked stoned. The cops think he's the reason Andrew was kidnapped. Didn't you know that?"

"I did, but that doesn't mean he tried to kill you and Lucia."

"Who else could it be? Nobody else was there every time something happened," said Lucia.

Aaron ran off to the bar and I sat down, feeling tired again. Lucia had a point. No one else was around at all the incidents. He was diving with us during both scuba incidents and I'd seen him in the vicinity during both poisonings. Colin as a hitman. It was a little weird, but what wasn't in the world of crime?

"Colin is the suspect at the moment," I said.

"But you're not convinced," said Graeme, his fingers drumming the table.

"Not yet. We have zero evidence."

"We have motive," said Dixie. "He has gambling debts."

"That's true," I said. "It's probably him. Dad always says that crime is crazy, but it has a certain logic to it."

Dixie smiled. "If it looks like a duck, it ain't a freaking camel."

Mom burst into laughter and we joined her, causing half the restaurant patrons to stare in our direction.

Dixie dabbed her eyes with a napkin. "That was something my husband, Gavin, used to say."

Mom and I waited for her to start weeping, but she didn't. Her dark eyes were sad, but there was a remembered happiness in there, too.

"But it might be a goose," I said. "That's how my dad always finished Gavin's saying."

"I'm not sure what that means," said Lucia.

"It means that most murders are exactly what they look like. If it looks gang-related, it probably is, but it might not be the gang you originally suspect," I said.

"There are outliers," said Mom. "Thrill killers, for instance."

"You think a thrill killer was after us?" asked Graeme.

"Not for a minute," I said. "I think it's money."

"So Colin fits," said Lucia.

"He does, but we'll have to see when Tabora finds him."

"If he finds him," said Mom. "This island isn't exactly easy to search."

"As long as they find Andrew, I don't care," said Dixie. "So what about that tour?"

"I'm going to lay on the beach," I said.

"We're up for it," said Graeme.

I stood up. "I'd rather keep you in bed, but if you think you're up to it, I just need to do a wound check."

Lucia sucked in her lips and gave me the big eyes.

"What did you do?" I asked.

"I sort of took the packing out."

"Why in the world?"

"It was itchy."

I rolled my eyes. "I still have to check it."

"No more packing. It feels so weird."

"Are you going to be difficult?"

Graeme stood up and laughed. "Probably, but let's get a move on."

Lucia and Graeme led the way back to their bungalow. He seemed completely normal and she wasn't limping hardly at all. Mom and Dixie said they had to change and split off from us when we got there. Their bungalow was so clean, it was a relief after Joe's disgustarama room. Lucia laid down and unwrapped her bandage. There wasn't any pus, only good white granulation, a sign that healing was well under way.

"So?" asked Lucia.

"Alright. I give in. You're looking very good, so I won't pack it again. You have to keep it dry, though, and don't overdo it," I said as I rewrapped her thigh.

Lucia touched my hand. "Have you talked to my brother lately?"

"Nope. My phone died a watery death. Have you?"

"Only every day. I'm still not ready to tell him about the diabetes. Please keep it to yourself when you see him after we get back."

"Maybe I won't see him," I said.

It was Lucia's turn to roll her eyes. "Haven't you learned anything about our family yet? You will definitely see Oz. There's no way you can avoid it."

"So have you told him about the stabbing and poison?"

"Not yet. I'll tell him after Colin is charged," she said.

"Sounds reasonable," I said. "Just between the three of us, assuming Colin is charged, will he make it to trial?"

Lucia sighed. "I doubt it. And I won't have any say in that decision. Aunt Calpurnia won't ask me my opinion."

"So she really runs the whole deal."

"Just between us, yes. She'd like you."

"She'd scare the crap out of me," I said.

"I doubt it," said Graeme. "You don't appear to scare easily."

I nodded, but I wasn't sure I agreed. What was scared anyway, if it didn't have an effect? I'd been afraid for my life plenty of times. There were other times I should've been terrified, but I was too stupid to know it. Either way it didn't seem to make much difference to me. I didn't have an off switch. I just kept going, whether it made sense or not. I didn't want to meet Lucia's Aunt Calpurnia, though. It just wouldn't be healthy.

I left after giving them a lecture on hydration and resting. Lucia and Graeme nodded, but they were listening to me about as much as I listened to Mom. I opened their door and found Aaron standing there, holding an extra-large glass.

"What have you got?" I asked.

"A synthehol smoothie. I invented it."

"Imagine that. What's synthehol?"

"Synthetic alcohol that doesn't get you drunk."

"So this is a fake drink?"

"No, it's real."

I took the drink. "You are so weird."

"Don't give it away."

"I won't." I sucked down half of Aaron's latest creation and went to change into my swimsuit. I found my remaining one-piece hung on the back of my bedroom door and it too had the seams ripping out. Was someone trying to tell me something? I wasn't too big for that suit, was I? I drank the rest of my smoothie and felt pretty good, despite the fact that I was busting out of my seams. How much alcohol was in that thing?

"Aaron!" I didn't let him in, but if he wasn't there, I would've been shocked.

"Yeah!"

"I thought so. What was in that smoothie?"

He listed about twenty ingredients, including macerated blackberries, but only a shot of chocolate liquor. "You hungry?"

"Not anymore." I found Chuck's gift bag still stuffed in my suitcase and pulled out the teeny bikini.

Groan.

It fit like latex and I've never felt so obvious in my life. Then there was another obvious thing in the room. An idea that had never before occurred to me and I felt kind of stupid even thinking it, but once that thought got in there, I just had to ask.

I peeked around my door to find Aaron standing there with, you guessed it, another fishdog. Gross. "Aaron, why do you follow me around?"

"Tommy told me to."

"Is that the only reason?" *This is so stupid.* "You're not like in love with me or something, right?" I asked, wincing.

"Huh?"

Sigh of relief. Aaron in love was too bizarre to be seriously contemplated.

Wait a minute.

"Aaron, is there another reason you follow me around? I mean, a reason besides Dad."

"Yeah."

I waited and predictably nothing happened. "Okay. What is it?"

"Chuck."

"What about him?"

"You won't let him follow you, so I gotta do it."

I ducked back in my room and put on my cover-up, which looked like used Kleenex. So Chuck wanted me stalked. Why did everyone think I was so incompetent? I hadn't gotten killed yet. I hadn't even gotten that close, only within say three hairsbreadths. Not too bad. I came out and Aaron followed me to the beach, right on my heels as usual.

"When did Chuck tell you to follow me?" I asked over my shoulder.

"He didn't."

I spun around and waited for Aaron to stuff the rest of his dog down his gullet. "So why are you following me for Chuck, if he didn't ask you to?"

"He wants me to."

"How do you know?"

"I know."

Okay. That's about as clear as chocolate ganache.

Hmmm. Ganache.

I found the perfect spot on the beach and ordered a Monkey Lala. Bruno was raking the sand in front of The Aviary and I suffered a wave of guilt. It didn't happen very often, guilt, but something about Bruno made me feel worse than the time I stole Dad's car, drove it around with fifteen friends stuffed in it like a clown car. They were drinking White Russians and guess what got spilled? The smell was unbelievable. Dad still couldn't talk about that without veins popping out on his forehead.

Confession is good for the soul or so they say. I'd never found that to be true, especially after being grounded for three months, but I thought I'd give it another go. I handed Aaron my drink and squared my shoulders. Aaron started to get up.

"Don't follow me," I said. "I can handle this alone."

Bruno spotted me at ten paces and leaned on his rake. I bit my lip and tried to look more regretful than I felt. I did feel guilty, but I wasn't sorry. Now that was a familiar situation for me.

"Bruno, I have to tell you something," I said.

"Yes."

"I broke into your room."

"Yes."

"You're not surprised?"

"No." His face was as impassive as Aaron's usually was.

"Why not? How often do people break into your room?"

"Never."

Usually when I made that sort of confession there was a lot of yelling. I didn't know what to do with the quiet, but the guilt was definitely worse.

"Do you want to know why I did it?"

"It doesn't matter. You invaded my privacy."

Oh, yeah. Privacy. I had so little of it, I forgot that other people did.

"My mother was going to put you on the terrorist watchlist to keep you out of the U.S."

His eyes widened just a smidge. He was surprised. Thank goodness.

"She's crazy. She would've done it. I had to show her your work. It was the only way."

"My work is private," he said.

"It still is," I said. "It's only Mom and she's not that bad."

"You said she's crazy."

"Well, there's that, but she'll back off and leave you alone."

As much as she leaves anyone alone. Cringe.

Bruno went back to raking. I was not forgiven and it sucked. I settled back on my chair with itchy guilt weighing on me and with it unreasonable anger. I guess I could've let Mom go all Mama Bear on him. Is that what he wanted? Dixie came down and told me they were taking off for their tour and I watched Lucia and Graeme get into a water taxi with Mom and Dixie. At least that felt good. They were okay. It was our second to last day and we were almost in the clear.

I woke up with a fresh sunburn an hour later with three guys standing over me. I squinted at them.

"Haven't you heard about sunscreen?" asked Mauro.

"The only sunscreen that works for me is called a tent. What happened? Did you talk to the right people?"

Spitball laughed and scratched the grey stubble on his chin. "I wouldn't call them right, but we put the word out."

"We bought a disposable cell phone. That's the number we gave," said Mauro.

Joe sat on the edge of my lounger and put his hands over his eyes. "What if it doesn't work?"

"It'll work," I said. "Most kidnap-for-ransom victims are released when the ransom is paid."

"How long before they call?"

"I'd give it a couple of hours. They have to get the message, think it over, and come up with a plan."

Aaron jumped up and ran up the stairs to the restaurant.

"What's wrong with him?" asked Mauro.

"He probably thinks you're hungry," I said.

"He's right. What do you think he'll make?" asked Spitball.

"There's no telling, but it'll be just what you need."

"You're lucky to have him."

"So I've been told." I rubbed Joe's back. "Have you called Andrew's family?"

"No." He got choked up and his voice came out in a tight rasp, "They can't do anything. It'd be like torture."

"Damn straight," said Spitball. "We get him back first, then tell them."

"I agree," I said. "My cousin Chuck's trying to get down here to help. He couldn't get a direct flight. Last I heard he was in Venezuela."

"Your cousin flew all the way to Venezuela?"

"Last time we talked he was getting on a flight to Nicaragua. He's busing from there."

"You got quite a family," said Spitball, checking his oversized dive watch. "We got a crew going to Mary's Hole in fifteen. Be back in a couple of hours. The shop can get us if you need."

Mauro gave Joe a cheap cell phone and they went down the beach to *La Isla Bonita Two*, bobbing around in the water, and talked to Alex the captain. Joe hunched over the phone and stared at the blank screen. I patted him. "Take Aaron's seat. He won't mind. I won't tell you to relax, since it's not possible."

"No kidding." He continued to stare at the phone. "Does your dad handle a lot of kidnappings?"

"Hardly ever."

He glanced up. "I saw on the news that two thousand kids get abducted a day."

"They do, but those are mostly custody disputes. I meant situations like this. There aren't many kidnap-for-ransom cases in the States. Dad only handled one that I know of."

Joe moved onto Aaron's chair. Every muscle in his body was tense and he gripped the phone like it was his only oxygen line. We watched the waves come in and out. I managed to turn off my brain by reviewing procedures like stitching and wound care. I found such details distracting. Joe couldn't calm himself until Aaron came back. He carried a large serving tray laden with multiple dishes and laid it on the small table between our chairs.

"You ready?" he asked, rubbing his hands together.

Joe didn't answer. He stared out at the ocean, gripping his phone.

"We are," I said. "What did you make?"

"Mac and cheese with cheddar, gruyère, and parm. The second dish is spätzle with cabbage, onion, and bacon. Where's Spitball and Mauro?"

"They had a dive."

He humphed but laid a crisp napkin in Joe's lap.

"I don't know if I can eat," said Joe.

"One taste and you won't have any problem," I said.

Aaron gave him a ramekin of mac and cheese and he took a tentative bite. "Wow."

I took a generous bowl of spätzle. Just what my swimsuit-splitting body needed. "Thanks, Aaron. Is that mustard in the spätzle?"

"Country dijon. I made it myself."

"You're a freak."

"You want dessert?"

"If I want to go home in a cargo plane," I said, poking my pudgy thigh.

"Huh?"

"Not right now."

Aaron ran off. Probably to make dessert anyway. Joe finished his mac and cheese and then polished off two bowls of spätzle. "What does he put in there? Crack?"

"I'm guessing valium. Feel better?" I asked.

He slurped down the last noodle and said, "I'm still freaked, but I do feel better. Spitball's right. You're lucky to have him."

We both leaned back, watching Todd and Tracy's kids smack the crap out of each other on the diving platform. The other kids slid into the water and swam away. There seemed to be a ten-foot radius around those kids at all times. Todd and Tracy were snoozing on the sand and didn't notice. Even if they were awake, I doubt they would've cared.

"Those kids make me want to get a vasectomy," said Joe.

"They are repulsive," I said.

Joe leaned back and closed his eyes. Aaron's food was working its magic. With the aid of butter and bacon fat, I turned my mind off and went to sleep. A couple of hours later, the phone rang, and every cell in my body went hot. Joe sat up bleary-eyed and stared at the cell phone in his lap but didn't touch it.

"Answer before they hang up," I said.

He tried to give me the phone, but I pushed it away. "They're expecting you."

Joe licked his lips and pushed the answer button. "Hello." He went silent and then said, "I want some proof that you really have him." He paused and then his eyes teared up. "We'll be there." And he hung up.

"Well?" I said. "Do they have him?"

"Yeah, they do."

"Did you hear Andrew speak?"

"He said, 'Hey, onion butt'."

"Onion butt?"

"My nickname in college," said Joe.

"How did he sound?"

"In pain and scared shitless."

"What's the plan?" I asked.

"We meet tonight at the dive buoy in Half Moon Bay. They want the money in a waterproof bag attached to a float. They'll put an address with Andrew's location in another waterproof bag with a float. We drop at the same time."

"What time?"

"Seven thirty."

"We have an hour and a half. Can I have that phone?" I called Tabora and told him the plan. He'd gotten the money, proceeds from a drug buy the Coast Guard had interrupted. He couldn't resist telling me how he took it out of the property room in his daughter's back-pack. If I didn't know better, I'd have thought Tabora was having fun. I could hear the squealing tires as he drove toward La Isla Bonita and hung up so he wouldn't die on the way.

Joe gathered his towel and water bottle. "Tell me again how this is going to work."

I gave him the phone and said, "It will work because most ransom victims are returned alive. Think of it as a business. If they kill an American, there will be some serious outrage and attention on the island. They don't want that. They want money."

"But some don't come back."

"That's true, but I'm not worried."

Liar, liar, pants on fire.

Joe blew out a breath and then sucked another one in quick. "You're going on the boat, right? You're the only one with experience."

"I have experience with criminals, not with kidnappings, but yes I'll be there."

"Good. Let's go find Mauro and Spitball."

The two dive masters were cleaning equipment and closing up for the night. Joe told them the plan and Spitball got a float he wouldn't mind losing. Tabora showed up with two other cops armed to the teeth. Pinto wasn't one of them, so I was happy. Spitball packed the money into double Ziplock bags and then put them inside a large neon yellow float bag. Aaron showed up with caramel volcano cakes and we ate while we waited. I'd never seen time go so slowly.

Thirty minutes to go and one of the office ladies came into the dive shop. "Miss Watts, your mother is waiting in the restaurant."

I found Mom sitting at her favorite table, holding court over Lucia, Graeme, Dixie, and, most surprisingly, Aunt Tenne and Bruno.

"What's going on?" I asked, not standing too close in case it wasn't going as well as it looked.

"It's our second to last night and we're having a celebratory dinner," said Mom. "Sit down."

"I can't. I've got to do something."

Her eyes narrowed. "No, you don't. Sit."

Behind Mom, Mauro and the others walked onto the beach and began loading tanks and BCDs onto *La Isla Bonita Two* as a cover for our operation. If you looked closely, you could see the weaponry concealed inside the officers' fishing vests.

"I'm going diving," I said. "With Aaron."

Mom relaxed. "Aaron's going?"

"Yes, Mother. My keeper is going."

"We'll see you later then," said Dixie.

I turned to go, but stopped to ask, "What are we celebrating?"

Mom beamed. "Bruno's returning to the States with us."

Dixie shrugged her shoulders at me and seemed bewildered by the turn of events. Good. Mom must not have told her about Bruno's work. At least he could have a tiny bit of privacy, not that I thought it would last. Aunt Tenne kissed Bruno's cheek and he responded with pleasure. Sure it was quick, just a flash really. He did a tiny lean toward her and smiled slightly. It was the right kind of smile, symmetrical and crinkled around the eyes. Any worry I had about Bruno disappeared.

"I'm glad to hear that," I said. "Welcome to the crazy, Bruno. I wish you luck."

"Mercy!" said Mom.

I cackled and ran down to the beach. It wasn't completely dark but close. Only a sliver of sun was above the horizon, leaving shimmers of orange on the water. Spitball met me beside the boat. His eyes darted around and he was practically vibrating with excitement. He was happier than a pig in shit as Grandma George would say.

"Remind you of the old days?" I asked.

"Hell, yeah. Lock and load, girl." He moved aside and I climbed on board. Alex sat at the rudder. Mauro and Joe sat midship in front of two tanks each with BCDs tucked under the benches. It looked like we were going for a night dive until Tabora and his guys got onboard in civilian clothes and broad-brimmed hats pulled low.

"Very stealthy," I said.

"This is an authorized operation, but no one needs to see the weaponry. " He pointed to the darkening ocean. "When we're out there no one will be able to see who I am."

That wasn't comforting. It reminded me of the tagline from *Alien*: "In space, no one can hear you scream." I gave myself the shivers with that thought.

Mauro patted the seat beside him and Alex started the engine.

"What's wrong?" asked Joe. Aaron's food had clearly worn off and his muscles were taut.

"Nothing. Just thinking about the ocean," I said.

"Don't," said Mauro. "The vastness will overwhelm you."

"Have you ever lost anyone?"

"Never."

It was all I could do not to lean into him and try to soak up some of that experience. "But things happen in the water."

"Rarely, but when it does it's usually due to panic or bad decision-making. A couple of kayakers disappeared because they went out when a storm was coming in and didn't stay close to the shoreline. It happens."

"There's no storm tonight," said Joe.

"No," said Tabora, sitting next to him. "It's clear. We'll make the exchange quietly, and I'll radio shore. I have a team ready to retrieve Mr. Thatcher."

"Where's Pinto?" I asked.

"As far from this as possible."

We all waited, but Tabora didn't elaborate. Aaron climbed onboard, chewing a huge wad of Bubble Yum and wearing the world's oldest and shortest swim trunks. Luckily, he was wearing a Batman tee. Aaron without a shirt was a scarier thought than the ocean at night. Spitball climbed aboard and Alex eased out into open water. We zipped over the darkening water through the low-speed channel and into the open ocean. The sun made a last blaze across the water and dipped out of sight, leaving us in increasing darkness.

CHAPTER FIFTEEN

Alex cut the engine and we drifted to a stop. Mauro flipped a switch and a small floodlight jutted a yellow beam out into the darkness like a sword. We sat in silence, listening to the marker buoy bump against the hull. Spitball pulled out the float bag with money and sat it in the middle of the boat and we all stared at it.

"Listen," said Spitball.

We held our breath. There was a hum in the distance, faint at first but growing louder fast.

"There they are," said Mauro. He went to the prow and shut off the floodlight. I gasped at the sudden darkness. Spitball fired up a hand-held floodlight and pointed it down between the dive markers. The other boat cut its engine and for a moment there was only the sound of waves slapping against hulls. They cut their lead flood, too, and then a handheld swept the water. I could only make out the faint outline of the boat. It was about the same size as ours, but without the canopy.

Joe stood up, his legs shaking. Spitball heaved the float bag into his arms. Joe turned in the direction of the other boat and yelled, "Andrew Thatcher!"

"Tabora, stand up!" yelled a man from the other boat.

Tabora's shoulders twitched, but he stood up and faced the other boat. I expected gunfire or accusations of treachery, but nothing happened.

"We have the money!" yelled Joe.

"Throw it in!"

Joe kneeled on the bench seat and shoved the bag over. It hit the water with a big splash. Spitball got out a long hook and pushed the bag away from our boat. There was another splash, this time much smaller. A pole pushed a small orange square through the water.

Mauro grabbed my arm. "Do you hear that?"

"What?" I whispered.

Spitball looked back at us and mouthed, "Shit."

Then I heard it. Another boat coming in hard behind us, a big cruiser with multiple floods.

"Pull it back!" yelled someone from the other boat.

"No!" yelled Joe. "They're not with us."

There was a loud squeal from a bullhorn and someone yelled, "Stop where you are!"

I yelled at Tabora, "I thought this was authorized!"

"It is!" he yelled back.

The kidnappers fired up their motor, their hook pulling the orange box back toward outstretched hands. Spitball kept pushing the money bag toward them.

"Get it! Get it!" they yelled. But they weren't reaching for the money, only their own drop.

Andrew's life was in that box. Another foot and it would be gone. Tabora was screaming at the cruiser. Spitball was screaming for the kidnappers to take the money. I pushed Joe out of the way, scrambled up onto the side of the boat, and dove in. My body sliced into the warm Caribbean water. I swam underwater toward the box and then my head broke the surface. Screaming all around. Gunfire behind me. I swam with everything I had toward that small orange square. Hands reached for it. I stretched out and batted it away under the water. A man fell overboard, his mouth open in a scream, his throat exploding into a blossom of blood. He hit me and I went under. A hand had me by my cover-up, dragging me deep into the blackness. I bit it and the hand released.

On the surface, I saw the square and another body in the water. I grabbed the square.

Mauro screamed, "They're going to ram us!"

"Go, Alex!" yelled Spitball.

More gunfire. The hook struck the water, narrowly missing my shoulder. Aaron was on the edge of our boat. He saw me.

"No!" I screamed.

He jumped. The little freak jumped. I swam to the left, my lungs burning.

Our boat rocketed forward and the cruiser kept going. The kidnappers on the other boat were screaming, but they didn't get out of the way. The cruiser hit them dead middle, splitting the little boat in half with a tremendous crash. Bodies flew into the water, wood and metal flew everywhere like deadly fireworks.

"Get the money!" someone yelled from the cruiser.

"Aaron!" I screamed, but he didn't answer.

Oh my god. I got my partner killed.

"Aaron!"

Floodlights from the cruiser swept the water. Who the hell were they? They weren't ours and sure as hell weren't the drug dealers' friends.

"Find her!"

Pinto. He was in the cruiser. My chest hurt so bad I thought my heart seized.

"I heard her! She's here in the water!"

I went under as a floodlight came close and then I bobbed back up again. I couldn't think what to do. Maybe the cruiser didn't kill Aaron. Maybe he was only hurt. I couldn't leave him, but Pinto was looking for me. I clutched the packet to my chest in a total panic. What did Mauro say about panic? I didn't know. I was panicking. There was a gasp behind me as someone surfaced.

Please don't let it be a crazy freak.

"Hey."

It was a crazy freak.

"Aaron," I said. "Are you hurt?"

"No." He sounded surprised at the suggestion.

"Why did you jump in?"

"Cause you did. I think they want to kill us."

"You think?"

More floodlights switched on and there was another hail of gunfire. More screaming.

"Mauro's gone," said Aaron.

"Swim to shore. Now."

"It's a long way."

"You got a better idea?"

Aaron started swimming just the way you'd expect. He did the dog paddle. I did the sidestroke, but I wasn't doing much better than Aaron. My cover-up was weighing me down. As soon as we got out of the range of Pinto's floodlights, I ripped it off, held the packet in my teeth, and swam. The shore seemed so far away and I was tiring. Aaron passed me. I couldn't believe it. That Yoo-Hoo swilling, hot-dog-munching doughboy actually passed me. That was it. No more Monkey Lalas. More jogging. Okay. So I'd never jogged before, but I intended to start as soon as I survived.

An island version of the song "Time After Time" drifted across the water and I stopped to focus on the shore. A resort twice the size of La Isla Bonita had come into view. The place was lit up so much that it glowed and accentuated the darkness that surrounded us. It wasn't so much the darkness around me as the darkness below me that got my heart pounding again.

Aaron kept dog paddling toward the shore in that slow steady way of his. It probably never occurred to him that the world below his belly was hungry. I started again, less tired and more determined. The box in my mouth made me drool from having it open for so long. I probably looked like I had rabies, but I couldn't drop it. I'd had my doubts about whether or not the drug dealers would hold up their end of the bargain, but they'd tried in the face of disaster to get the box back. Andrew's whereabouts were in there and he was counting on us.

It took at least another half hour before my feet touched sand. The party was in full swing at the resort. No one noticed two swimmers coming out of nowhere. We glided into the glow of the resort and I stood up, gasping and clutching the box. I struggled over a small dune and wiped stinging sea water out of my eyes. At that point the guests had noticed us. Every occupant of every table on the wide veranda was staring down. I walked up to the steps and braced myself on the handrail.

A man I took for a manager came down, frowned, and said, "I'm sorry. I can't admit you. We have a dress code."

I sucked in a breath. "Call the police."

"Excuse me?"

"Call the police. There's been…" I paused. What should I say? I wasn't sure exactly what happened. "There's been an accident."

"What kind of accident?" He was looking at my chest when he asked.

I stuck my face in his. "The kind where people get shot. Call the damn police!"

He jumped back startled and a couple of tourists rushed down the stairs. "Can we help you?" asked the woman, a blond my mother's age.

"I need a ride," I said.

Aaron collapsed on the stairs and raised a hand like he was in third grade.

"What?" I asked.

He gurgled something.

"Fine. *We* need a ride. Do you have a rental by any chance?"

The man stared. "Yes. Why?"

"Have you heard about the kidnapping at La Isla Bonita resort?"

"Of course." The woman took a towel and wrapped it around my shoulders.

I held up the box. "The victim's location is in this box. I have to get to him. The ransom exchange was botched. They didn't get the money."

"Oh my god."

"We can't get involved with that," said the man and he certainly didn't resemble any white knight I'd ever known with a beer belly and a sneer of distaste.

"Look. Andrew could be dying. If you ever thought you could be a hero, be one now. You can save him."

"Fucking A!" yelled a voice beyond the railing of the restaurant. A young man with floppy brown hair and dimples jutted into view and grinned. "Let's do it!"

I hauled Aaron to his feet and dragged him up the stairs into a restaurant that could've been in Manhattan, it was so formal. The young man stood up next to a table chock full of family. Only family can look that disapproving.

"Timmy!" said a woman in starched white. "You're not going anywhere with this woman."

"Timothy, Mother, Timothy. I sure as hell am. This vacation is about to get fun and I'm not going to miss it."

"We're having fun!" yelled his mother.

"I played canasta today, Mom. I was thinking about setting my hair on fire, just to make sure I was alive." Timothy snatched car keys off the table, grabbed my hand, and led me away from his shouting parents and grandparents. We ran through the resort with no sand walkways with Aaron huffing along behind us. Timothy found a red Toyota Camry and opened it.

"You're for real, right?" he asked me.

"I'm for real. Do you have a GPS system?"

"Sure do."

I got in, soaking the leather seats. Aaron got in the back. "You hungry?"

"No!"

"I'm starving."

"Of course, you are." I peeled off the plastic on the square and popped it open. Written in block print was an address, not in Coxen Hole as I expected, but in Milton Bight. I punched in the address and Timothy peeled out, just as his father ran into the parking lot, waving his arms.

"Your parents are going to be pissed," I said.

"They usually are. I think they like it. Did anyone ever tell you that you look just like Marilyn Monroe?"

"Every day of my life."

He blushed. "Sorry."

"Don't be. A fact's a fact."

Timothy increased his speed and broke every traffic law ever invented. I put on my seat belt.

"How come you were at the ransom drop thing?" he asked.

"I'm a nurse."

And a lot of other things I'd rather not get into.

"What happened?"

"I'm not sure. Another boat showed up and started firing. They tried to ram us and got the kidnappers' boat."

"Holy shit. That is cool."

I grabbed the door handle as Timothy passed a truck on a blind turn. "I'm sure I'll think so later."

We sideswiped an old wagon and ran down a clump of six mailboxes.

"Or maybe not. Please slow down," I said. "It's important we remain alive long enough to get to Andrew."

"Is that the victim's name?"

"Yes!" I screamed as Timothy slammed on the brakes and we did a three-sixty.

"There it is," he said, driving into a private drive with an oversized gate.

I jumped out and peered through the twisted pink metal spokes. The house was a grand Spanish-style mansion, perched on the edge of the sea. The house was dark, except for the exterior lights around the property. I jiggled the gate and rang the bell. No one answered and I stepped back to view the gate and fence. I'd climbed my share of fences, but that was a big one. And I had on Chuck's bikini.

I leaned into the car. "No one's answering. I'm going over."

"Screw that!" said Timothy with a grin I'd seen on my dad's face more than once. "Step back."

"What are you going to do?"

"Hold on, dude!" Timothy hit the gas and rammed the gate. I would've screamed, but I was too astonished. He reversed and rammed it again, that time busting through and shooting shards of metal onto the manicured lawn. I ran through the hole and yelled, "Are you crazy?"

"Don't sweat it. My dad will pay for it." Timothy got out and surveyed the damage with satisfaction.

"You're pretty confident," I said.

"The way only a senator's son can be. Let's find Andrew."

I helped Aaron out of the car. He was all blotchy and stunned. I grinned. "And you thought I was bad."

"I'm starving," he said.

We ran down to the house and started banging on doors and looking through windows. None of the shades were drawn and I didn't see anything suspicious. It looked like the house was a vacation rental and currently empty. Not a bad place to stash a kidnap victim.

Timothy picked up a large river rock. "Let's break a window."

I took the rock from him. "Let's not." I insisted we circle the house, checking all the windows. Every room was dark and something about that made me think Andrew wasn't in there.

"Garage," said Aaron. He was munching on a Snickers bar.

"Where'd you get that?" I asked.

"Pocket."

"Isn't it waterlogged?"

"Yep."

I shook my head. "You are so weird. What were you saying before?"

"Garage."

And there it was, a separate building fifteen yards from the house and it had an interior light on.

"That's it!" yelled Timothy and before I could stop him, he ran headlong into the door, ramming it with his shoulder. It didn't break, but Timothy did. He bounced right off and landed on the concrete, writhing in pain.

"You have issues," I said, standing over him.

"Could be," he said.

"I wish I had my lock picks."

"You have lock picks?" Timothy sat up, rubbing his shoulder.

"I have an interesting family, too." I walked around the side of the garage and found a window. On my tiptoes, I could see in. The garage was empty, except for a man leaning against a wall. Andrew. I banged on the window, but he didn't move. I bit my lip and assessed him. He wasn't tied up or restrained in any way. One of his hands was propped up against a pipe to hold him upright and there was quite a bit of blood on his pale blue polo and the floor. I thought I detected breathing, but I couldn't be sure.

Aaron came around to stand next to me. "He in there?"

"Yes and he doesn't look good. Timothy do you have a cellphone on you?" I yelled.

"Yeah."

"Call the police and give them this address. Tell them we need an ambulance."

Aaron picked up a big rock. "Now?"

"Now."

He hurled it through the glass. I got Aaron to donate his shirt and cleaned the rest of the glass out of the frame. He boosted me up and I climbed through, dangling until I managed to find a spot with no glass next to the wall and landed there.

"Andrew," I said.

He was awake now, but in no way focused. "Who is it?"

I knelt beside him and took his pulse, slow, real slow. "It's Mercy Watts. Do you remember me?"

"The hot one?"

"Not right now, I assure you. Did they drug you?"

"We should've paid those guys," he said quietly.

"You couldn't know. The police are coming." I heard a siren in the distance and relaxed for a second until the thought that it might be Pinto entered my brain. No. He was on the third boat. I was safe as far as he was concerned. I opened the garage door and Aaron and Timothy came in.

"Dude," said Timothy. "You are fucked up."

"Yeah," said Andrew.

I started examining him. He had a blunt force wound to the back of his head and considerable trauma to the face, but nothing on his torso to explain the blood. I checked one arm and then looked at the other, the one holding him up against the pipe. Andrew's dark skin had concealed it well. His hand was the source of the blood. I went around and touched his grotesquely swollen hand. Something had been done to it, but I couldn't tell what. Maybe a hammer to break all the bones?

"Andrew, I'm going to move your hand, so I can examine it."

"No, you can't." His voice had weakened.

"I'll try not to hurt you, but I have to look."

The sirens got closer and then twelve police trucks pulled into the driveway. The next thing I knew I had fifteen automatic weapons pointed at me. We put our hands up and the cops rushed in.

"I'm Mercy Watts. Call my name in. I'm working with Tabora."

"We can't find Tabora," said the lead officer, not anyone I recognized.

"He was at the ransom drop. Something went wrong. There was another boat there."

"Ransom drop. What are you talking about?" he asked with his weapon still on me.

"This is Andrew Thatcher, the kidnap victim. We made an exchange for his location tonight."

He dropped the weapon. "You say Tabora was in on this?"

"Yes, of course he was. He gave us the money to exchange for Andrew," I said.

"How much money?"

"Twenty thousand dollars' worth of lempira," I said. "Please, I'm a nurse. I need to examine Andrew."

The lead came forward, his black military boots crunching bits of glass. "Go ahead, but I need to question him."

The cop asked Andrew how he was taken, who it was, etc., but Andrew didn't have any answers. He barely remembered being at The Aviary the night he was taken. The men wore masks and had accents. He couldn't identify them. I took a closer look at his hand, still braced against the pipe. It was oddly dimpled in the center with a raw wound. Weird.

"Andrew, did they shoot you in the hand?" I looked back and his head had dropped onto his chest.

"What happened?" asked the cop.

"He passed out. Where's that ambulance?"

"They're coming. That doesn't look like a gunshot wound to me."

I nodded and the hand stayed right where it was on the pipe, even with Andrew out cold. "Shit." I looked at the back of the pipe. The tip of a screw poked through the metal. "They screwed him to the pipe."

The cop took a look. "Shit."

"That's one way to make sure he didn't get away," I said.

Timothy squatted next to me. "Those are some serious freaks. What'll we do?"

I stood up and looked around the empty garage. "We need a power drill."

"Gross."

"We've got to unscrew him."

The lead yelled for his men to find a drill ASAP. The ambulance came screaming into the driveway and the EMTs arrived at the garage with a stretcher. Must've been their turn to have it.

I introduced myself, while they assessed Andrew and started cussing.

"Do you have any painkillers with you?" I asked.

"No," said the younger one.

The older EMT, a man in his fifties, wouldn't look at me. He had something.

"We don't care what you've got or why you've got it. We need to get this man's hand off this pipe." I looked at the lead cop. Correct?"

The cop ordered everyone out of the garage and the EMT said, "I have chloroform. It's illegal, but I keep it for extreme cases."

"Go get it."

He went out to the ambulance and came back with a small bottle and a rag. Now I've never used chloroform and didn't even know anyone who had. I'd have to trust the EMT and it wasn't a comfortable feeling. Andrew was awake again, looking worse by the minute.

"Andrew, we don't have any regular pain meds, but we have to get your hand off that pipe," I said as calmly as I could.

"No. No. Don't touch it." Andrew began shaking. I couldn't imagine the pain he was in.

"Listen. We have chloroform. We can knock you out to do it."

His voice shook. "Okay."

"Timothy, go see if they came up with a drill, or a screwdriver?"

He ran out and got an ancient electric drill from someone. "They broke into the house and got it."

I asked for alcohol and the younger EMT, who looked like he really didn't want to be there, got it and started pouring it all over the drill bit. That's what we had, one drill bit. He handed it to me and I was ready to do it, but I avoided power tools like herpes.

"How does this thing work?" I asked.

"You've got to pull the trigger," said the older EMT.

I offered it to him and he backed up. Ah, come on. I was surrounded by guys and none of them wanted to use a power tool. What kind of universe was I in?

"Fine," I said. "How do I unscrew with this thing?"

Andrew groaned. "Oh, god."

Timothy took the drill from me and did something to a ring near the bit. "I'll do it."

"You'll do it?" I asked. "No, thanks. Someone with medical training should do it."

"Nope. It was meant to be. My parents think I'm a genius, but the only class I ever got an A in was Shop. Besides, I weigh more than any of you. Sometimes you've got to put some weight into it."

"Okay." I was queasy. It was bad enough trusting an EMT with illegal chloroform, now I had a senator's son unscrewing a man's hand.

"I'm ready," said Andrew, but he sounded anything but ready. Who could blame him? My bad vacation was nothing compared to his.

"Chloroform him," I said.

The EMT poured some liquid from the bottle onto a gauze pad and held it to Andrew's face. He jerked back away from the light sweet smell.

"Just breathe it in," I said.

Andrew forced himself to breathe and in a few seconds he was incoherent.

"Isn't that enough?" I asked.

"No. He can still feel pain," said the EMT.

It seemed like forever before Andrew slumped over, pulling on the hand and the EMT took the gauze away. "Now he feels nothing."

The younger EMT brought in an oxygen tank and fixed a mask over Andrew's face.

The older EMT and I gloved up and retracted the tissue around the wound and the younger one sprayed in saline so we could see the screw. It was buried pretty deep in the tissue and was lodged in Andrew's third metacarpal.

"Go ahead, Timothy. Unscrew him," I said.

Timothy was right. He was meant to do that job. He stepped right up. The bit fit well enough and Timothy had enough weight to make sure it grabbed and the screw was extracted in twenty seconds.

We got Andrew on the gurney and in the ambulance in some kind of land speed record. The ambulance peeled away, leaving black tire marks on the previously pristine driveway.

"You going?" asked Aaron from a corner in the garage, still chewing on his Snickers bar.

"No," I said. "There's nothing I can do that they can't."

He put the wrapper in his pocket. "Not true."

"I agree," said Timothy. "You just saved that guy's life and you're wearing a bikini. Smoking hot by the way. Very James Bond."

"Thanks, but I'd rather be wearing sweats or pajamas or any kind of clothes really."

"Let's go find you some then."

We started to leave the garage, but the cops held us back, saying they needed to take us in for statements. I handled it well, which is to say I teared up and begged. So they took brief statements and let us go. Timothy drove us to La Isla Bonita with a grin on his face. "You cry to get your way often?"

"Not as much as you'd think," I said, snuggling up with my still damp towel. I was all relaxed. Andrew was okay and a little crying never hurt anyone. I just wanted to go back to my room, eat a cheeseburger, and pass out like an EMT had chloroformed me. It was not to be. Timothy pulled onto the resort's drive to find it blocked by every police vehicle that hadn't been at the resort house.

CHAPTER SIXTEEN

The situation at La Isla Bonita wasn't bad as I originally expected, but then again, I expected it to be pretty bad. Spitball, Mauro, Tabora, and his men had paddled their way back to the resort in a life raft after Pinto shot at them. Apparently, there are only so many bullets an engine can take. They managed to slip away when a trio of boats on a night dive came by and heard the firing. They'd arrived about the time we'd been unscrewing Andrew.

We found them in the restaurant, still wet but looking pretty pleased with themselves. Spitball was holding court with six beers in front of him. A cop with a plethora of insignia on his shoulders was trying to interview him, but he was doing a pretty good job ignoring the frustrated official. Tabora spotted us and made his way through the crowd with Mauro and Joe following. Joe's face was so drawn and exhausted, it looked like he'd lost ten pounds on the boat.

"Finally," said Tabora. "We got word that you found Andrew, but little else. What happened?

"We swam to shore and Timothy gave us a ride to Andrew," I said, indicating my chauffeur, who'd lost interest in us and was busy smiling at a pair of waitresses.

Tabora shook his head. "I was sure you lost the box. Hell. I was sure I lost you. How is Andrew? Did he identify the kidnappers?"

"He'll be fine eventually. They screwed his hand to a pipe and no, he can't identify anyone."

Joe grabbed Mauro's shoulder to steady himself. "Did you say they screwed his hand to a pipe?"

"I did."

"Where is he?" He glanced around like I might've left him on the sand behind me.

"Coxen Hole hospital," I said. "Mauro, can you take him?"

Mauro hugged me and whispered in my ear, "I'm glad you're okay." Then he left with Joe.

Tabora scratched his chin. "Screwing someone to a pipe. That's a new one. What about the money?"

"We don't have it," I said. "You didn't pull it back in?"

"We were busy trying not to get killed."

"What about the kidnappers?" I asked.

"The Coast Guard found three bodies so far, but more may turn up."

"You know it was Pinto in the third boat, don't you?" I wrapped the towel tighter around my shoulders. "I'm guessing the money is with him."

He shook his head. "I don't know how he found out what we were doing. I only cleared it with the highest levels and told no one else. They're searching for Pinto as well, but I don't think they'll find him."

"How far could he get?"

"It's a big ocean." He put a hand on my shoulder. "I'm sorry I suspected you. On this island, I've learned to suspect everyone."

"Don't worry about it. As long as Pinto's out of the picture, I'm happy," I said.

Tabora left to go to the hospital and that's when Mom saw me. She stalked over with an empty glass. "Night dive, huh? You lied to your mother."

"You'd think you'd be used to it."

"Never. You could've told me."

"Yeah. I don't think so," I said. "Were you worried I was dead?"

Mom snorted. "Those scoundrels couldn't kill you. You're too difficult. Besides, you took Aaron with you. Poor little Aaron." She burped.
Mom was martini drunk.

"You wanted me to take Aaron, remember?"

"No, I don't." Mom hugged Aaron. He looked confused. So was I.
She squashed his face between her hands. "Look at this face."

I try not to.

"Mom, how many drinks have you had?"

"We're celebrating! It's finally happened." Mom grabbed me and
whispered, "I didn't think it would, but it did."

"What happened exactly?" I asked. "Aunt Tenne getting a
boyfriend?"

She shoved my shoulder, hard, and I nearly fell over. "No, silly.
Everything is different."

"What is?"

Instead of answering, Mom tried to drag me into the crowd. Not
going to happen. "Mom, I don't want to party. I just want a cheeseburger and bed."

Aaron ran past me to the kitchen. "Aaron!" I yelled. "I didn't
mean..."

Mom continued to yank on my arm until Bruno showed up with
one of the robes they gave people at the pool. "Just go," he said.

I slipped on the robe and let Mom lead me. She doesn't drink like
that often, but Bruno was right, there was no stopping her when she
did. We ended up at a table with the Carrows and the Gmucas along
with Aunt Tenne and Dixie. They'd all had more than a few. Bruno
prudently disappeared. Nothing is more obnoxious than a bunch of
drunks when you're sober. I put myself into a corner and Dixie, the
least tanked of all of them, scooted close.

"They found that Colin," she said. "He was dead drunk in an alley. I
heard some officers talking about it."

"Did they get any information about Lucia and Graeme?" I asked.

"I don't think he was conscious."

The waiter brought me a Monkey Lala without me asking and I
sipped it slowly. Maybe it was over. They had Colin. He didn't seem to

have a brilliant criminal mind, but every attempt on Lucia's life had been botched. That had idiot written all over it.

"Guess what?" said Dixie, her new blond hair glinting in the soft light of the table candles. "I'm going to write a book."

"Huh?" I couldn't focus. What were we talking about?

"I'm going to write about Gavin's cases. Fictionalized, of course."

"You want to be a crime writer?"

"Why are you so surprised? I was married to a detective and I have all his files."

I couldn't have been more surprised if she'd decided to be a stripper. Dixie wasn't like my mom. She had nothing to do with Gavin's life in crime. They didn't discuss cases. She wouldn't even answer the phone when he went private.

"I never thought you were interested in crime," I said.

"Gavin being out there scared me. I hated it, but now he's gone. It will be a kind of memorial." Dixie ordered another drink.

I'd rarely heard such a bad idea. Dixie wasn't ready for the stuff Gavin had in his files. He'd seen the worst humanity had to offer. I'd filed for him during high school and college for extra money. Every once in a while, I took a peek and immediately wished I hadn't. Some things were better left to the professionals.

"Are you sure about this?"

"I can handle it. Carolina's going to come over and we'll pick a case together. No child molestation cases." She took a big drink. "That's rule number one."

I could think of another twenty rules, starting with no looking in Gavin's case files. Aaron brought me a double cheeseburger and ran back to the kitchen. I ate slowly, savoring every flavor he put in there, since none of them were crab, and thought about Dixie. It was a new start. Maybe that was what Mom was going on about. Dixie being different. But it'd only been two months since Gavin had been murdered. I knew from experience that you can make new starts. You can make them over and over again. You can change your hair, your clothes, practically everything about you, except that one thing that can never be changed. A person is gone and the person you would've been, had they stayed, is gone, too. My person was David, son of Dad's partner, Cora, and my first boyfriend. He disappeared when I was sixteen and a man was sitting in prison for killing him, although his body had never been found. I knew David was dead. He had to be, but I still missed him and the life he was supposed to have. Nothing changed that. Nothing I'd found anyway.

I leaned back against the deck railing and watched the laughing tourists. Lucia and Graeme got up to dance. He appeared to be entirely recovered and Lucia, although slightly gimpy, danced happily. Her long dark hair swayed behind her back. Her cheeks were rosy and I could see her brother, Oz, in her. The thought of him made me smile. Dad would've been quite displeased at the sight. We were going home the day after tomorrow. I would buy a new phone and I would tell Oz his sister wasn't being abused. There was a lot of satisfaction in that, even if he was a Fibonacci.

The next morning I slept in and celebrated not having cops banging on my door by taking out the two stitches in my forehead. Dr. Navarro had done a good job and the scar would be minimal. I decided it would give me character, and then used Aunt Tenne's phone to check on Andrew. He was resting comfortably, but they had to do surgery to extract multiple metal shards from his hand from the screw removal. Several bones were broken in his hand and ribcage. He also had a bad infection. Luckily, their last medication shipment included IV antibiotics. Navarro said Andrew wouldn't be released for several days. Then I remembered to call Pete and managed to catch him between patients. I told him about my phone's death and he told me about the flesh-eating virus he got to check out. He didn't hold anything back, but I did. The Lucia situation would be better told when it was all over.

After eating a fantastic breakfast, I watched Mom take over Bruno's life by supervising the packing of all his paintings. I expected him to be angry or at least withdrawn, but he stood in a corner chatting with Aunt Tenne and the Carrows, acting like the whole process had nothing to do with him.

One painting wasn't packed. It stood on an easel off to the side, still shiny with wet oils. I couldn't stop looking at it, because I sat center, holding an overflowing glass with my head tilted down, smiling. Aaron was behind me in shadow, but definitely present. The rest of my family crowded around the table. Mom, Dad, Aunt Tenne, Dixie, Myrtle and Millicent and in the corner my cousin, Chuck. They all crowded in, looming over me, smiling and laughing.

Close up I saw more people woven into our clothes, some living and others not. Gavin's face was in Dixie's sleeve. Grandma George was in a flower Mom was holding. There was another face, one I never expected to see. Aunt Tenne came up behind me and wrapped her soft arms around me. "I told Bruno," she said. "I almost didn't, but I changed my mind. I was right, wasn't I?"

I blinked back the tears. Bruno had put David in me. His smiling face was concealed in my shoulder and my face was slightly inclined toward him.

"Is that you or what?" She squeezed me tighter.

I nodded unable to speak and slipped out of her grasp into the sunshine. I walked on the beach until it ended at a coral cliff and returned to sit by the pool with a memoir of living in Paris, balanced in my lap.

Lucia sat beside me and offered her leg. "What do you think? Spitball has that dry suit. I really want to go diving."

My chest tightened. The Dad feeling was back again full force. Colin made sense, but I don't know, something wasn't right about it. "I'd feel better if you stayed on dry land."

"Fibonaccis always dive in." She grinned. "Besides, this is my last chance."

I took off the bandage. The wound was closing nicely, had no smell, and no oozing. "It can't get wet, not even a little."

"It won't. Spitball says it'll be totally dry. The suit will be filled with air and we won't go very deep."

"Alright, but if you feel any discomfort, you have to surface. Who's going with you?"

"Graeme, of course, Spitball, your mom, Dixie, and Linda Gmuca. Frankie's too hung over."

What could I say? I have a feeling? Even to me it would've sounded ridiculous. "Stick close to Spitball."

She leaned over and hugged me. "They have Colin, and Graeme called the police station. They said he's not getting bail."

"Thank goodness for that."

Lucia left with only a slight limp. She was resilient, I'd give her that, or maybe it was being a Fibonacci. They always come out on top, no matter what. I settled back on my chair and read about Christmas in Paris. I'd like to try a cone of hot chestnuts and wander the wide avenues without a care. At some point, Aaron showed up with nachos. They looked great, but had on them the hated crab, so I ate some chips from the protected bottom to make him happy and declared them the best ever. Let me tell you even the chips with no crab touching them, had the essence of crabbiness. That stuff is pervasive.

One of the office girls came to tell me there was a phone call for me in the office.

"Miss Watts," said Tabora. "I have some bad news."

I held my breath.

"Colin denies having anything to do with the attacks on the Carrows."

"Do you believe him?"

Tabora tapped something on his desk in a slow, hard rhythm. "I do. I've been in contact with the FBI and they found no indications of bribery in his bank accounts and no connections to the Fibonaccis or any known associates."

"So he's just a drunken gambler," I said.

"I believe so. How are Lucia and Graeme this morning?" he asked.

"Fine. I had breakfast with them. They're convinced that it was Colin."

"It's not Colin and I have no leads."

I put my head on the desk and kept the phone to my ear. "I was afraid of that."

"What about you? Any ideas?"

"Not really. Nobody had access during every incident."

"Except the husband and then he was poisoned," said Tabora. "I'm coming over to conduct more interviews. My life would be much easier if you were leaving today."

"Mine, too, I suspect. I'll be at the pool," I said.

We said goodbye, I thanked the office staff, and left the frigid air-conditioning of the office. The gate guard's eyes passed over me briefly as I passed. The resort's security was good. No one got hassled. Unruly cruise ship passengers were booted posthaste, but they couldn't do anything about those who were allowed inside. Although it was a small boutique resort, there were quite a few guests and staff, all of which would have to be cleared. I didn't envy Tabora. Plus, by the time he got the job done, we'd be gone.

I headed for the pool, wishing I'd heard from Chuck. I assumed he wasn't calling Mom because she wasn't supposed to know about all this, but it made me uneasy just the same. The pool had filled up with guests while I'd been gone. A young mom and her fat baby were in the shallow end, learning to splash. Her toddler, in pigtails and a saggy-bottomed bikini, giggled on the side and tried to work up enough courage to jump in. Other guests smiled and yelled encouragement. "You can do it!" Dixie only noticed me when I blocked her sun. She was in my spot, reading my Paris book. She smiled and then it dropped off her face. "Bad news?"

I told her Tabora's thoughts and she shrunk back into the chair, wrinkling her nose.

"Hey," I said. "You want to write about crime. How about a little help here?"

"The crimes I'm going to write about have already been solved. I'll know who did it. That's a lot different than being amongst a resort full of suspects."

Aaron ambled into the pool area, wearing a brand-new shirt with the La Isla Bonita logo and carrying a small platter. I'd never seen him in anything new before. Whoever had picked it out had gotten the wrong size. The shirt went to the bottom of his stone-washed shorts.

"Brownie," he said, holding out the platter.

I took a big juicy one and said, "How do you always know when I need chocolate?"

"It's a gift."

"Yes, it is," said Dixie, taking a tiny brownie that matched her waistline. "We were just talking murder."

"Huh?"

"Colin didn't try to kill Lucia and we're back to no suspects," I said.

"I hate to say it," said Dixie, "but what about Joe or Andrew? They were around for every attempt, weren't they?"

"They were on a dive boat for the second poisoning, but I'm not sure about the first one," I conceded. "Do you have a cellphone on you?"

Dixie gave me Mom's phone and looked longingly at the other brownies.

Just eat another one, woman. No one cares if you gain a pound.

I called Chuck first and got his inbox. Damn. Then I dialed a second number and a polite hello came out of the phone. Totally unexpected. I looked at the number to see if I'd made a mistake. No. Right number.

"Uncle Morty?" I asked.

"Oh, it's you." Uncle Morty's gruff was back in a big way. "What do you want?"

"Why were you nice when you thought it was Dixie?"

"She cries. What do you want? Getting bored in paradise?"

"Not hardly. I don't have time to explain everything, but I need you to look up a couple of guys for me ASAP."

"Got a couple of hot dates?" he asked.

"When do I ask you to look into my dates?"

"You should. You dated some real douchebags."

"Whatever." I gave him everything I had on Joe and Andrew and told him I'd pay whatever he wanted as long as he was fast as in five minutes fast. That got him interested like nothing else. I'd spent half my life avoiding paying Uncle Morty anything.

"I suppose you don't want me to tell Tommy. Ain't gonna happen, sister," he said.

"I don't give a crap who you tell. Just do it."

He hung up on me. At least I could always count on him. He was back in three minutes with some preliminaries. Just normal stuff, bank account information, hospitalizations, degrees, loans. Nothing remotely helpful. Neither were in the kind of debt people killed to get out of.

"That's not going to do it." I took a deep breath. "Any connections to organized crime?"

"Define organized crime."

"The Fibonaccis."

Uncle Morty let out a string of curse words so loud I had to hold the phone far from my ear. Dixie wrinkled her nose again and Aaron snorted. He was used to it from their years of gaming.

"Are you done?" I asked.

More cursing.

"Are you going to help me or not?"

"Already on it. Tommy's going to kill you."

"Yeah. Yeah. Anything?"

"Nah. No arrests of any kind. They both bailed out a guy named Colin Rodwell for various misdemeanors, nothing to connect with the mob. What have you gotten yourself into there?"

"Are you sure there's nothing?"

"If I say there's nothing, there ain't nothing. Tell me the situation."

I did as he continued to curse. I left out the part about Chuck and his connection, Spidermonkey. If he knew that I went to someone else, even Chuck, I'd get nothing out of him for any amount of money. I did give him a complete list of everyone on both scuba trips and everyone Aaron, Dixie, and I had seen on the beach.

"So nobody was at each incident, except for that Colin, Joe, and Andrew," he said. "It could be someone you don't suspect. I'll get the resort registry and check every damn one of them."

"Call Dixie's phone, if you get anything," I said.

He grunted and hung up. Crabby bastard. Dixie's hand inched toward the brownies. I plucked one off the platter and dropped it in her lap.

"Mercy!"

"Now you have to eat it. No wasting," I said.

"I've eaten too much on this trip already."

"Please. You're practically anorexic. Eat the brownie. Gavin always did. You can put that in the book."

She laughed. "He never met a dessert he didn't like."

"Or a burger," said Aaron.

"Or a beer," I said.

Dixie got all misty. "What should I call him, my main character? I can't call him Gavin, I suppose."

"Ulysses," I said. "After his favorite general and the kid, Ulysses Jones."

"What kid?"

"The one he got exonerated in that horrible rape case. He did it pro bono. He really liked that kid."

"I never heard about that one," she said, quietly.

"Now you'll get to know Gavin all over again." I took another brownie and the toddler ran over, clapping her hands.

"Brownies! Brownies!" she crowed.

Her mom turned red and rose out of the water, carrying her chortling baby. "No, no, Bea. That's not polite."

"It's alright," I said. "Can she have one?"

Mom came over, still blushing. "I'm so sorry."

"Really, it's nothing. We have lots. I'm Mercy. This is Dixie and Aaron. Aaron's a gastronomic genius."

"I'm Laurie and this is Elissa and Beatrice." Laurie looked at Aaron's terminal bedhead and oversized tee as if she doubted my endorsement.

"Seriously, they're delicious," I said, offering up the platter.

Laurie nodded to Bea. She took a brownie with a squeal of delight and said something that might've been thank you. Baby Elissa smacked her lips and her big sister gave her a bit of the brownie.

Dixie smiled at Beatrice's chubby cheeks and tummy. "Where's your daddy today?"

"Zooska!" Bea announced.

We looked at Laurie, who had given in and taken a brownie. She was a little glazed over, the way I always got when Aaron made me chocolate. "Scuba," she said at last. "He's going on the Hole in the Wall dive and then we'll switch. I'm doing Turtle Crossing later."

"That's a great idea," said Dixie. "You switch back and forth, so you both get to dive."

"It's worked out well so far. We haven't missed anything."

Dixie and Laurie chatted about the dives she'd done so far. I stopped listening at some point. A word kept bouncing around in my brain. Switching. Switching. Everything went quiet for me, everything but that word. Switching.

Oh my god!

"They're switching!" I yelled.

Everyone jumped.

"What in the world?" asked Dixie.

I grabbed her arm. "Dixie, they're switching. It's two murderers, not one."

"Murder?" said Laurie, clutching little Elissa tighter.

"Who is it?" asked Dixie.

"Todd and Tracy. The Land's End couple."

"The ones with the horrible kids? No way."

"Yes. It has to be. One of them was at every single incident."

"Nobody would go on vacation to kill someone and take their kids," said Dixie.

"Can you think of a better cover? Have you seen them today?" I asked.

"I did," said Laurie. "Tracy was walking into town a little while ago."

"That leaves him free and Lucia's going to dive again." I bit back every curse word Uncle Morty had ever taught me, shoved the platter into Dixie's lap, and jumped up. Dixie's phone started ringing. "It's Morty!" she yelled, but I was already running. When was that dive leaving? Mom told me, but I didn't remember. I ran full out, past staring men and angry wives. The bikini was holding out, but let's face it, it wasn't designed for such explosive bounce. I braced my chest with my arm and put on my last ounce of speed.

I skirted the dive shop. It was empty, except for Marcella, the assistant manager. I ran to the desk, gasping.

"You should never run," she said. "Especially in a bikini. It's not safe."

"When...does...Hole...in...Wall—"

"The Hole in the Wall dive? They just left." Marcella checked her watch. "You missed it by twenty minutes, but we're—"

"Oh shit!" I looked at the dive board. Under Hole in the Wall was the list of divers. Mom, Lucia, Graeme, and a few others. There squeezed in at the bottom was Todd's name. He was on the boat.

"Call them," I said. "Todd did it. He's trying to kill Lucia."

She stared at me.

"It's him. He stabbed her. Call them!"

"Aaron?" she said, looking past me.

Aaron was there, so red-faced he looked about to pass out, but nodding furiously.

"Call them now! They have to abort the dive," I said.

Marcella picked up her portable VHF and radioed *La Isla Bonita One*. After a minute, Alex answered. Marcella told him to abort, but they were already down. "What now?" Marcella asked.

"Are there any other boats in the vicinity with divers ready to go down?" I asked.

She asked Alex and he said no. They were alone for the moment and he didn't bring dive equipment for himself.

"Where's Mauro or any of the dive instructors? I'll take anyone."

"I'm here." Mauro came out of the storage room, rubbing oil on himself.

"Do we have a boat available?" I asked.

"I'm prepping Two. Why?"

I told him about Todd and before I could finish, he was grabbing a BCD, tank, and weights. He thrust the set into my arms and then got his set that was always prepped. We ran for the beach, bypassing the golf carts. I've never run carrying that much stuff in my life. It must've weighed fifty pounds, but somehow, I did it. I ran into the water behind Mauro and handed him up my equipment. Aaron was behind me, but I stopped him.

"Call Tabora and tell Alex that if any other boats come, he should tell them to go down immediately and get Spitball's group to surface."

"I got to go with you," said Aaron.

"Not this time." I climbed on the boat and Mauro fired up the engine. "Call Tabora!"

We raced out of the resort's small harbor. The wind tore at my hair and we hit the waves so hard my teeth slammed together, shooting pain through my jaw. Hole in the Wall couldn't be that far, if they'd left and been down in twenty minutes, but they had a decent head start, at least twenty-eight minutes now. A lot could happen in twenty-eight minutes.

Lucia stay with Spitball. Stay with Spitball.

We passed several boats coming back from dives. Everyone smiled and waved. We kept racing and came around an outcropping of coral. The La Isla Bonita boat rocked in the water next to a series of buoys. Alex jumped up and waved. Another boat came in from the other direction, twice the size of our boats and fully loaded. Mauro cut the engine and guided us to the side of One.

I popped open my bundle and began hooking up the equipment. Mauro was behind me and completely suited before I had all my equipment together.

"Lloyd's here!" yelled Alex.

Mauro lowered his mask and sat on the side. "Tell him!" He dropped over.

I clipped on my BCD, did my checks, and waddled into position. Alex was yelling at the other boat, presumably Lloyd's. The boat came around and I saw a guy about Spitball's age hooking up a set of regs as I dropped into the water. I sunk. I'd forgotten to inflate my BCD. I pushed the inflation button and popped up. Then I deflated as fast as I could without exploding my eardrums. Mauro was on the bottom, rotating slowly. He'd started off to the right before I reached the bottom. My fins touched the sand and I caught sight of Mauro's fins disappearing between two coral walls. Hole in the Wall was nothing like my other dives. It was all canyon as far as I could see and I did not want to go in there. The walls went up ten or fifteen feet and bulged out in dark, rounded shapes that reminded me of thick brownie batter. Not welcoming in the least.

I slowed my breathing and went in, swimming through a corridor with plenty of cubbyholes and twists and turns. I couldn't catch up with Mauro. He knew where he was going and his long legs propelled him much faster than my short ones. So far, I hadn't seen another diver other than Mauro. Where were they? What if they went in a different direction? I was breathing way too heavily. I checked my gauge. I'd already used up 500 psi of air. Not good.

Calm. Calm. Breathe in. Breathe out.

A shadow went over me and I jerked to the right, running into some jagged coral. It gouged my shoulder. I really missed my penguin suit. A diver dropped down in front of me. Lloyd from the other boat. He gave me the okay sign and I gave it back. He turned and sped off into a tunnel. I didn't know where Mauro had gone. Lloyd's fins were already out of sight. There was no way I was going in that hole without Lloyd right in front of me. I went straight with fingers crossed. The maze of coral went on and on. Sometimes it opened up to a sandbar with schools of lovely fish and stingrays loafing, hidden in the sand. Then it was back into the maze. I came around a tight turn and nearly ran into Lloyd. He indicated that he hadn't found them yet. We went in different directions. The maze walls got higher. I had to swim under bridges and came to a short tunnel. It was either go through or go back. I could see out the other side, so I stuffed the fear down.

There are no sharks in there. There are no eels in there. You're okay.

I swam in. Mauro had taught us in class what to do if we vomited into our reg and for the first time I thought it was a real possibility. My stomach was clenched and if it was possible to sweat underwater, I was doing it. The tunnel was longer than I realized and for a minute I was in darkness—anything could've been in that hole. I focused on the light at the end of tunnel. I was getting there. Getting there. Getting there.

And then the light went out.

CHAPTER SEVENTEEN

I bit my reg so hard, my jaw made a cracking pop. I couldn't go back. The tunnel was too tight. Forward. I had to go forward. A sliver of light. My breathing was so loud in my ears. Using too much air. Trapped. No the sliver got bigger and then only covered half the light. Another dark shape came from the side and I saw a tank and a firm belly. Hands frantically saying, "Okay?" Mauro! The first shape moved farther away and I saw something white in the black.

I reached the end and swam out in a burst between two divers, Mauro and Spitball. Spitball was clutching his side. The white hilt of a knife stuck out from between his fingers. Mauro gave Spitball the sign for which direction. Spitball pointed into a canyon and Mauro shot into the gloomy opening. Spitball told me he was going to ascend. I gave him the okay sign and he gave it back although his face was distorted in pain. How could I leave him?

Another diver entered the sandbar. Mom. I pointed at Spitball and the knife and darted after Mauro. I caught sight of him after a hundred feet and banged on my tank with my fingernails. He turned and indicated I should go left and he would go right.

Fantastic. Alone again and now with well under 1000 psi.

I swam into the crevasse that looked like a place that eels would love. Love to bite me, that is. Who was I even looking for? Lucia or Todd? I ran into a dead end, reversed, and took another. The coral walls were lowering and I saw a huge amount of bubbles rising in the water above a wall. I swam up, a good ten feet in depth change. My ears screamed in protest. I swallowed, trying to clear them as I went over the top. There was another canyon below me, but no divers in sight, only a huge amount of bubbles coming from under a ledge of black coral. I dipped down. The pain in my ears intensified. I held my nose and swallowed. My ears popped with such pain that I yelled and lost my reg. I arced my arm and snagged the loose tube as I reached the ledge where the bubbles were. I thrust the reg back in my mouth, but before I cleared it, I saw them. Two divers backed into a crevasse, one behind the other grasping them around the waist. Arms were flailing. A hand from behind came at the front diver's face. Lucia's face. The back diver's hand got past her flailing arms and yanked the reg out of her mouth. It spewed, free flowing oxygen. The other diver clamped his hand over her mouth and nose and I got a look at his face. Todd, his face distorted in anger and determination. I clawed at his arm and they came barreling out of the crevasse, knocking me back against the coral opposite. Todd kicked up to ascend. He was trying to blow her lungs out.

I grabbed Lucia's dry suit and pulled her back down. Todd fought hard and dragged us both up a foot. My vision changed. Wavy lines at the edges. I wasn't breathing. My reg was still flooded. I couldn't let go. Lucia thrashed and kicked me hard in the gut. What little air I had blew out. The dry suit material slipped in my hands. I couldn't hold her. I grabbed Todd's weight belt instead. He was still trying to swim up, so I yanked him down as hard as I could. They both came down and we were head-to-head. My vision was going black. I grabbed his reg, but his teeth were clamped tight. One last chance. I seized his mask, ripping it away from his face and flooding it. Todd jerked back and released Lucia, frantically trying to get his mask back in place.

I punched my reg and it cleared explosively. I sucked in a breath and nabbed Lucia's reg floating in the water beside her head. Her eyes rolled back. I forced it into her mouth and cleared it. The jolt of the clear brought her back. She put both hands over the reg and breathed deeply. Todd came at us. He snagged her hose and yanked it hard. Her head whipped to the right and for a second I thought he had broken her neck, but she kept ahold of her reg. A blade flashed in the water and then her hose was free, spewing bubbles. He cut the hose. I've never seen a look of such panic in anyone's eyes and I've been in plenty of ERs and witnessed unbelievable pain. Lucia experienced pure terror in those moments and it would stay with me forever.

I yanked her spare reg out of its spot and thrust it into her face. She wouldn't spit out the other reg. She was beyond her training. The terror had taken over. I tried to pull it out. No. She wouldn't release it. Todd crashed into the coral ledge. Mauro had him by the BCD and was punching him in the face. I didn't think you could punch somebody underwater, but you can. Blood exploded from under Todd's mask. I let go of Lucia and grabbed Mauro's punching arm. He had so much trust, he actually dragged me forward with his last punch to the side of Todd's head.

I screamed into my reg, "Help!"

Mauro let go and turned to Lucia. He grabbed her mask and flooded it. She instantly released the reg and he popped her spare in. I held her shaking body and we turned back to the ledge. Todd was gone in one of five directions. Mauro gave me the ascend signal and I nodded. He went in search of Todd and we went up slowly. I put a little air into my BCD and then into Lucia's. By the time we got to twenty feet, she'd managed to slow her breathing. We were face-to-face. Her eyes locked with mine. We were both weeping as we floated upward and I had a curious feeling of not really being there. That this all hadn't happened and when we broke the surface it would all disappear.

I looked up to gauge our depth and saw a body hit the water next to the hull of a boat about fifty feet from us. The man swam back up and treaded water. We were still fifteen feet down and I had to watch as a boat sped away from the other two. The man in the water, maybe Alex, swam to another boat and was gone. We broke the surface and I inflated both our BCDs fully and spit out my reg. Lucia didn't. I hugged her and then began towing her to the closest boat.

"Mercy!" yelled an unfamiliar voice.

I looked back and saw Lloyd on *La Isla Bonita One* with Spitball. He eased the boat to us and practically dragged Lucia on board by her BCD. I climbed up under my own power, but just barely. My legs went wobbly when my feet touched the deck and I ran into a canopy post.

"Grab that girl, Lloyd," said Spitball. He was sitting on the deck with a bloody towel pressed to his side.

"I'm okay." I lurched over to a bench and collapsed onto it.

"The hell you are."

"You're the one who was stabbed." I dropped my tank and unclipped my BCD. "Was that Alex in the water?"

"Yeah," said Lloyd, gently wiggling the reg out of Lucia's mouth. "He's on my boat."

"Did Todd throw him off Two?" I asked. "Where did he go? We've got to get him."

Lloyd laughed, left Lucia, and turned the boat. "That's the spirit. I like you."

Lloyd kicked it into high gear and we followed Todd's wake. From the look of it, he was going back to the resort. Not a great escape plan, but his family was there. We saw the boat when we came around a curve in the island. He was almost to the resort, but he was going too fast.

Please let him crash. Come on. No trial. Just a bloody spot on the sand.

He cut the engine.

Damnit!

But he was too slow after all and the boat went straight at the beach. Sunbathers ran screaming as he hit the sand. The boat stopped just short of the restaurant deck where a family stared with hamburgers halfway to their mouths. Todd tumbled over the side of the boat and ran.

Lloyd cut our engine at the right time and we glided in, barely nudging the beach. I staggered to the side and climbed up.

"Where the hell are you going?" yelled Spitball.

"After that piece of shit," I yelled and stood on the side.

"Ah, hell. I'd seen that look before. Somebody's going to die."

"Not me." I jumped and trudged through the waist-deep water

onto the beach. Twenty shocked tourists stared at me. "Where'd he go?" I asked.

They pointed to the alley beside the restaurant and I got a surge of energy. I ran down the alley, cut through the dive shop, and ran toward Todd and Tracy's room. At some point I became aware of someone huffing and puffing behind me. I looked back and there was Aaron, red-faced but keeping up.

Todd and Tracy's room was open. They were all gone. A man yelled from the end of the path. "They're driving away!"

We ran down to the office but didn't see them. There was only a golf cart there. None of the resort vehicles or cabs.

"Shit!" I couldn't believe it. I'd lost them and they had two kids in tow. I'd never live it down. Oh the hell with it. I turned the corner and ran down the lane, trying to catch sight of them, but they must've turned a corner. I screamed in frustration.

Aaron drove up beside me in the golf cart, holding a frosty drink.

"We can't catch them in that!"

He blinked and took a sip.

"Fine!" I got in. "Floor it!" And he did. It was not an impressive amount of speed and I was embarrassed by the whole deal. Aaron drank his drink and we went up the lane.

"You know we're chasing a would-be murderer, right?" I asked. He was so calm; I had my doubts.

No answer, just another sip.

"Where'd you get that drink?"

"Alfie."

"Who's Alfie?"

"The guy who gave me the drink."

"You are driving me crazy!"

Aaron gave me the glass and it wasn't half bad. Not that it made up for a family four-pack escaping me, but it was some form of comfort.

"You know we're never going to catch them in this stupid thing," I said. "If you tell Dad or Chuck that I tried to chase down a murderous family in a golf cart, I will never speak to you again."

"There they are," said Aaron, pointing to the other resort golf cart making a turn onto the main road into the West End. They were trying to escape in a golf cart. They were stupider than me.

Yes!

Todd and Tracy looked back and spotted us. I waved and their kids flipped me off. Nice! We followed them through the streets of the West End, past bars and tacky tourist shops. We were about twenty yards apart, but Aaron and I couldn't get any closer. We passed a couple of tourist cops, standing next to their bicycles.

"Stop them!" I yelled.

They smiled and waved. Oh my god! What does a girl have to do to get some assistance?

Aaron hung a right.

"Where are you going?" I asked.

"Shortcut."

"We've been on this island for nine days. You don't know any short-cuts. Turn around. We're losing them."

Aaron took back his drink and kept driving.

"Aaron!"

"We're on an island."

"What?" I asked.

"Where are they gonna go?"

Ah crap.

"They could get on a flight," I said.

"No seats available."

"Or better yet a boat. This place is chock full of boats. They could escape to the mainland or Utila."

Aaron slurped up the last of the drink and gave me the empty cup. He took a sharp left and there was no golf cart.

"I can't believe we lost them. On the upside, our so-called partner-ship is at an end."

"Tommy says we're partners," said Aaron.

"Not after this he won't. You've committed the ultimate offense. The criminals got away."

Aaron took another sharp left. "There they are."

The other golf cart was only five yards ahead.

Damnit. I didn't know whether to be happy or pissed off that he found them.

Aaron had it floored, but we couldn't get any closer.

"I can run faster than this," I said.

"Okay."

Ah crap. Now I have to do it.

I waited until Todd's cart hit a hill, then I jumped out and ran to them. I grabbed the back post and swung up beside Tara, who proceeded to smack me.

"Stop it, you little hooligan!" I yelled.

So, naturally, Tyler started smacking me, too. Those little hands hurt. Dad was right. I should've brought my taser. I'd have tased that kid. I'd have tased him good. I climbed onto the back seat, despite the rapid-fire smacking and got in position to leap onto Tracy, who was driving. Then Tara bit my leg and Todd turned in his seat and started whacking me with his wife's purse. I had brief flashes of tourists watching us go by with open mouths. Not my finest moment.

I got my feet under me and lunged at the wheel. Then we both had the wheel and the cart started weaving left and right. A cop car pulled up beside us and blared the siren. Ear-splitting, but I wasn't letting go.

The cop's window went down and he yelled. "Pull over!"

"I'm trying!" I yelled back.

The siren blared again.

"It's over, idiots!" I yelled.

"It's not over, slut," yelled Tracy.

"Slut!" I lunged, ramming into Tracy and knocking us both out of the cart and into the cop's passenger door. He stopped just before we went under the rear tire. We lay there for a second, winded and dazed. A car door slammed and the cop yelled, "Freeze!"

I don't know where he thought we would go. My legs were tangled up in Tracy's and both our heads were under the car.

"Tracy!" yelled Todd.

"Do not move, sir," said the cop.

"I have to help my wife. That slut attacked her."

Again with the slut.

The cop yelled for someone to call the police station and the pebbles started biting my side. "Can we get up?"

"Shut up," said Tracy and she rammed my head into the bottom of the car. I got her in a choke hold and we rolled out from under. The cop was yelling. Todd was yelling. The crowd was laughing. I had her face smushed into the blacktop and a pair of Italian loafers walked up to my face. "This makes it all worth it."

Chuck. Freaking fantastic.

"Quiet," I said. "I'm subduing a suspect."

"You know you could kill her with that hold." He squatted next to us, revealing the paisley socks I bought him for Christmas.

"I'm okay with that," I said.

Todd begged the cop to shoot me and, frankly, that just made me squeeze tighter. The cop told Chuck to back away, but he flashed his badge while mentioning the Lucia situation. Then he put a handcuff on Tracy. "Let her go, Mercy. She's turning purple."

I did, but only because my arm hurt. Chuck hoisted Tracy to her feet and put her hands behind her back. She screamed that I was a maniac. Not a bad description given my current state. Chuck gave me a hand up. "You're a badass. Chasing people down in a golf cart. Tackling them in a bikini."

"I hope you're duly impressed," I said.

"You might want to fix your top." He grinned at me. "Not to mention your bottoms."

That completed my day. A crowd of at least a hundred had formed. Half had cameras and I had a breast hanging out and my string bikini was half unstrung. I fixed myself and glared at him. "You could've told me that immediately."

"And ruin the moment? I don't think so." He shoved a protesting Tracy in the cop car and tried to subdue Todd, who at that moment decided to go batshit crazy. He started stripping and yelled, "Don't touch me! I've got AIDS!"

"Dude," said Chuck. "If you don't put your pants back on, I'm going to touch you with my fist."

"You can't! I'm leaving! I'm going!" Todd kicked off his pants, much to the astonishment of his kids. Tara and Tyler were still sitting in the back of the golf cart with their mouths in Os. They'd never been so pleasant.

Todd made a move to dash by Chuck, who grabbed his bony

shoulder and squeezed. Todd went down on his knees, his dingus flopping. There's a picture I'll never get out of my head.

"He's touching me!" yelled Todd. "Police brutality!"

Chuck squeezed again. His long fingers dug in under Todd's collarbone and the weasel screamed like a five-year-old girl. "It's her! It's all her fault."

Chuck winked at me. "Now that I believe."

"It's her fault!" yelled Todd as the cop handcuffed him above his hairy butt. I've never seen such a look of revulsion on a man's face. Plenty of times on a woman's, but never a man's. Maybe guys are harder to gross out.

Chuck and the cop yanked Todd to his feet. He kept on yelling about me and how everything was my fault. I guess it was from his point of view. He wanted to kill Lucia and I ruined it. It was the first time fault sounded good.

"Yeah. Yeah," said Chuck. "You would've gotten away with it too, if it weren't for that meddling blond."

The cop shoved Todd in the back of the car beside his still screaming wife and leaned against the door. He wiped his round face with a red handkerchief and looked me over. "Are you Mercy Watts?"

"Your reputation proceeds you," said Chuck.

"And follows me," I said. "I'm Mercy. Why?"

"Tabora's a fan." He grimaced at the kids, who were still in some form of shock. "I guess I've got to take them in." He looked at me hopefully.

"Nope. Not a chance. Those demons are going with you." I pointed at the lovely bite mark on my calf.

"I had to try," said the cop.

"I won't hold it against you."

Aaron walked up carrying an open to go box filled with baleadas. "You hungry?"

"So you were off getting food while I was wrestling the suspect to the ground?" I asked.

Aaron shrugged and offered the baleadas to Chuck and the cop. They each took one.

"Remind me why you're my partner."

"Tommy says."

"Right."

The cop herded the now crying Tara and Tyler into the car. I promised to be available for statements at La Isla Bonita whenever he wanted to take them, so I didn't have to go to the station in a bikini. Chuck volunteered to go, saying he had to discuss extradition. He'd been ordered to take Todd and Tracy back to the States. The cop drove off and the crowd dispersed, looking vaguely disappointed that there wasn't a second round of bikini wrestling.

"Wait a minute. You knew they did it and you didn't call me?" I asked.

"My phone and luggage were stolen in the Managua airport. Then I got on a bus. By the time I got another phone, I was here and nobody was answering. Besides, I knew you could handle it."

"What if I didn't?" I asked, hands on hips.

"You did. I assume Lucia Carrow is still alive."

"She is, just barely."

"Works for me. I'll see you two at the resort after I sort this whole jurisdiction thing out."

"The Honduran government has jurisdiction. The crimes happened here," I said.

"But the conspiracy started in the States. Did Pete tell you about his patient that was shot at Plaza Frontenac?

"Don't tell me that was supposed to be Lucia?" I asked.

"Witness descriptions match Todd and we've proved he was in St. Louis driving a rental car that also matched. We're hoping the Hondurans would rather get Todd and Tracy off their hands than deal with them."

I got in Tracy's golf cart to take it back to the resort. "Mind telling me why they wanted to kill Lucia?"

"You haven't figured that out?" He grinned, looking quite rakish and handsome, despite his rumpled clothes and the bratwurst-shaped bruises on his face or maybe because of them.

"I've been busy trying to keep people alive, for your information."

"They were trying to save their own skins. Todd and Tracy are accountants to the Todaro family. We think they were cooking the books and were about to get caught," said Chuck.

"I thought they were crazy, but they stole from the Mafia? That's suicide."

"I agree, but that's what it looks like. After the Fibonaccis had Angelo Accosi killed, they hatched the plan to kill Lucia as revenge."

"What?" I said. "They thought killing her would make them even with the Todaros?"

"Looks like it."

"Nobody works like that, especially not the mob. Lucia isn't equal to an underboss. She's a civilian. That would start a war between the families."

"What can I say? That was their plan." Chuck got in his rental car and sped off. Aaron stayed next to my cart, chewing.

"We're leaving, Aaron," I said and he trundled off to the other cart and I followed him back to La Isla Bonita. He ate the entire time.

CHAPTER EIGHTEEN

I parked my golf cart next to Aaron's, picked three more embedded pieces of gravel out of my thigh, and climbed out like I'd aged thirty years, complete with the old man groan. Aaron gave me his empty to go box and ran away as fast as his little chubby legs would carry him.

"Thanks!" I yelled after him.

I tossed the container in the recycling bin and told the girl in the office that we'd brought back the carts. She barely looked up from her *Vogue España*. Okay. Catching would-be murders 0. Beauty tips 1. I left and walked down to the scuba shop to find out if anyone knew how Spitball was doing. I assumed he was at the hospital as any normal person who had been stabbed would be. Spitball wasn't normal. He was at the counter, explaining how the open water certification process worked to a new group. His side was bandaged with what looked like an old sheet. There wasn't any blood, so that was good. He saw me standing at the top of the stairs and waved. Then he finished with the newbies and they signed up to start the course the next day.

One of the women asked, "May I ask what happened to your side?"

"Just a scratch. Got to be careful when you're moving equipment."

Everyone nodded in agreement and left the shop. Spitball grinned at me. "So here she is, the conquering hero."

"Well, we got them, if that's what you mean," I said. "So you're calling that wound a scratch?"

"Ain't nothing. I got worse fighting for the last pork chop. Five brothers."

"You should be at the hospital."

"I been there before. No, thank you."

"Can I take a look?" I asked.

"If I got a problem, I'll call you. So did Todd and Tracy confess?"

"No, but it looks bad for them. My cousin showed up and he's trying to get them extradited back to the States."

"If he really wants to punish them, he should leave them here. Honduran prisons ain't no joke."

"I bet, but the States want them. How's Lucia?"

"Shitty. Todd came within a hair of killing her. She went hysterical on the beach and Graeme wasn't there. Luckily, your Aunt Tenne stepped up and got her back to her room before people started asking too many questions."

"You've managed to keep this quiet? You were stabbed. Not to mention all the attempts on Lucia and Graeme."

"Hell, yes, we kept it quiet. This is our business. Todd and Tracy ain't our fault. I'm not gonna let those bastards drive tourists away."

"It's going to be all over the news. Maybe you can drive the tourists in. You'll never get murdered on our watch. You know, that kind of thing. Notoriety is a draw," I said.

Spitball scratched his stubbly chin. "You might be right. La Isla Bonita, the safest resort on the island. We've never lost a tourist."

"Are you saying some resorts have lost tourists?"

"It happens occasionally. You can't stop stupidity."

I left Spitball mulling over marketing and wandered down to Graeme and Lucia's bungalow. I knocked and Graeme answered the door. Wracking sobs burst out behind him and drove me back a step. That and Graeme's appearance. His eyes were puffy and bloodshot.

"Mercy, thank god it's you. What happened?" he asked with a raspy throat.

"We got them. Todd and Tracy are in custody. It's over now."

He hugged me so hard that all the air whooshed out of my lungs. Just that made it all worth it, even the pebbles still embedded in my butt.

"Mercy," called out Lucia.

"Yes, it's me." I could see her stumbling out of bed behind Graeme. "Don't get up."

"She should get up," said Aunt Tenne behind me. I turned to see her with Mom and Dixie. They reminded me of the three Fates, all wise in their own way.

"I don't know," said Graeme.

"I do." Aunt Tenne came onto the porch and walked right past Graeme, bumping him into the door frame with her wide hip.

Before I knew what was happening, Mom, Dixie, and Aunt Tenne had gotten Lucia dressed, combed her hair, and powdered her nose. Lucia said nothing. I think she was too surprised. They hooked their arms through hers and led her out into the afternoon sunshine.

"We're going to get a drink," said Mom. "Care to join us?"

"Um..." said Graeme. "Maybe we should stay here."

"No, you shouldn't," said Aunt Tenne. "Life didn't stop. Let's live it."

Without another word, they went down the walk with Lucia, chattering about her lovely hair and what drink was best. Did she prefer ice or blended? Sweet or sour?

"I don't know what to say," said Graeme.

"That's okay. It wouldn't matter if you did." I steered him out the door. "They're going to do what they're going to do."

We followed them through the maze of paths to the restaurant. Mom ordered a slew of drinks and started to take Lucia down to the water. For the first time, she pulled back. "I can't go down there."

"Take it from me," said Aunt Tenne, "you have to."

"We'll be with you and Mercy's right behind. You've never been safer," said Dixie.

"What about me?" said Graeme. I guess he'd never been seen as incidental before.

"And Graeme," said Mom with a tone that said he was practically useless in such situations.

My family took Lucia down each step, slow but steady. She shook and Mom held her tighter. She cried and Aunt Tenne whispered encouragement in her ear. "Don't let them take the ocean away from you," she said. "It's too precious."

They stepped on the sand and Lucia's shoulders twitched. The three fates crowded close and walked her to the water's edge, stopping just short of the gentle waves. The water was its usual ice blue and the reflected light danced over our skin. I don't know what was going on in Lucia's mind, but mine was flooded with moments of panic. Remembered fear that was no longer real, but certainly felt real.

A boat went by and pushed in waves. My family held firm and the waves hit their feet. Lucia gasped and hands stroked her back.

"There. You've done it," said Mom.

"The water is perfect," said Dixie.

"It can't hurt us," said Aunt Tenne.

The waves kept coming, rushing around their ankles and creeping up their calves.

"Our clothes will get wet," said Lucia with a much stronger voice than I expected.

"They'll dry," said Mom.

Lucia stepped forward and the women of my family stayed right with her moving as one, the way they always moved with me. Right there. Ever present in love. Soon their hemlines were soaked and then their skirts floated up around their waists, twisting and flowing like petals around lovely stems.

"So these are the people who raised you," said Graeme, smiling.

"I think they're still doing it," I said. "I'm not done as far as they're concerned."

A waiter came up with a huge tray of drinks. "Where would you like these?"

We found an empty table next to some loungers and then waded in ourselves and delivered the drinks. Graeme and I didn't stay. Lucia didn't need us. We lay down on the loungers and watch the brilliant sun creep across the sky.

I fell asleep and when I woke, Chuck was in Graeme's spot, wearing touristy garb and drinking a Honduran beer. "About time. You're going to sleep away your last day on the island."

"I deserve a nap. A hundred naps. This was the unvacation."

"You look hot."

"That's less important to me than you think."

"What I think or whether you're hot?"

"Both."

"Liar." Chuck drained his beer and asked for a dark replacement. Since Honduras doesn't really do dark, he and the waiter settled on a Salva Vida.

I stole his beer as soon as it arrived and glared at him. "I'm not lying."

"Yeah, right. You want to hear about Todd and Tracy or what?"

"Or what."

Chuck ignored me, like the rest of the family did, and proceeded to tell me that Todd and Tracy hadn't confessed. I didn't expect that they would. This was real life not *CSI: Miami*. The surprise was that they wanted to charge me with assault, multiple counts.

"Was Todd wearing clothes when he made this request?" I asked.

"As a matter of fact, he wasn't." Chuck tried to suppress a belly laugh and failed. His laughter was contagious and I found myself giggling. "He kept stripping every time we turned our backs. He's really fast at it."

"What is up with that?"

"I've seen it before. It's some kind of panic reaction. Todd has lost it."

"Where are the kids? I can't stand them, but no one should see their parent having a mental breakdown."

"Tabora put them in his office, but they did see one stripping. They are going to need some serious therapy when they get back to the States."

"So the Honduran government agreed to extradition just like that?" I gave Chuck his beer back. I don't like Salva Vida, tastes like Budweiser. He drained the beer and ordered another. I asked for a

Monkey Lala and Chuck made fun of me. I didn't care if it was a girly drink. Hello. I'm a girl.

"In a manner of speaking."

"And what manner would that be?"

"I've got five seats on your flight tomorrow. Tabora's going to take them to the airport. They can either get on my flight or they're getting on a flight to the mainland. A prison bus will be waiting for them."

"This includes the kids?"

"It does."

"Easy choice there. How'd you get five seats on my flight?"

"Strings were pulled. The FBI wants Todd and Tracy in the worst way and they don't want to wait."

"They want them to testify against the Todaros. That's crap. Those idiots will get in the Witness Protection Program."

"Yes, they will, but it won't last long. Once Cosmo Fibonacci finds out what they tried to do, their days are numbered."

I said nothing about what Lucia had said about Calpurnia really being the head of the family. I don't know why, except that it felt like a confidence. I should've felt bad about Todd and Tracy's impending demise, but the memory of Todd's hand over Lucia's mouth was too fresh. Aunt Calpurnia could do what she wanted and undoubtedly, she would. I wouldn't complain.

We drank in silence until Mauro showed up. He smiled down at me, extra shiny, and I think he may have grown a few extra muscles since I last saw him.

"So is this the boyfriend?" he asked.

"Yes," said Chuck.

"No! This is my cousin, Chuck the cop."

Mauro gave Chuck the 'you're creepy' look until Chuck explained that we weren't blood-related and therefore free to date. I explained that that would never happen, but neither of them looked convinced. I sipped my drink and watched the dad of the fat baby and toddler make sandcastles for his children. Without Tara and Tyler the beach was quiet and soothing. I asked where Mom and everyone else had gone. Chuck said they were changing for dinner. Then he and Mauro got into a boring diving discussion about differences in regs. If it wasn't chocolate or a Monkey Lala, I had absolutely no interest.

Chuck poked me in the thigh. "We're going on a night dive. What do you say?"

"Hell, no." I'd had a couple by then.

"Come on," said Mauro. "It'll be your last hurrah on Roatan."

"I've had about fifteen last hurrahs, so I'm all full up. Have fun."

They got up, unfolding long, lean limbs, and left for the scuba shop. I watched them walk away. Their bodies were quite similar, but, of course, I preferred Mauro. He wasn't Chuck, an unmistakable advantage. Once they turned the corner, I settled in and truly began to enjoy my vacation. I swam. I played with the baby. I laid on the floating platform and Roatan became perfect.

CHAPTER NINETEEN

I walked into Kronos three days later. I couldn't contain my desire for one of Aaron's burgers any longer. Kronos was a Star Trek-inspired burger joint owned by Aaron and his business partner, Rodney. If you met them, you'd never think they were successful restaurateurs, but Kronos was packed even more than usual with cops, firemen, and some civilians. I slipped in behind a pack of St. Louis University students and kept my head down. Pete gave me one of his baseball caps and I'd tucked my hair up in it and wore a pair of over-sized aviator sunglasses. All I wanted was to pick up my burger in peace. I don't know why I thought I could do that.

"Mercy!" yelled a cop in uniform down at the end of the bar. I'd met Ameche during Gavin's murder investigation. He loved our connection. I was less enthused. The entire population of the bar turned and I was instantly surrounded and pummeled by questions. The story of Lucia's near murder was on every front page and Nancy Grace had taken up yelling about Roatan on every TV show that would let her. Lucia being a Fibonacci and my being a cop's daughter added to the appeal. We'd been featured everywhere. Then the other shoe dropped. I'd been videoed first climbing out of the water after the ill-fated ransom drop for Andrew and then tackling Tracy in the golf cart. There were posters. There were new fan clubs. YouTube videos editing out Aaron and putting me in Ursula Andress' Bond girl bikini from *Dr. No*. Sometimes I was nude. I was always embarrassing.

I fought my way through the crowd and flagged down Rodney, who was mixing Metaphysical Malts two at a time. He finished and came down to make my day better. "I told people you come here," he said, happily. "Our receipts are up twenty-seven percent."

"You are dead to me," I said. "Where's my burger?"

About fifteen guys offered to buy me lunch. I learned a long time ago never to accept free anything from men, it leads to bad behavior, not mine.

"No. No," said Rodney. "It's on the house."

"Thanks," I said, taking my bag full of happiness. Rod and Aaron were the exception to my rule. If either of them tried to feel me up, I'd take them straight to the hospital to have their heads examined.

I turned and started for the door with cameras stuck in my face and flashes going off like firecrackers. Rodney damn well owed me a burger. He owed me a dozen.

"Wait!" Rodney yelled.

I went back to the bar and set down my bag. "What?"

"There's a guy waiting for you."

The whole place erupted in laughter and followed by dozens of guys saying they were also waiting for me. Fantastic.

"Not you guys!" yelled Rod. "That one over there."

The crowd parted and I saw who was waiting for me. I knew I couldn't avoid Lucia's brother forever, but I did think I had a few more days. Oz waved to me and I sighed.

Just get it over with. He's not going to offer a payback now. Too public.

I was so wrong. You'd think I'd start getting used to it. I went over and slid into his booth and he pushed a malt in front of me.

"How'd you know I'd be here?" I asked.

He smiled, showing me his very white teeth. "You know how it is."

"Not really, but I guess I don't want to, do I?"

"I had to talk to you. We have business to settle," he said, leaning back and putting his well-tanned arm on the seat back.

"We really don't. Lucia's fine. Everybody's fine," I said.

"We owe you."

Oh shit. Dad is going to kill me.

"It's totally fine. We're even." I started to get up, but he put his hand on mine.

"Try your malt. I have it on good authority that it's your favorite. We need to discuss Lucia, in any case."

"I just talked to her this morning. She's doing well. There's nothing else to say."

"Is Graeme beating my sister? I have to know."

I'd totally forgotten the suspicions that got me to Roatan in the first place and I wasn't sure what to say.

Oz's hands curled into fists. "He is, isn't he?"

I took a sip of the malt, a slow one, giving me time to think. "No," I said. "He isn't."

Oz didn't relax one bit. "Explain the bruising. Explain why she won't talk to me."

"I'm not explaining anything to you. Lucia deserves her privacy, what little she can muster right now. She asked me not to tell you and I'm not going to."

His face fell. "She asked you not to tell me. Why? What is it? What's wrong?"

"Graeme is devoted to your sister. She's fine and that's all you need to know. She'll tell you when she's ready."

Oz relaxed ever so slightly. "She'll tell me?"

"Eventually. Now I'm leaving. Please don't stalk me anymore."

"I'm afraid not. Like I said, we've got business to settle."

Groan.

"My family wants to thank you for saving Lucia. It's a debt that can never be fully paid, but they intend to try," he said.

"Don't worry about it. I'm good. Lucia is starting a charity drive for Roatan medical supplies. That's all I want."

"That won't do it. My family will thank you. It's best if you agree," said Oz.

"I don't know how to take that," I said.

He smiled again. "It's the way it is and has always been. We're Fibonaccis and we owe you."

I stood up. "I really don't want anything. You've thanked me quite enough." I stepped into the crowd.

"Aunt Tenne," Oz called after me.

I stopped and turned back. "What?"

"You know what I mean," he said. "Sit."

I eased back in the booth, very aware of being surrounded by cops that knew my dad. "I really, really don't. Unless you're referring to her new boyfriend, which is fine. We like him. Please don't do anything to Bruno."

"You really don't know?"

"What did I just say?"

Oz opened a briefcase that was sitting on the seat beside him and pulled out a thick manila folder. He pushed it across the table and raised an eyebrow. I fingered the stiff paper, not sure if I wanted to open it, but my curiosity got the better of me and I did. On top of the stack was an eight-by-ten color photo of four very pretty girls posing in front of a '70s blue Mustang. Aunt Tenne was the girl farthest to the left and she was a person I'd never seen before, fit and shapely, glowing with effervescent joy like Mom.

"It's Aunt Tenne," I said. "She's stunning."

"Keep going," said Oz.

I flipped over the photo and underneath was a paper-clipped sheath of newspaper clippings. The top one was from the *St. Louis Post Dispatch* about a two-car accident and a picture of mangled cars in some brush. Below the cars were four school pictures. I didn't want to look any further.

"They're dead," I said. "All but Aunt Tenne."

"Yes. Your aunt and her three best friends were hit by a habitual drunk while driving to college. Her three friends were killed outright. Your aunt barely survived."

That can't be right. That couldn't have happened.

"But Aunt Tenne didn't go to college," I said.

"No, she didn't. She spent the next year having surgeries on her back and hips. There may have been some suicide attempts."

I flipped the picture back over and looked at Aunt Tenne as she once was, a person I never knew existed.

"My family wants to thank you," said Oz, softly.

"I don't know what you're saying."

"I think you do."

"So...is the drunk still alive?"

Oz pulled out a second folder, just as thick. It also had a photo, taken recently of a grey-haired man standing in front of a BMW dealership.

"Phillip Grint, the auto baron? Are you serious?" I asked.

"Keep going."

Underneath Grint's glossy print was a tiny article, barely an inch long, and it acknowledged that Phillip Grint, son of auto tycoon, Jonathan Grint, had been involved in a fatal auto accident involving four eighteen-year-old girls. None of the girls were named and there was no mention of an arrest. I leaned back as my stomach got queasy. "I don't want to think about this right now."

"Not much thought is required," said Oz.

"You're right. Aunt Tenne is fine. She doesn't even limp."

"I wouldn't bring it up, if that were true."

"It happened over thirty years ago."

"There's no statute of limitations on murder."

"Wasn't it a drunk driving accident?" I asked.

"That phrase covers a multitude of sins. I call what he did intentional and your aunt isn't fine." He gave me a third folder. "My family would like to help her as you helped Lucia. Give her her life back so to speak."

I didn't open the folder. "She has her life."

"But not much else. As far as we can tell your aunt has never waned or wavered in her grief. She visits her friends' graves regularly, brings them flowers, talks to them."

"That's okay. People do that." I wasn't so sure, but what else could I say.

"She drives by his house." He opened the third folder and there was a shot of Aunt Tenne in her car in front of a mansion with a wide manicured lawn and an ornate gate at the end of the driveway. "That's his house. She goes there and sits for hours. I don't know if he knows she's there. If he does, he doesn't care."

"When was this taken?"

"Three days before you went to Honduras. The anniversary was during your trip, but this isn't rare for her. I have it on good authority that she's there regularly. Several times a month."

Good god, Aunt Tenne. What are you doing to yourself?

"He didn't go to prison, Mercy. He didn't go to jail and he didn't get community service. He walked away and this wasn't the first time or the last. He hit a ten-year-old boy two years before and the boy lost a leg. His father arranged for Phillip to spend six weeks in rehab. Forest View Therapeutic Center in California. Thirty thousand dollars a month with personal chefs. It was the same with your aunt's accident. He went on vacation."

"The court agreed to that?"

"One way or another."

"Your family thanking me won't change anything."

"It'll balance the scales a little."

I looked through the pictures again. It wasn't fair. It wasn't remotely right, but as I looked another picture worked its way in, the picture of Aunt Tenne smiling with Bruno. On Roatan, she showed the same joy that I saw in that picture with her friends so many years ago. "Before we left, she said it was going to be different this year, that she was going to be different. You know what? She is different and it's not just Bruno. I hate that this happened to her. I hate that he got away with it."

Oz started to speak, but I cut him off. "I get what you're trying to tell me. This bastard has been happy for over thirty years and Aunt Tenne's been miserable. I've seen what it's done to her every day of my life. I just didn't know what caused it. But my answer is no. She's made a new start. If something were to happen to Grint, it would be all over the news. It might jolt her out of the good place she's in."

"Are you sure?" asked Oz. "He deserves it. You don't know half of what he's done."

I smiled. "You never know. I could change my mind. If I keep looking at these pictures, I might."

"What about your godmothers then?"

"Oh dear lord. Please don't say they have some horrible past that needs fixing."

He chuckled. "No. Their past is just fine. I was thinking of their present. The lawsuit."

"They'll win that." I finished the malt.

"Maybe. They are a little batty and this issue with you and your parents is troublesome."

"What issue?"

"All the money, your education, the house on Hawthorne. People are starting to wonder."

My queasiness increased. Shouldn't have drank all that malt. "Wonder what?"

"What exactly did your parents do to deserve such largesse."

"So do you have a folder on that, too?" I asked.

"Afraid not and it's not for lack of trying. Are you saying you don't know why the Bled sisters picked your parents?"

"Something about a favor. They don't tell me anything."

Oz dug out yet another folder.

"I knew you had another."

"Not on your parents' involvement with the Bleds. Open it."

Inside that innocuous folder was a copy of an internal memo dated two weeks before. It directed Internal Affairs to investigate Dad for possible misconduct in dealing with the Bled family. It said all resources would be made available and the lawsuit should be watched closely for information.

"Dad didn't do anything illegal," I said.

"Are you sure about that?"

Um, no.

Oz finished the last of his drink. "Things are easy for my family. We're born under a lucky star."

"I don't know about that. Lucia was nearly killed in Roatan several times."

"But she wasn't, because you were there. Lucky, don't you think?"

"Lucky you arranged it, I guess," I said.

"All the stars aligned. That's the way it is for us and sometimes we like to spread it around. My sister got lucky. I don't see why your family and friends can't be lucky, too."

I stood up. "We're lucky already. We don't need the Fibonacci stars for that. Thanks for the malt."

Oz smiled, stacked up the folders, and gave them to me.

I took them though I didn't want to read what they contained, so much unhappiness, except for Phillip Grint, he was way too happy.

"Calpurnia Fibonacci says you're welcome," said Oz, picking up a menu.

I hesitated. What did he mean by that? I nearly asked, but something stopped me, a little feeling that it was best not to know. Instead, I went for the door, having totally forgotten my burger. But Aaron was there with his hand on the door handle. He held up my bag in the other.

"Hey Aaron, why didn't you come to the table?" I asked.

He shrugged.

I glanced back at Oz, who was watching us. For the first time, I noticed there was a perimeter around his booth. The cops and firefighters kept their distance, but there was a feel of respect to it, a quiet knowing that some lines ought not be crossed. And I had crossed them. I'd walked up and sat down, like it was nothing. And it was definitely something.

"Do you know who that is?" I asked.

"Yeah."

I put the bag on top of the files and waited to see if he'd elaborate. He didn't. I don't know why I expected that he would. Aaron wasn't the king of information. He pushed open the door and practically pushed me through. "Say hello to The Girls."

The door closed and I turned to watch Aaron nod to Oz and head back in the kitchen. Aaron knew Oz? Or was he just acknowledging the power in the room? That didn't seem like Aaron. He barely acknowledged bathing.

I walked slowly home with the unsettling thought that I'd started something that I would never be able to end.

It took five hours. Not five days. Not five weeks. Five hours for the Fibonaccis to repay me. I'd like to say that was a record, but it probably wasn't.

The phone rang, waking me from a burger-induced coma.

"Mercy!" yelled Dad. "Get to the mansion. The alarms have been deactivated."

"Where are the guards?" I asked, instantly alert.

"The security company isn't answering."

"Did you call the cops?" I ran toward my front door, tripping over shoes and a sleeping Skanky.

"You're closer. Get over there and take the Luger."

"But—"

"There's twenty million dollars' worth of art in that house. Go! Now!"

I ran back into my bedroom and found the antique Luger my great grandfather brought back from World War Two nestled between two Christmas sweaters. Dad insisted that I be armed after Gavin got killed. I bypassed the Luger, despite Dad's orders, and chose the smaller Mauser. I yanked it out of the holster, found the clip in my handy box 'o clips, flipped off the safety, locked the slid and checked the chamber as Dad had taught me. I slapped the clip in and heard the ever so satisfying clack of the slide racking into place. Safety on, I shoved it in my pocket as I ran out of the apartment.

I bypassed my truck and sprinted across the street. A biker in full Tour de France wear saw me, swerved, and hit Stillman Antiques' oversized sidewalk sign, tumbling ass over teakettle. A car squealed its tires and there was the sound of crashing metal behind me. Stillman Kelley ran out of his shop's front door and yelled at me. "You aren't supposed to run!"

"It's me, Mr. Kelley, Mercy," I said as I stooped over the dazed biker.

"Dude," said the biker.

Mr. Kelley pulled out his cell phone and dialed 911 and then shook a finger at me. "Your mother can't run and neither should you. It's not safe for people."

My dad had banned running for Mom after she caused a three-car pileup. This was a first for me. Usually, I could get away with it.

"I didn't mean to. It's The Girls. Something's happened," I said.

The biker's hand came up and brushed my breast like I wasn't going to notice that. I smacked it away and he groaned.

"You're okay," I said. "If you can grope, you're fine."

Mr. Kelley pointed to the alley. "Just go. I'll handle this. You can only make it worse.

I resented that, but it was probably true. I ran through the alley and ended up on my parents' end of Hawthorne Avenue. It was quiet. I didn't see any crazed getaway drivers. Maybe it was a mistake. A power outage or something. I sprinted down the Avenue under flickering gas lamps. It was safe. There were no drivers to distract.

I found Myrtle and Millicent's gate open. My feet crunched the dead leaves on the wide front walk as I ran up to the house in which I'd been born, a 1920s Art Deco mansion that was one of a kind to say the least. It had geometric ironwork that suggested Egyptian hieroglyphics, three story conservatories, and more green marble than you've ever seen, outside a quarry.

I flung open the door and almost fell over the enormous pile of luggage in the foyer. It was The Girls' luggage, hat boxes, trunks, twenty-four pieces in all.

I pulled out the Luger, just in case. "Myrtle! Millicent!"

No answer. I ran through the big empty rooms with all the furniture and priceless art covered in starched white sheets. Everything looked intact. All places filled. The house was enormous, so it took a while, but I finally found the intruders by the smell of baking cookies. They were in the kitchen, two little old ladies wearing Prada and colorful silk aprons, because that's practical to bake in.

"What happened? What's going on?" I set the Mauser on the marble pastry table and gasped for air.

Millicent eyed the pistol and patted her silver hair, elaborately swirled going-out hair. "Whatever do you mean, dear?"

"What are you doing here? The alarms are off. The guards are gone."

"We sent them home and the alarms wouldn't hush up, so we shut them off. Technology is such a fuss."

"But why?" I asked.

"It's over," said Myrtle.

"What is?"

"The lawsuit. Brooks dropped it two hours ago. We wanted to surprise you."

"Holy crap! Why?"

The Girls grasped the heavy pearl necklaces that encircled their necks. "Mercy, please."

"Sorry," I said. "Um.. Why'd he drop it?"

Please don't say he's dead under mysterious circumstances.

"He just changed his mind," said Myrtle. "Perhaps he realized you don't treat family that way."

I seriously doubt it.

Millicent came over and hugged me. "You don't seem happy, my darling girl."

I hugged her back, feeling how tiny and delicate she was. Sometimes I forgot how old they both were. I really shouldn't do that. No one goes on forever. "I'm thrilled, but curious."

"His lawyer didn't say why and, oddly enough, he's going to pay all our lawyers' expenses," said Myrtle.

"I don't care why," said Millicent, "just as long as I don't have to answer any more questions. Those lawyers have no shame. They seem to think there's no such thing as privacy."

Myrtle gave me a madeleine cookie, fresh from the oven. Heaven.

"What did they want to know?" I asked.

"They kept asking about Uncle Josiah's house and your parents, as if Brooks has a right to know our private matters. It is our money and it was our house. It's none of his business what we choose to do with either."

Myrtle opened the oven and a wave of heat filled the kitchen. Lovely after the house had been cold and alone for two months.

"So," I said, "why did you give them the house?"

Millicent gave me the same look that made me quiet in French restaurants and airports since I was little, but I was no longer little. I wanted to know.

"The house was an amazing gift. I just want to know why you gave it."

"You are as bad as the lawyers. We raised you better than that."

You think so, but not really.

Myrtle slid in another pan of madeleines and set the timer. "Come, dear. Help us unpack. We picked up some chocolates from Bissingers, your favorite dark chocolate caramel suckers."

They aren't going to tell me. Why is this such a secret?

"Mercy?" said Myrtle.

"Of course. I'd unpack the Ringling Brothers for those suckers."

We went through the house to the foyer. I met a couple of panting cops on the front steps and explained the situation. Then I called Dad and rearmed the alarm. The Girls picked up hatboxes and I got a couple of suitcases and followed them up, up the wide staircase as I had done all my life. The white sheets blew up off the paintings as we passed and I got glimpses of their beauty. A lovely welcome home.

Millicent reached the second floor first. "I think we should go on vacation to celebrate. Mercy, you need a vacation."

"I just got back from vacation." Not that it was all that relaxing.

"That was a beach vacation. You're not a beach girl. You burn. You need culture, art, architecture."

"I know," said Myrtle. "You need Europe."

I couldn't argue with that, although I wondered if they were just trying to distract me from the house question. The internal memo popped into my mind. The Girls were out of the woods, but what about Dad? "Maybe we should just lay low for a while."

"Why should we? Life is short, even if you live a long time. We should know."

"What do you say to Prague or Vienna?" asked Millicent.

"I'm thinking Venice," said Myrtle.

They didn't need an answer. They would decide the destination and I would go along, which was fine with me. "Just promise me one thing."

"Anything." Myrtle kissed my cheek.

"Promise there won't be any murders or crimes of any kind," I said.

"Why ask us?" Millicent smiled, wrinkles wreathing her pretty face. "You're the one who controls that."

Groan.

The End

PREVIEW

Double Black Diamond (Mercy Watts Mysteries Book Three)

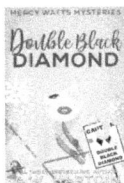

"I should have your problems."

Raquel, known as Raptor by those who knew her well, stood behind me. The smell of her stale coffee breath filled the staff room. It went well with her natural aura of evil and unjustified anger. I stuffed my water bottle in my backpack and turned to face her.

"I'd like to give you some of my problems, Raquel. Maybe you'd do better with them than I have," I said.

"You wouldn't give me the time of day, Mercy." She tossed her dark curls over her shoulder and brushed past me to get her purse out of her locker and her stethoscope clanked against the metal. She cursed under her breath and glared at me as if it were my fault.

"Not true." I smiled. Raptor hated smiling on general principle, so I did it as much as possible in her presence. "It is now 7:23 AM and I'll even tell you the day. It's Sunday."

"Smartass."

I threw back the last of my cold coffee, wiped out my mug and tucked it in beside my water bottle. "I can't deny the truth."

"You've been complaining about Colorado all night and I'm sick of it. You act like getting an all expenses paid skiing trip is some kind of punishment or something."

I sighed. In my case it kind of was a punishment, a punishment for dating someone long enough that he decided I absolutely had to go on a trip with his parents, not that I expected Raptor to understand that. I don't do well with parents, especially mothers. They could get crazy about their sons and for some reason they seemed to think their baby boys needed protection from me especially. I expected a week of suspicion and sly insinuations.

"It's been a long night. Can we just snipe at each other another time?"

"You know where I'll be this week?" Raptor hissed at me.

Bitterville? Panties-in-a-twist town? Vinegar village?

"Here in ice cold St. Louis, not skiing with my doctor boyfriend and his rich parents."

I'm sorry for St. Louis.

"Well, gotta go," I said as our boss, Odetta, poked her head in.

"Mercy, make sure you stop by Mr. O'Quinn before you go. He'll be hell on wheels, if you don't," said Odetta.

Raptor threw up her hands and stalked out. "Unbelievable."

"Don't mind her," said Odetta. "She just hates you."

"Don't I know it. I'll see Arthur on my way out," I said, going out the door. Odetta and I watched Raptor walk away. She even walked angry.

"What is it with you two?" asked Odetta as she tied her long black braids with a red ribbon.

"I arrived at nursing school two minutes before her and took the dorm room she thought should've been hers by virtue of GPA."

"That's it?"

"That and I continued to breathe afterwards," I said. "Call my service if you want me back after Colorado."

I was a PRN nurse, which meant I was a glorified temp. I never knew where I'd be from week to week.

Odetta glanced at Raptor stepping into the elevator and then raised an eyebrow at me. "You'll come back?"

"I'm used to her and I like the floor."

"Then I'll make the request."

We said goodbye and I took a left toward Arthur O'Quinn's room.

The old guy would probably be asleep, but it wouldn't hurt to check. I pulled open the door to his private room and the smell of three thousand flowers flowed out into the corridor. I tiptoed in and peeked around the drawn curtain. The thin man on the bed with the covers drawn up to his chin was surrounded by more flowers than I'd ever seen in one room. They were everywhere, vases on every flat surface, including equipment. Arthur's eyes were closed and his breathing was shallow but steady.

"Is that Chanel No. 5 I smell?" he said softly.

I bit my lip and his hazel eyes fluttered open.

"Don't worry, Miss Watts," said Arthur. "I know exactly who you are."

"Glad to hear it," I said.

"When will you be back?"

"In one week if Odetta schedules me." I made a face.

"Colorado's beautiful this time of year."

"It's not Colorado I'm worried about."

"They'll love you."

"Mothers never like me. Even my own is on the fence."

"I doubt that. I like you, and I'm hard to please. Ask any nurse on this floor," said Arthur, his eyes closing again.

I did please Arthur, but it wasn't a fair competition. I had something that no one else had. No one except my mother, that is.

"Sing me to sleep, Marilyn," he said with a gentle smile.

"Alright as long as you know I'm not really her," I said.

"I know. You just take me back to my youth and a time before all this." He waved at all the monitors keeping track of his bodily functions.

I took off my backpack, got out a tube of shiny red lipstick and smeared a thick coat on. I might look exactly like Marilyn Monroe, but I couldn't sing like her without the lipstick. I dropped the backpack and sallied forward, singing "Diamonds are a Girl's Best Friend", complete with all the arm movements and tush wiggling. Arthur lit up the way he only did when his late wife Joanna was mentioned.

"It's uncanny," he said. "You have the voice, everything. If I didn't know better, I'd think Marilyn Monroe was here in my room."

"Wearing scrubs and tennis shoes?"

"It didn't matter what she wore, she was something special, like you."

I brushed the gauzy hair off his pale forehead. "Not like me. It's just the face God gave me."

"He chose wisely. She would've liked you."

There was no arguing with Arthur about the differences between me and Marilyn. And who was I to argue anyway? Arthur actually knew the late bombshell. In another life, he'd been an assistant to her favorite photographer and had seen her frequently throughout the last years of her life.

"I've got to go," I said.

"Did they tell you? I'm at the top of the list."

"I heard. Your kidney will show up any day now."

"I hate the thought of someone dying so I can live," Arthur said.

"It's the only way, so let's concentrate on you living," I said.

"Will you be here when it happens?"

"If I'm in town I will."

He closed his eyes and took a deep breath. "Good."

I grabbed my backpack, slipped out, and closed Arthur's door quietly.

"Mercy."

I jumped and turned. Odetta was standing in the corridor, clasping her hands.

"You scared me." I patted my heaving chest.

"Can we talk?" she asked.

"What about?"

Just then two women came running down the corridor. The first was Philippa, my friend and fellow nurse, and the second I didn't recognize. Philippa was still in her favorite pink polka-dotted scrubs from the night shift, but her companion wore grey sweats, a battered bubble coat, and a pair of worn-out Nikes.

"She's gone," gasped Philippa. "I saw her leave the garage."

"Who?" I asked.

"Raptor." She glanced at the other woman. "I'm sorry. Raquel."

"It's okay. I know how she is," the other woman said and that's when I recognized her. It was Raquel's older sister, Cecile. She was a senior in nursing school when I was a freshman.

The three of them stood together looking at me, but none seemed inclined to say anything.

"So...you wanted to talk to me," I said.

"Yes." Odetta glanced around like she was expecting someone to sneak up on us. "Let's go in an empty room."

She led us down to the next vacancy and closed the door. Cecile was shaking and Philippa put her arm around her shoulders.

"Okay. Now you're just freaking me out. What's going on?" I asked.

"Do you know about my son?" asked Cecile in a quavering voice. She pulled a snapshot out of her pocket and handed it to me. In the center was a brown-haired little boy clutching a teddy. He looked up at the camera with an impossibly wide grin and gapped teeth.

"Keegan?"

"Yes, but he doesn't look like that anymore. You know his diagnosis?"

"Not the particulars. He has Dravet syndrome. Philippa told me."

"Do you know what the diagnosis means?"

I swallowed and tried to think what to say to this mother shaking before me. She knew what it meant. Was it any good to pretend that it was something else?

"It means he'll never have a life," I said softly.

Odetta began crying and turned away, but Cecile looked me right in the eye. "That's right."

"I'm so sorry. How old is he now?" I asked.

"He just turned four."

I wanted to ask more questions, but I was afraid of the answers. Cecile wasn't there because Keegan was doing well. Dravet syndrome was a kind of walking death. Children were diagnosed usually in their first year of life and it was all downhill from there. The afflicted could suffer hundreds of seizures a day. It affected every part of their lives and the lives around them. There was no cure and no approved treatment.

"He's gone into status," said Philippa.

I nodded like I truly understood what that meant for Keegan, for Cecile. It varied from patient to patient.

"They can't stop the seizures," said Cecile. "They go on for over an hour now and they happen almost constantly. He's lost his ability to speak and to stand or walk."

"The neurologist thinks it's beginning to affect his cognitive abilities," said Odetta, turning around and wiping her eyes.

I waited, but no one continued. Tears rolled down their faces and they watched me. I wasn't crying yet, but I was on the edge.

"I get the feeling that you want something from me," I said.

"I wouldn't ask if I wasn't absolutely desperate," said Cecile. "It's so bad. I think...I think he's going to die."

"What can I do?"

"You're going to Colorado," said Odetta. "When you told me, we came up with a plan, but it won't work without you."

I didn't like the sound of that. Whenever someone came up with a plan for me, it was a bad thing.

"What do you want me to do?"

"Have you heard of Alice's Answer?" asked Cecile.

Now I had it. Alice's Answer was a cannabis oil being used to treat seizure disorders. It was only made in Colorado where it was legal.

"You want it for Keegan," I said.

"It's his only hope," she said.

"I guess it is. What exactly do you want me to do?"

"It's still illegal in Missouri. No one can import. It would take forever to get special approval, and we don't have that kind of time. I can't afford to move to Colorado. Keegan's father, he left. He couldn't handle it. The insurance isn't covering Keegan's care completely. There's just no money, and I have two other kids to think of."

"And bringing it across state lines is a crime, state and federal," I said.

"Yes, but it's his only hope. I don't want to ask you, but..." Tears flowed out of Cecile's eyes in a continuous stream.

"Why me?" I asked, even though I already knew the answer.

Cecile broke down and Philippa answered, "You're going to Colorado. You'll be right there."

"And my dad is Tommy Watts."

"If you were caught, he could get you out of it."

"My dad's a retired cop, that doesn't make him the all-powerful Oz, although he thinks so."

Cecile straightened up. "I can't get caught. I'm the only parent they have left."

"I'd do it," said Odetta. "But I've got kids of my own. We need my income."

"I offered," said Philippa.

Cecile shook her head. "No. If you went to jail your mother couldn't handle it."

Philippa's mom had early onset Alzheimer's. When she was coherent, Philippa was the light of her life.

"And...you have the Bleds," said Philippa.

I'd known Philippa since high school. She'd never once tried to use my connection to the Bled family for her own purposes and that was saying something. A lot of people had no such scruples. Myrtle and Millicent Bled were my godmothers and wealthy to the extent that most people couldn't imagine. People were always contacting me trying to get to them. I knew how desperate the situation was if Philippa was willing to do it. I would've asked about other family members, but I imagined they would be in the same boat. Incomes were needed. Mothers and fathers were required. I, on the other hand, was single with an influential father and connected to one of the most powerful families in the state, if not the country. It had to be me. Plus, when Raptor found out, she would lose her damn mind. Raptor would owe me. It might be worth a stint in jail just for that alone. I didn't know what my parents would say if I got caught, but I decided I didn't care. Keegan wasn't going to get brain damage, if I could help it. My parents would just have to deal.

"I'll do it."

Read the rest in Double Black Diamond. Available now.

ABOUT THE AUTHOR

USA Today bestselling author A.W. Hartoin grew up in rural Missouri, but her grandmother lived in the Central West End area of St. Louis. The CWE fascinated her with it's enormous houses, every one unique. She was sure there was a story behind each ornate door. Going to Grandma's house was a treat and an adventure. As the only grandchild around for many years, A.W. spent her visits exploring the many rooms with their many secrets. That's how Mercy Watts and the fairies of Whipplethorn came to be.

As an adult, A.W. Hartoin decided she needed a whole lot more life experience if she was going to write good characters so she joined the Air Force. It was the best education she could've hoped for. She met her husband and traveled the world, living in Alaska, Italy, and Germany before settling in Colorado for nearly eleven years. Now A.W. has returned to Germany and lives in picturesque Waldenbuch with her family and two spoiled cats, who absolutely believe they should be allowed to escape and roam the village freely.

9 781952 875052